SOLDIER OF FORTUNE
MAGAZINE PRESENTS:

MICHAEL WILLIAMS

A TOM DOHERTY ASSOCIATES BOOK

This is a work of fiction. All the characters and events portrayed in this book are fictional, and any resemblance to real people or incidents is purely coincidental.

DOORGUNNER

First printing: April 1987

A TOR Book

Published by Tom Doherty Associates, Inc.
49 West 24 Street
New York, N.Y. 10010

ISBN: 0-812-51202-2
CAN. ED.: 0-812-51203-0

PRINTED IN THE UNITED STATES OF AMERICA

0 9 8 7 6 5 4 3 2 1

FOR BACHLER WHO RETURNED WITH THE LIVING

FOR ROTHEL WHO RETURNED WITH THE DEAD

FOR SMOOT WHO NEVER RETURNED AT ALL

ROOKIE

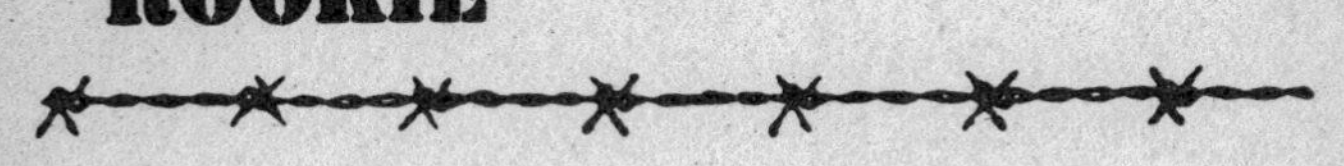

I.

Harsh sounds disrupted the smooth, rhythmical beat of the blades, snapping Carl out of his reverie. The helicopter began to shake and vibrate unsteadily thirty feet above the ground.

"What the hell was that?" the pilot's voice boomed through the intercom.

Oh, God, they'll never let me fly again! Carl fought down a rising panic and tried to swallow the knot in his throat as he keyed his mike. "Sir, we hit a dead tree limb to the rear on my side."

"Damn!" Carl saw the pilot glance back in his direction, teeth clenched, the rest of the face unreadable beneath the dark visor.

The aircraft commander quickly set the Huey back down in the clearing, stabilized the RPMs, and shut down the engine. The shirtless, darkly tanned platoon leader of the infantry unit that they had just resupplied wandered back out into the small landing zone.

"Short trip, huh?" He grinned at the pilot, who was scowling at the ends of the chopper's blades.

Warrant Officer Raymond Jessup ignored the platoon leader and yelled for Pfc Carl Willstrom, who was standing on the opposite side of the ship, staring at the jagged end of one of the rotor blades. Carl braced himself and came around the ship's tail section.

"What the hell happened, Willstrom? Why did we hit a tree on your side after you cleared me up? Maybe the tree moved?"

"Sir, I thought we had enough room to clear it," Carl lied. He hadn't even noticed the seemingly harmless dead tree as he sat there in his gunner's well contemplating the glorious life of being an aerial warrior.

"If you want to fly with this outfit," Jessup growled, "you'd better get your head out of your ass and learn how to do your job! And fast, or I'll have you on the shit-burning detail for the rest of your tour in Nam!" Jessup disgustedly waved him back to his position and stomped past the smiling platoon leader.

"Hey!" called the platoon leader. "You gonna make it out or would you like reservations here for tonight?"

"We'll do just fine." Jessup swung up into his seat. "We just lost a couple of inches off the ends of the blades. It'll be a shade bumpy and vibrate like hell, but we'll make it back."

Carl closed the copilot's door and headed back to his gunner's cubbyhole, aware of the following stare of the crew chief, Sp5 Morris. That was one person he didn't need for an enemy. Carl made a quick mental comparison. At a light 145 pounds on a five-foot ten-inch frame he knew that Morris, a stocky Chicago tough type, could nail him to the wall. And might after the way Carl had screwed up the crew chief's helicopter.

Shrugging off the stare, Carl brushed back his dark hair and slid the olive-drab flight helmet over his head. The pilot was already talking, a strange-sounding mixture of speech and squawking static that Carl was still getting used to.

"Let's get it right this time," Jessup said. "Clear?"

Carl carefully scanned the 180-degree arc, his area of responsibility, to make sure there was nothing to interfere with the blades, be it man, beast, or tree. "Clear right."

The pilot glanced over his shoulder at Carl, seemed satisfied, and cranked the engine.

The Huey lifted off the ground, rotor wash blowing dust and dead grass into the treeline as the chopper rose straight up between the tall trees flanking the narrow LZ. Once above treetop level, Jessup nosed the ship over, giving a momentary impression of diving back into the jungle before she leveled out. Turning toward Tay Ninh, the pilot eased the army-green workhorse across the treetops at a bumpy seventy knots.

Carl sat at his gun with the barrel slanted down at a 45-degree angle, watching the blur of the lush green jungle rush by, a scant twenty feet below the chopper's skids. Low-level flying, going *lima-lima* in chopper jargon. A damn sight more exciting than flying around at two or three thousand feet beating holes in the clouds. Down here was where it was at. Here just below him was the darkness of the jungle, the home of the elusive enemy, Victor Charlie.

One of the old veteran gunners had told him that low leveling over the double or triple canopy jungle made it almost impossible for anyone on the ground to hit you if you avoided the larger clearings and kept your airspeed up. Still, it was more exciting down at this level, imagining what the silent trees were protecting.

"Damn," he said quietly to himself. "Almost did it again." Drifting off in his fantasies had already gotten him in one bind today and he didn't want to try for a double. He was going to catch hell when they got back. Captain Ranes, the maintenance officer, would go through the roof and come down right on Carl's head with his size 13 boots. Carl's heart sank even lower. Repairing combat damage was one thing, but this . . . a rookie screwup!

It was bad enough being a lowly rookie and catching all the flak traditionally dumped on a new guy. Now, on his third day of flying, he had committed an act that would make him a target for more than the regular abuse. This wasn't the way it was supposed to be at all. In youthful exuberance, he had volunteered for helicopter duty to experience the thrill of aerial warfare, to earn the silver aircrew wings. He hadn't expected to be a butt for jokes and to be run ragged by his fellow aircrewmen.

Fellow aircrewmen! Some kind of comradeship this had turned out to be. He had wanted so badly to be part of the team, accepted by the others as a gunner, a member of an elite group. But they weren't ready to accept him yet, and after this, maybe never.

The platoon sergeant had told him in a gruff but fatherly sort of way that the razzing and tricks wouldn't last too long, that it was all part of the Game. Oh, yeah, it was part of the Game, all right . . . to the others. On his second day in the unit, one of the crew chiefs had told him to run over to the maintenance tent and get five gallons of rotor wash to clean the main rotor blades with. The parts clerk at the tent had told him that all solvents and cleaning fluids had been transferred to the motor pool, so off he had gone to the far end of the company area where the motor pool was located. The motor sergeant had told him that he could have as much rotor wash as he needed, but first Carl would have to get a requisition form from the orderly room with the appropriate approving signatures on it.

At the orderly room, Sp4 Donnelly, the company clerk, eased his skinny frame back in his battered metal chair and laughed at him. "You newbies are all the same! You dudes don't know jackshit about nothin'. Rotor wash is your blade wind, man. It don't come in no bucket."

Leaving the orderly room with a slow heat building up, he had seen the motor sergeant talking to a couple of mechanics and pointing in his direction. He couldn't hear what was said, but both men suddenly started laughing, shook their heads, and went back into the work bay.

A sudden change in the helicopter's attitude refocused Carl's attention to his duties. The pilot had put the ship into a climb as they neared the cultivated areas of the villages outside of Tay Ninh. At two thousand feet they leveled off, the blades still beating choppily at the air. From that altitude Carl watched the patchwork-quilt design of the rice paddies and the dusty, narrow, ribbonlike roads dotted with small antlike figures scurrying about, ignoring the flying beast above them.

Carl remembered the crew chief's lecture from his first day of flying and shifted his attention from the scenes below to the horizon. The crew chief had drilled his point home, attempting to impress Carl with the dangers of coming back into the seeming safety of the base camps.

"Charlie's only part of the problem, kid. You've got to

keep your eyes open for all the other aircraft, 'cause a midair will sure as hell ruin your whole day. The control towers do a pretty good job keeping everybody straight, but mistakes happen. You 'specially gotta watch out for the VNAF pilots. Those crazy dink bastards never check with the towers. They just take off any damn time and direction they want."

Aside from the old-timer's warnings, Carl had heard enough stories about the Vietnamese Army and Air Force to make him more than a little skeptical about their abilities. With that in mind, he carefully scanned the surrounding airspace as the pilot received final landing clearance and swept the ship over the wire and earthworks into safe harbor.

Carl stripped the machine gun, the tool of his trade, off the pole mount, hefted the twenty-three-pound weapon over his shoulder, and moved around to the left side of the ship to pick up the crew chief's weapon. As the doorgunner it was his job to take care of both machine guns, keeping them clean and operational. The crew chief was supposed to do the routine maintenance work while the gunner attended to the weapons, but frequently the two men would work together to speed things up. There would be no working together today, though. The maintenance officer had already arrived and was talking to the pilot and the crew chief as he examined the abused blades. Jessup told Carl to get the guns cleaned up, and Carl didn't need a second order. With both of the M-60s over his shoulders, he quickly headed toward the arms room and lost himself in the motions of stripping and cleaning the guns.

He had just barely made it back to his hootch, a far cry from his Texas home but extravagant by Vietnamese standards, when Sp5 Regis stuck his head in the hootch door. The thin lips of his hawklike face curled up in a contemptuous smile.

"Another rookie screwup," he said, shaking his head in mock disgust. "You'll probably be dead by this time next week . . . if Sergeant Wooden lets you fly that much longer. He wants to see you over in his hootch ASAP and he's pissed off right now, so you better get your ass in gear."

Sergeant First Class Alvin Wooden, the platoon sergeant, the only person who hadn't been hassling him up to this point. *Well, hell. Guess I'm on everybody's shit list now.*

Wooden was waiting in the hootch for him. At thirty-six Wooden looked like a man of fifty, seventeen years of service turning the dark brown hair to a dull gray and creasing the face with a network of lines. His gray eyes were unreadable, only a studied stare, as Carl presented himself.

"Okay, Willstrom," he began in a slow monotone. "I know your eyes are okay because you passed a flight physical to get here, so would you kindly explain to me how you put that helicopter into a tree?"

Carl had been trying to figure out how to answer that one. Wooden must have heard a thousand excuses and would see right through anything that Carl might try to make up. "I don't know how it happened, Sergeant. I guess I just wasn't concentrating and didn't see the tree. I told the pilot that I thought we could clear the tree, but . . ."

Wooden's calm suddenly broke, his fist slamming down on his ammo crate table, cutting Carl off before he could finish. "Listen, soldier! This is no game over here. People die because of mistakes like that. I don't give a damn if you get shot all to hell or blow yourself up, 'cause you're the new guy in the platoon and I don't know much about you yet. But I do know those other people on that chopper and I do give a damn about them. I don't want to see any of them get wasted because some rookie fucked up. We all make mistakes one time or another, but Nam is one place you don't make too many. I'm gonna give you another chance tomorrow. You'll be going up with Regis on 312 and he's gonna be watching you every step of the way. If I get a report that you screwed up on anything—I repeat, *anything*—you're going to be the platoon's shit detail man until I can get your ass transferred out of here. Any questions?''

Carl shook his head. Wooden studied him for a moment and then dismissed him with a curt wave of his hand.

Back in his hootch, he sat on the edge of his cot pondering the miseries of being the only new guy in the platoon, when Regis once again found him.

Smug, self-confident to the point of arrogance, Regis made no attempt to conceal his contempt for Carl. He planted himself in front of Carl, commanding the rookie's attention. ''All right, newbie. We got a log mission for the 1/7 Cav tomorrow out near Katum. Lift-off at 0600, so make sure you've got the guns and ammo on the ship at least fifteen minutes prior. I want the cans filled to the top and an extra thousand rounds under the seats. 312 just came out of maintenance today and is empty, so you're going to have to hump all the ammo out to her. Smokes should still be on board, but check 'em anyway. The place we're going is about sixty klicks north of here and damned close to the red line.'' He paused for a moment, seeing a puzzled look on Carl's face. ''Red line—Cambodia to you—a place we ain't supposed to be. Anyway, there's been a lot of shit happenin' in that AO, so double-check the guns. We'll take a test fire on the way out if we got time.''

Without waiting to see if Carl had any questions, Regis turned and headed for the door, then stopped and turned back toward Carl. ''One more thing, rookie. Don't screw up on my ship.'' He gave Carl a malicious smile, clearly conveying the unspoken message that he hoped for a mistake, then left, leaving Carl to his thoughts.

The morning air was cool and invigorating, giving Carl a savored moment of refreshment that a troubled sleep had failed to provide. He had made it through the early morning routine without incident and now sat at his position as the Huey began to gain altitude over the quiet, deceptively peaceful panorama of Tay Ninh Province. From high enough up it could have been a rural scene from anywhere, a patchwork design of browns and greens, farmers in the fields. The jungle made the difference. Full-strength NVA regiments could be hiding under that green curtain, moving freely as he rode through the sky.

The feeling of the cool air across his face reminded him of one of the reasons he had volunteered for duty as a doorgunner. The idea of being able to get into the action with a fair degree of comfort had appealed to him. The glory of war from the skies was somewhat reminiscent of a past age when daring young men had taken to the air in their flying machines over the trenches of a war-torn Europe. Defying death in the skies and then returning to the comfort of a base at night, exchanging stories of the day's adventures and enjoying the camaraderie of fellow fliers. That was the way to fight a war!

His sympathies went out to those on the ground, the grunts, who had to hack and slash their way through the jungles in the sweltering Vietnamese heat. Tales that he had already heard of booby traps, leeches, spiders, and an endless list of deadly snakes only served to further emphasize the advantages of being a doorgunner.

Looking down from his vantage point, it seemed hard to believe that there was a war going on. Quiet down there and, to Carl's relief, quiet up in the ship. Regis hadn't made any remarks and neither had the pilots. Carl hadn't flown with either of them before, but he knew that the copilot, Warrant Officer Nelson, was a fairly new arrival, just barely a month in-country. His light blond hair and watery blue eyes set in a pale face gave him a choirboy appearance, out of place in the aerial war chariot. In contrast, the pilot, First Lieutenant Harris, was an army recruiting poster come to life. Square-jawed, six feet on the mark, with close-cropped black hair and a deeply tanned face marking him as a veteran. With over nine months in-country, Harris was on the downhill side and classified as a "two-digit midget," ninety-nine days or less. Carl felt reasonably safe with the experienced pilot at the controls even if the rest of the crew might not feel too secure with Carl as the right side gunner.

Halfway to their destination, the pilot overflew a free-fire zone and let Regis and Carl check their pieces with a couple of quick bursts. With no particular target to shoot at, Carl simply pointed his barrel down at an angle and pulled back on the triggers of the butterfly grips, sending a short stream of the 7.62mm bullets earthward. The tracers appeared to arc and bend back ever so slightly, burning out before they reached the jungle below. Carl enjoyed the feeling of power that the guns gave, the power of death that the dark metal spoke of when it made itself heard. Of course, other men held that same power, but that was what gave the excitement to what Carl perceived as a deadly game. To his untested spirit the Game only partly consisted of trying to destroy the enemy. The most challenging part was the ability of those small brown men to destroy him, a quarry that could fight back most effectively as helicopter loss statistics showed. The *Stars and Stripes* paper he had seen the other day said that over twelve hundred helicopters had been lost so far in the war. To Carl, that just added spice to the Game, even though he hadn't seen any action yet.

Fifteen minutes past the point where they had conducted their test fire, a reddish-brown blur gradually took shape as a circular dirt ring, 150 yards in diameter, dotted with 105mm artillery pieces and a battery of the earthshaking eight-inch self-propelled guns. A small island of brown in the midst of an ocean of green, Fire Support Base Gray was temporary home to the 1st Battalion, 7th Cavalry, one of the division's infantry battalions. From the relative safety of the fire base, companies, platoons, and squads invaded the jungle, Charlie's domain, in search of the enemy or at least his war materials, hidden in their underground caches. Today, 312's mission was that of resupplying the units in the field with the necessities: ammunition, food, and most important, water.

"Blue Grass Six, this is Papa One Two, over." The pilot's voice crackled through the earphones of Carl's flight helmet.

"Papa One Two, Blue Grass Six X-ray, over," came the squawked garbled reply from the base below.

"Roger, Six X-ray. This is One Two. We're your log bird today. What have you got for us? Over."

"One Two, Six X-ray, we have class one for Alpha Six's location. Come on down and visit, out."

With the preliminary radio exchange over, Lieutenant Harris put the chopper into a steep downward spiral, dropping quickly to avoid tempting any ground fire. Carl had been told several times why it was done that way and understood the necessity, but understanding didn't keep the guts from churning on the way down. At least he didn't get sick as he had the first time his pilot had made the same kind of approach. He had spent his first break between flights scrubbing the wind-smeared puke off the chopper's floor panels. Another gunner had told him that after the first time it rarely happened again. Carl sincerely hoped it was true.

The grunts were ready for them when they hit the ground. While the pilot talked to one of the infantry officers and consulted his map, the grunts loaded on case after case of ammunition, some 7.62mm for the M-60 machine guns, 5.56mm for M-16s, and two cases of frags. Carl watched the rough-looking lot pass the cases along in a daisy chain. Shirtless for the most part, darkly tanned, the soldiers were already sweating profusely in the early morning heat. The sweat streaming down their backs and chests carried away the dirt and grime like small eroding rivulets. But the cleansing effect was only momentary. No one could stay clean for long in a place like this.

In five minutes the ship was loaded and balanced to Regis's satisfaction. Lieutenant Harris was talking to the crew over the ship's intercom. "Seems like one of their elements had a little visit from Charlie during the night. Some small-arms fire and a few mortars around 0400. They've got patrols out around their NDP, so stay alert." He looked back over his shoulder, deliberately focusing on Carl. "I don't want any friendlies getting shot up!"

Ten minutes later they were circling a jungle clearing half the size of a football field while Lieutenant Harris tried to raise the ground unit on the radio. After the second try he received a response.

"Papa One Two, this is Alpha Three Six Romeo. Over," the unit's RTO replied from below.

"Alpha Three Six Romeo, Papa One Two. We are inbound your location with Class One. Request smoke. Over."

The radio operator on the ground relayed the request, and a few seconds later a plume of yellow smoke drifted lazily up from the northeast corner of the clearing. The pilot identified the yellow smoke, and the RTO confirmed correct identification. Down again, tight spiral right into the fading smoke. It was easier every time, Carl thought, just like the man had said.

As the helicopter touched down, half a dozen men ran out from the treeline, bent low to the ground, shielding their faces against the blowing dust and grass. Forming a daisy chain, they quickly off-loaded the supplies and vanished back into the closed protection of the jungle. As the shadow of the last man disappeared into the trees, an officer and a fully loaded soldier came trotting out to the ship. The soldier, a tall lanky black, clambered on board. Despite his bulky pack, he made himself comfortable with an ease that bespoke of many helicopter sorties. The black grinned at Carl and yelled above the noise of the ship's engines. "I'm going home, Jack! Orders came down yesterday! Back to the World!"

Carl smiled back and nodded his head in approval. The *World*, that which existed everywhere outside of Southeast Asia. The goal of every GI, to make it back to the World alive, and with all the important parts still attached.

The pilot had received the same information along with an outgoing mail pouch from the infantry officer and was ready to lift. "Clear?" questioned Harris. The crew chief replied instantly; Carl took a second longer to be sure. No trees, no grunts by the tail rotor. Up and away.

Halfway back to the fire base the radio crackled to life. "Papa One Two, Blue Grass Six X-ray. Over."

The copilot took the call. "This is Papa One Two. Send it. Over."

"Papa One Two, Six X-ray. One of our elements in

trouble. Mechanical ambush, enemy situation negative. One line one, one line two. Extraction urgent at following coordinates. I send, Tango Lima one five six, three four two. Contact Charlie Two Six on this net. How copy? Over."

Harris answered while the copilot quickly located the map coordinates. "This is Papa One Two. Solid copy. On our way . . . Break . . . Charlie Two Six, Papa One Two. Over."

An urgent voice came back instantly. "Papa One Two, Charlie Two Six. We monitored your traffic. Line two has to go now. Will pop smoke on your command. Over."

"Charlie Two Six, Roger that. At your location in zero three mikes. What kind of LZ do you have? Over." As the pilot finished speaking he nosed the chopper until the airspeed indicator was showing 120 knots. Their short-timer passenger looked startled, then worried.

"What the hell's happenin'?" he yelled at Carl.

"Medevac call," Carl yelled back over the increased turbine noise. He saw the man's reaction, read the silent 'Oh, shit, I'm too short for this' in the soldier's expression. Even a new guy could understand that feeling. Medevac meant injuries, injuries usually meant action, and any man riding a chopper back to the rear to catch that freedom bird to the World didn't want to get sidetracked into a place where he could die.

Lieutenant Harris's voice caught Carl's attention again. "Man on the ground says our LZ is a wide spot on a trail. They're taking down trees with C-4 so we can hover down, but it's still going to be a tight fit. No sign of Charlie, but the area's only secure about thirty meters out, so stay alert." Again Harris looked over his shoulder, staring hard at Carl, who felt compelled to respond with an affirmative.

The radio squawked again. The platoon leader on the ground advised Harris that they could hear the ship, and Harris requested a smoke. After identifying the color and getting confirmation, Harris put the ship into a steep dive, pulling out sharply less than fifty feet above the treetops. Hovering down, the crew chief kept up a steady chatter advising the pilot of his clearance. Carl followed his lead, and the Huey settled down amid ragged stumps and potentially hazardous flying debris from the blasted trees.

Even before the skids touched down, the infantrymen swarmed out of the trees on both sides with their bloody burdens. On Regis's side two soldiers threw a poncho-wrapped oblong on board. Carl's attention was focused on the writhing mass of pain being laid on the floor at his side. A young trooper with what once was blond hair was wearing a bizarre wig of tangled hair dyed red, edged with ragged flaps of skin and perforated with fragments of skull. Carl felt his stomach churn and rise, fought hard to suppress the surge, and forced it down again. Cursing at the burning sensation, he looked back at the soldier, wondering how the man could still be conscious with what looked like a death wound. Despite the ugliness of the wound, he felt drawn to the sight, and studied the man. In the frozen seconds of time, his eyes took in the bloodied fatigues, the peppering of jagged holes in them, the convulsive jerks of the arms and legs. One leg seemed odd, mismatched with a blood-soaked T-shirt wrapped around the ankle.

"Here, catch," a voice yelled, and Carl automatically caught the tossed object. Out of context, it took him a moment to realize that he was holding the injured soldier's boot with the foot still in it, raggedly severed at the ankle.

He was frozen for a moment with the grisly relic in his hands, but the pilot's request for clearance cut through his numbed mind and pulled him back to the task of getting the ship out of the LZ. Once at the top of the trees, Harris ran the ship all the way to the red line, staying low and fast. At one point he made a sharp bank to avoid a solitary spire of dead wood, causing the wounded soldier to slide diagonally across the floor before being grabbed by the short-timer. The wounded grunt had stopped thrashing, but was still breathing fast and shallow. The same course deviation that had caused him to slide had also rolled the corpse, partially unrolling the olive-green poncho. For a moment Carl stared at the ruined head, no longer resembling anything human, and then he abruptly leaned out over the edge of the helicopter and retched, splattering the remains of his breakfast along the chopper's tail boom.

When the heaving subsided, he fell back weakly against the compartment wall and stared at the short-timer. The man met his eyes and gave him a humorless grin, then moved closer so he could be heard without shouting.

"You'll get used to it, my man. It happens all the time in the bush. These guys was probably the point and the slack men." He pointed to the head injuries and the amputated foot by Carl's feet. "Looks like a high-low booby trap. More'n likely some of our own shit that Charlie found and rigged. Glad as hell I'm gettin' outa here." The last was barely audible to Carl. The black's face became expressionless and, finished talking, he moved back toward the center area, staring at the floorboards.

The rest of the flight passed without incident. The wounded trooper lay motionless, a small pool of blood gathering at his side only to be whipped and spread around by the airflow. Carl's stomach had settled and he was feeling the absence of his meal. He heard Harris call up the Blue Grass element, telling them that the ship would be off station for refueling after dropping off the casualties. Carl absently wondered if they were going to chow down while they were off station.

Nelson, the copilot, radioed in to 15th Medical Battalion at Tay Ninh, giving them the casualty status. Then he switched frequency, raised Tay Ninh Control, and requested priority landing clearance to the dust-off pad.

The medics with a stretcher rushed the ship just as the skids touched down, and quickly but gently eased the wounded grunt onto the stretcher. As they hurried back into their sandbagged building, another pair of medics, in less of a hurry, loaded up the corpse and the severed foot. Carl never found out the fate of the injured soldier, even though he wondered about him. The old-timers didn't give it a second thought. Unless a man was from their own outfit, there was no interest in him after he passed out of their hands. That was the way it was, part of the mental survival.

Carl's thoughts kept drifting back to the scenes on the

chopper, but he didn't let it get to him and did his job well enough to stay off everyone's blacklist. Shortly before dark, the 1/7 battalion CO gave the pilot a "well done" and released them for the day. After topping off with fuel in Tay Ninh, Harris piloted the ship back across the active and hovered into 312's revetment, a steel planking and sandbag shelter. While the pilots and Regis began doing the postoperation maintenance checks, Carl busied himself with some old rags and a water can. There was the matter of removing the remains of his earlier aerial disgorgement from the length of the chopper.

Regis inspected his efforts, nodded as if satisfied. "Okay, Willstrom, now take care of the guns."

Carl considered that a small triumph. He hadn't been razzed about getting sick, and Regis had even called him by name instead of "rookie" or "newbie." With a bit of snappiness to his step, he headed for the solvent barrels with the two machine guns. They weren't too much trouble, having only thirty or forty rounds fired through them, and Carl had them back together in a short time. A light coat of oil and an operation check added the final touch. He liked the look and feel of the M-60, and for a moment he saw himself in a fantasy, manning his gun, delivering a withering hail of fire, beating back the surging communist hordes. The flame-flashing barrel was a scythe of death, reaping its harvest. He smiled at the fanciful flight, glad that nobody could read his thoughts.

After securing the guns, Carl wandered over to the company mess hall and joined the other crews who were coming in for late chow. Regis was already there, talking to Jolley and Smith, fellow platoon members. They stopped for a second when Carl walked in, then Regis acknowledged him with a slight nod and resumed talking.

"Rookie did all right today," Regis was saying, "even if he did try to paint the tail boom with his guts!" They all laughed, but at least it was a friendly laugh, tinged with a hint of acceptance. Carl smiled, flushing, and sighed inwardly. Back to "rookie" again, he walked over with his tray to join them.

II.

The next five days were long and boring, making Carl understand what his father had told him. A veteran of two wars, his old man had said that war frequently consisted of long hours of brain-dulling boredom interspersed with brief moments of sheer terror. Most of Carl's experience so far was on the boredom side of the scale, and he thought a moment of terror would be a welcome relief. The first thrills of flying were over, and although he was still fresh and eager every morning, there was no action. Five days of quiet resupply missions for various line units, shuttle runs for ship parts, and working on the ground was eroding the Red Baron, silk-scarf image. Working with Sp5 Jolley on 372's periodic maintenance wasn't too bad, though. Jolley was an easygoing old timer who had already done a year in Nam and was halfway through his first extension. The carefully cultivated handlebar mustache was his trademark, and the dark aviator's glasses lent a dashing air to his appearance.

Working with Jolley, Carl learned the ropes of the helicopter trade and was gaining the acceptance of the other crewman. Aside from the stigma of still being a newbie, only one obstacle clearly separated him from the rest of the platoon. He was still a cherry-boy, untried by the baptism by fire. Jolley, the old man of the platoon crews at twenty-two, assured Carl that he would receive that ritual in the very near future, and Carl had the impression that the crew chief had his own intelligence network.

With 372 finished, Carl returned to his hootch, the corrugated steel and sandbag abode of the second flight platoon. Except for Jolley, the entire platoon was gathered there, the crews seated on the cots, Sergeant Wooden and the platoon leader standing in the middle of the floor area, waiting.

"Jolley on his way?" Wooden asked as Carl came through the door.

"He'll be up in just a minute, Sarge. He was finishing up the logbook when I left him." One of the other gunners made room for him on the edge of a cot. "What's going on?" he whispered to the man, Sp4 David Smith.

Smith, a young redheaded kid from Ohio, flashed him an excited smile. "We got a big combat assault tomorrow! Apache scouts found a big-ass bunker complex near the red line and we're gonna hit it. The LT's gonna brief us as soon as Jolley gets here."

The LT, First Lieutenant Gonzales, was a short, wiry figure. His leathery, dark brown skin would almost allow him to pass as a Vietnamese. He started his briefing when Jolley's feet hit the rough plywood floor. "Listen up, troops. We've got a hot one tomorrow. I have already briefed all the pilots in detail, so you'll just get the basics. Hunter-killer teams from 1/9's Apache Troop spotted a large complex forty-five klicks northwest of here. The complex is just on our side of the red line and may extend across into Cambodia. The scout ships reported receiving moderate ground fire from our side, and the gunships reported heavy automatic-weapons fire from the Cambodian side. All of our platoon's ships will be utilized plus four ships from the first platoon. We'll have a heavy arty prep and air cover from Blue Max. The CA will be made with three sorties from two companies of the 2d Battalion, 5th Cav. Enemy contact extremely likely, so make sure those guns are ready. Lift-off at 0600. That's all I've got. Sergeant Wooden will give you the assignments."

Wooden finished up his list, told the crew chiefs who their pilots would be, and instructed everybody to be at the mess hall by 0500, flight line by 0530.

With all of the details out of the way, the meeting broke up, some of the men heading straight for their bunks, others gathering to talk about the mission. Carl opted for the cot and tried to get some sleep, but it stubbornly resisted him. He tossed and turned, sweating freely in the muggy heat of the night, and the butterflies in his stomach refused to still their wings.

"Opening-night jitters," he muttered to himself, and tried closing his eyes again. No good. A series of violent mind photographs flashed through his brain, every imaginable disaster that could happen out there. His test under fire would put to him all the unanswered questions. The sweat came from more than the Vietnamese heat. What would he do, how would he hold up, if the shit hit the fan? Despite his fantasies of furious action and heroic struggles, he was filled with self-doubts. He wished fervently for sleep to claim him, but the restless sleep that finally came did little to refresh him.

Sergeant Wooden came through the hootch at 0440, rousting the troops with an air of happiness that Carl found disgusting at such an early hour. Most responded at once, up and into their Nomex flight uniforms. A few had to be shaken twice, and Carl thought that they looked as exhausted as he felt. Dressing was a barely conscious act, and he felt like he was wandering in a fog as he staggered to the washing troughs to shave. The first splash of cool water cleared his head and brought him back to life. Quickly shaving, he washed up, threw his kit back into the hootch, and made it to the mess hall.

Carl went light on the food, his stomach undergoing the same kind of turmoil that his mind had during the night. There wasn't much talking around the tables. Men ate quickly, gulped down their coffee, juice, or warm milk, and hurried to the flight line.

Carl joined the other gunners at the arms room, drew out the machine guns, and strode down the line between the two rows of revetments until he found 372. Jolley and the two pilots had just arrived and were starting the preflight checks. Critical oil levels, push-pull rods, safety-wired nuts and bolts. The list seemed endless to Carl. A thousand different things that could go wrong, any one of which could kill him just as dead as an enemy bullet.

He mounted the M-60s and stepped out of the revetment to flag down the mule, the army's workhorse version of a go-cart, that was bringing around the extra ammunition. Carl lifted off six of the two-hundred-round ammo cans and stored them under the crew seats. That brought them up to three thousand rounds for each gun, five cans on each side plus two thousand bullets in the minigun cans that were strapped onto the gun mounts.

At 0530 they were all ready. Warrant Officer Simmons cranked the engine and adjusted his sunglasses on his crooked nose. Carl had heard that the misshapen object was the result of a chopper crash Simmons had survived when he was a rookie. WO1 Peters monitored the instruments while Jolley ground-guided the ship out of the revetment and then sprang aboard. Simmons hovered over and eased 372 into her spot of the single file line up on the edge of the airstrip. Captain Slough, first platoon leader and flight leader for the mission, made all the clearances and lifted off, followed, in trail formation, by the other nine ships. Once out of the traffic pattern, the flight leader, code-named Yellow One, climbed to two thousand feet and ordered an echelon left formation. This gave Carl an excellent view of all the ships ahead of his as they took on the diagonal configuration. For Carl, on his first assault mission, it was a breathtaking sight. The ships cutting through the skies between the billowing white clouds above and the soft green below sent a thrill through him. He had been gripping the handle of his gun, but noticed that nobody else was. All the other guns he could see were barrel-down, held in position by barrel clips on the pole mounts. At this altitude no one was worried about ground fire.

Once down at the 2/5's home, FSB Collins, all the choppers shut down and Captain Slough called for all the aircraft commanders to meet at his ship for a final briefing with the infantry S-3. As the minutes crawled by, Carl could feel a knot tightening in his stomach and tried to lose it, re-oiling his gun, checking the ammo belts, joking with Jolley and the copilot. Jolley didn't seem to feel any pressure. Hell, why should he? This was old hat for him. But the copilot, Carl sensed, was as nervous as he was.

Peters was another of those recent arrivals, only a few weeks longer in Nam than Carl and equally inexperienced under pressure. Like many of the warrants, Peters looked too young for his rank. Not quite twenty, he was just a few months older than Carl. The smile on his face as they talked didn't match the uneasiness in the blue eyes. Carl wondered if Peters could see the same thing in him and decided to put his flight shades back on.

They all looked up at a shout and saw the ACs returning. Off to the right the lead elements of the infantry companies were filing out of the fire base, splitting into six-man groups and making for their designated ships. Simmons gave the whirling hand gesture as he approached, indicating crank time, and Carl hurried to the tail section to get the blade untied. With the blades clear and the grunts standing just outside of the rotor sweep, Peters fired up the turbines. When all the ships were cranked, Carl gave his group the signal to load up. Quickly, the grunts piled on, sleeves rolled down, rifle muzzles pointed either up or out. They situated themselves so that they could un-ass the ship in a hurry. Everyone was expecting this to be a hot LZ, and none of the infantry wanted to be on the chopper long once they hit the landing zone. A hovering Huey loaded with grunts made a hell of a good target.

Carl looked at the six men on the ship. Grunts. The men who bore the brunt of the fighting in all wars. All shapes and sizes, from skinny dudes who were barely heavier than their packs to towering football-player types. Most of them had a worn look about them, an oldness in the eyes matched by their faded drab jungle fatigues. A few surface tears and patches, but still holding together, just like the men who wore them. One of the six stood out in his dress. A young kid with a peach-fuzz mustache and fair complexion, untanned by the tropical sun. The jungle fatigues had that sheen to them that marked a newbie. His eyes weren't those of an old soldier repeating an endless task. Worry, fear, darting around the interior of the ship, trying to find reassurance.

Carl understood the feeling but couldn't offer any comfort. The pilot was giving them instructions, taking his mind away from the troubles of others. "No fire restrictions on the first sortie. We'll be going in staggered trail. LZ is long and narrow so we'll be close to the treeline. Count on little guys waiting for us and hope the artillery prep gets some." As if on cue, the artillery batteries opened up, and the 105s and 155 guns roared out over the noise of the ten helicopters, spewing out their deadly message from steel throats.

On the lift-off order from Yellow One the ships all hovered up, and like a line of ducks following their mother, they rose into the sky, regrouping at two thousand feet. This time the gunners were all on their weapons, barrels out, ready for action. Here and there in some of the choppers Carl could see grunts sitting on the edges of the open compartments, legs dangling out over empty space, their own weapons pointed out. Everyone was going to be blasting when they came down on final approach.

One of the grunts yelled and pointed back to the rear of the flight formation. There they were: the escort service, four AH1G Cobra gunships, from Blue Max, the division's aerial artillery battalion. The grunts were all smiles as the slender shapes closed in on the flight. The Cobras would take up where the fire base artillery left off, two ships at a time diving down to provide close support for the lift birds. Carl had never seen the gunships in action before, but their fame was legendary in Vietnam. Their rockets, automatic 40mm grenade launcher, and three-thousand-rounds-per-minute electric machine guns made them deserving of their reputation.

Simmons keyed the intercom. "LZ at one o'clock." Carl looked out forward and just to the right of the chopper's nose, and saw the long brown gash in the jungle and the flashes followed by clouds of gray and white smoke where the artillery rounds were impacting.

Again the radio crackled, this time with the flight leader's command for the staggered trail formation. That would keep the ships out of a straight line but still close enough to get the entire flight down at the same time and give all the gunners clear fields of fire.

The flight went into its final turn and began the descent just as the artillery barrage stopped. The Cobras swept by Carl on their way in, making their first pass to clear the area for the lead elements. Yellow One gave the firing order that Carl had been eagerly awaiting when the ships were ten seconds out from the LZ. "All Yellow elements, go hot!" Twenty M-60 machine guns erupted, accompanied by an assortment of infantry weapons.

Carl, riding in the seventh bird, lost his tenseness and became caught up in a shooting frenzy, firing long arching bursts into the already battered treeline. For a few seconds the only thing that registered in his mind was the path of the tracers ripping into the jungle, then, remembering his training, he slowed down and let the gun chatter off shorter bursts. The second Cobra section rolled in, expending their rockets ten to twenty meters inside the treeline, miniature lightning flashes against the green darkness. No fear, no nervousness now, only a slight puzzlement. So far there had been no return fire. The LZ was a natural gauntlet and should have been an ideal place for Charlie to have a welcoming committee.

Yellow One was almost on the ground, all the ships were into the landing zone, and a Cobra section was just pulling out of its gun run when the spell broke. With a sudden fury that made Carl scream, unheard in the battle din, white flashes lashed out toward the choppers from the entire length of the LZ. He screamed once more, heart pounding, but not in fear or surprise. Defiance! Action, targets, not trees. Somewhere far away, one part of his mind was watching the events unfold, everything moving in slow motion, every detail standing out as if under microscopic focus. Photographlike exposures printed into his mind as another part of his awareness carried on the war of reality.

A steady white flash in the trees directly opposite him

demanded his attention as the ship moved into the enemy's line of fire. Trailing the position slightly, Carl depressed the triggers on the butterfly grips, adjusting his aim by the tracers, walking his fire right into Charlie's muzzle flashes. For an eternity of milliseconds Carl dueled with enemy guns until the chopper was past that obstacle and hovering down, with more enemy fire coming from slightly to the front. Carl shifted his fire to the new targets, letting loose a long stream of fire to cover the infantry as they scrambled and leaped from the chopper.

Three of the six men on board jumped off from his side, dashed a few steps, and dropped to the cover of the ground, returning Charlie's fire. Unloaded and cleared, the chopper lurched up, giving Carl a better angle of fire, and for the first time he became aware of other actions going on around him. Infantry fire teams were trying to maneuver toward the treeline, and Cobras were still rolling in with their suppressive fires. Another muzzle flash drew his attention and abruptly ceased as he poured a hail of fire into its concealed position. For a moment he kept up the rain of bullets, and then with a yell of triumph he angled at another target, his heart still pounding furiously.

Somewhere close by, an explosion sounded over the machine guns, and a frantic Mayday signal started over the radio, interrupted by a second, more violent explosion.

"Jesus Christ!" The pilot jerked the ship hard right, almost brushing the tops of the trees on the way out. "Yellow One, Seven. Six just took a hit and blew up!"

"Yellow Seven, Yellow One, Roger. Break . . . Yellow One Zero, One. Over." The last ship in the flight responded, and Carl heard the flight leader instruct the ship to check for survivors as it went by. For a long few seconds no sounds were heard, save the cutting blades and turbines, as the flight climbed to altitude to regroup.

"Yellow One, Yellow One Zero." The voice from the trail ship paused for a moment, then continued, terse, emotionless. "Negative on survivors. They're all gone."

Gone. One ship, four men, snuffed out just like that. The helicopter was from the first platoon, and Carl really hadn't gotten to know his own platoon that well yet, much less the others. Still, it was a sobering jolt into the reality of sudden death. Men from his own company, only a few seconds in front of his ship. The chill of death washed away the remaining battle heat in Carl's mind.

On the way back to the fire base for the next load Carl monitored the radio channels, drinking in all the details. Two Cobras remained on station and Carl could hear the background fighting when the grunts made calls to the gunships to direct their fire into areas of increasing resistance. From the traffic Carl had the impression that the fighting was the heaviest toward the north end of the LZ and that the grunts had only secured the south end. One message concerned the ill-fated first platoon ship. A field medic had braved the enemy fire to check out a body that had been thrown clear of the chopper, but the report from Yellow One Zero was only confirmed. No survivors.

Picking up the next load of troops, Carl felt the excitement begin to build again. For a brief moment, a twinge of guilt assailed him and he tried to rationalize the anticipation of more action with the reality of death already done and death still to come. "Fuck it." They were dead, he was still alive, and there wasn't a hell of a lot else to say.

The chattering radios told of a changing tactical situation on the ground. After a prolonged stiff initial resistance, Charlie had not faded away into the jungle as he usually did. The north end of the landing zone had definitely become a rallying point for the enemy, now confirmed as being North Vietnamese regulars. Only the southern section was secure, and the GIs in the first lift had suffered heavy casualties.

Yellow One instructed the flight to split into two groups, the first four ships and a medevac bird making the first sortie. The remaining ships, including Carl's, would stay aloft until the lead group started out. That would put him right behind the second group's leader, and if his ship were to the right of the lead . . . His fingers tightened involuntarily on the butterfly grips. No obstacles between him and the consolidated NVA positions, a full field of fire both ways.

While the first group made its approach, Carl listened in on the steady stream of radio traffic as the first flight hit the LZ.

"Taking fire from fifty-ones at one o'clock! All Yellow elements break hard right on lift-off."

"Yellow One, Yellow Two. We're hit and down. No control response. We're getting out!"

"Two, One. Roger . . . Break . . . Yellow Five, did you monitor? Over."

"One, this is Five. Roger, we'll pick up Two's crew. Out."

Carl heard other ships reporting hits on their way out, but he had his own concerns now as the second flight began the approach. The staccato sounds from the AK-47s and Chicom machine guns pierced through his helmet phones, and long series of flashes from dead ahead gave him his targets. Screaming at the grunts to stay back in the cargo bay, Carl swung his right leg down onto the skids and pivoted his M-60, firing right past the copilot's door. The grunts plugged their ears against the head-splitting blasts in the close confines of the cargo area while the copilot, ears protected by the flight helmet, gave Carl an excited thumbs-up. "Tear 'em up, gunner!"

Carl continued laying down a protective net of lead until the ship was a few feet from the ground. Then, for a helpless moment, he had to cease fire to allow the grunts to scramble out. A split-second glance through the front windshield revealed the wreckage of Yellow Two off to the left and a flash of moving figures as the crew of that chopper sprinted from tree cover to launch themselves into the protective womb of Yellow Five. The boots of the last grunt cleared the deck and Carl began to spray hell again in a small arc, nose to two o'clock, as the flight began to lift out.

Simmons banked the ship hard right, giving Carl a dizzying view of a small section of the LZ. He spotted the bodies of several GIs lying motionless in the grass, one sprawled on his back, one knee bent and propped up, arms outstretched beside his head, looking for all the world as if he had just lain down for a nap in a lush meadow. Only the dark red stain covering most of his chest provided the testimony of death.

A quick rush of radio calls informed the flight leader that some of the second group's ships had also taken hits and the ten that had started the mission were reduced to seven as Yellow Eight had to make a forced landing just short of the fire base. No injuries, just one more ship out of action.

Carl noticed that the first flight group was still sitting on the ground at the fire base even though the grunts were all on board, ready for the third and final sortie. Once again the tactical situation had changed, and Carl gathered from the command and control traffic that the NVA were finally beginning to roll back into the jungle. The men on the ground were slowly moving up, encountering and clearing bunkers against thinning resistance. One Cobra section had rearmed and was working over the northern part of the LZ in front of the advancing infantrymen. Another gunship had been dispatched to provide security for the downed Yellow Eight until a ground security and recovery team could get there.

With the enemy pulling back, the flight leader decided to take all seven ships in for the last landing. This time each ship would carry at least seven, stronger ships taking eight to make up for the loss of the other three choppers.

Loaded and ready to go, Carl began to feel a physical change washing through him. During the first two lifts, his senses had been absorbing everything that happened like a sponge, and now, in this momentary lull, an ice-cold hand reached into him and squeezed the sponge. Reaction flooded out. He could feel the blood draining to his feet and knew that he must be turning pale. A cold heat enveloped his body, dizziness, spinning, legs shaking uncontrollably, and for a second he was afraid that he was going to pass out. Stay calm. Breathe deep. Suck in that air. Fighting hard for control, he felt a fresh cool current of air as the ship began to move, and a fresh current of life flowed through his body in that instant.

Going in this time seemed anticlimactic. No muzzle flashes, no instinctive chattering of AK-47s, no radio calls "taking fire." Back to their usual form of fighting, Carl thought. Fade back, fade away . . . till next time. He noticed that despite the relative security of the LZ, the grunts still didn't screw around getting off the ship. Most of them were jumping off before the skids ever touched ground and dogging for the trees. The bodies he had seen earlier had been carried back to the far south end of the LZ along with the wounded.

Carl pressed his mike button to give Simmons a "clear right" when the ship was suddenly jolted by a thundering explosion. A fiery blossom sprouted a scant ten meters to the right front of the ship, propelling blasted earth and shrapnel in volcanic simulation. Sensory input imploded into his head, grunts diving to the ground, the copilot jerking in his harness, his agonized scream mixing with the booming reports of more mortars impacting amid the helicopters.

"Yellow elements, One. Up and break hard left. Out." Discipline and training showed as the flight made it up and out together, but Carl didn't have time to reflect on it. Peters was still screaming, hands over his face, head jerking violently from side to side.

"I can't see! My eyes, God, I can't see!"

Jolley was already moving up behind the copilot, ripping an aid kit off the wall as he came. Carl remained frozen for a split second, then scrambled across the separating space.

"Grab his arms!" Jolley yelled above the turbines. He was trying to restrain the wild thrashing, but couldn't get the arms pinned to check the wound. Carl grabbed frantically at the right arm, then managed to corral the left and pinned them to the sides of the seat while Jolley slipped the seat retaining pins out.

Simmons had already broken away from the flight and was running the ship all the way up to the red line speed, making for Tay Ninh. Carl hoped it would be fast enough. When Jolley had tilted back the seat, both crewmen got a good look at what was left under the shattered visor. Peters's struggles began to subside and Carl was aware of what was happening.

"Shock!" Jolley unlocked the safety harness. "Help me get him out of this and down on the floor!"

Struggling awkwardly, lifting and twisting, they got Peters in a prone position on the dirty floorboards. Jolley unstrapped his chicken plate and propped up the man's feet while Carl used his to throw over the torso. Not much warmth but it would have to do. Jolley plugged his helmet wire into the copilot's mike jack.

"Mr. Simmons, his visor is shattered all to hell and there's plastic shit in both eyes. There's a piece of shrapnel sticking out of his left eye and too much blood to tell much else. He's still alive but I'm afraid to try to get the helmet off."

"Roger. Just try to keep him from moving. Can you see any other wounds?"

Jolley looked over his body, then glanced questioningly at Carl, who shook his head. "No, sir. Nothing we can see."

What was visible of Peters's face was deathly pale between the blood flows across the cheeks and down the neck. Carl figured he must be unconscious and hoped he would stay that way. Wrestling with the screaming man, fighting down those bloody arms filled with agonized strength, had almost unnerved him. He glanced up over the empty seat and for the first time noticed the jagged holes in the Plexiglas, one large one and several smaller ones, from the shrapnel. Looking back down at the still figure, he said a silent thanks that he hadn't been hit and felt an immediate wave of guilt wash over him. *Damn, shouldn't feel guilty for thinking like that. Everybody took the same chance, just the breaks of the Game*. Carl knew it could just as easily have been him, and it might be the next time. He didn't want to end up like Peters, though. Like most of the "Wobblies," the warrant officers, Peters was barely older than Carl's nineteen years, and from what Carl could see, the young flier was probably going to spend the rest of a long life without sight. Reality was a far cry from the movies and television where people died quickly or bore their wounds in stoic silence. The silver screen didn't show the agonies of the Peterses and the footless infantry soldiers of the wars. Still kneeling, gently holding the copilot's arm, he recalled the short story he had written for his high school literary magazine. A written extension of his private fantasy world, it was about Vietnam, but not this Vietnam, not the reality.

Peters was still alive and unconscious when they reached Tay Ninh's dust-off pad and delivered him to the medics. They couldn't stay around to see what his condition was because the pad had to be kept clear. There were inbound choppers with more of war's harvest from the same place that they had come from.

Simmons repositioned the ship to the POL point, and while Carl refueled the ship, Jolley did a quick walk-around inspection to see what kind of damage the ship had suffered. As he came past Carl, he bent down, slapped Carl on the leg, and pointed just below Carl's gun mount. Carl took a step back and saw the two neat little holes, about eight inches apart.

"Looks like AKs or thirty-ones," Jolley commented. "Good thing they weren't up about two feet or you might be singing soprano."

Carl nodded vigorously. Two feet higher . . . an involuntary shudder rippled through his guts and groin just thinking about it. That was another one of those things that never happened to anybody in the movies.

Simmons checked with company operations, gave them 372's status, and was told to return to the company area. The mission had been completed and the rest of the flight was on the way back. Being the first ship back in made them first in line for repairs unless one of the other birds had priority damage. Captain Ranes, the maintenance officer, was there at the revetment to meet them.

"Sorry to hear about Peters. At least he'll go home

alive,'' the big man remarked, and then turned to business. ''What's the damage here?''

Jolley took over, pointing out what he had found on the surface. ''Seven holes in the body, mostly just sheet metal work. Both upper and lower windshields on the right side'll have to be replaced. We got two hits on Willstrom's side that probably punctured the fuel cells.''

Ranes glanced at Carl with a good-natured smile. ''Well, at least this time the enemy did it.''

As they went over the ship in more detail, Carl asked about the condition of the rest of the flight. No other injuries, but the loss of four men KIA and one serious WIA was more than enough. Jolley told him that that was the heaviest piece of action the company had seen in over four months.

''Less VC action, more and more North Vietnamese coming across from Cambodia. Gonna make life hard on the helicopters, and keep the maintenance crews damned busy,'' Jolley said as they heard the news that two of the downed ships were salvageable and were being slung in by the massive Chinook helicopters.

After providing what help he could, Carl unhitched the guns and hurried up to the solvent barrels. He could see the rest of the ships coming in and wanted to get his weapons cleaned up before the place got too congested. The machine guns appeared to be in good shape, no broken springs or worn rods. The main chore was simply to scrub off the carbon deposits from the eight or nine hundred rounds that each had fired.

Scraping off the grime kept his hands busy, and the familiarity of the task gave him time to review the day's events. He had waited, expected some kind of reaction, the shakiness when the adrenaline quits pumping, but nothing came. Maybe the drain after the second lift had left nothing in his body to react with. Maybe, and a smile crossed his face, just maybe he was tougher than he thought. The hot LZ had been his cherry popper in spades and he had held up. Scary as hell now that it was over. Some of his people had died and he had survived, gave the enemy blast for blast . . . maybe even killed some. Did that enemy gun quit firing because of the grunts, was it snuffed by a gunship, or did the NVA simply clear out? From a moving helicopter it was hard to tell if the gunner silenced the concealed position, but Carl found himself hoping that it had been his long burst that cut off the enemy gunner. This business of not knowing bothered him.

He had joined the army for the express purpose of coming to Vietnam to fight the communists. Hell, they had to be stopped somewhere. Far away, in another world, he had taken it for granted that he would kill men in Vietnam. That was part of the test and ritual of manhood in a hundred cultures through six thousand years of history. In the books he had read, the histories of wars and warriors, this was the way it had been. Men fought and died or emerged victorious to make their mark during their time. But this, what he had experienced, was not as clear as it should have been. True, he had fought, but what came of it? He had done his job well and hadn't panicked under fire. Those slow-motion instants in combat had made him feel more alive than ever before, but there was something missing. The ultimate conquest of human predator over human predator had not been fulfilled. He snapped the guns back together. Next time.

After chow that night, Jolley invited him over to the little hootch that served as a small club for the enlisted men. Most of the other gunners and crew chiefs were there, already swapping war stories. The scrap lumber and wire mesh oasis was stuffy, smoke-filled, but nobody minded. All of Vietnam seemed stuffy and smoke-filled on some days. At least there was a large ice chest and cool drinks.

Carl took a seat on an ammo crate while Jolley got the beers and exchanged friendly obscenities with other old-timers. Picking up snatches of several conversations, Carl heard numerous liberties with the facts of the day's action and also noticed that no one was mentioning the lost crew, a gunner and chief who had probably been here last night.

Another mental survival tactic, letting the dead go without forgetting them.

"Hey, rookie!" Regis stumbled over, already under the influence of too many of the 3.2 beers, half supported by Jolley. "Rookie," he shouted again, drawing the attention of all in the club. "Hear you did good up there today, slick. Jolley says you didn't let no shit get to you." Carl nodded, started to say something, but Regis cut him off. "Rookie, today you sure as hell got your fuckin' cherry popped. Me and Jolley, as senior old-timers in this damned asshole of the world, hereby declare you to be no longer a fuckin' rookie. We"—he smiled drunkenly—"further declare that you have earned the right to be called by your name. What the hell's your first name? Oh, yeah, Carl. You are now yourself, Pfc Carl Willstrom."

Regis's speech was followed by a few cheers, good-natured jokes, and two beers, one thrust into his hand and the other ceremoniously poured over his head. Ritual. Rites of manhood. A warm feeling flowed through him, this acceptance, the belonging. He laughed, spluttering in his beer, raised his glass in mock salute, and drained it.

Captain Slough, the mission's flight leader, wandered in before the men got too sloppy and after only a few seconds of shouting for attention, managed to get everyone quiet. Regular army in appearance, polished boots, stiff hat, and white sidewalls, he was also regular army in his actions, from what Carl had heard. Tough but fair, led by example, all the things an officer was supposed to be, and respected by the men.

"Gentlemen, I only want to take up a few minutes of your time. Just a quick debriefing on today's mission. From what I can see, it looks like most of you are in the right frame of mind right about now." He paused for a moment for the ripple of laughter, accepted a beer from one of the gunners, and continued. "The companies we inserted are in complete control of the LZ, and at last light all enemy contact had been broken. Latest word in reports that the grunts were finding large bunkers, well stocked with rice, medical supplies, munitions, the usual materials. One type of material not there. Very few weapons, individual or crew served, have been found. S-2 confirmed that it was an NVA regimental staging area and thinks the heavy resistance was a covering action, main force units evacuating their priority equipment back into Cambodia. The 2/5 commander reported a body count of twenty-seven NVA, and numerous blood trails into the jungle could raise that higher by morning." Again he paused, looked around, met the eyes of the men. "Friendly casualties were bad. The ground forces lost eight men killed and fifteen wounded. And of course, we lost four of our own. Mr. Sellers, Lieutenant Koblotski, Sergeant Allen, and Specialist Washington. The word received from 2/5 said that an NVA got them with an RPG. For what it's worth, a GI nailed him a second later. As some of you know, Mr. Sellers was getting short, thirty-nine days left, and his wife just had their second baby four months ago. We'll be taking up a collection for the family after the memorial service tomorrow night. At least the other men weren't married. Mr. Peters, the new copilot on Jolley's ship, is going to live and may even have partial sight in his right eye. The left eye is gone and that is his ticket back to the States." He took a long drink, leaned back against the wall, and went on. "Men, it was a tough day down there but you did a fine job. The 2/5 commander gave you an 'atta boy' and hopes to see you again soon, which brings me to my closing remarks. The platoon leaders and sergeants are being briefed right now for tomorrow's missions. If your ship is still flyable, you will be up again tomorrow, so take it easy on the suds." Draining the last of his own beer, he departed without ceremony, leaving a silence in the small hootch.

Men stared at their beers or sipped them slowly, thinking of the dead, their own futures, or wondering what kinds of missions they would draw tomorrow. Carl, Regis, and Jolley finished up their drinks and headed back to their hootch in silence. Carl was thinking more about his own chances of survival than about the men already dead. Before coming to Nam, he had heard that helicopter crews had a very short life expectancy. Since his arrival in the unit, however, not a single man had been killed until today's action. Regis said that the Yellow Six crew were the first fatalities in over two months. The grunts had it a hell of a lot harder, but for some reason, everyone thought choppers were an exceptionally bad risk. Every now and then, when gunners were in short supply, division infantry troops would be offered a chance to get out of the boonies to be doorgunners. There was rarely an overwhelming rush of volunteers, so the job was usually open to anyone else who could pass the flight physical.

Some of the grunts had taken the job; other gunners came from the ranks of the pencil pushers, truck drivers, cooks, and a dozen other MOSs. Carl himself had been trained stateside as a 63 Charlie, a track and wheeled vehicle mechanic. He smiled as he thought back about that. Man, that recruiter had sure seen him coming, told him that as a 63 Charlie, Carl would get to drive all those tanks and APCs. It sure sounded good at the time, but after four months of training with those things on the maintenance end, he knew that there had to be something better. That second day in-country at the division replacement center had saved him. Grouped together with a hundred other new arrivals, Carl had listened to two groups of visitors at the center. Both had worn distinctive uniforms that set them apart from the files of troops in the issue jungle fatigues.

The first speaker was a massive black soldier wearing the stripes of a first sergeant on his camouflage uniform. On his head was the black beret, the sign of the U.S. Army Ranger battalions. He gave a colorful, impressive speech. Simply, he was looking for volunteers for "H" Company, 75th Rangers. Current assignment orders were of no regard. Anyone who thought they were good enough would go through a crash Ranger course with airborne training in-country and upon successful completion would be assigned to the division's attached Ranger company.

The speaker for the second group was not quite as colorful as the Ranger, except for one item. The olive-brown flight uniform was topped off by a black cowboy hat, a real Stetson, decorated with silver braid and gleaming brass crossed sabers. He represented the division's helicopter battalions and squadrons and informed his captive audience that there was a shortage of doorgunners in many units. His offer was basically the same as the Ranger's, and neither of them saw the need to explain why there were shortages. Conceding that the Rangers had a formidable reputation, the flight officer pointed out that there were certain advantages to being in a helicopter unit. Regular meals, decent bunks to come home to every night, relatively comfortable working conditions, the chance to earn the silver flight wings, and as a final bonus, extra money in the form of flight pay.

Something about all of that had appealed to Carl, and when the formation was dismissed, he reported to the flight officer, who had set up shop at a small field table. Two days later he had arrived at Tay Ninh base camp.

They hit the hootch just in time to catch the tail end of Jerry Cooper's latest war story. Cooper, a heavyset, sandy-haired man, was the crew chief of 578, the ship that had taken an engine hit and plopped down in the LZ.

". . . and I got my ass out of that bird, man. I thought sure as shit that baby was gonna blow up. I only got 150 more days to go here and I damn sure don't want to make my DEROS in a body bag. At least I'll be down for a couple of days now while they're getting me a new engine. That was enough for one week."

"At least you're alive right now," said Corning, a lean Cajun with a deep scar running across his left cheek from mouth to ear. "471's crew ain't never gonna see the World again. Washington and me was in the same platoon for a while and he was a damn good gunner. He was getting short, too."

"One thing about it," offered Regis, still feeling his beers. "Poor bastards probably never knew what hit 'em. Better to go fast than take the long dive alive or burn."

The others all muttered their agreement. Carl wished that Regis hadn't brought that up. His two worst fears had just risen up like twin specters of doom. He hadn't told anyone about his fear of heights, a fear that he confronted and dealt with, seeking out the heights to defy. And fire! That was the worst of all. No man should have to die an agonizing death by flame, but in the helicopter business it was a very real threat.

Wooden disrupted the dismal chain of thought and brought everyone's attention back to mission routine, rattling off a few assignments for Regis and the others in the hootch. A psy-ops mission for one, command and control for another, four men left, and to these Wooden finally turned his attention. "Jolley, right after breakfast, you take charge of Dulles, Jones, and Willstrom and start fixing up the platoon bunker. The sandbags around the back end look like some of you knife-throwing commandos have been using 'em for target practice, and some of them are just plain rotten. I've got three hundred new ones waiting to be filled." Ending on that cheerful note, Wooden advised them all to get some rest.

After seven hours of filling one green bag after another, Carl decided it would have been easier to just rebuild the whole damn bunker. The old crew chief laughingly assured him that the bunkers did have their uses. They made a quiet, private place to take some of the hootch girls, or a relaxed place to smoke some of the pot that was so plentiful in Nam. "Hell, Will. Every now and again we even use the bunkers to hide from some of Charlie's 'fall out of the sky' stuff. Kind of odd about that," Jolley remarked as he tossed the last sandbag up to Carl. "We haven't had any incoming in over three weeks, since just before you arrived. I don't know what's holding them back. They're sure as hell not bashful about shelling us most of the time."

Despite the Vietnam orientation, he still didn't know that much about what the Vietcong and North Vietnamese had. Jolley's length of time in Nam had provided him with a wealth of information, and like most of the old-timers, he had encountered firsthand just about everything that the little brown men had in this sector.

"Charlie's got three basic items in his toy bag that he tosses in here. You got your Chicom 82mm mortars, the 122mm rockets, a local favorite, and the 120mm mortars. We been known to get a few 60mm mortars and an odd assortment of recoilless rifle rounds. On really special occasions we've even had flying garbage cans, a big 240mm mother that they haul down here from up north."

Carl was impressed by the arsenal but didn't say so. He had gotten the impression from others that the company had been leading a charmed life against incoming rounds and the men in the unit seemed a bit disdainful of the potential threat. The company area had taken a few hits, but in the last nine months no one had been even slightly injured as a result of incoming. Inexplicably, their sister company, at the far end of the airstrip, had lost over a dozen men killed and wounded because of mortars and rockets during that same period. The flying stuff could reach a man anywhere, and avoiding it was largely a matter of luck. Carl hoped that he would always be at the right place at the right time. Only way to survive the Game.

In the mess hall they shuffled through the chow line, watching the cooks throw the food on the trays. Melted Jell-O, warm Kool-Aid, malaria pills, and salt tablets made it a meal for the record books. A record of how many times a man could eat the same thing and never notice the taste. Halfway through this delightful repast, the company commander gave Carl a momentary diversion from his food.

Major Garvin, a plump, round-faced man with a double chin and a short crew cut, reminded Carl of one of the old Three Stooges. But he was their commander and Jolley said that he wasn't bad for a lifer, so when he called for everyone's attention they respectfully gave it. "Gentlemen, a quick announcement while we've got most of you together here. The memorial service for the men of 471 will be held at 1930 hours, outside in front of the TOC bunker. I'd like everyone in attendance unless duty requires you elsewhere. Carry on."

After Garvin retook his seat in officers' country, the usual buzz of small talk resumed as the troops finished up their meals and relaxed a bit. Carl cleaned off his tray and then decided it was about time to clean himself off.

Stripping off the dusty uniform, he wrapped the olive-drab towel around his waist, grabbed his soap dish, and joined the stream of men going to the several shower rooms. Throwing the towel over a nail, he turned the water valve and ignored the first rush of reddish-brown water that poured from the pipe. Gravity-fed from old airplane wing tanks, the water was always a little rust-colored at first, but at least it was cool. Nobody minded. It was another one of those fringe benefits of having a base camp to call home. As he scrubbed off the sweat and grime from the sandbag detail, he noticed that not all of the brown was washing off. About damn time, he thought. Finally starting to get that Vietnam tan, at least above the waist. Made him look more like an old-timer, taking away the new-guy paleness.

Stuffing the grubby fatigues into his laundry bag, he slipped into a clean flight uniform and was reading through a day-old copy of the *Pacific Stars and Stripes* when Jolley stuck his head in the door and yelled for him.

Reflecting on the ritual, Carl thought it was the most moving ceremony he had ever seen. A long table had been set up, draped with a deep velvet cloth and punctuated in the center with a gleaming silver crucifix. On either side of the cross were positioned four flight helmets, visors down as if to shield the visages of the lost. As the fading light of the setting sun cast its final shadows, the chaplain read a short eulogy for each of the four men. Then the major gave a more personal tribute to each of the fallen men, urging the surviving comrades to carry on and honor the memory of the dead. In a final unforgettable moment, the last ray of the sun disappeared, and the company snapped to attention to render a final salute as the mournful notes of taps drifted through the air. Carl's eyes were unable to focus clearly because of a film of moisture clouding them, and some of the men who had lost close friends let the tears run freely.

It reminded Carl of the almost romantic quality of death and farewells given to the warriors of old. But, he thought somewhat soberly, being blown apart and charred at the same time wasn't quite the same as the way men died in the old stories and legends of heroes. He wondered what the books would say about this war when it was all over.

Carl celebrated the end of his first full month in-country on the second of August. Only 335 more days to go, hardly a short-timer, but at least he was one month closer to the goal of most GIs, that magic DEROS, date estimated return from overseas. That was if he didn't extend. Most men were happy to get any kind of drop, but Carl, partly under Jolley's influence, was already considering a six-month extension. Of course, he realized that his whole attitude might change in the next seven months before he would even be eligible to put in for an extension, but he didn't anticipate any change. He was where he wanted to be and thought that doing Nam duty was a damn sight easier than the stateside routine.

He also finally got to put on the aircrewman wings. Earlier in the week, he had logged his twenty-fifth hour of flight time and now the silver wings were his. Silver on paper. He didn't mind that they were the same subdued black insignia as everything else. It was just important that they were there above the left pocket, occupying what had been an embarrassing void. No longer a lame duck.

Carl had the opportunity to experience more of the boredom of war as the days dragged by. There were a few combat assaults, but the LZs were cold and the only company ship that drew any fire was a third platoon ship on a sniffer mission near the red line. Incoming mortar rounds hit the base one night, but they were all impacting around the south end of the base. Carl joined the rest of his platoon on top of the bunkers, where they drank their beer and watched the light show. It looked more like a small Fourth of July celebration than an attack, flashing lights, glowing streamers of hot metal striking through the dark. It was very unreal and distant seeming, hard to imagine that on the other end of the airstrip men from their sister company might be dying.

Cooper had explained what the sniffer machine was, but Carl still wasn't sure if the crew chief was giving him the straight story. A mechanical bloodhound that picked up ammonia concentrations seemed a little farfetched. When they picked up the sniffer operator and his machine from the division's chemical unit, Carl was afraid to ask the man how the machine worked, but Cooper, sensing Carl's disbelief, asked the operator to explain the process. Satisfied with the explanation, Carl helped strap the sniffer box inside the ship, and the pilot took the ship off to its assigned search zone.

Flying low-level patterns over the target grid, Carl kept his gun angled out, fingers on the triggers. They were in a free-fire zone, an area that was clear of friendly forces, so any targets that moved or any detection marks on the sniffer box were in open season. Cooper told him before lift-off that the easiest way to confirm enemy troops on the ground was to fire a few bursts into the jungle when the machine registered a mark and hope that it would draw return fire.

Suddenly, the operator spoke into his headset. "Mark, large!"

Olsen, the only black warrant officer in the company, made a mark to indicate the location on his map while Carl and Cooper both fired quick machine-gun bursts almost straight down into the jungle. No response. Carl had hoped that there would be, but Cooper had told him that the NVA and VC weren't fools, and that experienced Charlies knew better than to return fire to a helicopter that might be shooting blind.

"Mark, larger . . . mark, same," the operator said, this time quieter and in a less excited voice.

"Going hot," Cooper advised the pilot, and both of them fired longer bursts, covering more territory. Carl leaned out over his gun mount and finished his firing with a fast arc down and to the chopper's rear. He hung out there for a moment, empty space below him, and tried to penetrate the double canopy jungle with his eyes. No return fire, nothing visible.

Coming across the airwaves, as if from a great distance, Carl heard a faint voice on the FM frequency. The almost inaudible voice was repeating a message, and Carl slid back onto his seat, pressing one hand to the side of his helmet for better hearing. The pilots and Coop had heard it, too, a call sign identifier trying to contact an unidentified aircraft. The message repeated once again and now Carl could detect the note of urgency in the weak transmission.

"Unidentified aircraft vicinity Whiskey Tango 4685, this is Red Sword Three Six Bravo. You are firing on friendly forces. Over."

Simmons sighted over his crooked nose at Olsen's map. "Check those coordinates relative to our position," he ordered. Olsen plotted the location given by the Red Sword caller and pointed it out to the pilot. Simmons nodded and relaxed a bit. "That's well outside of our search area. Somebody out there somewhere is screwing up. Just to be on the safe side, though, contact Red Sword One Six and check out this Three Six Bravo element."

Olsen called into the One Six, the local battalion commander, and received confirmation that there were no friendlies in the search zone. Carl heard the Red Sword leader tell Olsen that he hadn't been in contact with the Three Six element for over two hours, but that their last reported position had placed them four klicks west of the search zone. Nobody on board the chopper said anything, but Carl knew they were all thinking about the same possibility. Down under all that jungle where everything looked the same, it was easy to get lost, but to be almost three miles off would be hard for even a rookie platoon leader to do.

"Mark, large," the operator reported, looking ahead at the pilot.

Simmons glanced back at his gunners for a second. "Short burst, straight out," he finally ordered.

Cooper fired off a quick flash and Carl followed suit, the eagerness to fire suddenly diminished. Again no return fire, but their short bursts were the cue for the faint transmission.

"Low-flying helicopter vicinity Whiskey Tango 4685, this is Red Sword Three Six Bravo. Cease fire, cease fire! You are firing on friendly forces!"

Simmons immediately ordered no more firing, contacted the cover ship and told him that they were aborting the mission and coming up to altitude. At two thousand feet, Simmons leveled off and began a sweeping orbit over the search area.

"Time to find out what the hell is going on down there," he told Olsen. "Red Sword Three Six Bravo, this is Papa One Niner. Over." An acknowledgment came back an instant later and Simmons pulled out his CEOI, the communications codebook. "Three Six Bravo, Papa One Niner. Authenticate Zulu Tango. Over."

"Papa One Niner, Three Six Bravo. Roger, stand by." The unseen voice was still weak but much calmer sounding now.

Carl didn't know how to use the CEOI yet, but he knew what was going down. Someone on the ground was in the wrong location and Mr. Simmons was checking to make sure that it wasn't an English-speaking Charlie trying to get over on them. NVA operators had been known to find unit frequencies and try to screw up operations with fictitious radio messages. If the man on the ground was who he said he was, then he should be able to respond with the proper authentication code in a matter of moments. If the correct code answer wasn't received, the gunship that was flying cover would roll in, spitting death.

Almost ten seconds passed before Red Sword replied with the correct authentication code. It could still be the enemy but the chances were less likely now.

"Three Six Bravo, Papa One Niner. Did aircraft in your vicinity depart the area? Over."

"Papa One Niner, Three Six Bravo. Roger that. Aircraft has moved off but we can still hear it. Sounds like it went up. Over."

"Three Six Bravo, that was our aircraft. Do you have any casualties? Over."

Carl let out the long breath he had been unconsciously holding. Nobody on the ground had been hit. Simmons went back on the air. "Three Six Bravo, Roger, understand no casualties. Be advised, your radioed position is not your actual. Pop smoke and we will give you your correct position. Over." As he finished the transmission, Simmons shook his head and made a quick bet with Olsen on the chances of the platoon leader being an OCS rookie with less than three weeks in-country.

Three Six Bravo came back on the air telling Simmons that he was popping green smoke. Simmons cursed explosively. "Goddamned idiot!" He quickly pressed his mike button. "Three Six Bravo, negative. Negative on that green smoke. Check your procedures with your Papa Sierra. Over."

Carl recognized the cut-down and wondered how the platoon leader on the ground was feeling. Simmons was telling the man over the airwaves to get some advice from his platoon sergeant on the proper use of signals.

"That young man is going to get someone killed if he doesn't get his shit together in a hurry," Simmons was saying over the intercom. For Carl's benefit he added, "Any Charlies nearby working this frequency could toss out a green smoke just to make things confusing. Take a lesson from it, gunner, and don't be afraid to ask someone how to do a job right."

With the communication security problem resolved, Simmons continued his orbit until he saw the new smoke and confirmed the ground unit's location. Olsen encoded the location coordinates and sent them off, whereupon the pilot turned the ship away, toward the new search zone that the local battalion commander had cleared for them.

IV.

Carl was lying on his cot, trying to ignore the heat and the resulting sweat standing on his naked and well-tanned torso. Across the base camp, some five hundred yards distant, a 155mm battery was conducting a fire mission for some battalion out there in the countryside around Tay Ninh. Back in Texas, he could never have gotten to sleep with that kind of racket going on. Funny how after a while, a person could get used to the heat, the constant thundering of the big guns, the ground shaking from the devastating rain of B-52 bombs. Must be like adapting to the noises of living on a big-city street. It was almost 2100 hours and it was still at least 85 degrees, humidity was close to the same number, and in the poorly ventilated hootches there was no breeze to stir the sticky air. Some things weren't bothered by the conditions, though. Carl could hear some of the denizens of the darkness scuttling across the hootch. Rats, hunting for their nightly feasts. There was more than enough garbage to ensure that there would never be a shortage of the foul black rodents. Better they should have enough to eat, Carl thought. If they didn't get out scraps and garbage, the little bastards would probably just pick up the troops and carry them off for a snack. They were sure as hell mean enough to try, and Carl had developed a healthy respect for the Chihuahua-sized animals after seeing a couple of cornered ones. Every now and then, someone would try to shoot one with a .45 when the rats got too bold.

Suddenly, a loud explosion ripped through the stillness, interrupting Carl's rat contemplations, sending him flying off his cot, rolling onto the floor. More surprised than scared, he lay there for a moment, started to crawl toward the door, and collapsed prone, covering his head as another blast went off close by. Incoming, not outgoing. His mouth felt dry but his brain was working logically. More explosions were crashing nearby, men were screaming and shouting, footsteps pounding past the hootch, fading down the wooden walkways.

He low-crawled toward the door again, reached it, shoved hard with one hand, and came up on one knee to make a sprint out to the bunker. A shrill whistling sound made him flatten out again as a tremendous blast rocked the hootch, taking away his breath. Momentarily dazed by the force of the blast, he lay in the doorway for a second, until Jolley, crawling out from under his cot, scrambled over to him, jerked Carl to his feet, and roughly propelled him out of the hootch into the platoon bunker.

Jolley held him up to the dim red light bulb illuminating the bunker and gave him a quick once-over. Carl blinked uncertainly several times, trying to get his eyes to focus, finally succeeded, and assured Jolley that he was all right. At that moment, Sergeant Wooden dashed into the bunker, fleetingly silhouetted by the reddish-orange flash of a mortar. The big man was breathing hard and struck Carl as looking a little ridiculous, dressed only in his olive-drab boxer shorts and unlaced jungle boots, but then, so were most of the other men in the bunker. Carl knew that for them, there was nothing unusual about the incoming. They were already comfortable and talking quietly among themselves until Wooden got their attention.

"All right," he yelled, and then lowered his voice to a less deafening level. "Roll call. Let's see who's missing." Only three men didn't answer the muster, and two of them, Cilino and Corning, were on reaction force duty for the night. They would be down at the flight line with the security detail, protecting the helicopters from possible sappers. The only man unaccounted for was Sp4 Dulles, a gunner who quartered in the hootch next to Carl's.

Over the echoing explosions of the continuous incoming, Cooper spoke up. "Dulles wasn't in his hootch when the shit started. I saw him heading for the showers just a couple of minutes earlier."

"All right, Coop, come on with me and let's see if we can find him," Wooden said as he finished lacing up his boots. Both men moved to the narrow bunker entrance, and one at a time, staying crouched low to the ground, they slid around the entrance barrier and disappeared into the darkness. Carl and the others settled back into low conversations, speculating on the possible damage to the buildings and ships. Every few seconds an explosion sounded and the talking would stop or the speakers would raise their voices over the din. The single red light bulb cast an eerie glow across the interior of the bunker, creating a vision of a fragmented hell with half-visible demons of red and shadow.

"Hey, it stopped. Now we can see if we still got a place to sleep," said Regis. He and Jolley both agreed that it was probably safe to emerge, and as they filed out, they encountered Wooden and Cooper with Dulles. Dulles was a dark-skinned kid from the Midwest, and in the light of the flares going off around the perimeter, Carl could see that the already dark skin was even darker than usual. The man had lost his towel during the attack and his entire body looked incredibly filthy. His contorted face told Carl that he was in pain, but Carl couldn't see any wounds because of the slimy, wet, mudlike substance covering most of his body.

"Get a light on in the hootch, hurry!" growled Wooden. "And get some towels and water."

Carl made way for them as they half carried, half dragged Dulles into the battered hootch. As they passed close to him, Carl caught an unpleasant odor, absolutely foul-smelling. Shit! Dulles wasn't covered with mud, he was coated with a liberal cloak of human feces. Fighting back against the stench, he crowded into the hootch with the others to see the sorry-looking spectacle.

"Son of a bitch!" Regis exclaimed. "What the fuck happened to him?" he asked, staring at the foul-looking unfortunate. Wooden didn't bother to answer, just hastily laid Dulles down on the wooden floor, directly under the unshielded glare of a bulb.

Cooper blew out a deep breath, turned his head aside, and inhaled deeply, then offered an explanation. "He must have been coming back from the showers or just leaving the latrine when the first rounds hit. We found him about ten feet from where the latrine used to be. Nothing there now but splinters and crap. Rocket must have landed dead center on the place and blown a shit barrel all over him. Damn, what a fuckin' mess. Somebody get me a rag or something."

Smith dumped a bunch of rags and towels by Wooden and handed one to Cooper, who wiped some of the muck off himself and then knelt by Dulles, trying to remove smears of excrement.

"Damn," Wooden swore quietly. "Here, try to get this mess around his leg. Careful!" They could all see the red blood beginning to mingle with the brownish-yellow paste on his left leg, a sickening palette, with the tip of a piece of wood protruding through the flesh and waste. Other wounds became visible as more of the filth was removed, but none looked fatal. "I don't think there's anything here that's going to kill him, but you two get him cleaned up a little more and get him over to the medics," Wooden ordered, looking at Regis and Cooper. "They'll need to take care of the piece in the leg and dress him up to make sure he doesn't get killed from infection."

With the indication that Dulles was going to be okay, Jolley couldn't resist saying what Carl was thinking. "Man, I've heard of people getting their shit blown away, but this is ridiculous." There were a few half chuckles, and when even Dulles cracked a pained smile, everybody broke into open laughter. It was a relief that the situation could allow a moment of humor.

There was only one serious casualty, one of the maintenance people who almost lost an arm, and Carl thought that they had been pretty lucky. A couple of the hootches had sustained light damage, and much to Carl's annoyance, a large number of those freshly stacked sandbags around the hootch and bunker had been shredded. More sandbag details, he thought to himself, just a little irritated with the enemy's game tonight. "Some game," he muttered, straightening up his cot. "I swear, Jolley, I'm gonna kick some Charlie's ass if they start messing with my sack time."

Jolley just laughed at Carl's indignant tone. "You and what army, Will? You ain't going to find the bad guys running around in the woods with little signs on their backs saying, 'I'm the son of a bitch who shot up Willstrom's hootch.' Course if they'd organize this little war like a good football game, then we'd all have programs to tell us who the players were. Might even be able to tell who's winning!"

Carl's brief irritation disappeared, and he had to join in the laughter, seeing a ridiculous image in his head of the little brown men with their AKs and numbered black pajamas swarming across a field. He wondered what the final score would be and if the time clock would ever show zero seconds to play. In high school he had always worried that the war, in its sixth year, would end before he could get to Vietnam. Two years later it was still going on and he was there with it, a part of it.

Two months in-country made Carl feel like a real old-timer. The bona fide veterans still kidded him from time to time, but then they always razzed anybody who had to stay in Vietnam twenty-four hours longer than they did. Carl didn't mind. He wasn't the low man on the totem pole anymore. A new recruit, fresh from AIT in the States, had arrived a week earlier and been assigned to Carl's platoon. Carl participated in the traditional tricks played on the newbies and greatly enjoyed sending the rookie, Pfc Scott, on errands looking for fifty yards of flight line. The rookie got a little pissed at some of the jokes and jokers, but nobody gave a damn about how he felt. Carl knew what everyone else, except Scott, knew. It was all just part of the Game.

The only problem with the Game was that it wrote its own rules and changed them whenever it wanted. Carl was beginning to think of the Game as something animate, intelligence without control. Even in the random actions of the Game, one rule stayed fairly constant, he thought, remembering his own blade strike. Rookies do stupid things. Nine days after being assigned to the second flight platoon, Pfc Larry Scott, from Tulsa, Oklahoma, walked into the spinning tail rotor of a chopper. The rotor blade, almost invisible at 12,000 RPMs, killed him instantly. A week later nobody even remembered his name.

V.

"Jolley, why don't you get the hell out of here?" Cooper asked as they sat around the ammo crate table in the club hootch.

"I keep telling you, Coop, it's like this," Jolley explained. "If I went back stateside after this extension is up in forty more days, I'd still have nine months to do in the green machine. And that's nine months of hassle that I don't need. Stateside duty means regular haircuts, salutes up the ass, daily shaves, and all that other spit-and-polish crap. I don't think I could handle it. 'Sides, this last six-month extension gets me a free thirty-day leave, and when the extension is up, I'll get a two-month drop. When I leave Nam for the last time, I'll be finished with Uncle Sugar's green team for good."

"Sounds like a number one idea," Carl interjected. "I'm thinking of extending, too, after I'm down to 120 days."

Cooper couldn't keep from laughing at that. "Will, you've still got a lifetime to go over here! Hell, if I had as much time left as you do, I'd go and shoot myself. You'll still be here when the damn VC DEROS."

Carl just grinned back at him and downed the rest of his beer. He didn't care what Coop or anyone else thought. He felt that Jolley's reasons for extending applied to him as well. And of course, there was the thrill of the action. He knew that line of thinking was almost juvenile, bugles and glory stuff, but it really was there. A certain excitement that was difficult to explain, but that was part of the unspoken reason why Jolley and others like him were doing extensions or repeat tours.

Cooper shifted his heavy frame around on the grenade box chair and looked at Carl more seriously. "If you're really serious about this extension crap, you might as well be crazy all the way and extend for scouts. All them fuckers are a little crazy."

"What are scouts? Sounds like cowboys and Indians," Carl said.

"Damn close," Jolley commented. "Remember those lightweight choppers at the POL point the other day? The ones that looked like an egg with a hard-on. Those were OH-6s, recon ships from the 1st of the 9th Cav. They spend all their time hovering around the treetops trying to get someone to shoot at them. Coop's right. They're all a little loose in the head."

Carl decided to store that information away and see if he could talk to some of these "scouts."

The three finished up their beers just as Wooden found them, reminding them that they all had an early crank time for what promised to be a long day of combat assault sorties. The briefing earlier had made it sound like the mission would be a cakewalk, probability of contact about zero, so there wasn't the usual tension of the night before a big CA. Carl felt relaxed and sleep came easily, the regular pattern of outgoing shells working as well as falling raindrops to lull him into oblivion.

* * *

By the time they had finished the third sortie, Carl was already bored. There had been an hour delay in lifting off the first sortie. Then the "LZ" that they hit was a huge, open clearing, almost a klick square, nothing but lush green grass to land in. Just on principle the doorgunners blasted the area as the ships came in for the first time. Carl sprayed his fire aimlessly out into the grass and the far distant treeline, watching the tracers disappear into the LZ's green carpet. The fire from the Cobra section and the lift ships didn't cause any secondaries, no mines or booby traps hidden in the grass. As they hovered down, Carl leaned far out to search for any of those unpleasantries that Charlie might have hidden out there. Not all booby traps were of the exploding nature, and while pungi stakes might not have a serious effect on the choppers, they could be deadly to infantry troops jumping off the ships into the waist-high grass.

The first troops were off without incident, and after that, there was no more firing in the LZ. The mission became a bus run, the only danger being the threat of relaxing too much and letting something stupid happen. All week it had been like this, milk runs with hardly a hundred rounds fired during the whole time. When it got like that, Carl found it difficult to keep his mind on task hour after hour and finally borrowed a trick from some of the other gunners to add variety to the routine. Some of them were skid riders, standing out on the skids of their ships, no safety straps, nothing connecting them to their ships except their feet on the skids and their hands on the gun grips. The pilots didn't seem to mind, as long as they didn't lose anyone, and so far, they hadn't. Carl had tried it a couple of times in past days, on short hops, approaches, and lift-offs.

As the fourth load of infantry clambered aboard, Carl slipped out of his gunner's well and planted both feet firmly on the skid, gripping the M-60 with one hand and hooking the other onto an ammo can strap. Clearing the pilot up, he steadied himself as the ship hovered up and nosed forward. For a moment he experienced a breathlessness as he looked down at the ground, which was rapidly falling away below him. His grasp on the butterfly grips tightened for an instant, and then it was past. He could feel the increasing pressure of the air rushing by, tugging at him as the chopper began to pick up speed. His old fear of high places tempted him to climb back into the safety of the helicopter as the ship approached the thousand-foot mark, but a sense of defiance kept him out there, poised over the abyss.

The grunts had their eyes glued on him, a couple of them grinning at him, others regarding him as if he were crazy. Confirming that thought, one of the troopers, a freckle-faced kid with tufts of red hair under his helmet, shook his head and yelled at him, "You a crazy son of a bitch!"

Carl grinned back and felt the eighty-knot wind peel his lips back. The constant strain of standing against the airflow finally forced him to climb back inside as the helicopter hit the fifteen-hundred-foot mark.

During the remaining lifts he continued to ride the skids and began to feel comfortable enough to hang on with only one hand. The grunts continued to regard him as if he were crazy or just idiotic. Most of them thought the ships were dangerous enough without adding extra risks. A couple of the gunners in other ships were watching him and gave him a thumbs-up sign when he swung back up into his well for the final time. That felt good, but he wasn't ready to try some of the stunts that he had heard of other gunners doing. Soon, but not yet.

The usual buzz of rumors abounded in the mess hall, rumors of war's end or a big push, it didn't make any difference. Someone at Carl's table said that there had been another big NVA supply cache found near the Red Line that might mean action for them. Carl could hear the conversation at the next table centering around the Paris peace talks and speculation that the war would be over by the end of the month. Carl laughed at that, and Regis, who had also been listening, bounced a biscuit off the speaker's head, starting a short biscuit artillery duel between the two tables.

After the biscuit barrage, Smith ran a hand through his tousled red hair, shaking out crumbs, and changed the subject to something less violent. "Will's gonna get his ass blown away if he rides those skids into a hot LZ."

"No sweat, Smitty. Will's learning the ropes pretty fast. Don't think he's going to do nothing like that," Jolley said. Then, looking at Carl, he went on. "Riding the wind can be a lot of fun, but a hot LZ isn't the place for games, right, Will?"

"Damn straight. Hell, I'm not a fuckin' rookie anymore."

"Roger that, Will," Jolley confirmed. "About the only time a man needs to be on the skids in a hot LZ is when he's firing straight to the front, blowing out the peter-pilot's ears, and I know old Will has done just that on one occasion. With these pole-mounted guns it's mostly easier to stay inside and swing the gun. When I first got here, we used the regular infantry model M-60s and those long monkey straps. Man, we could walk the skids, sit on 'em, and fire our guns any damn direction we wanted, 'cept up, of course. Still, these pole mounts aren't too shabby. Strap on a bigger ammo can, belts don't get tangled quite as easy, and that bigger ammo can might stop a few AK slugs."

"Hey, Sarge! What's happening?"

Wooden had entered the mess hall and looked around until he had spotted Carl's table. He was approaching them with that "Glad I found you" expression when Regis greeted him.

"Oh, shit!" Jolley exclaimed, pretending to hide under his hat. "Maybe if we ignore him he'll go away."

"No can do, Jolley," Wooden laughed. "But not to worry, GI. What I got won't bother you at all. Some of these other fine gentlemen here might find this of interest. Got a mission for you, Corning. Line company in contact out at that new cache site and they've requested a flare ship. I've got a couple of loaders putting the flares on your bird right now. Take Willstrom along. He hasn't done a flare mission yet, and this is as good a time as any to learn. Jessup and that new lieutenant, Richter, are your pilots. Crank in thirty minutes. Enjoy your evening," he added cheerfully, and departed, leaving Corning and Carl to gulp down the rest of their meals.

They hustled back to the hootch, grabbed their flight gear, and picked up their field jackets. Night flying at altitude, even in Vietnam, made for a cool time. Stopping by the arms room, Corning helped Carl with the machine guns and they jogged down to 641, Corning's Huey. Warrant Officer Jessup and Lieutenant Richter, a rookie of ten days in-country, arrived just a minute later and began the preflight checks in the rapidly fading light. Jessup had greeted Corning with a thin-lipped smile, and nodded to Carl, fixing the gunner with a disconcerting stare from brown eyes that matched the close-cropped hair. Carl broke the exchange and busied himself with checking the guns and ammo. He still felt a little uncomfortable around Jessup. He had only flown with Jessup twice since the blade strike incident, and he knew from the way the pilot looked at him that he still didn't have the man's complete trust.

He felt his face flush red as he thought about it. Dammit, there was no reason for the warrant to do that to him. Carl knew that he had been doing a good job ever since then and resented the unspoken feeling. Well, fuck him and the horse he rode in on, Carl thought, determined not to screw anything up on this mission.

With most of the checks out of the way, Corning gave Carl a crash course on flare drops. He quickly went through the altitude fuses, how to hook the flare cables to the rings in the floorboards, and most important, how to toss the flares out without getting tangled up or hanging up a flare under the ship. Carl tried desperately to remember all the information and started to ask a question, but Jessup yelled impatiently and it was time to lift off.

Last light had already fled from the jungles when they arrived on station over the grunts' NDP, their night defensive position, near the site of the cache. The grunts had marked their position with flashing strobe lights, concealed from view by unfriendly eyes on the ground, but easily visible to the men in the chopper. From three thousand feet up, Carl could see sporadic flashes from the infantry's perimeter, the red tracers cutting a glowing path in the darkness and being answered by green tracers, AKs, and light machine guns, from NVA firing from unseen positions. Carl could tell from the fire he could see that the GIs must be in light brush or a clearing, and the NVA were hidden under a heavier canopy of jungle. Mixed with the tracers was an occasional eruption of flame marking the impact of 40mm grenades from American M-79s. The entire spectacle seemed unreal, like a silent fireworks display set against black satin.

Silent from here, he thought, but it must be damn noisy and hot for the men on the ground. He listened in as the radio crackled to life and a voice on the other end gave them a situation report. The voice sounded very confident of its position, calm and disciplined. It requested that flares be dropped at eight-minute intervals. From Corning's crash course, Carl remembered that the eight-minute interval would give the ground unit continuous semidaylight, robbing the NVA of the element of darkness, until the ship ran out of flares.

"What happens when we run out of flares?" Carl asked over the intercom.

Jessup answered him after acknowledging the ground unit's request. "We're going to circle around here at four thousand feet and drop until we run out or until our twenty-minute fuel light comes on. If contact gets heavy, we drop the flares out at four-minute intervals and keep the whole damn area lit up like a football stadium. When we get down to our last eight flares, let me know. Bravo company is supplying the relief bird and they'll be ready to go when they get my call. While they are on station, we reload, refuel, and grab a cup of coffee. Any more questions?"

"No, sir," replied Carl, somewhat surprised at Jessup's

long and patient explanation. "I think you covered just about everything I can think of."

"Okay, then let's get to work. Chief, set the fuses for 3500 feet and hook up. Lieutenant Richter will monitor elapsed time and tell you when to toss."

"Roger that, 3500 feet it is," Corning responded, and indicated to Carl that he should set the first one.

Carl pressed his intercom button. "One more question. Can we get any better light back here?"

A dull red beam of light suddenly illuminated the fuse settings. Corning kept the red-lensed flashlight on the flare as Carl carefully set the giant dormant candle. "Don't want too many bright lights up here," Corning explained. "Just in case Charlie brings in a big gun, we don't need to make ourselves a target. Once the flares start going off, Charlie won't be able to see us unless he's at the right angle."

Carl nodded his understanding and slid across the floor, cradling the flare in his arms as Corning snapped the narrow flare cable to one of the tie-down rings on the floor. The crew chief moved to a position between the pilots and gave Richter the ready signal.

"Now!"

Carl hefted the flare with both arms and pitched it as far out from the ship as he could, feeling the release cable snap against his leg as the flare broke away and disappeared into the darkness. For a few seconds the ship swept silently across the night sky with only the dim green interior lights of the instrument panel offering illumination. A bright light suddenly blossomed below them, filling the cloud-covered sky, and like a small sun, the flare lit up the scenario beneath them.

Descending slowly, spinning lazily under the parachute, the flare cast a flickering and uncertain light over the jungle. The trees almost seemed to be moving like dancing shadows, as if the forests of Macbeth's castle had somehow been transported across time and space to this remote corner of the world.

As the flare drifted ever earthward, Carl was able to see

small dark splotches on the ground, the American defensive positions, amid isolated stands of trees in a semiopen area. Occasional green tracers from the surrounding tree-lines drew bursts of fire and laserlike tracer lines from the individual fighting positions. During the lifetime of the first flare, Carl had gotten a fairly good idea where many of the NVA were firing from. With the flare sinking lower and fading out, Richter gave the order for the next drop. Again, Carl gave the heavy cylinder a forceful toss, and the second flare burst into full brilliance half a minute before the first one fizzled out.

"Here they come." Jessup spoke low and calmly to the crew.

Corning pointed down and away, Carl following the direction, saw the white streaks climbing past them, disappearing into nothingness.

"Fifty-ones," Corning whispered into his mike.

"How far can those things reach?" Carl tried to sound nonchalant, as if he were merely curious.

"Don't worry about it. They're just shooting to let us know that they're down there. Chances of taking a hit are about zip," Jessup said. "But knowing where they're at might be useful. I think I've got a fix on their position." He broke off the intercom and contacted the ground unit, advising them that there was a heavy machine-gun position about six hundred meters west of the NDP. With an approximate grid location, the grunts might be able to put some heat on the .51 with mortars.

Corning spoke up, answering Carl's still unanswered question. "They're good up to about three thousand feet, maybe a little more if the gunner is really good and it's in the daytime. Past that they're not very effective. Course, that's generally speaking. Some strange shit can happen up here. That's why we stay high on these drops and don't show our running lights."

The night dragged on with only occasional exchanges of fire on the ground and nothing directed at the ship. Finally, Jessup put in the call to their sister company requesting that the relief ship crank up and head out. Carl counted four flares left when the Bravo company bird arrived on location and took over the mission. After a brief radio exchange alerting the new ship to the last known .51 position, Jessup turned 641 toward Tay Ninh and pushed the ship across the moonless sky. Only Richter broke the silence when he reported that the twenty-minute fuel light had come on. Less than ten minutes out of Tay Ninh, that didn't even bother Carl, who had slipped back into his gunner's position as the ship descended.

It felt good to be able to take off the jacket again and relax after the unaccustomed coolness of the high night flight. After refueling and loading up another batch of flares, they hit the mess hall and enjoyed the warm coffee mixed with occasional light conversation. Carl enjoyed the opportunity to talk with the pilots with no one else around. It was almost like ordinary people, civilians, talking to each other, not officers and enlisted men. Jessup was even friendly under the circumstances.

It was almost midnight when the shadowy form of the Huey lifed off and left the lights of Tay Ninh behind. Only a few minutes passed before the distant dots of fire, the other ship's flares, became visible on the dark horizon. Jessup called up the chopper and let them know that their relief was only three minutes away. Barely a minute had passed from the radio message when Richter spoke excitedly into the mike.

"Look at that! What the hell are they doing?"

Carl and Corning both looked up from the flares they were preparing and peered through the front windshield. At first glance Carl didn't notice anything except a brightly burning flare. Then, in the flare's glow, he realized that the helicopter was staying with the flare as if they were connected. Even as the thought completed itself, the excited voice of the other ship's pilot broke over the radio.

"Mayday! Mayday! This is Yankee One Three. We have a flare hung up under the skids and burning. Can't get it loose." The pilot's voice steadied. "Two Six Charlie, give me some strobe markers. Making an emergency landing at your location."

The ground commander acknowledged the order as the flare ship went into a steep dive, spiraling down with its unwanted beacon. Jessup radioed and told them that he would try to provide air cover and asked if they wanted any flares for the landing attempt. Carl could feel the tension in the other pilot's reply. He didn't want to make himself any more of a target than he already was.

"Gentlemen, man your guns," Jessup ordered. "We're going down to fifteen hundred feet. Lay down heavy on anything you see coming up at the other ship. Don't fire into the strobe positions. Let's do it!"

As if on cue, they saw the first of the tracers searching the sky for the flare ship and disappearing into the glow of the floating candle. White tracers, the .51 that had fired on them earlier, Carl thought.

Jessup continued to drop the ship, putting it into a slow counterclockwise orbit allowing Corning to give covering fire to the other crew. Carl felt frustrated, unable to do anything from the banked angle he had. Only the darkness confronted him, but he held on to his gun grips all the same, listening to the harsh report of Corning's gun as he fired long burst after long burst into the location of the enemy's antiaircraft weapon.

A brilliant white streak of light raced past the helicopter out to Carl's front. Corning's efforts were distracting the NVA gunners. Carl's heart raced even faster as more of the deadly lights shot past them.

"He's got our general location from the flash. Chief, cease fire! Gunner, we're coming hard right. Get ready to take over."

Jessup banked the chopper sharply and moved into a clockwise orbit, presenting Carl with an awesome sight. The plummeting flare ship was still brightly lit up by its unwanted passenger, and the green and white tracers were rising up to meet it, like fiery moths drawn to a kindred flame. The infantry unit was pouring out a heavy volume of fire trying to cover the hapless ship, their red tracers making crisscrossing patterns with Charlie's weapons. To the Christmas colors, Carl began his own contributions, firing down at the muzzle flashes directed skyward. All sense of time and space dissolved, nothing else in the world existed outside of those red-white flashes and the dark steel of his own gun. Flash! Fire! Flash! Fire! A hundred rounds burned through the barrel, then another hundred. Carl became aware of his surroundings again, the fast pulsing and pounding of blood and heart. With more control he began to fire shorter bursts, trying to pinpoint the enemy firing positions. The .51 suddenly shifted its fire from the flare ship back to Carl's bird, the brilliant white flash-flash-flash reached out and white tracers ripped through the air just missing the ship. Carl was pumped up, too excited to be scared, and kept on firing until Jessup broke off and banked back to the left.

"That guy's accuracy is starting to improve, Chief. We're bothering him right now. Let's see if you can blow the bastard away!"

Carl listened to the rattling gun and found its noise comforting. He was still gripping his own weapon tightly, now afraid to relax, wanting to keep up the pace of the action to fight off the sudden feeling of cold sweat. He tried to concentrate on other things, and the crackling radio gave him a focus. For the first time in over a minute, the flare ship's pilot was transmitting, frantically, without call signs.

"We're almost down! Taking lots of hits . . . casualties . . ."

A huge explosion abruptly cut off the transmission, an explosion easily overshadowing the machine gun even at this distance. Carl stretched around the transmission wall and stared down at the blazing inferno below.

"My God," Richter breathed quietly over the intercom. For a moment there was an eerie silence. Corning had stopped firing, the guns on the ground were stilled, only the whumping of the chopper blades kept the world alive. Pieces of flaming debris were falling to earth, in and around the NDP, a hundred small flares made of the dismembered Huey.

"Motherfucker!" Corning's yell could be heard throughout the ship as he began the war again with a violent spray, triggering reaction from those on the ground.

"Get a flare set for fifteen hundred, fast!" Jessup commanded.

Carl scrambled out of his seat, set and hooked the flare, then thrust it out as far as he could. He quickly rigged up another one and positioned himself on the floor at the edge of the cargo bay. Down below, only a dozen or so larger pieces of the helicopter were still burning, casting strange, twisting shadows against tree stands. The pop of the flare's parachute signaled a new light, paling the others into mere candles. The flare's light from just below the chopper revealed a stark scene of shades of black and white. Helicopter wreckage was scattered over a larger area than Carl had thought, most of it just west of the GIs' defensive positions, but a few twisted pieces had landed in the middle of their perimeter.

The firing had reached full peak again and more tracers were shooting up toward the ship. Carl, holding nothing but the flare, wished he had his machine gun, or at least an M-16, to fire back with. He glanced over at Corning, who was still pouring fire out. He couldn't see the man's scarred left cheek, but he knew from the chief's clenched jaw that the long scar must be stretched tight and pale across the facial bones.

"Two Six Charlie, this is Papa One Seven. Over."

The RTO on the ground acknowledged Jessup's call. "Papa One Seven, Two Six Charlie. Over."

"Two Six Charlie, what's the situation down there? Do you know what happened?"

"Papa One Seven, Roger. No casualties my element. No survivors from ship. I saw a fire flash run from the flare into the ship's belly while they were still about one hundred feet up. Then she exploded. That's all I know. Over."

"Two Six Charlie, Papa One Seven, Roger. Out." Jessup switched to his intercom. "Sounds like they took some hits and had the fuel cells ruptured, sprayed fuel out, hit the flare, and the flame followed the fuel trail back to the cells. Richter, notify Bravo company in case they didn't monitor. Also, tell 'em we need another flare ship on standby. We're still on a mission. Set flares for thirty-five hundred."

As soon as Richter completed the call to Bravo's TOC, Jessup got back on the horn to the ground unit to check on possibilities of body recovery.

"One Seven, this is Two Six Charlie. We have one at my location, and possibles outside our perimeter. We still are in contact, so negative on recovery at this time. Will send out patrols at first light. Keep the flares coming."

Jessup acknowledged the message, reached the proper altitude, and ordered the drops to resume.

Radio contact with the replacement ship had been laconic. No one on either ship wanted to say any more than was needed. Carl knew how the men on the other ship must be feeling. He figured that by the time he ran out of flares they probably would have expended most of their ammunition, as well.

Throughout the rest of the night the ships beat back and forth from Tay Ninh to the mission site. As usual, the enemy activity had tapered off before dawn, and the NVA had melted away into the jungle. Jessup decided to remain on station to pick up the bodies as the first light patrols moved out to recover whatever might be left. He dropped the ship down to a thousand feet, and from that distance Carl could see that the grunts were finding less than entire bodies, tossing pieces into body bags.

Unexpectedly, the Bravo flare ship returned to the scene and contacted Carl's ship. "Thanks for sticking around, One Seven, but we'll take them back. They're our men. Out."

Jessup rogered the transmission and left it at that. Words wouldn't mean much. He notified the grunts that he was departing and rose away from the scene of the night's deaths.

Carl tossed and turned, trying to sleep in the stifling heat of the Vietnamese morning, but every time he nodded off, a vision of a burning chopper with flaming, thrashing men tumbling out thrust itself into his mind, jolting him awake. The first time, he jerked up in his cot with a choked-off scream and startled a hootch girl who was cleaning up. She jumped back with a shrill yell of her own and stood by the door, eyeing him suspiciously as he stared around, sweat streaming down his face, eyes unfocused. Finally, she decided he was harmless for the moment, shook her head, mumbled something about GIs being dinky-dau, and went back to work.

"Damn right, mama-san," Carl grumbled back. "You bet your ass I'm crazy. That may be the only way to be over here." She ignored his comments and he collapsed back onto the sweat-stained cot. Hell, those guys probably died instantly in the explosion. Dead flesh didn't feel the burning fire. Still, the dream haunted him, and finally around noon he got dressed and left the hootch.

He wandered over to the TOC and stuck his head in to see what was happening. A radio operator that he knew slightly flashed him a gap-toothed smile and waved him in. Roccoli, shortened to Rocky, finished talking to some ship on the radio and turned back to Carl, brushing back a tangle of dark, wavy hair.

"Hey, Will! That area you guys were at last night is catching all kinds of hell today. A company from the 227th put in a CA near that cache site this morning, and they're getting their butts shot off." He got up off his makeshift stool and pointed out an area on the large wall map about two klicks from the Cambodian border. "They've been going in right around here"—he circled a spot with a grease pencil—"about a klick west of the downed flare ship, and it sounds like they hit another supply area, big, maybe regimental. Already lost one Huey and the NVA are shelling the LZ from across the border where nobody can touch them. That's a real pisser."

"You figure those jokers in Washington will ever let us roll into Cambodia and kick some ass on those dudes?" Carl knew what the answer would be. It was a sore point with all the Americans who worked the border areas.

"You know that as well as I do. Ain't nothing but a money thing. If they turned us loose in Cambodia, Uncle Sam would be shelling out big bucks every time we hit a rubber tree. And you know Uncle Sugar don't want to waste money on rubber trees when he could be using it to pay out life insurance on all the troops who are getting wasted by the dinks hiding out in those rubber plantations."

"Yeah, but Rocky, what are we fighting for over here? Are we banging our heads against the commies or are we fighting dollars?"

Rocky snorted derisively. "Grow up, Will. You been here two months already and you ain't figured it out? What have you seen happening around here? You ever stop and look at these people?" Rocky's smile was gone now and he was starting to heat up. "These dink sons of bitches could care less whether they're communists or not. Damned ARVNs cut and run when the shit hits the fan, and half of 'em would slice you up if you turned your back on them. They don't want us here and most of us don't want to be here. Only thing keeping us here is a bunch of bastards who got a lot of money tied up in this place. I'm telling you, Will, ain't none of these gooks worth a damn and sure as hell, ain't none of 'em worth dying for!"

"I don't know about that, Rocky," Carl began uncertainly. "The people here have been fighting for a hell of a long time. Maybe they're just tired of war and want to be left alone." Seeing that his remarks weren't being very well received, Carl thought of something that needed doing and took his leave. Rocky's statements bothered him. He had begun to suspect that defending the principles of democracy and protecting the freedom-loving masses of South Vietnam were not the real issue. He knew he was naive in some respects and sometimes a little too idealistic for his own good, but he could see that something was wrong. The way many of the Americans treated most of the Vietnamese people wasn't exactly the way Carl thought proper for men who were supposed to be defending those same people. He hadn't actually seen it happen, but he had heard of prisoners, suspected VC, being thrown out of choppers, of helicopters and grunts using civilians for target practice, burning hootches, killing water buffalo, and all just for the hell of it.

He countered that last thought. It wasn't just for the hell of it. He had seen the same thing before in the history books. The clash between cultures or political philosophies had an established pattern. Contempt from one side directed at the other, and with it sometimes an element of fear. He considered the position of the Jews in Nazi Germany. Labeled as inferior to the Nordic ideal, they also were feared as one would fear something vile and unclean. He had seen it in places other than the history books. The same feeling had been felt in Texas, the blacks, the Mexicans, all considered by some to be inferior, yet threatening. At least in the States, the law kept some degree of control over peoples' actions, but Vietnam wasn't the States. The restraints of normal society were gone and these little brown and yellow people with their strange gibberish and customs were slightly less than human in some eyes, much like the Indians of the old West. And he was beginning to see that many GIs, far from home, drafted into a war they wanted no part of, had modified an old saying: "The only good gook is a dead gook."

VI.

The first light of the new dawn was just beginning to break across the base camp. Carl was up early and relaxing under the cool spray of water in the empty shower shed. He paused for a moment outside the shower and gazed off into the distance toward the Rock. The Rock, Nui Ba Den, Black Virgin Mountain, any of those applied to the solitary mountain that thrust itself three thousand feet up above the flat miles of rice paddies and jungles. Carl had flown all over Tay Ninh Province and around a few others as well, and he knew this was the only mountain in a sixty-mile radius of Tay Ninh. She made a magnificent sight at this time of the early morning, barely visible and shrouded partly by the rising mist. A surrealistic vision, it seemed a place of legends, wandering spirits, demons, or gods. In reality, it was home to a small detachment of Americans, guards, and operators of a communications relay center. By night it was a hub of activity for the VC, who reportedly had well-hidden tunnel complexes throughout the mountain. VC and NVA observers used the Rock as a fire direction center for mortar and rocket strikes on the base camp. It had other uses. The best one Carl could think of was the service as a beacon, a signal that home was nearby after a long day.

He pulled out a fresh set of Nomex, the supposedly flame-retardant flight uniforms, dressed quickly, and joined the other crews at the mess hall for slightly green eggs, barely warm bacon, and warm milk in melting wax cartons.

"Hell, if we really wanted to win this damn war, all we'd have to do is fly over Charlie's positions and drop our food on him," Regis said after almost choking on a piece of overdone bacon. "It looks like somebody already napalmed this food. Guess they had to make sure it was dead."

"Can't throw food at the dinks," Corning replied with a grin. "It's against the Geneva convention to use inhumane weapons on the enemy. Besides, if we threw our food at them, can you imagine what they'd be throwing back at us? Man, that *nuoc mam* is some nasty shit. I can't figure out how these people can eat that stuff."

"If you clowns don't get your butts in gear, that's exactly what I'm going to have the cooks fix up for you when you get back!" Sergeant Wooden was standing in the doorway staring at the bulk of his platoon.

"On our way, Sarge," Jolley said quickly, and led a general rush for the door and the waiting ships.

Carl hooked up with a short, stocky crew chief from

New Mexico. Sp4 Martinez, part Apache, part Mexican, was the only Chicano in the platoon aside from the platoon leader, Lieutenant Gonzales. Carl had flown with Martinez once before and had been impressed with the kid's knowledge of helicopters. He seemed like a straight trooper, but he didn't talk much with the others, preferring solitude in his free hours.

Lieutenant Harris was piloting the ship today, one of his last missions. He already had his orders for stateside and was due to rotate out in two more weeks. Warrant Officer Ashley completed the crew list and Carl had an idea that it would be a pretty safe flight. Ashley, a tall rugged-looking young man, had been around for a few months and was just about ready to qualify as an AC and get his own ship. With an experienced copilot and a pilot who was getting super short, the shuttle missions had to go smooth.

As senior aircraft commander in the platoon, Harris had been given charge of the three platoon ships, and he designated one of them to haul the battalion commander around while the other two took care of lifting out the dead and wounded and the enemy supplies.

The LZ nearest the main concentration of captured equipment had been blasted out of thick jungle with demolition charges, and was a tight fit for both of the ships to land in at the same time. Carl kept a sharp eye out for hazards as they descended into the clearing with the help of ground guides.

"These guys look like they've been through the wringer," Carl stated as a tired, ragged group of soldiers trudged out of the trees with several body bags. The grunts looked completely exhausted, drained and empty, a faraway stare in the eyes of those who had enough energy to raise their heads. Again, Carl was thankful that he had gotten into helicopters. Some of the men, now dumping the lumpy green bags on the floor, looked more animal than human, unshaven for days, encrusted with sweat and red dirt. Must be a hell of a way to live. More coming. A half-dozen walking wounded struggled out to the chopper and crawled on board, shoving the olive-drab bags around to make themselves as comfortable as their wounds would allow. The worst cases had been medevacked out hours ago and none of these men would be out of action for long, Carl guessed. A few shrapnel wounds, minor lacerations, just good enough for a Purple Heart and a couple of days back in the rear. Carl had a pretty good idea what most of the grunts would tell the army about where to pin the medals, if they had a chance, but the couple of days back in the rear was a different story.

Several more soldiers appeared from the trees, these carrying bundles of AK-47s roped together. The weapons looked to be brand-new, and Carl's mind began scheming. The AK-47, Charlie's standard assault rifle, was a well-made piece of machinery, according to what he had heard from GIs who carried them. Made with few moving parts, they were ideal for jungle warfare, easy to clean, hard to jam, and rugged. He eyed the forty or so AKs that had been thrown aboard and wished that the wounded men had gotten on the other ship. A couple of the men in the platoon had AKs, and Carl wanted to add himself to that number. That regulations had a section about not using captured weapons didn't matter. Platoon sergeants and pilots frequently looked the other way. The Chicom rifles made good backup weapons, and if they got lost, nobody got hassled.

At the fire base everything was off-loaded quickly and both ships headed back in again. No more wounded or body bags, only captured equipment.

Martinez keyed his mike. "Look at what these dudes are bringing in. Got two of them bad mothers."

Carl leaned around the transmission wall to see several troops sliding in two long-barreled machine guns, very businesslike with their antiaircraft sights and ribbed barrels. Even though he had never seen one up close, he knew that these had to be .51s, Charlie's main antiaircraft gun in this part of Vietnam. "Two less to shoot at us with. Now all they got to do is find all the rest of those things and it'll make the sunny skies of Nam a whole lot safer."

"By the time this war is over, not even Charlie's gonna

be able to find all the metal that's buried out in the jungles,'' Harris said, laughing. ''People are going to be finding leftover stuff from this war a hundred years from now.''

That was easy to understand. With supplies being hidden all over the place and some enemy units getting annihilated, some of the caches would remain in their tunnels for years to come. But not this load. Carl wondered what happened to all this captured material and decided again that a few missing pieces wouldn't be noticed. So far, though, no opportunity had presented itself. The infantry had long ago learned that chopper crews were not immune to the time-honored traditions of thievery between units, and they had a guard on each load of equipment.

Finally, after the sixth sortie of the day, the items of major importance had all been lifted out, and the less critical material was started on. This time there was no guard along, and even though it wasn't much, Carl requisitioned a small Chinese medical kit and a gray Chicom ammunition can. According to the markings, it contained 550 rounds of the Russian short 7.62mm bullets. If he could ever get his hands on an AK, the shells would be useful. If not, then he could always trade it off to someone who needed it.

The next load was more of the same stuff along with several bags of machetes. One bag split open as the soldier threw it on the ship, and the crude-looking tools slid across the floor. They were simple of design, solid, one-piece, all-metal construction with square tips and flimsy Chinese-made sheaths.

Carl helped the soldier collect them and pile them into another stained rice bag.

The grunt, another tired, filthy man, managed a worn smile of appreciation for Carl's small help and shoved one of the machetes toward him. ''Here. A souvenir from Uncle Ho.''

Carl nodded his thanks and accepted the present like a kid getting a new toy. He felt only briefly guilty about ripping off the other items. What the hell, they wouldn't miss those items anyway. He slid the machete under his seat with his other pirated booty and recovered them with his field jacket.

Carl's ship had just departed the LZ with the first load of troops when the battalion commander, in the third ship, made contact with them.

"Commander says that one of the security platoons at the far west edge of the bunker complex has made contact with an enemy force of unknown size, so keep a sharp eye out. We're going to have to speed things up," Harris informed the rest of the crew, and then switched to his own TOC's net to request three additional ships.

Carl switched his radio to monitor the infantry frequency and after following their communications for a few minutes, realized that a very serious situation was developing at the LZ.

Harris was back on the intercom, conferring with the copilot and doing some quick math. "We've only got forty minutes of light left at the most, and those other ships won't be able to make it in less than fifteen minutes. There's still almost a full company, ninety troops, on the ground. We're going to daisy-chain them out, one ship at a time. Fast in and fast out. Stay loose on the guns. It could get a little sticky toward the end, and gentlemen"—he paused and glanced back toward Carl and Martinez—"I want to make it back to the world as scheduled, in one piece."

Carl nodded his agreement and continued listening to the men on the ground. The last couple of extractions would probably be the toughest. It would be dark by then, and from what he could understand, the enemy pressure was increasing on the security platoons. One bright spot appeared as the extra lift ships radioed that they were inbound and had two Cobras along for support.

The daisy chain began and the infantry on the ground blew out a few more trees to make it easier to get two ships down at a time instead of only one. The Cobras were to remain on station while the lift ships shuttled men out, but with the fading light and the close proximity of the enemy, supporting fires from the gunships would be difficult.

Going in for the second time, Carl could tell that the defensive perimeter was shrinking. Too much firing going on close to the LZ. The NVA were trying to tighten the knot on the steadily decreasing GIs. The smoke grenades that the troops had been using to mark their own positions were now all but useless for directing gunship fire.

The third time in, Harris went back to his original plan of one ship at a time to reduce the risk of a midair collision. He spoke quickly, precise orders for each member of the crew. "Running lights off. Gunners, fire only if you can see their muzzle flashes directed at us. Grunts are holding a tight perimeter around the LZ only. We're going in."

Looking forward, Carl could see an occasional green tracer streak across the area of the LZ. The LZ was only a dark shape within an even darker form, and as they closed in, Carl spotted the dull red dots weaving in the darkness, marking the locations of the ground guides with their red-filtered flashlights.

Carl felt the dryness in his mouth, the speed-up of his heartbeat, and made an extra effort to stay calm and collected. He forced a drill through his mind, going over his instructions, actions to be taken in the event of contact. Controlled and ready, he gripped the butterflies as the ship settled down into the clearing and was immediately rushed by three phantom figures from each side. The thin defensive line around the LZ was six men thinner, and even in the dark Carl could tell that at least two of the grunts were wounded.

Other soldiers, facing outward, had opened up with heavy fire to cover the ship's landing and departure, and Carl could see the suppressed flashes of their weapons strangely lighting the jungle. It seemed to be having the desired effect. He couldn't see any return fire coming in as the ship hovered up and forward.

The dark outline of the jungle was looming up in front of the ship when all hell broke loose. Fire erupted from several sectors simultaneously, AK-47s flashing brilliant white from less than sixty feet, spewing lead into the chopper. Carl vaguely heard men yelling, someone screamed. A ripping sound, bullets tearing through the thin metal skin of the ship, and the sound of his own gun blazing back filled his ears. An invisible fist suddenly slammed him back against the wall, his head jerked violently, and he fought desperately to cling to his machine gun, holding the triggers down and sending a red stream of death into the flash of the enemy muzzles.

I'm hit. I've got to be hit, he thought, but could feel no pain. Shock, the only answer, but he didn't care. He kept pouring fire and the enemy's muzzle blast suddenly winked out. "Got you, you bastard," he muttered under his breath, and shifted his fire toward another target. Then they were out over the trees and leaving the clearing behind, the pilot's voice sounding in his earphones.

"Cease fire! Cease fire! Everybody okay?"

Carl suddenly began to shake violently as a wave of fear and a growing sense of dull pain washed over him. He let go of his gun grips and clasped his hands together, pressing tightly, trying to stop the shaking, trying to feel out the pain.

Martinez had reported that he was okay. "But I think one of the grunts is dead. Took a hit just as we cleared the LZ. His buddies are checkin' him out but it don't look good."

Carl finally found that he could still talk and after a few seconds of cautious searching reported that he was still alive. "My chest hurts like hell and my head's still a little fuzzy. Think my chicken plate must've stopped a couple of rounds. I think I got one of 'em!" The last came out exultantly, viciously, and elicited an approval from Martinez, who was still keeping tabs on the infantry casualty.

"Don't hurry on his account, sir. Charlie nailed him clean."

Carl looked around the wall at the soldiers in the chopper and in the dim light of a red flashlight beam above the dead man, he could see the exhaustion, the fear, and something else that he couldn't quite name on the faces of the survivors. In some of those hollow eyes, a look of resignation, men who know their fate. They had made it out of one small sector of hell, but there were a hundred other places, a hundred other times still to go through. Those expressions, the dead soldier unmoving on the wind-whipped floor, countered the fleeting feeling of victory over the unseen enemy that he was sure he had hit. In subdued silence they made their way back to the fire base and dropped off the grunts.

The other ships were taking their turns hitting the LZ, so Harris stayed on the ground for a few minutes to check for battle damage.

"Nothing serious," Martinez told Harris. "Maybe a dozen bullet holes, all sheet-metal stuff."

Harris nodded, wiping away a bead of sweat from his dark, tanned face. "None of the warning lights have popped. Everything seems intact. Looks like you had a close call, gunner," he said, pointing at Carl's chicken plate and shining his light on it.

Martinez whistled lowly, and Carl stared down at the scarred body armor. There were deep gouges almost dead center, marking the spots where AK bullets had struck him. That was what had slammed him backward, and that was what had been responsible for the momentary crushing pain he had felt.

"Shit!" It was the best he could manage. Eight inches higher and the copper-jacketed rounds would have ripped through his neck. Eight inches lower . . . "Shit!" He remembered the tearing pull he had felt against his head, and pulled off his flight helmet. "Marty, shine your light on this." A long bulging furrow had been plowed through the upper right side of the fiberglass helmet.

"Damn, Will! Those dudes almost got you. You must have somebody looking out for you or else you really been living right!" Martinez shook his head as if he couldn't believe Carl's luck, and Carl was equally amazed that he hadn't even been scratched.

"Time to go!" Ashley yelled, beckoning to Harris. The young copilot's blond mustache had a sickly green tint from the instrument lights, and Carl thought the warrant's whole face had a deadly green pallor about it. He shook off the feeling that something wasn't right and scrambled on board, plugging in his mike just in time to hear Ashley on the intercom bringing Harris up to date.

"Everybody's taking fire coming in and back out, and it's getting heavier. All ships have reported hits and we've got several casualties. We're taking out the last load, six packs and a platoon leader. Harris," he continued with a trace of nervousness, "those gooks are going to be all over our ass when we start pulling up. The platoon leader said he'll pop a trip flare off just before we make short final. It may light us up a little but it'll give the Cobras a solid mark and with a little luck, might even blind some of the little bastards for a few seconds."

"Sounds like a hot time in the old town," Harris replied with an edge in his voice. "Damn it all! I'm too fuckin' short for this kind of thing. Chief, you men heard what Mr. Ashley said?" Carl and Martinez both rogered an affirmative and the pilot continued. "I'm holding you two responsible for my butt. Once we get those troops on board, I don't want to hear those guns slow down until we're a klick away from that place!"

Listening to the pilot, Carl knew the pucker factor was running high with everyone. When that last group of soldiers made a break for the ship, there wouldn't be anything holding the NVA back except the two Cobras and the doorguns. And the last time in had been hairy enough! He checked the Velcro straps on his chicken plate and hunkered down experimentally to see how much of his body he could hide behind the large ammo can. Not enough, he decided, but anything would help. That was one of the drawbacks about helicopter duty. Once the enemy had you in his sights there was no cover to drop to, no place to hide.

On final approach Carl tried to find enough moisture in his mouth to spit, but it was dry as an old bone. All the stops were coming out this time and his body was already reacting to the anticipation. His temples were pounding in the tight confines of the helmet. He wasn't even aware of his rapid breathing until the first rocket blast from the gunship made him start. At the same time, a sudden splash of light signaled the trip flare going off just to the front and below them. The sounds of automatic-rifle intensified as both the grunts and the NVA cut loose with everything available. Out of the corner of his eyes he saw the magic red line of minigun tracers as the Cobras rolled in closer, throwing out an incredible shield of fire, a hundred rounds per second.

As if purged by the flame of the Cobras' weapons, the feeling of fear and nervousness washed away, leaving him calm and clear-headed, already swinging his gun to bear on enemy positions.

"Go hot!" Harris almost yelled into the intercom, sending Carl and Martinez into their individual duels against the AKs and the RPDs.

Carl held the triggers down, locking in on one flash for a second and shifting to another, trying to suppress as many different spots as possible. In the light of the flare he could see the outlines of the few remaining GIs, backs to the chopper, firing out into the jungle for all they were worth. Firing around and over them as the ship touched down, Carl covered them as they broke position and, bent low to the ground, dashed for the chopper. Carl had the feeling that the entire ship was one big duck in a lopsided shooting gallery. An agonizingly slow duck. Nothing was moving at the right speed. Flashes, like a thousand Roman candles, were blasting from the too-close treeline. His gun seemed to move slower and slower as he fired in a huge arc, not even trying to pick out targets now. Yelling that they were loaded and clear, even the ship seemed to be a victim of this slow-motion nightmare.

A dark form materialized on the edge of the jungle,

then another, less than forty feet away, moving at a charge in frozen seconds of time, firing from the hips, firing death straight into the chopper. In the instant of eternity that it took for Carl to bring his gun to bear, he could hear screaming from inside the chopper and a screaming voice in his own brain. "I'm dead, I'm dead. Why aren't they hitting me?" Then the screaming broke out, exploding from his lungs, savagely, incoherently, sustained by the pounding blood and a berserker's fury.

Leveling the steel death at the nearest figure, he cut through the shadow, its arms pitched up, sending the rifle turning through the air as the man collapsed to the ground. The second shadow was still firing and Carl suddenly was hammer-smashed again, but kept hold of the triggers, and in the light of the flare he watched the brown man's head explode as he caught a full burst from Carl's gun. With the blood frenzy still burning through him, he kept firing at the falling figure, the bullets twisting and jerking the dead flesh in a grim dance.

Climbing away from the LZ, still firing, the red tide began to recede and the urgent voice of the pilot broke into his field of awareness. Tracers were still following them, but his was the only weapon still firing, and Harris was trying to raise the crew chief.

Carl let up on the triggers and listened for Martinez's reply, but nothing came from the ship's left side.

"Willstrom, you okay back there?"

"A little banged up, sir," Carl replied, feeling the first time a burning sensation in his neck. Something warm was trickling slowly down to his chest under the chicken plate. The pain was only mildly uncomfortable, and putting his hand to the left side of his neck, he determined that it was a minor wound, probably a piece of bullet that had struck his plate. "I'll be all right. I'm going around to check on the chief."

"Make it fast and then get up here and check the copilot," Harris ordered quickly. "I think he's hit."

Carl scrambled across the grunts and switched on the

helicopter's interior lights, illuminating this last, exhausted group of soldiers and the crew chief's compartment. Martinez was slumped over sideways, and as Carl tried to move toward him one of the grunts grabbed his leg, yelling and pointing to another soldier. Carl's glance went from the sweating, dirt-streaked face of the man holding his leg to the still form on the gray-silver floorboards. Looking closely in the low-intensity light, he could see the gaping, ragged hole in the man's abdomen, unreal colors of greens, blacks, and yellows marking the internal organs. Some of the intestines were protruding up through mangled skin flaps, and another soldier began the drilled-in, automatic first aid, covering the wound with a large bandage from the aid kit.

Carl grabbed at Martinez's mike cord, yanked it loose from the chief's helmet plug, and keyed the mike, turning Marty's head at the same time. "Sir, we've got one grunt shot all to hell, gut wound! Martinez is still alive, breathing. I can't see any blood. May just be unconscious, hits on his chicken plate. I'm coming forward now." He pulled the crew chief back toward the cargo bay, made sure he wouldn't fall out, and then worked his way over the huddled-up grunts until he was at the console between the two pilots.

Ashley's seat belt was locked down, holding the copilot back against the seat, but his head was inclined forward, chin almost touching the chest. Carl leaned around from the left side, tilting the limp head back and raising the visor. The fair-skinned officer's eyes were shut, as if in peaceful sleep, but there was a small trickle of blood coming from the corner of his mouth. Carl carefully slid his thumbs under the bottom edges of the helmet, spread it open, and lifted it off Ashley's head, which slumped onto the left shoulder. There, on the right side, just above the ear, the light blond hair was matted and bloodstained around the dark entry hole of a bullet. Still, warm blood was running down the neck and covered Carl's hand as he felt the neck for a pulse, knowing there would be none.

Feeling no emotion, strangely detached from the concentrated world of pain and death inside the helicopter, he looked at the man's helmet, noting the small, neatly drilled hole on the right side of the olive-drab headpiece. For the second time in his brief flying career, he had lost a copilot. He plugged in Ashley's mike cord, glancing across at the pilot. He could tell from the pilot's expression that Harris already knew the answer to the unasked question, but he said it anyway. "He's gone, sir. Took a head shot. Must have killed him instantly."

Harris stared at Ashley's body for a second, then nodded. He glanced at Carl's neck and then fixed his eyes on the distant lights of Tay Ninh. "We'll take this bunch straight to 15th Med. Pass that on to whoever's in charge. You don't look too bad, so the company medics can take care of you when we get back. Until then, you're the crew. Check Martinez again and do what you can to help out the troops."

Carl rogered, located the platoon leader, and passed on Harris's message. The young lieutenant looked up from a minor injury that he was working on, catching Carl's eyes. He had seen Carl checking the copilot and knew that the warrant officer was dead. For a moment they held the exchange, soldier to soldier, each having lost a portion of the soldier's family. Then the lieutenant silently nodded his thanks and bent back to his task.

Carl slid across into Martinez's position and reached under the seat for the canteen that many crewmen carried for those "just in case" situations. Martinez was still out. Carl pulled off the crew chief's helmet and dumped some of the cool water over his face. Another quick splash and Carl was rewarded with a brief flicker of the eyelids. Then the eyes came open all the way, and Martinez just lay there, disorientation and puzzlement registering in the black eyes.

Glad that he didn't have a second corpse on his hands, Carl grinned at the still fuzzy trooper and helped him into a sitting position.

"Feel any pain anywhere?" Carl yelled above the engine noise.

"What happened?" Martinez asked dumbly, not hearing Carl's question. He shook his head slowly from side to side, up and down. "What happened?" he repeated.

"We almost got our shit blown away. From the looks of it, you took a couple of hits on the old plate. Probably saved your ass, but put you under for a while. Those chicken plates earned their money tonight. We're on our way back into Tay Ninh now. One of the grunts is in bad shape. Ashley's dead." It came out as accepted fact.

Martinez's obsidian eyes flickered toward the cockpit, then down at the floor. "Bad shit, man. He was a cool dude. Knew his stuff and didn't hassle no one."

It was as good an epitaph as any. Carl figured the words didn't apply to everyone. There were a few who knew neither their job nor the forces they tried to control. That kind didn't always last and were never mourned. Carl nodded his agreement and moved back into the cargo bay to lend a hand. A young soldier with shaking hands was pulling a tattered poncho over the body of the gut-shot soldier. Carl hadn't figured that the kid had a chance. He was just glad to still be counted among the living. One more time, once again a survivor. And a killer. He wasn't sure how he felt about that. There was no doubt about it this time. He had wasted two of them at close range, almost died at the hands of one of the NVA if not for the chest protector. The memory sent a shiver down his spine. The key word, *almost*, the difference between life and death. "Fuck 'em," he finally muttered. "Game rules. They lost, I won."

VII.

"Hey, Carl!" Jolley came running toward him from the orderly room, waving a handful of papers. Carl stopped on the walkway and waited for the old-timer. "Got my leave orders! I'm heading back for the World in six more days. All them round-eyes better clear the streets." He flashed a leering smile and curled a tip of his handlebar mustache. "Lieutenant Harris and me are going down to Tan Su Nhut on the same day. Only difference is, he has to stay back in the World and I only have to stay there thirty days and then I get to come back here for some rest!"

Carl laughed with him. "Jolley, you're a crazy bastard. How are we going to keep this war alive without you for the next month?"

"You're a hell of a person to be calling me crazy. With locos like you running around, I'm sure life won't be too dull until I get back. I was rapping with Harris about that shit you dudes got into last week. The man said you were really together when it counted. Maybe you even had your stuff too much together. Even when Ashley died, you didn't seem much bothered. You really dig this war, don't you?"

Carl studied Jolley for a few seconds as they walked, the old crew chief's eyes unreadable behind the silvered aviator's glasses. "Hell, you've been around this place for a long time, Jolley. I don't think you'd be sticking around if you didn't have the same kind of feeling. Yeah, I do dig it. I was scared shitless some of the time out there last week, but it was also a real turn-on. I thought Charlie had me by the balls, man. But there was such a rush at the same time. I was going fuckin' crazy, yelling and firing 'em up. I was scared, thought I was dead for a minute and I can't wait for the next time." Reliving the experience afresh made his blood heat up, and his voice deepened. "It's the Game, Jolley. I feel bad about the guys who get wasted and worse for their families, but this is war. That's what it's all about. Going up against somebody else's guns and coming out on top makes me feel . . . alive. Someone once said, 'For those who have faced death, life has a flavor that the sheltered will never know,' or words to that effect. I don't know who the dude was, Jolley, but those words were about people like you and me. The flavor is the risk. You know it and I know it, and I guess we're both a couple of crazy bastards."

Jolley just smiled. "You're right on all counts, slick. Idiots both. You sure as hell can get fancy with words when you want to. You ought to write a book about this place one of these days. Damn sure better put me in it somewhere. It's all gotta be good, though, or I'll kick your ass!"

Carl just laughed with him. "Right on. Maybe I will write about this. You just make sure you get on back over here, so I'll have something to write about."

Jolley pulled off his sunglasses, wiping off some imaginary dust. "I'll tell you something, m'man. You don't need me around for writing. You been here less than four months and you've already seen more action than some dudes who are finishing up their tours. Before you arrived, we had been on a long dry spell without much action, and now we're in a hot cycle with you collecting a lot of the heat. You keep ending up in the wrong place at the wrong time, or depending on your point of view, it might be the right place at the right time. You may not have heard, but you're getting a reputation, some good, some bad. Chopper crews are a superstitious bunch, and you've already had two copilots shot up on ships you've flown on. I heard one pilot telling a rookie Wobbly that the surest way to get his cherry busted was to have you along as the gunner. You're making a name for yourself, slick, so we got to give you a fitting name. You know, a minute ago you were talking about acting all crazy and weird and that sounds like a good handle to me. Willstrom's too damn long, but that's easy to handle. Weird Willy! I like it.'' He slapped Carl on the shoulder, smiling, pleased with his creation.

''Does that mean I've got to act weird all the time?'' Carl asked in mock seriousness.

''Damn straight it does. You got to be the craziest fool here and keep all these rookies in line until I get back.'' He nodded his head, repeating, ''Weird Willy. I do like the ring of that. Let's hit the club and make it official.''

Carl's fourth month in-country was greeted by the beginning of the monsoons, the torrential rains common to tropical jungle areas. It began with a regular pattern as every day in the late afternoon the dark clouds would release their burdens, suddenly and violently. The old-timers had told him that in a few more weeks the rains would be almost continuous. He could hardly wait. It was already miserable enough. The hootch roofs leaked, the mud was six inches deep, and the pounding rain split open the older sandbags, washing the loose sand down to the base of the hootches to add to the mud.

''Look at all that damn rain. If people ever saw that much rain back in Texas, they'd be out building arks.'' Even as Carl spoke, another sandbag gave up the ghost, hammered relentlessly by the driving rain. ''Looks like more sandbag details, Coop. Jolley cut out just in time. Right now, he's back in the World somewhere, chasing some round-eye women, sleeping in a real bed. Hell! Even got flush toilets and hot baths! I wonder if he feels guilty about enjoying all that good life, knowing that we're up to our balls in muck, defending freedom?''

''Yep, I can just see that son of a bitch feeling guilty. He probably can't even remember our names right now.'' Cooper shifted his heavy frame around on the cot, trying to get comfortable. ''He's sitting in a bar right now, drunk out of his mind, telling some broad about how he's winning the war single-handed. Giving her the old line about 'shipping out for the front tomorrow.' He might as well enjoy it. He's gonna pay for the ride later. Six more months to do when he's had his fun. You couldn't pay me enough to keep me in this hole a day longer than I have to be here. And if the army wants to give me a drop, I won't argue."

A splashing and stomping sound attracted everyone's attention to the hootch door as Sergeant Wooden burst in. He shook off some of the water and left a dripping trail as he moved to the center, demanding attention.

"Well, gentlemen," Wooden began with a smile, the kind that said "Guess what you have to do?" "To some people this may be an unpleasant assignment, but try to look on it as a travel opportunity. TOC just got a call from division maintenance in Phuoc Vinh. They just got some parts in for your ship, Coop, and the old man wants those parts here tonight so that maintenance can get your ship off of Red X and ready to fly. Since the parts are for your ship, I figured it was only fair to let you go get them. Willstrom looks bored, so why don't you take him along as gunner. Jessup's your pilot and you'll be taking Jolley's bird. Get your gear and move out. With a good tail wind you might make it back for regular chow."

"Thanks a lot, Sarge. How'd you like to get fragged in the next thirty days?"

"Don't even joke about that!" Wooden retorted. "I'm already getting paranoid enough without my beloved platoon trying to do me in. I may spend the next thirty days hiding out in the bunker." This was the last month of his second full tour in Nam, and he had told everyone that it should be his last. With only three more years left to go before he had his twenty in, he didn't really think the army would send him back to a combat zone again.

"Aw, don't go and hide on us. I promise not to pull any pins. You're not bad for a lifer, I mean career soldier," Coop said, laughing. "I guess we can let you slide on by this time. C'mon, Wild Willy, let's go play in the water."

"That's Weird Willy," Carl corrected him.

"Right. Probably gonna be Wet Willy by the time we get back from Phuoc Vinh. Jolley's bird don't have no doors, does it?"

Carl shook his head, threw on his poncho, and put on his flight helmet as a rain hat. It sounded like it was raining even harder than before, if that was possible. He muttered a few choice words and followed Cooper out into the storm.

The wood-planked walkways were almost useless, having sunk into the ever-softening earth. A whipping wind neutralized the protection of the poncho, and Carl gave up trying to keep dry. The mission was a real pisser. If it had been a combat mission, he wouldn't have minded so much, but to have to put the guns on in this weather for a bread-and-butter run seemed like a wasted effort.

Once in the air, Carl tried again to keep from getting completely soaked. He huddled up as tightly as possible and kept his visor down for protection against the stinging raindrops. The field jacket that he had brought along had long ago lost its water repellency, but it was better than nothing at all, and served as a good windbreaker when gusts buffeted the ship. Every time that happened, the ship would get knocked out of trim for a few seconds, allowing wind and rain to pour into the bay area, adding to the general unpleasantness of the trip.

Definitely a miserable mission, he thought, watching the raindrops splatter against his gun. The wind pushed them around the curving of the barrel and sucked them out into open space again in a continuous flowing spray. Carl didn't like the idea of being in the air in bad weather. The ease with which the wind tossed the chopper around made him feel like a tiny passenger on a frail piece of straw in a hurricane. The long, slender blades of the ship hardly seemed adequate for keeping the fragile mass of sheet metal and its four occupants suspended in the turbulence of the monsoon storm.

Carl breathed a deep sigh of relief when Jessup finally brought the ship to ground on one of the pads near division maintenance. Safely on the ground, he relaxed and worked out the stiffness from his shoulder muscles. Cooper and Jessup dashed off through the rain in search of parts and the usual paperwork, leaving Olsen, the black copilot, and Carl to watch after the ship. The half hour that Carl had figured for ground time crawled by, and the parts chasers didn't return.

Just as total darkness pulled her shroud over the skies, Jessup dashed into the chopper, soaked to the skin, and in ill humor.

"Goddamned supply people! Took half an hour to find the asshole in charge. He'd already quit work and was soaking up suds at the club. Son of a bitch knew we were coming and needed those parts tonight. Coop's bringing them out in a jeep in a few minutes. I almost had to threaten the chump to let us borrow the jeep. Let's get this bird cranked. I want to get out of here as soon as we're loaded."

Carl untied the rotor blade and swung it out just as Cooper slid to a stop in the jeep. Cooper waved for Carl to give him a hand, and while the driver stayed dry in the jeep, the two crewmen made several trips, loading the heavy boxes onto the ship.

"Thanks for all your help, slick!" Cooper yelled at the driver. As they jumped aboard the chopper, Cooper flashed a smile at Carl. "I hope these guys don't ever need any favors from us. Usually, they're pretty good about helping us out, but they got some new jerk in charge who thinks his job stops when they tell us they got our parts."

Jessup was cleared for takeoff and the tower advised him that there were severe storms toward Tay Ninh, electrical and heavy turbulence up to six thousand feet. Jessup acknowledged and thanked the controller, then lifted off into the darkness, the running lights transforming the rain into a shimmering shower of silver and sapphire droplets.

Once out of the traffic pattern, Jessup started a gradual climb up through the dark sky, leveling out at seven thousand feet. There was nothing visible below, no ground, no lights, nothing but a swirling darkness. He felt like the entire ship was suspended in limbo with no substance of reality to hold on to.

"We're at seven thousand, Chief. I don't think the best shot in Vietnam could hit us at this height in this kind of weather. Why don't you and the gunner move inside a little more?"

Carl didn't wait to be asked again. No point in staying wet at that altitude. The only hazard that high up would be from some other aircraft flying through the clouds. They still had to stay alert, but at least they were above the storm's worst area.

Far below and around the ship, lightning lit up the sky, and in one particularly brilliant flash Carl saw that dead ahead the storm was swelling up to meet them again. He pointed toward the front, tapping Cooper on the arm, but the vision had already faded. "Looks like it's getting worse up there," he yelled, not using the intercom. "You know, Coop, this kind of stuff scares the crap out of me. No way to fight back."

Cooper just grinned at him and started to say something when the ship suddenly plunged sickeningly, sending Carl's stomach to his throat. For a long second the ship dropped through the air pocket, yawing from side to side. Carl grabbed hold of a seat pole and reached out with a free hand to help Cooper steady himself. When the chopper steadied again, Cooper slid in as close to the center of the troop seats as he could get, pulled up one of the seldom-used seat belts, and strapped himself in.

"That kind of shit scares you, huh? Don't feel like the Lone Ranger, man. A few good shots like that could overstress the blades, pop them rotors right off!" He grinned unpleasantly at Carl.

Carl joined him in the center of the ship and hooked up a belt. "You're full of all kinds of good news, aren't you?" He felt ill at ease enough without those remarks. His dread of heights was starting to crush in on him, tightening his chest with every pitch of the ship. It wasn't so much the idea of dying that bothered him. It was that long fall, the screaming helplessness of plummeting thousands of feet, the stretched seconds in which to think. That was what bothered him. He preferred low-altitude flying but he had to go where the ship went, and over the last few months he had conquered his fears until now. At least, everyone else seemed worried, too. The lack of chatter between the pilots showed that they were tense and on edge, but they stayed in control of the ship despite the storm's best efforts.

A long, torturous hour after leaving Phuoc Vinh, the ship finally pulled into home port. Even the unabated rain, still falling in sheets, couldn't dispel Carl's joy at being on solid ground again. Swinging out of the seat and planting his feet on terra firma, he quickly went about stripping the guns from their mounts and, leaving the others to do the postflight, stepped out through the ankle-deep water toward the arms room, anticipating a warm meal and a hot cup of coffee.

VIII.

Might as well be at a regular army base back in the World. No enemy action in almost three weeks and Carl was getting restless. The monsoon rains were still in full swing, and many field operations were being geared down. He had made a few routine combat assaults in name only. There had been no one to assault against, therefore no combat, unless shooting up the silent trees could be considered as combat. He figured he must have shot holes in at least a hundred of the leafy, towering denizens. And oddly enough, not one of them had returned fire.

Hawk-faced Regis had survived his year and departed in fine army tradition. A blowout party had left the crew chief in a drunken stupor, and Carl had half dragged, half carried Regis out to the helicopter the next morning for the flight to Bien Hoa.

On the heels of his departure had come a cycle of replacements, more newbies. Carl's platoon picked up a new gunner and a crew chief, both fresh from their respective AITs. A new copilot had joined the platoon, a young kid who had just turned nineteen and looked every day of it. The new warrant, bright blue eyes, wavy brown hair, boyish grin, made Carl feel like an old war-horse at an ancient nineteen and a half.

The army saw fit to give him a promotion to specialist 4th, and even better, from his point of view, he received his first combat medal for the action that had taken place when Ashley was killed. Secretly proud of the Air Medal with the "V" device and the Purple Heart for his neck wound, he accepted them with an outward indifference, as did others who were decorated for the same action. Collecting medals at the expense of the lives of others was something the crews didn't talk much about. It was considered bad taste, even if the awards were earned with great risk. The older veterans didn't like serving under or with men who were out for glory.

The platoon leader, Lieutenant Gonzales, was a one-digit midget, DEROSing in less than a week, and a senior lieutenant, Rawls, from the first platoon had been assigned to take over Carl's group. New faces were all around the company area, and Carl found himself to be part of an ever-dwindling force of experienced gunners and chiefs. Jessup and Cooper were both getting short, but not all of the experience was leaving. Jolley was due back in a matter of days, and Carl was looking forward to his return.

Even without enemy there were losses. The rules of the Game still remained constant concerning rookies. A rookie copilot from the third platoon blew his foot off with a dud M-79 grenade round at one of the major fire bases. The base, FSB Barbara, was a more or less permanent fixture just a few klicks from the Black Virgin Mountain. It was considered more secure than most and had a proliferation of dud shells around it. The story that Carl had picked up was that the rookie had taken a stroll outside the perimeter, found the 40mm projectile, and being a curious rookie, he had kicked at it. The impact of his foot set off the grenade and separated said foot from the end of his leg. That was the story that made the rounds. Everybody knew that the new guy probably never saw the grenade, simply hit it by accident, but since it involved a rookie the story was more entertaining than the fact, and typified the popular concept of rookie intelligence and behavior. Carl didn't feel at all guilty laughing with the others at Marty's retelling of the event in the club hootch.

The grim humor of some of the events couldn't be extended to everything that went on. A first platoon ship had to make a trip to Phuoc Vinh for spare parts, and Carl heard their radio traffic while he was shooting the breeze in the TOC with Rocky.

The pilot radioed in that they were encountering rough weather on the return trip and that the ship was going to return low level under the clouds at fifteen hundred feet. Rocky shook his head, tossing his oily dark hair. "Hope he knows what he's doing. I think I'd rather be up on top of the weather instead of trying to cut through it."

The radio crackled to life, the pilot reporting that they were entering a very low visibility area. Suddenly his voice rose, yelling at the copilot, forgetting that he was still transmitting on FM.

"Hey! Hey! Pull up, pull up! Don, let go of the controls! Chief! Get him off the controls!" The pilot switched to the guard frequency. "Mayday! Mayday . . ."

The radio abruptly went dead. Rocky scrambled to try to raise the ship, but there was no response. The operations officer scrambled a ship to try to locate the first platoon bird in the storm and sent a brief message over the guard channel asking for search assistance if there were any ships near the pilot's last reported position.

Carl had a pretty good idea what was going to be found. So did everyone else in the TOC who had heard the pilot's last frantic yelling. He had heard of it happening before. It sounded like the copilot had gotten vertigo, couldn't tell up from down, and froze on the controls after putting the ship into a dive. At only fifteen hundred feet it wouldn't have taken many seconds for the ship to plow into the ground.

A long hour passed before the search ship reported in. They had found the remains of the ship, bits of wreckage scattered over a large rice paddy area. No survivors, not even sizable portions of bodies, had been spotted. The search chopper's pilot reported that they were going to land and try to bring out the remains of the crew if they could find anything.

It was a sorry way to die. Carl knew the men who had died. The crew chief had been getting short, down to his last thirty days, and just a few nights earlier at the club hootch had been telling everyone that his wife and young son were driving out from Arizona to meet him when he arrived in Oakland.

Now, instead of a husband and father, all the family would get back would be a telegram and a Purple Heart. The man had been one of those who were drafted out of their safe, civilian lives, their jobs interrupted by the call of the nation. And Carl felt sorry for those men and even more so for their families. The RAs, the regular army enlistees, were there by choice and couldn't really bitch. Some, like Carl, were there because of the lure of the Game, with the understanding that dying was one of the major rules, and they accepted that risk. But, unlike the crew chief, many of the young volunteers had no responsibilities, no family back in the World depending on them to return safely. Carl wondered how the wives of the older career soldiers could live with that kind of life, husbands who might have to spend several tours in combat areas before they got their twenty or thirty years in. Seemed like a hell of a way to make a living.

Aside from his parents, Carl had no one to worry about him. No fiancée or steady girlfriend. Trying to stay close to someone halfway around the world was pointless, and there were enough girls in Nam to keep the juices flowing.

The five-dollar whores didn't provide much in the way of companionship, but they served their purpose. They also kept the medics dispensing penicillin in large volume. Carl had heard the same stories as all the others, and like most of the troops, he didn't ride bareback. He always carried one of those PX rubber packs when he went into town. He didn't want to go home missing any parts because of the Black Syph, or any other fanciful variety of VD.

"Hey, slick, you getting any of that yet?" Smith laughed and pointed to a new hootch girl.

Carl smiled, following the point, and shook his head. Her name was Kim. Vietnam was full of Kims. Carl thought she must be about sixteen, although it was hard to tell how old any young Vietnamese girls were just from looking at their bodies. That was one of the major complaints of most GIs about the women. Nothing up top, at least by American standards. Carl didn't care about the small breast size too much. He had always thought that Oriental women had a delicate beauty about them, and the months of close exposure to them had not lessened his appreciation of them. Admittedly, not all were raving beauties. Most of the women Carl had seen had lived hard lives, working and surviving from one war to the next. By the time they were twenty-five many were already old. But he did like the way the young ones looked, and with ulterior motives he had befriended Kim, and was learning about her.

He and Smith continued to watch her as she swept around the hootch, conscious of their stares. Her jet-black hair framed a slightly oval face with eyes to match the hair. Carl thought he could see a slight smile in them once when she glanced up at him.

"Kim! You and me, we go to bunker today."

She pretended to be angry and stopped sweeping for a moment to shake the broom at Carl. "Numbah Ten GI. Kim no go to bunker!"

Smith jumped up and made a dash at her, pinched her

on the butt, and almost made it to the door before she caught him with the broom.

Carl enjoyed the grab-ass as much as anyone, and watching Smith getting pasted with the old straw broom was something to laugh at. Smith tried to duck under one swipe, slipped and rolled half out of the door, bowling over an older mama-san with a load of clean laundry.

"Better get your ass out of here now, Smitty! You done pissed ol' mama-san off!"

A shrill stream of insults and curses followed the red-headed gunner as he dusted himself off and made a face at mama-san. She replied with another string of gibberish, and Carl wished for the hundredth time that he could learn to speak that language. The idea that Kim might help him to learn had some appeal to it, but for the moment she wasn't talking to him. He wasn't worried. He still had a long time to go on this first tour, and he was sure that he could develop something.

IX.

By some strange coincidence, Jolley's return ushered in a new cycle of action. The beginning days of December saw increased action levels all along the division's Cambodian border area.

"Guess they just been waiting for me to get back so they'd have some competition," Jolley remarked as the two flopped down on their cots. "Man, I've only been back in the saddle for three days, and those dinks have shot at me every day. Good thing they're lousy shots."

"Make you wonder if you did the smart thing, coming back here? Right now you could be sitting around stateside somewhere, fucking off, getting laid. Hell's bells, anything but getting shot at."

"I think we've had that conversation before, Weird Willy. I'll take the shooting." He laughed and gave his mustache a twist. "Anyway, I'm too damn handsome to die."

"Well, we'll see about that. Here comes Lieutenant Rawls. Maybe he's got a mission for you to go capture Ho Chi Minh." Carl was glad to have Jolley back, and enjoyed flying with him. He thought they made a great team, both a little crazy.

Because of his mustache, a huge, bushy, reddish mass of nonregulation hair under his nose, Rawls entered the hootch looking like a worried walrus. In a matter of minutes Wooden had assembled the platoon, and Carl could tell after the first two sentences that the mission was going to be a hot one.

"Gentlemen, the other platoons are receiving identical briefings right now on tomorrow's mission. Depending on the effectiveness of the arc light, enemy resistance may be anything from nil to moderate. We're going after an NVA main force regimental staging area. S-2 has information that NVA battalions from this regiment are preparing for a strike against one of the border bases and we're going to hit them first." He paused for a moment as a small cheer went up, then raised his hands for quiet and continued, a slight smile breaking the tension on his face. "An arc light will be going in on them at 0730 hours. We will already be in the air and approaching the strike zone with the first load of two sorties from the 2nd of the 12th Cav. As soon as possible after the dispersal of the dust cloud, we'll go in. Guns hot on the first lift only. Once in the LZ watch your fire. Vision will be at a minimum and we don't want you to shoot up any of our own ships. And please don't let your pilots land in bomb craters. After the first lift restrict your fire to identifiable targets only, and at all times, watch out for dud bombs. Our platoon has been designated to go on standby after the operation. We'll remain at the fire base for material and/or POW extraction, and anything else that might pop up. Questions? All right, Sergeant Wooden will give you your crew assignments and times."

Before anyone had a chance to start up the chatter, Wooden commanded their attention and passed out the crew lists.

When he called out Jolley's gunner, Jolley made a show of having his feelings hurt. "Sarge, I'm surprised at you. I thought for sure you'd want to be my gunner on a mission like this!"

"Son, you couldn't get me up in the air now. I'll be with you in spirit, though. After you fearless fliers take off, I'm going to hide myself in the TOC bunker and follow your heroic actions over the radio. Matter of fact, I might just take up permanent quarters in the TOC."

Carl couldn't blame him. With the renewed action had come more frequent rocket and mortar attacks on the base camp. With only fifteen days left on his last Nam tour, Wooden was definitely committed to making it home alive.

Carl found himself assigned to Regis's old ship, 312, but under new management. He had been paired up with a rookie, Sp4 Wiley, who had been in-country for about as many days as Wooden had left to go. Wiley had only flown for a week or so, and had come under some light AK fire only once, and that had been at extreme range. Carl didn't know much about him yet. He certainly wasn't very imposing looking and Carl had the feeling the newbie was already scared. The man's rookie-pale face was sweating slightly and his brown eyes darted nervously around the hootch until they focused on Carl. Standing up from his cot, he hurried across the floor, giving Carl a chance to look him over. He was about Carl's height but a shade lighter with nondescript brown hair and ears that looked much too large. Maybe it was the short hair that set them off. Carl didn't really care. He was more interested in his personality. Something about the rookie didn't set well with him. He silently wished he had been assigned with Jolley or Corning or any of the more experienced chiefs, but they were helping to break in new gunners.

It wouldn't do to pair up two newbies on a hot mission

if there was any alternative, and in Carl's platoon there were plenty of experienced men to draw on. The fact that the rookie would technically be in charge of him didn't bother him at all. He wouldn't put up with any shit from any rookie. He knew he would be more in charge of the new crew chief, and part of his job would be to ride herd on Wiley and look out for him. And here the dude came over, nervous as hell.

"Hey, Weird Willy"—he used the name as if it were a title—"are these arc lights really as bad as I've heard?"

Carl glanced up at him, casually motioning for him to have a seat. "Yeah, they're some bad shit, especially against positions that aren't well dug in. And they'll sure as hell fuck up anything at ground level." He saw Wiley relax slightly and brighten up at those words. He couldn't help adding, "Of course, you gotta figure that a regimental area is going to be well protected. Remember, these little dudes have been working out in the jungles for years, and they're used to this bombing business. You heard what the LT said. If we get lucky, the B-52s might waste most of 'em. Then again, it might just shake 'em up and piss them off." Wiley tensed up again, and Carl regretted having said that. No point in trying to scare the new guy before they even got out there.

"You really think there might be a bunch of them left alive after the bombs hit?"

This rookie is already starting to act flaky. "Look, Wiley, don't worry about it. If they're still there, then we deal with them. Hell, one of Charlie's regiments is only equal to one of our full-strength battalions, maybe only six hundred men. You take care of one half and I'll get the rest. Relax. The whole damn thing may just turn out to be a wild-goose chase. The NVA have a pretty good intelligence network, and they may already be gone by the time the air strike hits. You just keep your eyes and ears open and follow the LT's instructions. Don't shoot no friendlies, make sure of your targets, and you'll do just fine." He said it with more conviction than he felt. The new guy was already on the shaky side and was going to need a lot of support. Support that Carl might not be in a position to give if things got hot. He wasn't superstitious, but he was already getting a bad feeling about this mission. Cutting a guy too much slack could get the whole crew killed, and Carl didn't want his thread cut just yet. Not because of some rookie who couldn't handle the heat.

Wiley wandered back to his cot and sat down heavily, staring at the floor. Carl watched him for a few seconds, considering trying to say something else to relax the newbie, and then shrugged off the idea. Everybody's got to work that problem out himself.

Carl stripped down to the baggy OD boxer shorts and sprawled out on his cot. Wiley was still staring at the floor as if life had no meaning left, and Carl shook his head. "Do or die, rookie," he breathed silently, and dismissed the crew chief from his thoughts, drifting off to sleep.

The crisp morning air was almost a natural high. The smooth, steady beat of the blades was a Vietnam lullaby, comforting and relaxing. Carl hoped that it was having the same effect on Wiley. The kid was really tensed up, and hadn't loosened any during the morning chatter despite the pointedly reassuring remarks from Carl and the pilot.

WO2 Nelson had sensed immediately that something wasn't right. Carl had filled him in on the previous night's discussion and gave him his own opinion of Wiley.

Maybe once the mission got under way the new crew chief would loosen up. If the mission got hot, the new guy would either make it or break it. Carl himself was beginning to feel the stir of excitement in his blood as they neared the pickup zone. This one was a little different from the standard combat assault. Going into this LZ might be like sticking your head into a beehive after kicking it around. There could be some real angry people waiting for them when they hit. At the other extreme, it could be a human junkyard with only wrecked and torn flesh to greet them. The B-52 strikes employed saturation bombing in a very concentrated area, and the concussion alone could kill men caught above ground with no cover.

The ships landed in a wide, staggered formation at the fire base, and the first load of grunts rushed aboard, seemingly eager for action and blood. This represented a solid chance to catch a large NVA force and surprise those who had been planning to surprise them. Carl figured it could be a real turkey shoot, flying in on a disorganized and stunned enemy. One young grunt, face streaked with browns and greens, flashed a hungry smile at him.

"Gunner! Let's get some!" he yelled above the engine drone, raising a clenched fist.

Carl gave him a thumbs-up and patted the grips of his machine gun. "If there's anything left to get!" he said. He was hoping for action almost as much as his crew chief was probably hoping to avoid it.

At 2,500 feet with three minutes to impact, the flight leader started a wide swinging arc about ten klicks out from the target area. The counterclockwise orbit far away from the strike zone afforded Carl a sometimes view of the area. Nothing distinctive about it, no different from the other miles of stretching jungle, nothing to indicate that in 180 seconds the stillness would become an inferno of blasted hell.

Carl checked his watch again. Forty seconds, thirty, counting down. The bombs should be on their way down. His ship was on the target side of the arc when he saw the first flashes, a series of tiny instant lights like dozens of minute firecrackers bursting silently in the distance. With the sound of distant, rolling thunder the blast swept by the ships. Carl figured there was a shock wave with it, but in the lurching troop ships it would be unnoticeable this far away.

For a while his ship was in a position so that he couldn't see what was happening, and by the time the zone came back into his view the scene had changed drastically. All along the thousand-meter length of the strike area a huge, dark cloud was billowing up, debris and smoke rising toward the heavens.

On the next circle around, the towering mass of disintegrated earth had topped out level with the flight, thinning and dispersing in the upper wind currents. Carl stared at the massive testimony of man's destructive capabilities, the stark darkness of the cloud contrasting sharply with the purity of the blue sky.

Hard to believe that anything could survive down there, but he had heard stories reported by the *chieu hoi*s, VC and NVA who had come over to the other side, about men who had survived arc lights without any heavy cover.

He looked across at the grunts, who were smiling and laughing, pointing to the rising cloud and enjoying the show. He knew the line of their thinking. Charlie's getting his payback—in spades—and they were looking forward to the mop-up.

At a kilometer out of the LZ the flight came down to the treetops, and Yellow One gave the order to go hot as his ship began its final approach. With no visible targets, Carl was content to simply exercise the power of his weapon. If there were any NVA trying to crawl away from the impact area, the hail of fire from fifteen pairs of doorguns might just add a little to their miserable situation.

Just ahead of him Carl could see the dust rising from the first ships, and as his chopper, the seventh in the long trail formation, cleared the edge of the relatively untouched jungle, his mind inwardly boggled at the close-up destruction he saw.

Burned earth and shattered matchstick trees were everywhere. Craters, huge, gaping wounds in the earth's skin, almost overlapped each other. Smoldering brush and shifting shadows in the churned-up dust from the rotors gave the place the appearance of a dead hell with the Hueys coming in like swarming green insects rushing to a feast of death.

Carl continued to pour fire through the thickening dust, slicing his weapon in a narrow arc. With his vision drastically reduced, his ears picked up some of the slack, the rocket explosions from the Cobras, Wiley's machine gun chattering. A good sign. At least the new guy was on his gun. The grunts had pulled their OD first-aid slings over mouths and noses and were tensing for the jump-off.

No one reporting "taking fire" yet. "Damn!" The dark form sprawled on the ground a bare twenty feet away caught him by surprise, but he quickly swung his barrel on target. Not a GI, probably already dead. He fired a short burst into the body, saw it jerk with the bullets' impact. No doubt about it now.

"Coming down," Nelson said, pulling up to a hover.

Carl checked for any nasty surprises, stepping out onto the skids, looking under the chopper, and cleared the pilot down. Wiley proved his existence by clearing the left side. The ship rocked slightly from the GIs springing off before the skids hit the ground. Carl kept his gun trained over their heads as they rushed out a few yards and dove to the ground, weapons facing out, ready for anything or nothing.

Still no resistance, but Carl was getting a feeling, a nagging whisper in his mind. They were out there. There were still some alive.

Yellow One gave the command to lift off, and the entire flight came up, moving slowly past the prone grunts, showering them with more blowing dust. Carl could see the end of the thousand-meter strike zone just ahead, and as Yellow One passed it, Carl heard what he knew was coming.

"Taking fire! All elements, Yellow One taking fire at eleven o'clock. All elements break right!"

As Nelson started to make the break, Carl heard Wiley stuttering into the intercom. "Fire! Fire! We're taking fire!" Then the rookie's machine gun opened up as he remembered that he had the capability to shoot back.

Even though he didn't have any visible targets, Carl cut loose on the edge of the jungle below him, aware that as he started, the chief's gun abruptly quit. He started to press his mike button, but a sudden white flashing from an isolated crater drew his entire attention. Several muzzle flashes were coming from the tattered foliage ringing the crater, directed at the breaking ships. Barrel on target. Fire! Using his tracers, he walked his rounds into the middle of the multiple flashes, aware that gunners from other ships were sending their tracers into the same area. For a five-second count he held the triggers down, saw a body lunge up then drop, and the muzzle flashes stopped.

"Willstrom! Grab the rookie!" Lieutenant Richter was shouting in the mike and pointing back toward the crew chief's compartment urgently.

Carl released the gun grips and scrambled around the transmission housing, catching sight of Wiley's arm flailing convulsively, blood spurting from a severed artery just below the elbow, sending a red spray across the chopper. Wiley was screaming and tried to resist when Carl reached around and tried to pull the chief into the main cargo bay.

Carl grabbed at the jerking arm with his free hand, grabbed Wiley by the throat and forced him to the chopper floor, rolled on top of him, pinning the rookie down, and wrapped both hands tightly over the spurting artery.

"Artery!" he screamed at the watching Richter, as if the man couldn't tell. The front of Carl's uniform was streaked with blood, as was much of Wiley's Nomex, and despite Carl's desperate pressure, a rapidly growing pool of blood was spreading across the floor under the arm.

Wiley stopped his struggling for a moment after being pinned, and for a brief second Carl raised to shift his weight. In that second Wiley suddenly bucked and lunged like a maddened animal, twisting with an incredible strength for somone who had lost so much blood. His eyes rolled wildly, unnerving screams tearing from his throat.

Carl smashed him down to the floorboards, trying to use a forearm across the neck to hold the head still. His brain was screaming at him to knock the chief senseless before he kicked both of them out of the ship. But the part of his mind that was in control whispered to him in the face of the screaming madness. He couldn't relax his hold for even a second. He stuck his face right down into Wiley's, yelling at the man, trying to get his eyes to focus on him.

"Wiley! Wiley, it's all right! Look at me! Look at me, dammit! You're gonna make it! You're gonna make it! Just hang in there!"

"I'm gonna die! I'm gonna die!" The rest of the rookie's yell dissolved into hoarse gibberish, and the brief flicker of recognition that Carl's voice had sparked disappeared. Wiley's efforts seemed to be weakening but he couldn't afford to relax.

"Willy, we've broken formation and we're heading for Tay Ninh! Keep the pressure on that arm!" Richter's advice wasn't needed, but Carl wished that the copilot could get back to help, or that there were still some grunts on board. He nodded his head to show that he understood.

A splintered second of warning came, Wiley's body tensing like an overwound spring before it breaks.

"Noooooooo!" Wiley screamed like a soul in hell and made a superhuman surging body wrench sideways, heaving Carl off toward the center of the ship's floor. As Carl flew off, clutching wildly for the chief, Wiley arched back, rolling toward the open bay's edge.

Carl rolled to his knees, heart pounding, everything moving in slow motion. He moved forward, too slow, too slow, reaching out for Wiley. The blood-drenched figure completed a roll, and hung there on the edge, his face a horrible grinning mask of insanity. Carl's arm continued to extend, fingers stretching with a dreamlike slowness. Wiley rolled back slightly and disappeared into the empty space outside the helicopter, the last trace of the doomed man, a flapping left arm, beckoning in a final motion.

A bolt of unnatural fear shot through Carl, stopping his breath with the last Ahab-like gesture.

"Jesus Christ! Hard left!" Richter had witnessed the entire drama, helpless to prevent it. Nelson, unaware of the full story, responded immediately, banking the ship hard left without question. The steep banking angle gave Carl an almost straight-down view of the jungle a thousand feet below. For a brief moment, he thought he saw a dark shape far below, then it vanished through the leafy jungle top.

"What happened?" Nelson demanded, glancing over his shoulder at a shaken gunner.

Carl drew in a deep breath, calming himself, gathering his feelings into a controlled group again. His voice started with a slight shake. "Goddamned rookie freaked out. He went fucking crazy and rolled himself right out of the ship.

He's down there somewhere. I tried to hold on to him, but he just twisted away and rolled out, like he wanted to die!"

"Do we go down and try to spot the body?" Richter was looking down into the jungle as the chopper continued the sharp, banking orbit.

"Hell, I don't think we could find him," Nelson replied, his voice hard. "Willstrom, did you see where he went down?"

Carl, more recovered from the experience now, wiped some of the blood off his hands before replying. "Yes, sir, I think I caught a glimpse of him. He should be about a hundred yards to the east side of that small open area at eleven o'clock. Dammit! That dude had a blown artery, sir. He shouldn't have been able to throw me off like that. He just went berserk and I couldn't stop him. I should have punched his lights out or strapped him in or something!" The words poured out in a torrent, the emotional cork popping in his mind.

"Easy, Weird Willy," Nelson said quietly. "There was no way you could have known how he was going to react. He was shaky to begin with. No fault on you."

"He's right, gunner," Richter chimed in for Carl's benefit. "I saw the whole thing and you did everything possible under the circumstances. Two men probably couldn't have held him down."

Carl just nodded, not trusting himself to say anything. Maybe, just maybe they were right. He wanted to believe they were, he needed to believe it, that he had done everything he could have. Rookies getting themselves wasted by their own stupidity was one thing, a part of the Game, but he had actually had this man's life in his hands for a few moments. Even as the doubt tugged at him, he knew he would rationalize the events away, given time. That was just part of the survival method. He recalled the impression of fear and doubt that he had read in the rookie the previous night. Shit, the dude was so wired he'd never have lasted through a whole tour anyway.

While he sat there sorting things out in his head, Nelson kept the ship in a circle above the general area where

Wiley had disappeared, and contacted the flight leader, filling him in on the details and requesting instructions.

After a few, long silent minutes Yellow One got back to them. Carl followed the transmission from the crew chief's well, where he had taken up temporary residence. From Yellow One he learned that a pink team, hunter-killers from the 1st of the 9th Cav, had just completed a mission east of their location and were en route to help find and recover the body. Carl's ship was ordered to remain on station to direct traffic for the recovery.

Circling slowly above the jungle, nobody felt inclined toward conversation, and Carl, listening to the steady *whop-whop* of the blades, found that his defense systems were covering him after the initial shock of the incident.

He was reestablishing his identity within himself as Weird Willy, the crazy man, the gunner who survived while others he flew with sometimes didn't. Only a weak twinge of guilt hit him when he mentally added Wiley to the long list of rookies who hadn't been able to handle the pressures.

Cold-blooded. But that was the way it had to be. So far, he had been lucky. None of the men that he considered as close friends had been killed. He wasn't sure how he would react if one of them died. It didn't pay to speculate on those kinds of thoughts. Better just to concentrate on the living and being alive.

"Looks like our company is here," Richter said, breaking the silence. "Two o'clock."

Carl craned his neck around the transmission wall, looking out toward the right front, and spotted the two choppers flying toward them. The hunter-killer team, one of the small OH-6A observation helicopters and its deadly protector, a Cobra gunship.

"Papa One Four, this is Tango Two Two, over."

"Tango Two Two, Papa One Four," Nelson acknowledged. "Thanks for coming."

"Roger, One Four. We're ready to begin search. Low bird descending now. If you'll direct him into the general area, we'll get started. His call sign Tango One One, over."

Nelson broke off from the Cobra and established contact with the scout ship. "One One, maintain present heading. You're in line with target area, about one thousand meters out." He waited a few seconds as the ship closed in, then continued, "You're coming up on a small open space, five hundred meters to your front. My Golf element thinks our missing element may be one hundred meters to the Echo of open spot, over."

Carl listened to the conversation and watched as the small ship bypassed the open area of the east side and began a widening set of concentric circles, moving slowly and deliberately. Since their missing "element" wasn't trying to hide from anyone, Carl figured they should have no trouble locating the body unless there were others down there who might object to the close scrutiny of the scout.

Carl checked his watch. Fifteen minutes gone and no trace of Wiley had been seen. The bubble-shaped ship continued its ever-widening orbit with the Cobra shadowing it. Nelson kept their Huey up another five hundred feet to stay out of the way. Suddenly, Carl's attention was refocused on the smaller chopper. It went into a sharp right turn, began a tight circle, and then stopped, hovering in one spot over the treetops.

"Papa One Four, this is Tango One One. Missing element found."

X.

Carl had already cleaned and turned in his weapons and returned to help the pilots with the ship. He had worked with enough crew chiefs to get the routine down.

Nelson and Richter were almost finished when he got there. The floor and walls were still a mess and that would be Carl's job, but he had gotten used to cleaning up dirt and blood on the floors of all the platoon's ships. Two things there was never a shortage of, dirt and blood. And bullet holes.

"Might as well get the sheet-metal people out here," Nelson told him as he pointed out the battle damage. He ran a tanned hand through his blond hair, scratching at the back of his head. "This one just barely missed the shaft," he said, motioning at a small hole in the tail boom. "No problem with the hit in the engine cowling, straight through and out the other side." For a moment his blue eyes stared into Carl's, the pilot's once boyish face hardened by a half year of Nam, then he spoke. "We didn't check out the transmission wall yet, but I'd like you to get the sound-proofing stripped off, cleaned up, and check for holes in the wall. The round that hit Wiley may have gone through the arm and could be stuck in the ship." He pointed again to the holes. "Looks like all the hits came from Wiley's side. That first position that opened up must have done this. I remember that he didn't open up until a second after he told us that we were taking fire. For what it's worth, that extra second that he delayed might really have been what killed him."

Carl had picked up a scrub brush and was scraping some of the dried blood off the floor. He didn't reply to Nelson but simply nodded his head. He had already written the chapter off to experience. He was thinking about the body that the 1st of the 9th Blues, an infantry platoon, had pulled out of the jungle. His momentum when he crashed through the tops of the trees had ripped both of his arms off and snapped and twisted most major bone areas.

Despite the body's bad shape, Carl really didn't feel sorry for the crew chief. The man might have been dead before he ever hit, and if not, the impact would have finished the job instantly. More than the death itself, it was the timing that bothered Carl now. Somewhere back in the World in just a few hours, only twelve days before Christmas, Wiley's parents were going to get that telegram, that messenger that every parent dreaded. At least he hadn't been married.

He continued scrubbing up the ship and checked out the walls. If the bullet had gone through the chief's arm, it hadn't ended up inside the ship. No damage other than the two hits that Nelson had shown him.

He replaced the soundproofing and was getting ready to leave when he saw Wooden heading in his direction with another sergeant. "You making it okay, Will?"

"I'll survive," Carl replied. "It wasn't a picnic in the park, but I suppose you've seen it enough to know."

"Right. And I'll be glad to be getting out of here. Tired of seeing young kids die. Anyway, this is Sergeant Wells." He half turned toward the tall, lanky E-6 who was with him. "He's my replacement, just got shifted over from Bravo Company. Wells, this is Sp4 Willstrom, more commonly referred to as Weird Willy. Dumb as any new guy when he first got here, but he's turned into a damn good gunner."

Wells extended his hand and gripped Carl's firmly. "I won't be taking the platoon officially for three days. Meanwhile, I'll just be watching the operations and getting to know the people. Sergeant Wooden tells me that he thinks you're ready to make the move into a crew chief's slot. Think you can handle it?"

Carl cracked a smile for the first time in several hours. "Hell, yes, Sergeant. I've been working out with the crew chiefs a lot for the last couple of months. I think I know most of the stuff, and I've always got the TMs handy." The chance to crew a ship of his own meant more responsibility and a better chance for promotion to Sp5 if he did his job right.

"Okay, you've got the job. Sergeant Wooden and I were just talking over the situation and there's one ship in the platoon without a crew chief." Wells looked over Carl's shoulder at 312, then his eyes came back to meet Carl's with a questioning look.

When the offer had been made, Carl knew which ship he would have to take, but he didn't hesitate. "I'll take it!'' The strange feelings that he had felt before the mission, the uneasiness, the death of Wiley, didn't affect his decision. True, he was the third crew chief for 312 in less than thirty days, but it was a good strong ship. Regis had lorded over it, cared for it for six months, and never had any trouble. As for Wiley's death, everybody had to die somewhere, sometime.

''Good enough!'' Wooden exclaimed, giving him a slap on the shoulder. ''Get the logbook taken care of, and one of my last official duties will be to get some orders cut on you for the 67 November MOS.'' Then his voice grew serious again. ''Look, I know it's been a long day for you, but when you are finished with the logbook, come on over to the club. I'm buying. We'll drink a farewell to Wiley, a drink for your new job, and a beer for me 'cause I'm getting the hell out of here.''

''Right, Sarge. Probably do me good. Might even get drunk,'' Carl stated matter-of-factly, but Wooden shook his head.

''Don't overdo it, Weird. You'll be going up tomorrow. Do it with a straight head. I'd like to know everybody's still alive when I leave here.''

Ordinarily, the men didn't talk much about their comrades who died, at least not until some time had passed. Even rookies rated a day or two of peace, but word had gotten around about the bizarre death of Carl's crew chief, and some of the aircrews were curious about what had really happened. Several of them cornered Carl in the club and asked him directly what the real story was. He gave it to them straight without any added-on bullshit that usually accompanied war stories. The only part he didn't tell them about was the unreasoning dread that coursed through him when he thought about that last vision of Wiley. He wanted to forget that last insane grin on Wiley's face and the beckoning, the grotesque invitation to follow, of the flailing arm. He wanted to get drunk and forget about that part, but he knew that Wooden was right, and a fast drunk wouldn't help. After he laid the facts out, he changed the subject around to what had happened after his ship left the action.

"Weren't no big thing, slick," Jolley informed him. "The second lift didn't draw a single round. The boys on the ground covered the area pretty well and came up with a few POWs. They tossed 'em on my bird, got the floorboards all fucked up. Those NVA dudes were a mess. Two of them didn't look like they was going to make it, blown all to hell!" Jolley looked over at his gunner, who nodded agreement. "One of the guys guarding them told me that one of the dinks had been found just staggering around in a daze. They didn't find any resistance, man. That shows you what a hell of a number those arc lights can do!"

At that moment Lieutenant Rawls came through the doorway. "Listen up! All platoons, mission briefing and debriefing. Platoon sergeants"—he motioned in particular at Wooden and Wells—"get 'em back to the hootch."

"All right," said a weary Wooden. "You heard the LT. Move out!"

In the hootch, Rawls was studying a piece of paper, waiting for all the men to sit down and quieten. When everyone's attention was focused on him, he smoothed down the bushy, red mustache, kicked a leg up on an ammo crate, and cleared his throat. "First item. New platoon sergeant, most of you have already met him, takes over in three days." He waved toward Wells as he introduced him. "He'll be talking with you men, getting to know you, watching our operations, and give you a chance to get to know him. He's got a good record from Bravo Company and I'm glad to have him aboard, since our current man has grown tired of our company. Next item, the bad news. We lost a man today. He was pretty new to us and I didn't get much of a chance to know him, but he was still one of us. Memorial service will be tomorrow at 1930 hours in the mess hall. I'd like everyone to attend unless duty requires you elsewhere." He let out a long breath as if relieved to be done with that part. He again glanced at the piece of paper before continuing. "Next item. Today's mission. Unqualified success . . . ground commander passes on a 'well done' for the flight crews. The arc light did its job, completely smashing the NVA main force at that location. Final tally, forty-nine confirmed enemy dead plus lots of bits and pieces, seven POWs, a small assortment of AKs, RPGs, sixty-millimeter mortars, and a few light machine guns. At last report the infantry units were following up numerous blood trails, and the body count will probably increase. One of the company commanders asked us to pass on the credit to the gunners and chiefs for at least five of the confirmed dead found around a machine-gun position. Wiley was the only friendly casualty in the entire operation.''

He folded the paper up and slipped it into his pocket, letting the serious lines fade from his face for a moment. ''Next item. Our own Weird Willy has moved up in the world to join the ranks of those gallant aerial engineers, the crew chiefs. He's taking over 312 effective now.'' It was already old news, but the platoon gave him a mild cheer for the record, making him feel a little self-conscious. Rawls held up his hand for quiet. ''Last item. No signals for a Christmas truce or cease-fire. On the contrary, all indicators point toward intensified enemy activity around Tay Ninh Province, so you can probably look forward to a busy Christmas and New Year. Nothing heavy on for tomorrow, though, so I'll leave you to Sergeant Wooden for one of his last duties.''

Wooden handed out the assignments, detailing two of the ships to the operational control of the first platoon for a CA. He saved his new chief for the last. ''Nothing big for your first mission. You got a log mission out at Fire Base Green. Good chance to break in a new gunner. Kurtz will be your right side.'' He looked in the direction of another one of the rookies who had joined the platoon in the last week. ''Got that, Kurtz? You just listen to Willstrom here, do what he says, and you'll be okay.'' He turned back to Carl and shook his forefinger in a cautioning motion. ''Green's under attack right now. One of third platoon's ships is running a flare mission for them, so when you're out there tomorrow keep your eyes open. There might still be some activity around the areas you'll be in."

"Right, Sarge. Damn, it's a good thing you're getting out of here. You're getting to be a real mother hen." Carl laughed. "I'll make sure Kurtz brushes his teeth before he goes to bed and we won't stay out late after you leave!"

Wooden wrinkled up his nose. "All right, be a wise ass, just be a careful one." He gave a few more words of advice to some of the others and then left the crews to themselves.

Carl checked Kurtz out, remembering that he had been the gunner assigned to Jolley's ship for the arc-light sweep. He was shorter than Carl by a good three inches but a little stockier. Black hair was still close-cut, an indicator of how new he was to the outfit. He looked gutsy enough, and Carl thought the kid had an open, honest look. He rose to shake hands with the rookie and motioned for him to have a seat.

"I'm Weird Willy, new chief on 312. You were with Jolley on today's mission, right?" Kurtz nodded in response and Carl rolled on. "Was today the first time you've fired your weapon?"

"I popped loose a few rounds on a test fire the first time I went up. That was two days ago. Did quite a bit of shooting out there today, though," he said eagerly.

"Yeah, I think most everybody got off a few shots." Carl smiled, remembering the excitement of his first hot LZ. "Main thing is, were you shooting at anything or just spraying down the trees?"

Kurtz flushed and looked down at the tips of his boots for a second. "As a matter of fact, Specialist Willstrom . . ."

Carl cut him off with a snort and a wave of his hand. "Cut the specialist crap. You're not back in AIT, or did Jolley make you call him that?" It sounded like something Jolley might tell a rookie.

"It just kinda slipped out. Got used to talking like that to anyone who had a stripe back in the States. Anyway, I was fixing to say, I think the only thing I was shooting at was trees. I kept hearing about the NVA on the radio, but I never saw any, except for some prisoners the grunts put on board. Those poor bastards were in sad shape. I think one of them might have died while we were flying back in."

"That's what the Game is all about, Kurtz, fighting and dying. This may sound cold-blooded, seeing as how a man died on my ship today, but that's the way it is. And that's why I was asking you about your firing your machine gun. Real blunt about this. Wiley's shit was flaky out there, and I want my right side gun to be a good one, with no screwups. I may be a weird son of a bitch, but I intend to stay alive, *bic*?"

Even though Kurtz had only been there for a few days, he had already picked up on the local term for "do you understand?" "Don't worry about your right side, Weird Willy. I'll keep it covered."

Carl grinned at him and told him to get some sleep. Kid was definitely not like Wiley. Another one of these gung-ho rookies, full of dreams, hopes, idealistic. Kind of like he had been when he first came to Nam. Seemed like an awfully long time ago. He lay back on his cot and closed his eyes. Nothing. No haunting faces, no screams. He sat back up and unlaced his boots, wondering how his sleep would be. He wasn't sure how he felt, laughing and smiling with the others so soon after a death on his ship. One thing he did know. He was tired. The day had not been an easy one and he wanted an undisturbed sleep. Lying back again, he closed his eyes and let his mind drift into nothingness.

Gulping down the last of his coffee, he made a quick motion to Kurtz to follow him, and headed toward the arms room. He wanted to draw his own gun, and with the heavy steel over his shoulder, he strode down the flight line. His ship. The dark war-horse stood silently in its armored revetment awaiting its riders as the dawn broke.

Kurtz loaded up the ammunition while Carl linked up with Olsen and his charge, another rookie warrant named Chrissen, who had come in about the same time as Wiley and Kurtz. Another paleface, typically warrant type, young, slightly nervous, afraid of making a mistake while under the watchful eye of the experienced pilot.

While they were going through the preflight checks, Olsen began speaking to Carl, starting an overly loud conversation with a fast wink and a flash of white teeth. "Don't know what the problem is with Lieutenant Rawls and Sergeant Wooden. I can't imagine why they would send out a rookie peter-pilot and gunner on a mission with you along!"

Carl knew the drift the conversation was going to take, and he didn't mind. He was going to put yesterday's business into the memory books and continue to be Weird Willy. "Maybe they've got a kickback deal with the insurance companies or maybe they just like the people up at battalion to keep busy with lots of paperwork." He could see that both of the rookies were listening as they worked.

"Well, it's true that the army needs more paperwork, but I think it would be a little more considerate of them not to send rookie copilots up on the same ship with you. Look at it from my point of view. We need a few of the new guys to live long enough to become ACs so the rest of us short-timers can slack off a little and coast."

Kurtz slid the last box of ammunition in under Carl's seat and grinned at the two veterans. "Don't bother me none what you guys say. From what I've heard, it's only copilots that get hit when Weird Willy's around, 'cept for Wiley, and he was a crew chief, not a gunner, so I oughta be safe."

Olsen and Carl just laughed and Chrissen decided to ignore them all.

Approaching the fire base, Olsen radioed in to get the usual relative information. A tired-sounding voice told him that the enemy situation was negative, and the last contact with the enemy had been two hours earlier.

"Papa One Niner, be advised, first mission. We have seven line ones to go back to Tango November. They're ready to be taken out as soon as you can load and lift. Over."

"Things must have been pretty rough out here last

night,'' Olsen remarked on the intercom. ''When I was in the TOC Captain Rogers was updating me on the attack. Charlie dropped 150 to 200 mortars on their heads last night and then launched a ground attack in battalion force. The assault didn't get far but the mortar barrage did quite a bit of damage.''

''If I read him right, we've got seven corpses to take out, right?''

''That is correct. For a new guy, Chrissen, you're picking up the terms of the trade pretty fast, and speaking of new guys picking up things . . . Weird, does our new gunner know his duties about keeping the ship clean?''

Carl smiled and keyed his mike. ''I didn't tell him. Hell, I've only been a crew chief for twelve hours.'' He directed his voice at Kurtz. ''What he's talking about, rookie, is that you gotta keep the ship nice and tidy. When they load on those dead troops, they might make a mess. Part of your job is to clean up the blood and muck, make sure they don't leave any bits or pieces behind, and don't add to the mess if you can help it.''

''Hey, I may be a rookie, but it takes a lot to make me sick,'' Kurtz retorted. ''I'll do my job.''

Right, Carl thought to himself. ''Just 'cause you saw a couple of wounded NVA the other day don't make you immune to the flip-flops.''

Kurtz didn't reply to that and Carl returned his attention to the dark scar of brown earth that made up the fire base and the surrounding cleared area. It was situated in what had been a large clearing, expanded even further by the engineers so that an attacking force would have to cross a sizable open area to get to the base.

Flying in low, the ship passed over scattered work parties of GIs who were dragging small brown bodies to a central pile a hundred meters from the berm, the earthen wall that ringed in the fire base. A scarred and blackened bulldozer was already at work, scooping out the final resting place for the nameless dead of the enemy.

As the ship hovered toward the spot where their first lifeless cargo awaited them, Carl swung out onto the skids and waved at a grunt who had paused in his work to glance up at the chopper. The lone soldier waved back, extending the stiff, bloodied arm that he had just picked up and waving it as well. With Carl as an audience, he raised aloft the raggedly severed head of some unfortunate attacker, released it, and drop-kicked it a short distance through the air. Somewhere Carl remembered reading about groups of people who had used the heads of fallen enemies as playthings, grisly kickballs. He wondered if the rookie copilot had noticed the action. Probably not. With a view through the front bubble, Chrissen could see more than enough of the carnage. From what he could see, Carl figured there must be at least a hundred dead Charlies scattered around and in the body pile.

Once on the ground, grim-faced young grunts carefully laid the seven olive-drab body bags on the chopper floor. A wide range of emotions ran across the faces, and Carl could see the blending of anger, sorrow, and resignation in the eyes of some. Others were like masks, nothing showing through. Survivors. Stay alive, don't think about the dead. He understood the reaction.

When the last of the body bags had been loaded aboard, a young sergeant with a red mailbag and a smaller laundry bag in hand came hustling out of the fire base toward the ship. He stepped up on the skid shoe by the pilot's door, holding the laundry bag up. "Personal effects. I'll be going back to the rear with you, but I'm supposed to come right back out, so wait for me. It'll only take me about five minutes to deliver this stuff."

Olsen nodded and motioned him to get on. Leveling off above effective small-arms range, the ship turned toward home base, and Carl, slipping his barrel into its bracket, turned his attention to the grim contents in the cargo bay. One of the bags had a watercolor reddish-brown tinge forming at the head end of it, and dark fluid was beginning to leak from a small rip at the bottom edge. He shook his head slowly. The dude's head must be nothing but mush. Carl keyed his mike and leaned around the transmission wall.

"Hey, Kurtz! You gonna have a mess to clean up when they off-load these poor bastards. Take a look."

He watched as Kurtz looked around, spotting the leakage of bloody ooze spreading out from the bag. As it stretched away from the shelter of its former container, the winds began to catch at it, swirling patterns across the floor.

"Jesus!" Kurtz let out the exclamation softly. "What the hell happened to that one? Damn, I'm glad they got these guys in bags."

"Your time is just starting, rookie," Carl told him, remembering back to a time when another young rookie had caught and held a booted foot, separated from its owner. Long time ago. He thought Kurtz looked a little pale, and he glanced up at the copilot. Chrissen seemed to be concentrating on his flight duties, and hadn't looked back at the bags during Carl's conversation with Kurtz. Kurtz slid back into his position and remained quiet, only occasionally sticking his head out to look at his future, growing work.

The grunts who unloaded the bodies were a sharp contrast to the men who had put them on board. These were clean, shaven, rested, the lines of exhaustion gone until it was their turn to get back out in the bush. The young sergeant who had come along for the ride was still caked in red dirt, the knees and elbows of his jungle fatigues darkly stained from crawling and sprawling during the night's action. His face was partly clean from a quick shave, but the eyes were tired and the narrow face had a drawn and pained look to it. He left the chopper, and true to his word, was back in less than five minutes with a mailbag for the base and four newbies.

"Look at the purty soldier boys," Carl advised Olsen.

"Damn! They sure do shine, don't they? Makes Chrissen and your gunner look like old-timers." Olsen laughed.

Carl clicked his mike button twice as an affirmative. The new troops were almost painfully bright in their new jungle fatigues and spotless helmet covers. As they climbed uncertainly on board, Carl threw his hands up over his face in mock blindness.

Even the sergeant cracked a smile. No matter how bad things were, if you were safe and there was a rookie on hand, you could always find something to smile about.

"How long you figure they'll last?" Carl asked loudly.

The sergeant stepped back a pace, pushed his boonie hat high up on his head, and thoughtfully surveyed the newbies. "Long enough for me to get the hell out of here, I hope," he replied seriously, then looked at a smear of blood that Kurtz had missed. "Some of 'em may not last long enough to break in their boots if we have many more nights like the last one. Those dink bastards really hit us hard!"

"I could tell. Looked to me like you got more than your share of them, though."

"No shit," the sergeant snorted. "It's not hard to get a bunch of them when they come charging across two hundred meters of open ground. We knew they'd be coming as soon as their mortars lifted. They didn't care. Those crazies don't give a shit how many of 'em get wasted if they can just get a few of us." He looked at his charges, who were listening carefully to every word. He couldn't help but laugh at their open-mouthed stares. "I reckon these rookies will get put on the bits and pieces clean-up detail as soon as we get back. There's still gonna be lots of little chunks of NVA scattered all over the place, and they need to be cleaned up before they start drawing too many flies."

The newbies all looked uncomfortably at each other, and Carl could tell that some of them were wondering how much of this they were supposed to believe. "It's all true, troopies. You'll see for yourselves in about fifteen minutes. It is indeed a mess out there."

Cruising back toward the fire base, Carl hoped that Olsen would do something to give the rookies a little thrill, but the pilot just wanted to get the ship back and down, so he decided to show off with a little skid riding as they came down on final approach. He swung out, planting himself surefootedly on the skid, holding on with one hand to his machine gun, and making a casual show of checking out the area below the ship. The newbies stared openly, nudging each other, and Carl enjoyed the attention.

When the ship touched down, the sergeant rolled out and quickly herded his stumbling flock into the fire base. Carl watched them go, heads turning every direction, trying to take in all of the sights of this new world that they had only heard about. He silently wished them luck as they disappeared from view into the brown earth ring.

"It'll be about twenty minutes before our next sortie, gentlemen, so let's shut down and relax," Olsen suggested, winding the ship down. "Run a few checks on the ship and then you can take a look around."

After the ship had been checked out satisfactorily, Carl motioned Kurtz to follow him, and they took off, wandering around the perimeter, mingling with the work parties on clean-up detail.

Kurtz looked nervously around as Carl led him farther away from the base, toward the edge of the jungle, where a few grunts had gathered around the corpses of several dead NVA who were too far from the base to worry about burying. Carl felt a little out of place with his relatively clean Nomex amid the grimy, sweat-stained grunts, but they didn't seem to mind his presence. They were more interested in the contents of the various ammo pouches worn by the dead men. One of the dead NVA seemed to have some leaflets stuffed into one of the sections of his AK pouch. Carl moved on into the group, looking down at the lifeless corpse.

"From the way one of your sergeants sounded, these guys were really a bunch of hard-core dudes," he remarked, opening a line for conversation.

"Damn straight," a weary-looking corporal replied, spitting casually on the dead man's face. "Sons a bitches just kept on coming. Claymores didn't stop 'em, machine guns didn't stop 'em. Crazy bastards didn't slow down until they hit the wire. That's where we really ripped 'em a new asshole. These two must've gotten wasted early on.

See''—he pointed with the toe of a grimy boot—''they still got their ammo and grenades with them.''

Carl knelt down next to the dead Charlie, sweeping flies away from the eyes and mouth. ''See here, Kurtz.'' He slapped the rookie on the leg to make sure he had his attention. ''This is one dead Charlie.'' He knelt down even closer, breathing in the stench of the dead man, and made a pretense of carefully studying the small hole in the man's forehead. ''Aha! I found it, Kurtz. Look here, cause of death.'' He grabbed the cold flesh under the chin and jerked the head sideways for Kurtz to see. ''The man died from lack of brains.'' He laughed.

Kurtz stared for a second at the ruined remains of the back of the NVA's head where the skull had exploded out, then took a stumbling step backward, twisted and fell, retching violently.

''New guy,'' Carl explained, looking up at the grunts, who nodded knowingly and started cracking jokes at the expense of Kurtz and the dead Charlie.

As Carl stood up, letting the mangled head drop to the ground, the corporal bent low over the corpse, slipping his bayonet from its sheath. With a deft movement of the wrist he sliced the right ear from the unfeeling head and turned the head to the other side, exposing the other ear. He grinned up at Carl, the blade hovering over the dead flesh.

''Want this one for yourself or your friend?'' he asked, pointing in Kurtz's direction with the blade. ''We got more than enough to go around.''

The act itself didn't bother Carl. Even though it was against the Geneva convention, mutilation of the dead on both sides was almost a normal event. Some men took fingers or toes, but ears were the most common trophy, strung on a cord and worn necklace fashion by some. He was almost tempted to accept the offer, one more item to set him slightly apart, but the conditions of his job made him decline.

''I don't think my gunner would appreciate the gift just yet, and I've got two of my own. 'Sides, if I ever got shot down and Charlie got his hands on me alive and found me with that ear . . ." He let the statement go unfinished.

The corporal nodded, straightening up. "Yeah, I know where you're coming from, man." It was common knowledge that most men who were captured by the little brown men were navy and air force fixed wing crews flying over North Vietnam, but helicopter pilots and crews were also vulnerable, and there was no shortage of horror stories about what happened to some of those who were caught by the VC or NVA.

Carl glanced back down at the dead man and pointed to the ammo pouch that they had been searching through. "If nobody wants that pouch, I'd like to take it."

"No sweat, it's yours. We already got what we wanted," the corporal replied easily, holding out a hand toward one of the other men. The trooper handed him one of the leaflets that they had found in the canvas pouch. "Take a look at what the dinks wanted to leave behind for us to read." He thrust the paper toward Carl.

Carl glanced quickly over the page. It was an appeal to all allied forces in Vietnam to lay down their arms, refuse their orders, and demand an immediate return home. "I'll be damned. They got their own bullshit bombers." He grinned at the grunts. "We drop thousands of the same kind of crap on them, telling them to surrender. Guess they can do it to us. Anybody want to try this stuff out and see how far you get?" He offered the paper back, but the corporal waved it away.

"Keep it for shit paper, man. All we need is a few copies to turn over to S-2." He paused for a moment, looked across the field at Carl's helicopter, then back at Carl. "Say, slick. If you want some of this NVA stuff, maybe we can work a deal. You gonna be the log ship out here all day, right?" Carl nodded and the corporal went on. "You'll be heading back to Tay Ninh a couple of times probably and there's a few things we could use, mainly some smokes, if you got any left on your ration card."

"What kind of stuff are we talking about? If it's something I can use, I think we can deal.'' Carl knew the value of a cigarette in Nam and had used them for trading before. American cigarettes were as good as money in most parts of the country, better than money in some. Out in the bush paper script didn't mean much, but that last smoke had a lot of buying power. And that suited him just fine. Smoking was one of the habits that he'd never taken up, but he still managed to put his ration card to good use without going black-market.

''Hey, Mike, dump out the stuff in the bag.''

A grunt sporting a long, drooping mustache spread open a ragged laundry bag and turned it upside down, spilling out AK magazines, ammunition, pouches, and other small items. A longer object snagged and Mike pulled it out, drawing Carl's attention.

The corporal waved at the battle gear cheerfully. ''Mike figures to outfit his own VC hunting club back in the World, but I'm sure he'll be glad to trade off some of that crap for the good of his squad, right, Mike?''

''Long as I get my share of the proceeds,'' Mike grumbled. ''Take this piece right here, slick,'' he said, handing a battered AK-47 to Carl. ''The stock's all fucked up but the rest of the gun is in good shape. I got a nicer one back at the base, but I'm saving that baby. Gonna try to get that thing back to the States.''

Carl took the shortened weapon and looked it over closely. Only a few inches of the splintered stock remained on the assault rifle, but that could easily be removed by unscrewing the stock screws and then filing off the metal tangs. Make the gun easy to move around inside a helicopter. He jacked the bolt back, inspecting the chamber while the grunt went on.

''AKs are damned good weapons. They shake and rattle some, fire a little slower than the M-16, but I haven't ever had one jam on me, and I can't say that about those Mattel toys the army gives us.''

''So I've heard.'' Carl was delighted with the prospect of getting one of the Chinese-made weapons, but didn't want to appear too eager. ''What do you want for it?''

Mike looked at the corporal, who just shrugged. "Seeing as how it's a little busted up, how about three cartons, Marlboros if you can get them?"

"Since you already let me have the pouch and magazines, I think that's a fair deal," he hesitated, then added in something else that he had spotted, "if you'll throw in one of those web belts."

"Deal." Mike grinned and reached down to select one of several NVA belts that he had collected. They were similar to the GI pistol belts except for the aluminum buckle assembly with the star on the face. "We got enough of these suckers to stretch all the way to Hanoi. Go ahead and take it all with you, and get us the smokes when you can. Today, that is." For a moment his smile took on a threatening twist. "Just don't try to get over on us. We know your name and unit, man."

"No sweat, troops. I'll be good on the deal. Might want to do business with you again sometime." With the agreement concluded, Carl got their company and platoon and gave them an approximate time when he thought he might be able to deliver his part of the bargain. Then he slung the ammo pouch over his shoulder with the battered assault rifle and motioned to his still-pale gunner to follow him back to the ship.

Carl reached into his ammo can tool box, pulled out a screwdriver, and went to work on the stock. Throwing away the useless wood, he then began work on the metal tangs with his file while Kurtz looked over the belt and the AK-47 chest pouch.

"Hey, Weird Willy, look at this." Kurtz shoved the ammo pouch across the floor. "These guys write shit on their equipment just like we do!"

Carl stopped his filing and glanced at the pouch. In addition to the Chinese markings there was the date 1969 and the name Nguyen Van Tung in large block letters. Below the name was another set of words that Carl thought might be a name, but it was too faded to tell. The symbols below those were unmistakable, though. A pair of interlocked hearts.

He looked back up at Kurtz's face. "Well, rookie, I'm gonna tell you something. No matter what you hear from some people, those little brown guys that we're fighting against are people, too. I got nothing against them. They're just doing what Uncle Ho tells 'em to, just like we're doing what Uncle Sammy says. That business with the jokes and the ear back there was just part of the Game. I'm not saying it's right or wrong, I'm just saying that's the way things are. Old Nguyen here took his chances and lost, and from the looks of this pouch, I'd say he probably had a girl up north who'll probably miss him 'bout like any woman who loses her man." He stopped to let that sink in and went back to his filing.

Olsen laughed. "Weird Willy the Wise Man. A few more months and you'll probably have the whole war resolved!" The pilot rolled off the floor on Carl's side and watched his progress. "What the hell you going to do with that thing?"

Carl swung the barrel out toward the distant woodline, holding the weapon with one hand on the pistol grip. "This, sir, is going to be my backup weapon." He held it out for Olsen to examine. "You never know when something like that might come in handy. It'd be a hell of a lot easier to tote around than the machine gun if we ever got shot down, and it would be a lot more useful than those thirty-eights you carry."

"Point well taken, but you crew chiefs and gunners are supposed to do such a good job of protecting us that we'll never get shot down."

"Right, sir." Carl grinned. "But I think I'll keep it just the same. You never know when you might get a rookie gunner who doesn't pull his weight, or a newbie copilot who might crash us just for the fun of it! Anyway, if we've got some time to spare later in the day, I'd like to check this piece out, if it's okay with you."

"No sweat, I'd like to fire one of those myself if you've got enough ammunition." He handed the AK back to Carl, who nodded and passed the rifle on to Chrissen.

"Mean-looking weapon," Chrissen commented as he turned it over in his hands.

Olsen stretched and brought one arm down to pat one of the assault-rifle magazines. "Yes, it is that, and you'll be on the receiving end of its brothers and sisters quite a few times before your year is up. This is probably the same type of weapon that hit Wiley. I think it was all small arms, don't remember anyone calling any heavy stuff." Olsen glanced at Carl, who shook his head, then looked back at something that had attracted the gunner's attention. "Looks like the break is over."

Carl stuffed his new toy into the extra barrel bag and told Kurtz to get the blade. Half a dozen troops were coming their way, a sergeant in the lead, the others behind him, each carrying an assortment of ammo crates, C-ration cases, and water containers.

The sergeant, a rough-looking E-6, reported to Olsen and unfolded a map while the troops began loading on the supplies. "One of our platoons has been chasing down blood trails all morning and finally caught up with some slow-moving Charlies about here," he said quietly, indicating the location on the map. "They lost contact about ten minutes ago with a small enemy force and are awaiting resupply. Here's the coordinates and the platoon push. Their platoon leader says it's triple canopy, no landing areas, so I'll ride along with one of my men to throw the stuff off. That'll keep your crew guns free in case the dinks have gone to cover in the area."

Carl strapped on his chicken plate and went forward to slide the pilot's side armor into position, checking to make sure that Kurtz had done the same for the copilot.

Olsen cranked the ship up and while the RPMs were building he checked over the contents that the grunts had put on. Not enough weight to cause any over-balancing. Two cases of M-60 ammo, a like amount of 5.56mm for the M-16s, C-rations, ten artillery cannisters with drinking water and a last crate that grabbed his closer attention.

"Mr. Olsen, all this stuff is going to be dropped out, right?"

"Roger that, Weird. Why?"

"They got a case of grenades on board. Hope there aren't any defective ones packed in it. Might upset someone on the ground!" Grenades were well packed, but the idea of dropping a whole case from treetop level didn't sound like the best idea in the world. One faulty frag could raise all kinds of hell.

"No problem, GI." Olsen's voiced crackled back with a trace of amusement. "It's all government issue. Got to be good."

Carl gave a mental shrug. Probably no danger. The triple canopy would slow down the drop, and the underbrush, if there was any, would cushion the fall.

Olsen took the ship up quickly and made a straight line for the platoon's position, three klicks out from the base. Halfway there, he radioed in and requested a smoke grenade be popped to guide them over the correct location. The voice from the ground acknowledged the message and promptly radioed back that a violet smoke had been popped.

"Oh, man! I don't believe this crap," Olsen muttered disgustedly over the intercom, then switched back to the platoon. "Tango Three Six Charlie, Papa One Niner, negative on last transmission. Incorrect procedure. Pop another smoke and wait for my ID. Over." He turned to his copilot and shook his head.

Carl didn't have any trouble believing it. He had seen the same thing happen before. Some rookie platoon leader on the ground screwing up again.

"Papa One Niner, Tango Three Six Charlie. Be advised, second smoke going out now. Standing by for ID. Over."

Olsen fired back an acknowledgment, still pissed off about the radio security violation. Thirty seconds went by before the purple haze of the first smoke grenade filtered up through the dense jungle. It was so spread out that it was difficult to tell exactly where it had originated.

Another thirty seconds passed and Carl saw more purple smoke drifting up from the tops of the trees. More than one smoke alone could have produced. Olsen saw it, too.

"What the hell is that idiot doing down there?" He scanned the area closely, waiting for some other color, but nothing came through. He waited a few more seconds and then got on the horn to the ground unit. "Three Six Charlie, One Niner. All I can see is violet smoke, possibly from two places. Over."

"One Niner, Three Six Charlie, Roger that ID. That was the only color smoke we have. Sorry 'bout that, One Niner. We can hear you, but I don't think we'll be able to make visual contact because of the trees and the smoke that's trapped in here. Over."

Olsen glanced at Chrissen and signaled for him to reply. "Tell him that we'll hover around until he thinks we're over his position, then he can let us know and the sergeant can start kicking the stuff out. Can you gentlemen believe this?" he asked over the intercom while Chrissen was making the call. "I just want to get rid of these supplies and get the hell away from this joker on the ground. Being around people like that makes me nervous, and it could get us all dead if any of the dinks are still in the area!" He slapped one hand up against his helmet. "One color of smoke! Weird, you and the gunner keep your eyes open. See if you can spot anything through that stuff."

"Roger that." Carl leaned out as the ship hovered in toward the center of the purple haze and tried to focus his eyes through the treetops, looking for darker shapes, movement, anything at all, but it was useless. The triple canopy was an impenetrable barrier and the swirling smoke did nothing to make the situation easier. While he strained his eyes, Carl heard the ground unit commander break over the airwaves.

"One Niner, Three Six Charlie. Still no visual contact, but you're loud and I think you might be over my location or at least close enough for the drop. Over."

Carl glanced up toward the pilot and grinned, knowing what Olsen was thinking. One thought at least was comforting. If Carl could not see anyone on the ground and the grunts couldn't see them, then the enemy shouldn't be able to see them, either. He hoped. If some Charlie was in a position to get a fix on the ship, it would be a turkey shoot for a few seconds.

"Weird, tell that sergeant to toss off a couple of cases of Cs and we'll find out if close counts in something besides horseshoes and hand grenades."

Carl yelled at the grunt and passed on the instructions. Without bothering his helper, the sergeant tossed off the ration cases and settled back, watching Carl with a questioning look.

"One Niner, I think the goodies hit about twenty-five meters to the Sierra of my location. We heard something crashing into the bush. Stand by while I check it out. Over."

In the background noise Carl had heard men shouting and thought he even heard the ship's blades in there. He was beginning to get a little more nervous, totally in agreement with Olsen about this one. This was too long to be hovering over one place where there had been recent enemy traffic.

When the infantry platoon leader's voice came back on the radio, it was a much tenser man who talked to them. "Papa One Niner, Three Six Charlie," he called, hitting the call signs with emphasis. "Be advised, my security element has spotted movement right where I think you dropped the supplies. You've got Victor Charlies directly under you. Over."

Without waiting for instructions Carl pointed down to the sergeant, yelled, "Charlie!" and motioned him away from the bay opening. The sergeant scrambled up behind the pilot's seat and yanked the other soldier back with him.

Carl heard the rush of air as Olsen started to speak into the open mike, but the pilot's voice was cut off by the harsh reports of AK fire being directed at the chopper from directly below.

"Fire right below us," Carl yelled, and squeezed off a short burst before Olsen had the ship moving away from the area. He didn't need Olsen's cease-fire command. He knew the grunts were still down in the vicinity and could get hit if he tried to spray the NVA from anywhere except the close-in straight-up position that they had been in.

The unseen enemy was under no such restriction. Having given away their location, they continued to fire through the trees as the ship moved off, and from the sound of American weapons firing back, they were evidently engaging the grunts as well. Carl had a pretty fair idea of what was going on down there in the maze of jungle. Another of those typical deep jungle firefights, where neither side could see the other, even at relatively close distances. Blind firing, spraying down every motion, every noise from suspected enemy positions.

Olsen kept the ship circling around the action zone, content to monitor the radio traffic, and act as a spotter if the need arose, until some semblance of order had been restored.

"One Niner, Three Six Charlie, enemy contact broken off. My security elements are farther out and report no sign of the Charlies. We recovered the rations that were dropped and need the rest of it down here before we continue our mission. Over."

Olsen rogered the message, requested another smoke to get back on target, and IDed the expected purple smoke that finally made it through the tree barrier.

Despite the platoon leader's assertion that the area was secure, Carl stayed on his guns while the two soldiers on board hastily threw off the remaining supplies. Again, the elusive enemy had vanished into the hidden crypts of the jungle, but Carl knew that they were still close by. Not enough time for them to have gotten very far, especially if they were carrying any wounded with them. Of course, with all the American patrols out, there was always the chance that the NVA they had just brushed with might run directly into another unit before they could make it back to their staging area or bunker complexes.

Olsen turned the ship back in toward the fire base as the last of the water containers dropped through the treetops, and as soon as the ship was down, he turned over the controls to Chrissen and made a beeline for the operations bunker. Carl suspected that someone was going to hear an earful about the radio procedure being used by a certain young lieutenant out in the bush. If the Game let you live past the first mistake, you had to learn from it, he thought.

With the blades stopped and tied down again, Carl and the copilot did a fast inspection of the ship, mainly checking for bullet holes. On Kurtz's side he stopped to check out his rookie gunner.

"Didn't hear your gun firing back there, slick. What happened?" He fired the words in hard and fast, holding an expressionless face with the cover of the dark aviator's glasses.

Kurtz glanced down at his feet, then back up at Carl defensively. "Hey, man, there wasn't time. It all happened too fast"—he paused, pulling in another defense—"and I didn't want to take a chance on hitting any of the grunts."

"No time!" He looked away toward the distant treeline, teeth clenched in feigned disgust. He was glad Kurtz couldn't see his eyes. He straightened out the hint of a smile that was trying to spread across his face before he turned back to face the young gunner. "There was time enough for them to be shooting at us and you couldn't find enough time to let 'em know that you had a machine gun. We were directly over their heads for a good two seconds! That's enough time to get off at least one good burst, slick, and the rounds you put out in those seconds might be the ones that keep some Charlie from putting a bullet through your skull." Kurtz started to object, but Carl brushed his words aside. "I know. You didn't want to hit the friendlies. Were you listening to the radio traffic when the man said the Charlies were right under us, and that his position was twenty-five meters from the enemy?" He wasn't cut out to play the part of a heavy, even though he was enjoying himself, giving the rookie a hard time. He softened up and took the edge out of his voice. "Don't take it too hard, Kurtz. I think with some experience you'll be a number one gunner, but you've got to learn fast. You're going to have to react a lot of times, not think and then act. In this business, if you have to think about what to do, some time you may not live to do it.''

Kurtz nodded his head, a serious look on his face as if he had just learned one of the mysteries of the universe, and Carl broke a tight smile. ''Main thing is, we're still alive. Learn from your mistakes, 'cause I don't want my status to change on account of somebody else's screwup.'' With that remark, Carl closed the subject. ''Now, I'm going back out around the field to see what else these people got for me or see if there's any stuff still lying around. Want to come along?''

Kurtz shook his head. The business with the ear had been enough for one day.

Walking across the site of recent carnage, Carl noted that the bulldozer was almost finished with its work. He stopped and watched for a moment as the steel blade scraped the last of the lifeless bodies into the mass grave, their limbs twisting and flailing as they tumbled into the pit. He thought briefly about what he had told Kurtz, about the little brown men being human beings, too. Somewhere, those nameless dead were leaving behind mothers, sisters, wives, someone who might have cared for them, and those people might never know how or where their men had died. In time the jungle would reclaim the scarred land, and this final resting place for the remnants of a North Vietnamese battalion would be just another patch of jungle. That, too, was part of the Game. He turned from the gravesite and resumed his search for the spoils of war.

XI.

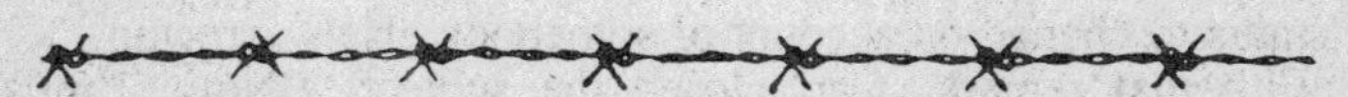

He scratched an "X" through another day on his short-timer's calendar. On the downward side of the first tour, his calendar was over halfway marked out on the side with the sexy women from *Playboy*'s Hall of Fame. He stared hungrily at the full breasts of Miss January for a moment. Good Lord! A round-eye with a figure like that could name her price in Nam and make a fortune without doing much work. He kissed the tip of his thumb and planted it on the blonde's breast, then flipped the page over to the back, where he kept a journal of daily happenings. He had just started up the log a month earlier and had developed the habit of making two entries on the days he was flying. A morning entry to tell whom he was flying with and the type of mission and an evening entry to sum up the day's events. Of late, the entries hadn't been too long. There had been a lot of small-scale action to fly support on, and most of the ships were logging flight time from dawn to dark. Even the nights were busy as the enemy activity in the province held at a fast pace, increasing the number of flare missions. Carl's entries showed ground fire being received by company ships almost daily, but hits were seldom and there had been no casualties since he had started the journal.

None of the crews were getting any downtime, but Carl didn't mind. New guys were still coming in and the constant flying gave all of them a chance to get broken in quickly. The steady influx of the new crop also kept the old-timers off the detail rosters on the rare occasions that they had a down day. He had already had three different rookies gunning on his ship and was taking up a fourth one today. He quickly penned in the information on his journal page. Scheduled for a routine log mission, it looked like a pretty calm day, nothing that a rookie should have any trouble with. He thought about his new gunner and shook his head, jotting the kid's name down. Pfc Slaker. He wondered how the scrawny soldier had made it through basic. At five foot four, Slaker was barely taller than his machine gun and didn't look a hell of a lot heavier. And dumb! Damn, he couldn't believe the army had really assigned this dude as a doorgunner. Ordinarily, even a rookie wouldn't have too much trouble on a simple log mission, but this one—he wasn't sure that Slaker really knew what was happening around him.

"Hey, Sarge, I got the guns. I'm ready," Slaker said slowly.

Carl looked at the midget gunner struggling with the two M-60s. At least the kid was trying. "Here, I'll take mine, and dammit, I've told you I'm not a sergeant. Just call me Willstrom or Weird Willy or plain old Weird, got it?"

This time Slaker didn't call him anything, just stared dumbly at the ground like a scolded puppy.

"Shit. Forget it and let's get down to the ship." If there had ever been a real-life Sad Sack, he couldn't have been a much sadder-looking case than this dude, Carl thought. Because of his small size, the army couldn't even fit him with a proper uniform, not that they were noted for matching people with the right size clothing anyway. Only two sizes in the army, too large and too small, and for Slaker even the too-smalls were too large.

Lieutenant Richter cocked one large, bushy eyebrow in Slaker's direction while they were doing the preflight. "That's supposed to be a soldier?"

" 'Fraid so, sir," Carl replied, watching Slaker fight the guns into their mounts in the most difficult manner possible.

"Well, do me a favor, Weird. When we stop to refuel, you take care of the job. You heard what happened when that rookie was with Lieutenant Harris the other day?"

"Roger that, sir. I'll take care of it." Word around the platoon was that Slaker had been topping off 641, and while the crew chief was signing for the fuel, Slaker took a break to stare around at the sky and let the fuel overflow, spilling quite a bit around the POL pad, before a shout brought him back to base.

Carl spoke to the rookie just before takeoff, making sure that the new guy did indeed know how to use the intercom. He could already see in his mind an assortment of calamities befalling them before the day was done. He hoped desperately that they wouldn't have to make any hover-downs into tight LZs.

The operations people at the fire base had advised that there would be a lot of supplies to be logged out to various locations during the day, so Richter decided to use the low-level routes from point to point to save on time and fuel consumption. As the ship headed back in for the next load, the treetops rushing by just below them, Carl heard the whooshing sound of an open mike, a hot mike, with no voice filling in the empty space. He glanced forward, saw Richter starting to look back, and then both heard the stuttering voice as Slaker tried to choke out a message.

"G-g-g-go-gooks!"

Richter jerked the chopper hard right, giving Carl a gut-wrenching pull and an excellent view of the Vietnamese sky. "Where at? How many?" he snapped.

The rushing air sound filled Carl's headphones again for a full second before the gunner got the words out. "Uh, I don't know. Maybe four or five of them, straight out on my side"—he paused, then remembered the directional words—"about three o'clock. They were in a small open spot crossing a log over that stream when we popped over the trees."

"Coming hard left, get ready, Weird," Richter ordered. He brought the chopper back to the stream that Slaker had mentioned and got their direction of movement from the gunner. From the crossing point he began a slow semicircular arc search.

Carl stayed tight on his gun, straining his eyes for a glimpse of anything unnatural, a motion, a darker shadow, a reflection. He was aware that his breathing was almost imperceptible, long, slow inhalations. He felt keyed but strangely loose, relaxed. He decided that he was really getting to enjoy this kind of life with its uncertainties and challenges. One uncertain item here, he thought, as he listened to Richter grill the gunner about the spotting. Slaker was pretty sure the men he saw were Vietnamese and he knew the weapons weren't M-16s. That was something to his credit, but some GIs carried pieces that weren't government issue.

Richter didn't want to take a chance on firing up any friendlies because of a rookie's mistaken identity, so he called up the base ops for a free-fire clearance while the search went on.

Carl heard the fire base's response a few minutes later. There were no friendlies in their current area.

"Let's do it, Weird. Recon by fire at intervals. See if you can get someone to bite. Right side, keep your eyes open! If you see anything, shoot and communicate. Go hot!"

Carl angled the barrel slightly and squeezed off a three-second burst into a darker section of jungle, probing, searching, hoping to get close enough to someone to spook them into returning fire and give away their position. Every few seconds in the arc, he fired another blast, reaching through the trees with the steel seekers, but nothing answered. Wherever they were, they could hear his firing and he knew that they would be aware of what was going down. His main hope was that he could put shots right on top of Mr. Charles. Maybe they had some rookies with them who would panic.

He tried to figure out where they might have gone once they realized they had been spotted. Did they book on down the trail to clear the immediate area, or had they gone to ground, trusting to the jungle for a cloak of invisibility? Even in the jungle it would be easier to detect motion than it would be to pick out a still figure on the jungle floor.

One area looked particularly promising, and he began to pump a stream of fire into it as they approached, then passed over it and left it behind. Still no response.

Here and there the trees were spread enough to give partial views of the ground, and while Carl kept firing at intervals, his eyes darted back and forth, checking out every break in the silent green wall. It wasn't as thick as some jungle areas in the province, and once he thought he had spotted something but the deceptive shadow that he riddled turned out to be just that, a shadow.

Finally, Richter decided that enough time had been lost. The grunts had the sighting location if they wanted to do anything with it. "Chances are, they're halfway to Hanoi by now," he remarked as he broke off the search pattern and took up a straight line heading back to the fire base.

Carl didn't think so, but he said nothing and kept his eyes peeled since they were still on the same course that they had been following when the initial sighting had been made.

"Hard left! Dinks at ten o'clock!" Carl suddenly yelled into the mike, using his foot on the floor button, as he swung his gun to bear on a dark form that was out of place against the irregular shadow patterns. He pulled back on the triggers even before the barrel moved into line and walked the rounds into the target in a continuous flurry of fire.

"Game's up, slick," he muttered quietly as the discovered soldier tried to bring an AK up into firing position. Carl saw only the steel of the gun and the form, no face, no features, no expression of a man who knew he was about to die. The M-60 tracers reached out and a tiny point of fire vanished into the form, followed by the unseen ball rounds, lacing the soldier diagonally from right shoulder to left hip, spinning him around and crashing him to the ground.

A surge of savage elation coursed through his frame, blood throbbing in his temples and neck. He continued to pour fire into the vicinity of the fallen man. Slaker had said four or five and the others had to be close by.

Richter kept the ship in a tight left circle over the area, but Carl couldn't spot any movement. He let up on the triggers and keyed his mike. "Scratch one Charlie, sir.

You should be able to see him on the next pass for confirmation. He's the only one I saw, though. No one else broke." Tough little bastards. To them the mission was always of prime importance. The dead man's companions down there wouldn't endanger themselves or compromise the mission to save one man's life. That was one of the things that made them so damn scary. Charlie didn't seem to give a damn about his own life or anyone else's, as long as the mission was accomplished.

"Okay, Weird, I've got him visual. Sure as hell looked dead to me. You've got yourself another confirmed kill."

In the helicopter phase of fighting, confirmed kills weren't that easy to come by because of the fast-moving nature of the airmobile operations. Frequently, the only targets would be shadows or muzzle flashes. Carl had already claimed a few confirmed kills along with a number of possibles, and now he could add one more definite to the list.

He pumped a few more rounds into the general vicinity of the dead man, widening his arc of fire, but no one took the bait. He was still pumped up from the contact and the kill, ready for more, but he was cooling with each passing moment as the jungle held on to its secrets. He recognized that he was going to have to get more control over his emotions, become colder, harder in his reactions. This battle heat business might get deadly in a prolonged engagement, but he enjoyed the thrill, the intense sensory experiences, the danger. Killing the little dudes before they could kill you was the main attraction of the Game. Some men just wanted to live, others he had seen or heard of lived to kill, but for Carl, it was seeing how close he could dance with death that gave the Game its spice.

Richter began to turn the ship away, back to its original course to the fire base, and Carl caught a last glimpse of his recent target. The man had had his chance. Not much of a chance, maybe, but he was carrying an AK-47, and if luck had been with him, he might have emerged as temporary victor over Carl. All it took was one bullet, lucky shot or deliberate aim, and the chopper could have gone down, and everyone on the ship could have died. Carl rubbed a gloved finger over the small scar on his neck, remembering back to a night in a small LZ, a flare, and a fanatical Charlie who had almost taken him out of the Game. He dropped his hand back to the butterfly grips and stopped the line of thought. Concentrate on matters at hand. He continued to scan the blur of the jungle rushing by under his feet while the pilot called in the spotting.

The unit commander took enough interest in the report to order a fire mission on the area. Carl figured that the grunts had been getting enough garbage from Charlie and were glad to be able to return some of the same.

The ground commander asked Richter to go back on station and adjust fire for the 81mm mortars that were being readied.

"Roger that," Richter replied, hopping the ship back and up to altitude. "This beats flying around getting the ship all dirtied up. Gives us a chance to watch our tax dollars at work."

Carl certainly didn't have any objections. All he needed was some popcorn and a Coke to complete the setting for watching the show. From his ringside seat he watched as the first of the mortar rounds impacted below. Small flashes of fire, miniature eruptions of smoke, and a faint sound of the explosions gave him the feeling that he was, in fact, in a theater watching some war movie.

Richter sent back a fire adjustment, watched the next set of rounds hit, and sent back a "fire for effect" order.

Carl finished off the day like a hundred others, sitting in the club hootch with a growing stack of beer cans, swapping stories with the other crews. Nobody worried about the rookie's feelings.

XII.

As much as he enjoyed covering the skies of Nam, there were a few pleasures to be found on the ground as well. The hootch girl, Kim, had been teaching him a few words of Vietnamese, and over the last few months more than words had been exchanged between the two. She had become Carl's girl-san and was generally considered by the others as being his property. She accepted the situation. It was at least a temporary security. Aside from the usual playful horsing around, nobody offered her any trouble, and that was about the best that any girl who worked around the army camps could hope for. The Vietnamese had been fighting wars for decades against outsiders, and the people had long since learned that for women and children to survive, they did what was necessary. The children stole or pimped, the women whored or found someone to look after them. Damn unusual to find any twelve-year-old virgins around army camps, and these were the places that many of the displaced refugees came to.

As Carl got to know her better, he found that Kim had come from a small hamlet up north, hit by both sides until there wasn't any reason for staying. Parents were both gone, dead, missing, she didn't know. She had worked her way south with other streams of refugees, toward the larger population centers, hoping to find work, but the bigger cities were already swollen with homeless, jobless people. Young and attractive, she had been desperate for work and had used her body as a bribe to get a job at the Tay Ninh base camp.

When she got that idea across to Carl, he had felt a brief surge of anger, but let it slide off and fade away. That was the way things were done over here and there wasn't a hell of a lot that he could do about it.

He wiped some of the oil off his hands on an already filthy towel and grinned at the young hootch girl. "Life's a real bitch, so enjoy what you can!" He grabbed for her wrist and pulled her close, unbuttoning the loose blouse that hid the small but firm breasts. She broke away from his grasp without much of a struggle, but didn't bother to rebutton the blouse.

"We go bunker, Carl?" She wasn't bashful about their relationship. She seemed to enjoy their lovemaking, and that was a new experience for Carl in Vietnam. The five-dollar whores in the towns took the money and lay there motionless for five or ten minutes until business was done. Then it was sponge bath and next customer. It satisfied the physical needs but that was about all. Kim was a whole different ball game. She enjoyed, she responded, she did whatever he wanted in the dim light of the cool bunker.

Carl nodded and they left the hootch together. He paused at the entrance of the platoon's bunker and yelled in to make sure he wasn't barging in on someone else's good times. When only silence greeted him, he ducked into the dark shelter, Kim right behind him.

He stripped off his shirt and pants, the boots having been left behind in the hootch, and pulled his already naked companion onto the musty-smelling cot.

Rolling her underneath him, he wasted no time. Vietnam was the land of the eternal quickie. The soldiers had to take what they could get when they could get it, even in the base camps.

He could just barely see into her eyes in the dim light, just enough to see that momentary flash of pain as he thrust into her. Then the eyes smiled with the pleasure of the movements, finally shutting as the fire inside increased for both of them. Carl felt the heat spreading through his body, felt her slender form thrusting back against his, and thrust harder, feeling the explosion building. With a low guttural moan, he erupted into the warm sheath of soft flesh, and slowed the movement, relaxing as the energy flowed out. For a few minutes, he and Kim lay there, beads of sweat forming and dripping off their heated bodies. Then Carl pulled out and rolled into a sitting position, resting one hand comfortably on a small brown breast, playing with the nipple while his body cooled off.

"Kim, you a numbah one girl. You sure know how to make a man feel good."

"I like make you feel good, Carl. You numbah one GI, not like some GI. You stay here, Kim make you feel good all time." She crept one hand over his leg and began caressing him slowly, tenderly, bringing him back to hardness. "Maybe you take Kim to America when you go home?"

The question wasn't a complete surprise. A lot of Vietnamese women wanted to go to the States with GI husbands. It wasn't something new with just Vietnam, he knew. Every war saw its share of foreign war brides, and this was no exception. He felt a bit too young to be getting married, even though the bait was tempting, but he wasn't about to turn her down flat while she was still holding on to some rather sensitive parts of his anatomy. And, he reasoned, by the time his extensions were all over with, he might be ready for some permanent company.

"You never know, Kim. Maybe so, maybe no. Maybe you get tired of me or VC shoot me. Or maybe sergeant kick my ass if I don't get back to work." He couldn't tell in the dark what her reaction was, or what she had expected, but when she spoke, her voice still sounded happy enough. This was just the first opening of the subject. He knew that Orientals were supposed to be a very patient people and he guessed that he would hear the same question quite often in the future.

They dressed and ducked through the exit back out into the bright midday sun. The fact that he had just missed lunch didn't disturb him too much. Not being able to savor whatever flavor of water buffalo stew, soup, or steak was no cause for regret. He was about to say something to Kim when he saw the lean and mean form of Sergeant Wells heading in his direction.

Wells had spotted them emerging from the bunker but

didn't remark on it. "Just about time to be back on your ship, Weird. Captain Raines says it should be all back together this evening and ready to fly tomorrow morning." He glanced down at Carl's bare feet and then at Kim, who was vanishing around the corner of the hootch with a load of laundry. "Hope your lunch was better than mine," he said with a slight grin creasing his face. "Now let's get on with some work."

"Roger that, Sarge. Wouldn't want to hold up the war effort." Carl went back into the hootch for his boots and headed out to the maintenance tent.

By the time 312 was all back together, it was chow time again, and having missed out on lunch, Carl felt the need for some kind of food to fill his grumbling stomach. The warm milk, gristly meat of uncertain origin, and the inevitable potatoes filled the need if not the desire, and he left the mess hall remembering back to a long ago time, a lost world where the inhabitants devoured rare steaks and barbecued ribs in sauce. And cold milk, cold beer, ice cream that didn't melt instantly, and Jell-O that held its shape. He paused at the doorway of the hootch, looked around toward the club, tossed a mental coin, and decided to turn in as soon as the mission briefings were done with. With his ship ready to fly again, he knew that Wells wouldn't leave him on the ground with all the action that was still happening out there in never-never land.

After the briefing, he flopped back down onto the sagging cot and drifted into a restless sleep. Fleeting distorted images hovered around the fringes of his mind, shifting from the ecstatic recollections in the bunker to darker shapes, barely visible. In one horrifying instant, a vision of Kim beckoning him into the cool darkness of the shelter turned suddenly into Wiley's insane death's-head grin and the arm, flailing, drawing him into a dark abyss.

He shot up, bolt-stiff in his cot, a cold sweat running in rivers down his body. His breath was coming fast and hard, and he fought down the speed of his racing heart.

Half an hour passed before he trusted himself to lie

down and try to sleep again. Dreams like that he didn't need. That madman's face was still hovering near, and it was over an hour before sleep finally claimed him and held him.

XIII.

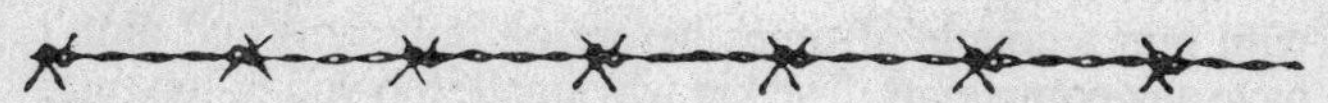

"All right, let's go. Rise and shine! It's a beautiful day out there and all of Vietnam's waiting for you!"

Carl dragged his body off the cot, glaring at Wells. "How the hell can anybody be so fuckin' cheerful in the morning?" He glanced over at Jolley who was already sliding into his Nomex. "Ain't there something in the Geneva convention about waking people up in the morning?"

Jolley laughed at Carl's disgruntled look, but gave him no help. "It's all part of that great plan of the army's. They teach cooks how to make green eggs and teach sergeants how to sound disgustingly happy when they're waking people up at some ungodly hour."

Even the old crew chief seemed too happy to suit Carl's mood and he considered sending a boot flying in his direction. Too much effort. He dressed and joined Jolley at the mess hall for the green eggs and the bacon that could have passed for old beef jerky.

"Hey, Weird, whatcha doing with that stuff?"

Carl dumped several of the stiff bacon strips in his shirt pocket before looking back at Jolley. "I might get hungry out there and get to feeling homesick for company cooking, or"—he paused with a crooked grin—"I might get shot down and captured. Always remember, save that last piece of bacon for yourself. Don't let the dinks take you alive!" He pulled one of the almost black strips back out and pointed it at his head.

Kurtz, who had just pulled up a chair, looked at him as if questioning his sanity.

"Like the man's name says, rookie. He's Weird Willy. At least he's acting better than he was when he first got up." Jolley looked at Carl as if he expected some remark.

"It was a bad night, man. Had some pretty heavy dreams, but I don't want to get into that." He dropped the subject, downed the last of his coffee, and headed out, stopping to tap his gunner, Riglos.

Riglos was fairly new to the platoon, but Carl had flown with him a couple of times before on milk runs and didn't have any complaints. The kid was small, too young-looking. Carl thought he looked more like someone who should be in the Boy Scouts than a soldier, but the rookie was eager to learn and caught on to his duties fast.

He followed Carl out of the mess hall, but hung a turn at the arms room to get the machine guns while Carl picked up his helmet and the spare barrel bag with his AK in it.

WO2 Simmons was already at the ship with another semirookie, a Second Lieutenant Carson. For a brief moment, Carl looked at Carson, thought about the gunner, and silently wondered where all the old-timers were now. Seemed like nothing but rookies, or at least people he regarded as rookies, left in the company. There were only four chiefs left who had been in the unit when he arrived, and one of those, Marty, was down to his last thirty days. Same held true for the officers. All the pilots who had been ACs were gone, as well as a lot of them who had been copilots when he had come in-country. Most of them had DEROSed stateside, but a few had ended their lives in this place, and he had been there with some of them.

He broke off his contemplations and went to work on the preflights with the two officers. "Any more word on what kind of mission we're running today, sir?"

"Same as last night. 372's going out with us. Pick up some Rangers at Loc Ninh and take them wherever they want to go." Simmons climbed down from his inspections on top of the ship. "I've got some ideas about where we're going, but I'll wait and see what the score is at the final briefing."

Carl nodded. He and Jolley had voiced the same thoughts that he was sure Simmons had in mind. Two ships, his and Jolley's, making a pickup at Loc Ninh for a Ranger drop without escort meant they were probably going to drop the Rangers along the red line. Loc Ninh was only a few klicks from the Cambodian border.

He was glad he had Simmons as the pilot, but then, he would have been happy with most of the pilots from his platoon. He and Simmons had flown quite a few missions together and had a good working relationship. Both trusted each other, a bond formed under the pressure of combat flights where a man had to trust his life to the other members of the crew. Carl visualized his pilots as shepherds, guiding the ship and its contents, the flock, safely in and out of wolf dens, while the gunners were the watchdogs, the bark and the bite under the shepherd's control. The only part of his analogy that bothered him was the fact that the shepherd could survive without his dogs in the blue pasture of the sky, but the faithful watchdogs didn't have much of a chance if something happened to the shepherds. He glanced over at the copilot with a half smile on his face. Sure hope our rookie sheepherder knows his job.

The twenty-minute flight through the cool morning air did more to refresh Carl than the previous night's sleep, and speculating on where this mission was going had him wired and ready for action.

As the ship touched down, Carl heard Carson speaking to the pilot, directing his attention to a narrow trail emerging from the orderly rows of tall rubber trees. Carl scooted around onto the troop seats to check out their passengers, who were filing out on the trail.

Well-worn cammies and gray, black, and green smeared skin gave them a very businesslike look. The lead man, a first lieutenant, carried a commando model M-16, a shorter version of the standard rifle, and wore a Gerber fighting knife strapped upside down on his harness. Tough-looking soldier, Carl thought, remembering back to a time when he had had a chance to try out for the Rangers. He smiled slightly, imagining himself as one of the men walking toward the chopper.

The lieutenant with four other men climbed aboard Carl's ship while the remainder of the ten-man group loaded onto Jolley's bird. The leader plugged in a headset and crouched between the two pilots with a map in hand. "We need to be dropped off right here," he said, pointing to a small circle drawn in red grease pencil. "It's a two-ship LZ, and I suggest a straight line route heading three-two-five degrees, low level, high speed. At one hundred knots we should be there in about fifteen minutes, almost right on top of it." He finished with an air of finality and started to replace his map, having marked the pilot's map with the location.

"Lieutenant, I was given orders that place me completely at your disposal," Simmons said, motioning the Ranger to keep his map out, "but I must point out that this little red circle of yours is a good fifteen klicks inside the red line. That's a little out of our jurisdiction."

"Not today, mister," the lieutenant answered unperturbed. "You are at my disposal and your job is to get my team to that location, now!" He added the last part with emphasis. "Radio silence after leaving Loc Ninh's control area. Let's move!"

"You're the boss," Simmons replied amiably. "Just wanted to make sure where we're going. All right, crew, you heard the man. We're taking the international tour today."

In the air Simmons headed straight out, advising 372 to fall in behind and maintain radio silence, and then Simmons himself went silent, leaving nothing for Carl's ears except the blades and the rushing air. He had suspected they might be heading into Cambodia, but a penetration of fifteen klicks was going to put them a long way from a safe haven if anything were to happen to them. No backups, no support! He didn't know what the Rangers were supposed to be doing after they got to the LZ and he knew that nobody was going to tell him. The army phrase "Know only what you need to know" applied in this situation. If the drop was successful, the Ranger lieutenant wouldn't want his mission jeopardized by some fly-boys who knew too much getting shot down and captured.

"One more item," the Ranger said, breaking into Carl's thoughts. "No guns unless absolutely necessary. If we make contact in the LZ, the mission's scrubbed and we get the hell out."

"Roger that, Lieutenant. Anything you say."

Simmons didn't sound unhappy, but Carl knew the pilot wasn't pleased with the orders that bound him to the Ranger's directions. The pilot was usually the king of his flying sky castle, like a ship's captain, and they weren't ever happy about being under somebody else's control. Simmons didn't raise any hassles and Carl didn't mind the temporary ownership. The chance for a trip into Cambodia wasn't something that came up very often, and it would be a first for him.

Even though the use of his gun was restricted, Carl kept his fingers hovering near the triggers and the steel barrel angled out, ready for action. He leaned out of his position and glanced back at Jolley's ship, which was staying right on their tail. From his angle the trailing ship took on the appearance of some giant insect, its Plexiglas multiple eyes staring unblinkingly back at Carl. Below both of them the ground swept by in a blur of green. He pulled back inside the ship, his eyes slightly watery from the force of the rushing air. A glance at his watch showed that they had been in the air for six minutes. They should be almost on top of the border. Every blurred tree that vanished below put them a step closer to Cambodia.

This must be old hat to the Rangers, he decided, checking out the men in the cargo bay. Four of them were sitting quietly, calmly watching the jungle go by or staring into space, each with his own private thoughts. The fifth man, the lieutenant, was squatting in a deep crouch, arms resting loosely on the back of the pilots' seats, watching the onrushing horizon that was Cambodia.

Simmons turned his head, spotting a terrain feature that was on the map. "Gentlemen, welcome to Cambodia. I hope your visit is an enjoyable one, and brief. Doesn't look a bit different than Vietnam, does it?"

"Same-same old jungle," Carl replied. Somehow he had expected it to look different and was slightly disappointed with the sameness of it.

"LZ should be coming up in seven more minutes, Lieutenant," Simmons informed the Ranger who had glanced at the map as they crossed the border. He merely nodded and continued to stare out through the front windshield as if he could already see the LZ.

The space separating the two ships and their destination shrank quickly. Closing in on the LZ, the Ranger tapped one of his men and held up two fingers, two minutes to target. He then keyed his mike and gave his final mission instructions to Simmons. "Stay on this frequency for the next ten minutes. If I give you an 'Execute Red,' you get this ship back to the LZ ASAP. If that situation arises, don't attempt to contact me, I'll call you when I can hear you coming. Remember, no guns in the LZ unless the mission is compromised."

Simmons gave him a thumbs-up and made sure that his gunners understood.

"LZ in sight, coming up in thirty seconds," Simmons warned. The Ranger nodded and moved to the edge of the cargo bay, throwing his legs over the edge, resting the worn jungle boots easily on the skids. The other four men took their places, poised, ready to jump off as soon as the ship was close to the ground.

Simmons pulled back on the stick, nosing the ship up, and dropped into the clearing. Carl kept a tight grip on the butterflies and scanned the edge of the jungle, half expecting his first visit to Cambodia to be greeted with a hail of gunfire. After all, this was a safe haven for the NVA, their home away from home. The treeline looked clear and he shifted his attention to the chest-high grass that was rippling and waving underneath the chopper's blade wash. Nothing that looked threatening.

With the skids still three feet from the ground, the Rangers started jumping off, rocking the hovering craft as they left. Carl looked forward as the last man left the skids, noticed an odd clump of foliage and started to call the pilot's attention to it.

He didn't have to. The irregular dark splotch of brush made itself the center of everyone's attention with a blazing muzzle flash from a well-concealed machine-gun position.

"Taking fire! Ten o'clock!" He swung his barrel, pulling back on the triggers even before it came into line with the target. No need for secrecy now. The mission had just been compromised and the ship was caught in its most vulnerable position, sitting at a hover less than twenty-five meters from the Chicom .51.

Sitting ducks! He couldn't believe that the NVA gunners hadn't already blown them out of the air. He kept his triggers back, pouring fire into the brush, but the weapon on the other end didn't let up. Every motion, every sound, seemed to drag out forever. Somewhere around him, he could hear men yelling, someone screaming. He was aware of the ship lowering into the grass and let off on the triggers just as the first of the Rangers hit the skids and vaulted into the ship. The man spun around, flattened himself to the floor, and began firing at the enemy gun while Carl squeezed off another short burst before the second man reached the skids.

The second Ranger leaped up, grabbing for the support pole, and jerked himself up into the ship, his face for a moment only a foot from Carl's. No fear, no panic, only grim determination expressed in the tight-lipped, dark-streaked face. Then his head suddenly exploded in front of Carl, a nightmarish vision of black and green smears erupting out in splatters of red blood, raw flesh, and the slick whiteness of shattered bone.

For a moment Carl was blinded by the spray of flesh and blood that splashed across his visor. Snapping out of a split-second shock, he shot his visor up and began firing at the unseen gun crew behind that white flashing tongue. His entire circle of awareness narrowed and focused along the thin, deadly line from the flaming tip of his gun barrel to the muzzle flashes from the brush. Somewhere in his mind he could hear Simmons yelling above the deafening volume of gunfire.

"Get that son of a bitch! Get him!"

The screamed words forced their way into him and became a part of his life as his universe closed back into the thin line. Nothing else existed in that moment of time and space. Only his gun and their gun . . . and the desire to kill.

"Die, motherfucker, die!" His own yelling broke the spell and brought him back to the larger world. The NVA gun abruptly stopped firing. The Ranger lieutenant threw himself into the ship. The other Rangers had piled in from the gunner's side. Radios were crackling, pilots talking, everything happening in a rush, flooding Carl with sensations.

Ten seconds. The whole episode couldn't have lasted more than ten seconds, but it seemed like an eternity. Simmons was pulling the ship out and away as fast as it could haul, and the cool rush of air helped Carl to clear his head. He was aware of the smear of wet, sticky pulp covering parts of his uniform, helmet, and lower face. He wiped some of it away from his chin, his arm moving with effort against a draining effect as the adrenaline flow shut down, leaving his body feeling weak and rubbery. His legs were already beginning to shake and he was glad that he had a seat and wall to lean back on.

For that eternal ten seconds, he had been there again, living life on the edge of that dark shadow, feeling alive in a way that he had only felt a few times before.

There, in the jungle's fringe, somebody else on another gun had been balancing on that same line until it rippled, pushing him off into the realm of death while Carl stepped back off the shadow line into the light of life.

He gathered his energy and pulled himself up to see what needed to be done in the aftermath. The dead Ranger lay crumpled up on the seat next to Carl unattended. No attention in the world would help him. One of the surviving four on his ship had been hit and was lying on the floor, his head cradled in the lap of one man while another worked swiftly, expertly over the man's leg. There was blood all over the floor and the uniforms of the soldiers, so Carl figured an artery had been hit. The Ranger tending the wound shifted to get better position, and for a moment

Carl saw the ragged opening in the flesh, high on the inside of the thigh. A tourniquet made from a belt had stopped the immediate gushing of blood, and the Ranger was ripping off the pants leg, strapping bandages over the wound. Carl couldn't see the other side of the leg, but the soldier was putting bandages there, too. The large slug from the .51 must have ripped all the way through, leaving entry and exit holes. Looking at the injured man's face, Carl decided that he must be unconscious. He appeared to be breathing shallowly, and underneath the camouflage paint Carl was sure the man's face was pale from loss of blood and shock setting in.

The lieutenant seemed to be uninjured and was back between the pilots with the headset on again. His voice was cold, hard, unexpressive. "Check the other ship and get us to 15th Med ASAP. One of my men is in bad shape."

"Roger," Simmons replied. "Weird, gunner, you guys still alive back there?"

"Can't kill Weird Willy that easy," Carl answered, sounding more confident than he felt. He heard the gunner check in, a little shaky, but still there. The copilot seemed to be okay and was looking around at the carnage inside the chopper.

Carson looked at Carl and pressed his mike button. "You sure you're not hit, Chief? I hope that's not your insides stuck all over your outsides!"

Carl glanced down at himself, imagining how he must look to the others. He raised a gloved hand and wiped away some of the dripping mess from his face shield before assuring the copilot that the blood wasn't his. "I'm fine. This poor bastard's had it, though. How's the ship?" He still couldn't believe that the enemy gunners hadn't blown them all to hell while they were sitting there.

"Not much left of the windshields," Carson informed him. "No warning lights on, no strong vibrations. I think we used up about all of our luck back there."

Our luck. Carl stared at the almost headless Ranger. My luck, maybe, not his. The bullet that he took might have saved Carl's life. No way of knowing for sure.

Simmons was on the radio with 372, and from what Carl could hear, Jolley's ship had come through without any casualties. "Anyone spot any fire coming from anyplace besides the .51 to our front?"

Carl waited for a moment, listening, but nobody spoke up. An unsupported heavy machine gun position seemed a little strange, but then, the whole damn war was pretty strange. The fact that they weren't all dead seemed strange to Carl. Maybe his fire had made them keep their heads down, firing only generally in the direction of the choppers. As far as he knew, the first Ranger to get back on the ship and himself were the only ones who had fired back, and only after he had pumped a hundred or more rounds into the position did it become quiet. They would never be able to come back and confirm whether or not the enemy position had been destroyed, but Carl had already given himself credit for the silencing. He hoped he had killed a couple of them to at least even the score. He glanced back at the wounded man who was being treated for shock now that the bleeding was under control.

Simmons kept the ship on top of the trees, leaving Cambodia the same way that they had entered it, low and fast. Carson had given him the heading to Tay Ninh, a long way off, even at red line speed.

At that speed, Carl knew that the chances of someone shooting at them were slim, so he concentrated most of his scanning on the surrounding airspace. The danger from other aircraft, hunter-killer teams in particular, was more of a threat. From time to time, he checked the activity inside the ship. Even through the facial camouflage, he could see a definite paleness in the face of the wounded soldier, a white death mask splotched with the shadows of the jungle.

Roads and traffic became more common below them as the silent race continued and Tay Ninh finally became visible on the horizon. A call to the tower got them clearance for a straight-in approach, priority landing at the dust-off pad and the medics were already standing by when the ship came down in a fast hover minutes later.

The Rangers off-loaded with their dead and wounded, vanishing into the medical building while the pilot lifted up and repositioned the ship to the POL point. 372, with no casualties aboard, had dropped her passengers at another pad and was already refueling, but waited for Carl's ship to finish, and both hovered back to the company area together.

Once inside their protective revetments with the engines cut, everybody began the exciting hunt for bullet holes. Carl's quick walk-around check while they were refueling had picked up half a dozen rips and holes in the skin, but with the blades stopped and the time for a closer look, more were becoming evident. The entry holes were all along the left side, from the pilot's windshield almost all the way back to the tail rotor. Carl joined the two pilots as they started their tour at the ship's nose.

"Jesus Christ on a crutch!" Carson's eyes opened wide as he stared at a pair of large .51 holes, neatly spaced about six inches apart in the nose of the ship. "How the hell did those dinks miss us? Man, they blew out the windshield, shot right through the battery compartment without hurting anything, and didn't get me on the way out. This is fucking incredible! I told you we used up our ration of luck!"

"No argument there. Beats the hell out of me how those shots could have passed through there without doing more damage than this." Simmons had lifted the battery compartment cover, visually tracing the path of the projectiles, noting the metalwork damage, and drawing an imaginary line to point where the rounds had passed on out of the ship. "Must've just missed the gunner and you." He lowered the cover and moved around to the left side, stopping by his door. A finger-sized hole at the back edge of the doorframe showed another near miss.

Carl leaned around into the cargo bay and let out a low whistle. He hadn't noticed it when he slid back the pilot's armor plate, but there it was. "Hey, sir, check this out! Blew a corner chunk right out of your plate." He shoved the sliding armor forward on its rail.

The top rear corner of the plate was gone, ripped away by the bullet that had gone through the doorframe.

Simmons looked at it thoughtfully and smiled slowly. "I'd always wondered just how much that plate would really stop. Never thought about setting it down next to a heavy machine gun to test it, though."

"Weird, looks like you got off lucky, too," Riglos said, pointing at still another hole directly under Carl's gun mount.

"This shit is gonna keep maintenance busy for a while," Carl said. "If that one didn't go all the way through, it must be stuck somewhere in the fuel cells. We'll check for an exit hole before we start ripping out the floor panels."

By the time they had thoroughly gone over the ship, they had found nine entry holes in the body and three exits marked by the jagged metal rays. One of the main rotor blades had a ripping hole through it and that was going to require some downtime to replace.

Carl slid his gun off the mount and handed it to Riglos, then picked up the logbook and started for the hootch, stopping by to see how Jolley was doing.

"Son of a bitch!" Jolley exclaimed, straightening up from writing something in his logbook. "What the hell happened to you?" He waved his hands in a gesture that took in all of Carl's uniform.

Carl glanced down. The chicken plate had taken most of the splattering from the head-shot Ranger, but quite a bit of the blood and ruined flesh had smeared into his lap and upper legs. Some of the grisly remains were stuck to his sleeves and his Nomex collar. He had left the plate in the ship, planning to wash it later when he came back with the maintenance crew, and had forgotten about the rest of his appearance. "The man on our ship that bought it was almost in my face when he got hit. I think I've got more of his head on me than he has left on him." He grimaced, now more aware of the odor of his coverings. The blood and other semiliquid splashes were beginning to dry, stiffening his sleeves and pants legs. "Guess I ought to get this rag off before it starts to draw flies. And if you think this looks bad, you should see the inside of the ship. Another one took a hit, cut an artery in his leg, so you know my gunner's got a mess to clean up.'' He looked over Jolley's ship with a careful eye. ''Looks like you didn't catch much shit. Did you earn any of your flight pay out there, or combat pay? You sure you were on the same mission as my ship?''

Jolley returned the smile, beaming broadly, and waved around the ship. ''Man, I'm too handsome to have my ship get shot full of holes. The gooks know better than to shoot at me.''

''Time to put on the wading boots. Shit's starting to get deep around here!'' Then he turned serious, the smile still there, but cold. ''I think maybe a few NVA died out there before they had time to learn to know better than to shoot at me.''

''I figured somebody must have hit their gun. They sure shut up in a hurry. Just as well for them, 'cause they'd have been in deep shit if I'd gotten a clean shot at them. Even though I am the greatest, there are still a few Charlies out there somewhere who don't know about me yet. They actually did put two holes in my beautiful ship.'' His face took on such a pained, serious look that Carl's grim smile had to fade and transform into laughter. This only made the old crew chief frown and shake his head in mock disapproval. ''Young rookies got no respect for us wise old warriors. What's the world coming to? My ship gets shot up and he laughs.''

XIV.

One day passed much like the previous day and the day before that. The rate of enemy activity had come to an almost total standstill. The slowdown in action cut down their missions, both assaults and supply, and Carl found himself in the air only four days in one ten-day stretch. Despite the pleasantries of a different kind of combat with Kim, he was getting restless from the inactivity.

"Hey, Sarge, I tell you, I'm going stir-crazy just sitting around here. Surely there's someplace in this country where someone needs a helicopter."

"Bitch, bitch, bitch! That's all I've been getting from you and Jolley lately. You two seem to think there's a war on or something. Don't you ever read the fuckin' papers? We're supposed to be letting the ARVN take over this action."

"Well, hell, even they need ships. Look, here comes the man. If he's got anything, I want it. Jolley's been here so long that he can't think straight, so I'm the natural choice," he concluded, knowing that Jolley would talk shit, too, if he thought it would get him off the ground.

Salutes passed casually around while Rawls slipped out a notepad covered with hasty scribbles. "Got any free crews for a run?"

Carl edged behind Rawls and started to flap his arms, hopping from foot to foot, insanely mimicking a ship's lift-off motions and simulating firing his machine gun at unseen enemies. He could tell that Wells was having difficulty keeping a straight face and he redoubled his efforts, adding sound effects which even the lieutenant couldn't ignore.

"I think, sir, in his own weird way, Willstrom is volunteering for the assignment. He must be getting desperate if he wants to fly for the ARVN."

"Nonsense, Sergeant," Rawls replied, turning to look at Carl. "I can see from the sparkle in his eyes that he's volunteering for this job because he is a dedicated professional who simply wants to help further the spirit of goodwill and cooperation between America and the patriotic warriors of South Vietnam." He almost made it without laughing. Most Americans troops, whether infantry or aviation, didn't much like working with the South Vietnamese army units. All too often, the ARVN were conscripts whose politics were questionable and who were frequently unreliable.

"That's me, sir," Carl said with a grin. "Dedicated, all that stuff."

"All right. Your crank time is at eleven hundred hours. Olsen will be your pilot, so link up with him over at the TOC. Should be an easy trip. The main idea is to fly around in circles while some ARVN paratroopers jump out of your ship." He paused, seeing Carl's strange look. "You heard me right. You know, the crazy assholes who jump out of perfectly safe flying machines. Even the ARVN have a few like that. They're a cut above the standard, but still keep a close eye on your gear. Sergeant Wells, round up a gunner to go along for the ride and let's get the show on the road."

Carl fired off a salute and got Wells to release Kurtz from a sandbag detail, a favor for which the young gunner would be only too happy to spring for a few beers at the end of the day. While Kurtz went for the guns, Carl stepped into the hootch for the barrel bag that he always carried with him. He hadn't found any use for the AK yet, but the bag contained an item that might come in handy for the trip.

The long, heavy steel operating rod from an M-60 machine gun made a useful tool for discouraging people from stealing things off his ship. Some of the crew chiefs favored the large eighteen-inch screwdrivers for that purpose. Thievery between units was a long-standing tradition in the American army, but having equipment ripped off by the Vietnamese was a different story, completely unacceptable. And they were notorious for it; thus, the weighted rod.

The guns were already on by the time the pilots got down to the ship, and Carl gave a disgusted snort when he saw his copilot. "Shit! That son of a bitch would have to be the one on the only flight available."

Kurtz looked up from storing away the ammunition. "Who you talking about, Weird?"

Carl motioned with a curt nod of his head. "That asshole with Olsen. Name's Sorden, butterbar, just got here a couple of weeks ago, and I've already flown with him once." The tone of his voice told Kurtz that the flight must have been less than pleasant, but he didn't get a chance to hear any more. The officers were even with the tail boom, Olsen flashing a brilliant smile across the black-as-night face, Sorden a study in contrast.

To Carl's way of thinking, Sorden was the in-the-flesh reality of the stereotyped rookie second lieutenant. On the previous mission, Carl had observed the man carefully, like he did every rookie that he flew with, officer or enlisted. At that time, Sorden had only been in-country for a few days and was on his first flight in Vietnam. Most rookies were usually a little nervous, but had the good sense to listen to their ACs and learn the facts of life, Vietnam style. Not Sorden. Fresh from OCS and flight school, he didn't need any tips from the pilot. He knew it all and made no secret of it. His whole appearance, the tone of voice, his attitude, all made it easy for Carl to develop an instant dislike for the man.

He knew most rookie butterbars were usually a little flaky until they had the chance to experience the realism of Nam and found that training doctrines were not written in stone. Some never learned. They died early, victims of their own ignorance, or sometimes victims of the men they led, frequently draftees who refused to be led on futile missions to useless deaths. Carl had decided after that first time up with Sorden that he was a prime candidate for that kind of end. Good thing he wasn't in a line unit. Carl glanced again at the object of his distaste as the pilots passed him. Certainly nothing there to inspire the confidence and respect of his subordinates. He was overweight, short, and the fat face had a perpetual, arrogant sneer stretched across it. Not for the first time, Carl wished that crew chiefs had some say in who their pilots were going to be.

Most of the pilots were good men, many young ones, the warrants who were just there for the flying game. There were a couple of regular army types and Carl had high opinions of most of them. They were cool under fire, fair in judgments, and didn't abuse their ranks. Without much observation, Carl decided that Sorden had none of those qualities. He had the feeling from day one that the man was an asshole, and the kind of officer who would hide behind his bars, pushing those thin pieces of metal as far as he could.

Olsen was going over the logbook with Sorden and discussing the mission. True to his expectations, Sorden was noisy and arrogant. "I don't know why we even put up with these worthless, slant-eyed bastards. Damn dinks don't want to fight at all. I don't trust any of them." The puffy face tilted in Carl's direction. "I want you to keep an eye on my equipment, Willstrom," he ordered, pointing to a camera dangling from the right side seat. "I don't want any of my stuff to come up missing."

Kiss my ass. "My ship, Lieutenant. Somehow, I take care of it. I'll watch the ship's equipment and my own. You watch your own stuff . . . sir." The word slid out slowly, no respect in it.

Sorden looked at him sharply, started to say something, then decided to ignore Carl's tone. Olsen was studying an oil-level reading intently, but Carl noticed the corner of the black pilot's mouth turning up in a slight smile. Carl knew that if he stayed on the line, no direct insubordination, Olsen would support him. He had heard some of the other officers making remarks about Sorden when they thought the enlisted men couldn't hear them.

In the air they quickly covered the short distance that separated the ARVN compound from the American base in Tay Ninh West. Hovering down the airstrip, Carl watched the Vietnamese pilots and crews strutting to and from their American-made helicopters. They made an impressive picture in their colorful flight uniforms. Red flying scarves, glittering badges of rank, silver-lensed sunglasses.

"Must be a parade in town somewhere," Olsen said as if reading Carl's thoughts. "However questionable their combat performance may be, you can't say that they don't look dashing."

Sorden's remarks hadn't been without foundation. Everyone knew that many of the ARVN weren't too hot about dying for the Republic, but there were many who were dedicated to fighting the communists. They either believed what the South Vietnamese government said, or in a number of cases they had firsthand experience with the methods of the Vietcong liberation of the oppressed masses.

One of the dashing figures strode across the strip to greet them at their landing pad and introduced himself with an almost blinding flash of smiling gold and white.

No wonder some of the grunts carried a set of pliers with them.

"I am Major Tran," he said in fairly good English. "My men already at drop zone, here." He held up a map and indicated a large open area near a small village just south of the main city. "We take six men up at one time. I stay in helicopter with jumpmaster to observe. My men need practice in jump from helicopter," he explained, still smiling broadly, eyes hidden behind the gold wire frame sunglasses. "I like to drop my men from one-five-zero-zero feet. It takes today ten trips for my company to jump. We go now." He laughed and pointed skyward, rotating his arm over his head.

Olsen smiled back, waved him aboard, and glanced across at Sorden. "We go now, GI."

After a leisurely short flight to the drop zone Carl sat back, making himself comfortable, and watched the glittering major as he spoke to his assembled paratroopers. Kurtz slid across the troop seats to join him.

"Little guy sure does get excited, don't he?" Kurtz flapped his arms, parodying the officer's animated movements and sweeping gestures.

"Well, what the hell do you think he's doing, slick? He's got to give those boys a fired-up pep talk to get them ready to fly out of our ship." Carl patted the seat as if it were an old friend. "It'd take a damn sight more than a good pep rally to get me to jump out of a perfectly safe helicopter."

The major was still yelling away enthusiastically when Carl decided that Kurtz might not be able to understand everything the man was saying and began translating for him. "He says, 'Now, today all you assholes are gonna jump out of a helicopter and some of you are gonna die!' " At that point the major gestured wildly with one arm pointing skyward. "Now he says, 'And all of you sorry fucks who survive get to do it again after the helicopter gets up in the air!' "

The major suddenly came to a dramatic and abrupt halt, a moment of silence, and then the troops gave off a series of spirited battle cries.

"What they saying now, Weird?"

Carl laughed and punched the gunner in the ribs. "Mostly, they're saying 'Fuck you, fuck you,' and some of them are yelling, 'Frag the major.' Looks like the party is about to bust up. Guess they're ready for a ride."

The major was hoofing it back to the ship, still flashing gold and ivory smiles. A fast step behind him came an older-looking soldier, not smiling. Got to be the jumpmaster. Must be a universal law about sergeants always looking pissed off. Farther back, the first lift of paratroopers stood, waiting patiently for the loading signal.

Carl slid out of his cubbyhole and moved over toward Olsen's door to catch the conversation between the pilot and the major.

"We ready to go now. No wind, I think."

"All set, Major. How about if they jump at five-second intervals on the eastern edge of our orbit. When the last man is out, I'll start a slow spiral down and you can watch from close up."

The major nodded happily, but Carl wondered if he had really understood what Olsen told him. While the major turned to wave on the first load, Olsen turned back to Carl, smiling as if he could read his thoughts. "We'll see when we get up there."

The six soldiers double-timed to the ship and loaded up in an orderly fashion without confusion, although a few of them were plainly nervous. Carl didn't think any less of them for that. He knew he wouldn't be there by choice. Back when he first had a chance to join the Rangers he would have gone for it, but not now.

The major joined his men, sitting for the moment behind the pilot's seat with the jumpmaster next to him. Still smiling, he gave Carl a thumbs-up sign, more gold glittering on his fingers.

"Major's all set, sir. Might not have enough power for a lift-off with all the gold this dude's wearing."

Olsen gave the controls to Sorden and the ship lifted easily into the air. Below them the remaining soldiers waved happily to their comrades, and dozens of smiling, yelling children danced about around the drop zone. Must be like a carnival for them. All the sharp-looking soldiers falling out of the sky in their puffed-out silk clouds. For the little brown-skinned children from the farming village the drop provided a break from the day-to-day routine of survival around fighting men from the several different factions.

Carl leaned out, waving at the small army of urchins. Mostly they were a dirty-looking bunch, the smallest ones naked, the older ones wearing a mixture of traditional peasant clothing and ragged army discards cut down to their size. He knew that if they had to shut down for any reason they would be overrun by a small horde of waifs, begging for C rations, cigarettes, whatever the GIs had that they were willing to part with. The Vietnamese kids were cute and Carl didn't mind sharing some of his stuff with them, but he would have to keep an eye open for small-time banditry, a way of survival for many of the street kids in the cities and refugee villages. And there was always the danger of some dark-eyed kid with a cute little smile coming up to the ship with a grenade. It had never happened to anyone he knew, but the stories had been around, and Carl believed some of them, examples of the tragic reality of Nam and one of the few things that shook Carl's idealistic picture of the war as a game of deadly stakes between consenting adults.

The ARVN, decked out in their tailored tiger-stripe cammies, were doing their last-minute equipment checks, readying for their moment of glory. At their jump altitude now, they were no longer laughing and joking with each other. A few nervous smiles, mostly silence, just like all the war movies Carl had ever seen with jump sequences. Maybe these guys saw the movies, too. No way to tell what they were thinking, but he figured it must be the same sort of thing that you could "hear" the troops thinking in the movies just before they stepped out into the empty blue sky.

Olsen let Sorden keep the controls so he could watch the show, and he gave the major the go sign. Tran shouted something to the jumpmaster, who, in turn, tapped the first jumper on the helmet.

The soldier cautiously positioned himself in the middle of the cargo bay, knees flexed, hands holding the knees of other troopers for support. The black eyes were glued on the edge of the ship's floor and Carl thought that the man didn't look properly thrilled about the prospect of jumping out of his wonderful ship. A second tap on the back of the helmet and the ARVN shuffled forward to the edge. The major yelled a command and with only a second's hesitation, the soldier pushed himself out and away from the chopper.

Even with the forceful push, the paratrooper came dangerously close to slamming into Carl's machine-gun barrel which was snapped down in its retaining clamp. The jumpmaster had seen it and said something to the rest of the men inside, pointing to the gun and making a shoving motion vigorously with his arms.

The next man moved up closer to the front of the opening and made a greater effort to push away, was successful, and was imitated by the next three soldiers. The last man must not have been paying close attention or was too wound up to give it his best. Carl watched in amazement as the trooper simply stepped out of the ship and promptly smashed into the gun mount with his shoulder. The impact sent him spinning wildly, cartwheeling out of control toward the brown and green patchwork below.

The major, the jumpmaster, and Carl all stretched out, watching with varying degrees of concern as the stunned trooper continued to tumble earthward. Finally, passing two of the men who had left the ship before him, the soldier got his fall under control and managed to pop his chute at five hundred feet.

The major slid back inside the chopper laughing, slapped the dour-faced sergeant on the shoulder, and said something that forced a smile from the tough, leathery face.

Olsen had been watching the small drama unfold, and at its conclusion he took over the controls, beginning a slow, lazy spiral down, following the billowing canopies.

On the ground for only a minute, Carl saw that the small army of children around the fringes of the drop zone had grown. "Check it out, sir. Every kid in the whole ville must be out here."

Olsen looked around at the mob of excited, waving children and waved back at some of them. "Yeah, look at the little beggars. They're already trying to shake down the ARVN for goodies, and this batch over here"—he pointed directly to the ship's front about fifty yards out—"they look like they're ready to rush us if I shut down the engine."

Sorden, who had been quiet for a long time, finally spoke up. "I wouldn't let them get any closer to us than that. One of those little bastards probably has a grenade."

"Right. If they take a step closer, I'll have Weird Willy blow their brains out."

Sorden's lip started to curl into a smile of approval at Olsen's statement, then realized that the AC was putting him on and fell back into a tight-lipped silence.

Carl looked away, smiling hugely. What an asshole! He knew that he was going to love hating this particular lieutenant.

The second load of paratroopers pressed onto the ship, rose into the sky, and made their jumps without incident. The story on the soldier who had hit the gun mount must have circulated quickly because no one else hit the mount. The trips up and back down and up again became routine. It wasn't until the fifth trip that Carl had a chance to see firsthand one of the reluctant ARVN that he had heard so much about.

One young trooper balked in the ship, frozen in the open bay, disregarding the angry commands and what must have been threats from the major and the jumpmaster. The kid was plainly scared; even Carl could see the fear in the black eyes.

Carl's eyes darted back to the jumpmaster, and the young soldier suddenly realized that the hard-faced sergeant was about to assist him in exiting from the aircraft. The reluctant soldier tried to dodge out of the way, lost his footing, and desperately grabbed for the support pole where Carl kept his smoke grenades and operating rod. His hands locked onto the pole as the rest of his body swung out over the edge of the ship, absolute terror in the contorted facial features. Nope, not quite absolute, Carl decided. Absolute terror set in as widening eyes watched the wickedly smiling sergeant unholster his .45 Colt and jack a round into the chamber, leveling the pistol at the young soldier's face. Still the terrified ARVN clung to the pole, the fear of the fall outweighing the threat of the jumpmaster. All eyes in the ship were on the sergeant, his pistol, and the miserable paratrooper. Carl couldn't believe that the sergeant would shoot the man, but the expression on the old veteran's face was cold. He said something in a low growl that Carl translated mentally as "jump or else," but the trooper only screwed his eyes shut and shook his head in a wild negative.

The sergeant shifted the aim, swinging his arm to the right of the soldier's head, and squeezed the trigger. The heavy automatic exploded harmlessly a foot away from the paratrooper's face, but his reaction was that of a mortally wounded man. He screamed and jumped away from the close-range blast, losing his grip and plummeting earthward. The major and the remaining ARVN scurried to the edge to watch his descent, and his companions all let out a breath of relief when they saw his canopy finally open far below. The major and his jumpmaster started laughing and smiling again, just enjoying the hell out of themselves. The remaining troops jumped like good little ARVN without any prompting from Smiling Jack, as Carl had dubbed the old sergeant. Maybe the crusty old warrior really would have shot him if the Americans hadn't been around. At least, the other soldiers seemed to think so and that was the important thing.

Back down again. There were still more troops waiting for their chance to prove their manhood. Olsen took control of the ship and made a flyby over one knot of excited children. Passing directly over their heads, Carl leaned out to wave at the crowd, and then to the delight of the children, he stepped out onto the skids while they were still a hundred feet in the air. He bowed and waved as they approached a second cluster of gleeful kids playing around some scraggly brush. Just as the ship's shadow crossed over them a flash of white light exploded into Carl's vision as fire, dirt, and grass erupted from the middle of the brushy area. As if by command, the small bodies around the explosion began dropping, some rolling, writhing, others jerking and then becoming still. Others, farther away, turned to watch in horror, some running to help, a few running away.

"Explosion! Right under us. Lot of kids are down!" Carl shot back into his seat just as Olsen slammed the ship into a hard left bank.

Sorden saw that Olsen was getting ready to take the ship down and glanced worriedly at the prospective landing area. "Could have been a mine or someone trying to hit us with a rocket. You're not really going to set us down there?" He looked across at Olsen, but the pilot ignored him, concentrating instead on the scene to their front.

Carl was back out on the skids, ready to clear down. Ahead of them he could see at least seven of the small twisted forms near the blast site. Some were being helped or comforted by other children while a hundred yards away the ARVN paratroopers were sprinting across the paddies to help.

Olsen dropped the chopper a rotor's length from the nearest of the injured kids, rushing out a string of rapid-fire instructions to Carl and the gunner. "Get the worst-looking cases on board. Tell someone we're taking them to

Tay Ninh and then start giving whatever first aid you can. Sorden, get me a landing clearance to dust-off!"

Carl jerked out the mike plug as soon as he heard Sorden's name mentioned and bounded off the skids just before the ship hit the ground. The ARVN major and Smiling Jack, right behind him, were yelling orders at the oncoming soldiers and rushing to help out the nearest casualties.

Crying children were everywhere, it seemed, but it was only the ones who were down that Carl bothered with. He came down on one knee next to a small boy, maybe five or six years old, who was lying on his back, knees folded up to his chest, rolling from side to side in pain, but not crying out.

"Hey, it's all right, kid, it's all right." Meaningless words, but he hoped the calmest voice he could muster would get through the language barrier. The kid never opened his eyes, but relaxed enough so that Carl could push his legs down. He gulped in a breath of relief, having already anticipated some gory mess. It looked like a relatively minor flesh wound through the side, ragged but not deep. This one could wait for the ARVN to truck him out. He waved one of the paratroopers over and sprinted off to another young victim only a few yards away.

The girl was lying on her side, the long dark hair tangled now and dirty. Carl rolled her gently over onto her back, his eyes drawn to her blouse by the contrasting colors, the simple once pure white now splashed with red splotches and smears. "Damn!" She couldn't have been more than eleven or twelve. The dark eyes were open, but unfocused, staring into nothingness as the lips moved with low, pain-filled moans. Blood everywhere, arms, legs, face, chest. Her body was like a sieve. He slid his arms under the small body, straightened carefully, and ran as smoothly as he could manage over the cluttered ground toward the ship. With each running step the precious life blood spurted from a bad wound in her left arm, but there was nothing that could be done for that. Her low moaning had stopped, even though he knew that each jolt of his feet must be causing more pain unless she was already past the stage of feeling.

The ship was filling up. Already five bleeding and frightened children had been loaded and two more were being rushed aboard, one held by Kurtz. He and Carl reached the ship at the same moment, Carl sparing him a quick glance. The gunner's face was almost as white as that of a badly mangled boy in his arms.

Carl laid the young girl down on the seat in his compartment and looked hastily over the scene. The worst of the cases were loaded. The major was already on board applying first aid to a small kid with neck injuries.

"Major!" He had to yell again to get the officer's attention, and then shouted out the pilot's instructions. Tran nodded that he understood and relayed the information to a scared-looking young ARVN who had just brought up the last of the wounded.

Carl plugged in his mike jack and cleared Olsen on his side, the gunner clearing the right. Olsen had his landing priority at 15th Med, and didn't waste any time with altitude, but stayed low level, heading straight in, while Sorden advised the medical station as to the number of incoming wounded.

Carl was trying to stop the flow of blood from the girl's arm. He ripped off a piece of her blouse and wrapped it tightly around the arm, directly over the wound, watching the splotchy red and white rag turn into a sponge of pure crimson. Her breath was coming shallow and fast; the delicate, doll-like features of the small face had paled from the onset of shock and loss of blood. It was coming from everywhere. Damn, she'll never make it. Too much blood. In addition to a serious wound in the abdomen and the already wrapped arm, there were terrible, ragged tears in the neck and upper chest, another on the right upper thigh. The once beautiful jet-black hair was also matting with dark fluid on the left side of the head, but he couldn't tell how bad that one was. Not enough material left of her blouse to bandage much with. He grasped the seat support pole with one hand and swung out around the pole, his body hanging out over the edge of the ship for a moment, nothing below him except air. Stepping over the other pathetic victims on the floor, he reached up and ripped the first-aid kit off the wall behind the pilot's seat and swung back into his station. He started to pull out an ammo can to prop her feet up with, then remembered the head wound and decided against it. He ripped off another piece of the blouse and used the shredded garment to bandage the wound along the thigh. At least no arteries had been hit. He shifted his attention up, ripped away what little remained of the blouse, and scanned the damage. The abdomen looked the worst, a gaping rip over five inches long, but at least none of the internal organs were pushing out. Nothing to do for that one but cover it up, which he did with a large dressing from the kit, mentally cursing himself for the tantalizing slowness and awkwardness of his movements.

Just above the tiny right nipple a small jagged fragment of steel was jutting out of the chest, at least an inch of it visible. Blood was slowly oozing up around the dark metal and he couldn't tell how much more of it was buried in the soft flesh. He decided to leave it alone, not wanting to start another major blood flow. He continued to work his way up the body, patching another hole just below the collarbone and then going to work on the freely bleeding rip in the girl's neck. Holding the blood-washed flaps of skin around the injury, he laid a large gauze bandage over it and taped it down as securely as he could on the slender neck.

Hang in there, kid. Hang in there. The doll-face features were still a waxy tan color, but the eyes were glazing over, the breath coming slower, hard to detect except for the slight rise and fall of the steel nipple jutting out of her breast.

Something wasn't right, too much blood still swirling around in the seat under the limp figure. His hands and sleeves and chest protector were covered with blood, but there was still more coming from somewhere. He desperately searched the frail form to find anything he might have overlooked. He slid one arm under her back, lifting her slightly, and ran his free hand over the back, feeling for the wound that he was sure must be there.

In the small of the back, just off center, his probing fingers slid into a warm, wet mush. "Aw, fuck!" His throat constricted, layers of coarse sand pouring into him, garbling the frustrated curse. He had to shake his head viciously to clear the strangling feeling and free his eyes from the blurring effect of moisture coating them. Then he was once more in control of himself, scared, but able to concentrate on his task.

It had to be the exit wound from whatever chunk of shrapnel had ripped through her abdomen. There was a regular fucking hole there, silver dollar size, and through it her life was draining out. He rolled her over on her side, just enough so he could get to the wound, and plugged it up, stuffing a wadded-up, green arm sling into the hole, pushing back into the body some of the mess that had been almost blown all the way through.

For a long moment he knelt there in the cramped space between his seat-turned-deathbed and the huge mini-gun ammo can strapped to his gun mount. He looked away from the child, unable to look at her face again, knowing there was nothing he could do.

Other things in the world regained their former status. They were already in Tay Ninh's control zone, other aircraft to watch for, be alert for the landing. He watched as they passed over the base green line, its guard bunkers and wire strands silently guarding. Closing fast on the medical detachment, he could see the cluster of medics and orderlies crowded around the dust-off pad with their stretchers, waiting for another harvest from the fields of the grim reaper.

Carl lifted the young girl up and pressed her close to him as he rose enough to pivot and sit on the edge of his red-covered seat. He opened the mike with the foot button and cleared Olsen down, felt the slight shudder of the chopper as the skids hit too hard, and, as though to echo that, a small convulsive spasm rippled through the torn body that he held. Her neck arched slightly, the small, tightly drawn lips opened in a silent cry, and she stiffened in his arms.

A medic reached out for her impatiently and Carl gave her up gently. The sweating medic took two steps away from the ship before realizing that she was dead. Carl watched as the soldier knelt down, checked for a pulse just to be sure, and then left the small body, cooling in death on the gray, sun-warmed concrete pad. He turned, glancing impassively at Carl, and came back to help with one who was still alive.

Carl sat there in his small cubicle feeling cold despite the heat of the day. He was still in control, but he felt numb, reacting automatically to the pilot's commands without really hearing them. Some part of him checked the space around them for obstructions. His eyes and mind were on the little Vietnamese girl whose life had poured from her body as he held her. He watched as the rotor wash from the rising ship dusted across her, whipping the torn clothes and the ragged bandages. Another medic walked over to her, picked her up, and followed the retreating swarm of people into the aid station. Carl's last sight of her was of the long black hair dangling down, the arms and legs swaying loosely like a thin, stringless marionette.

The Game had just made a play outside of the boundaries that Carl had thought existed. This wasn't the way it was supposed to be, and in the same instant, he cursed himself for being so naive. The Game had never excluded the innocents, the bystanders. To the contrary, it thrived on those who tried to stay away from the middle of the playing field, but were held by circumstances. He knew, of course, that civilians—men, women, children, the babies—had been dying in wars for thousands of years, but it was the first time that he had been a part, so close to the tragedy of dying children. How could any of the small brown children survive in this country where even their playgrounds were littered with unexploded bombs, dud artillery rounds, and deliberate booby traps. The kids had probably disturbed some old explosive device, a remnant of some earlier stage of the war, or even an earlier war.

Didn't really make a damn bit of difference what it was, he decided. The results were the same, whether it was accidental or a trap. A day of playful excitement for the children had ended abruptly, violently, in a lethal blast of fire and jagged steel. The dead wouldn't care what killed them, only some of the living would try to make some reason for it, fixing the blame on ill chance, on the nature of war itself. These people, the old survivors, were used to it.

Carl was still pondering over the wasted lives when Olsen brought the ship down for refueling. Carl walked around the ship, looking it over as a matter of trained habit. Kurtz was refueling, his visor down protecting his face against any splash-back from the JP-4, but Carl could see that below the visor the young gunner's skin was pale and his hands were trembling. The gunner, too, was covered with smears of blood from the children he had helped. Kurtz looked over at him. He couldn't see the eyes, but he felt the rookie's question. Why?

Carl shook his head slowly. No answers here, slick. He stayed by the gunner until the ship was topped off and then climbed back into his position.

"That's it for today," Olsen was saying as Carl plugged his helmet cord back in. "Tran canceled the rest of the drop. His men took out the rest of the injuries to a hospital at the ARVN compound and are making a sweep of the area for more garbage and trying to find parents or relatives." With that information distributed, he lifted the ship up, and back they went to the revetments, settling into the postflight routine, keeping their minds occupied with the work.

Kurtz dismounted the guns and set them aside silently. He headed off to the maintenance tent and returned promptly with a water bucket, setting it down heavily on the chopper's floor, sloshing some of the already dirty water over the bucket's dented rim. He didn't say a word to the others, just pulled an old brush from one of the interior storage holes and began scrubbing up the drying blood, the mute testimony of their pathetic cargo only fifteen minutes earlier. After a few minutes of almost vicious scrubbing of seats and floor panels the grim-faced gunner looked up questioningly at Carl.

Carl was reminded of a buffalo, the way Kurtz appeared, down on all fours, short and stocky to begin with, and looking pissed off at the whole world. He knew the feeling, he felt it himself, and he knew it must be harder on the rookie, still fresh with lofty ideals. Carl surveyed the ship's interior, forced a smile, and nodded approvingly. "Looks fine, Kurtz. Get the guns taken care of." He wanted to add something like, "And if you want to talk about it just come see me," but what was there to talk about? Fuck it! It happened and there wasn't shit he could do about it, except accept it and let it go. The memories would be there forever, but each man had to deal with that in his own way.

Kurtz felt the awkwardness of the moment, too, but ducked away from it, taking the guns and retreating to the arms room.

Olsen was filling out the logbook and saying something to Sorden in a sharp tone when Carl came around the nose of the ship. He didn't hear what was said, but the sound was low and angry. Both officers shut up when they saw Carl, and Sorden, scowling darkly, turned and stomped away.

Carl watched the man for a minute and then spoke. "Problems, sir?" he asked, not really expecting any answer.

Olsen glared at him for a second. Officers didn't discuss other officers' shortcomings with enlisted men, but Olsen was pissed about something and he wasn't regular army. The black warrant growled and spat with disgust. "That son of a bitch is a real asshole! He's trying to act like he's one bad dude, telling me that the sight of all those kids didn't bother him. Man, I saw his face. He was getting green around the gills just looking at them. And then he's got the balls to tell me, the fuckin' aircraft commander, that I jeopardized the ship and *his* life to save a bunch of 'gook garbage' who were just going to turn into VC anyway. If I have to fly with him much, I'm going to get a transfer. That man is going to be trouble, I can feel it." Olsen had cooled off somewhat and finally looked at Carl with a crooked smile. "I'll bet he don't like niggers, either!"

Carl was surprised by Olsen's answer, but pleased to hear that Sorden was regarded as an asshole by other officers. From other conversations he had overheard, he knew that some officers didn't care too much for Sorden, but to have an officer actually tell him directly was great. Of course, Olsen was the wrong man to talk to if a person was going to talk shit about the Vietnamese people. That was one of the things that Carl liked about the young warrant. Maybe being black was part of it. The man knew what it was like to be on the receiving end of prejudices like Sorden's.

For a moment they enjoyed a wave of laughter, then Olsen's face turned serious again. "What you just heard, I never said, got it?"

Carl gave him a big grin. "Solid copy, sir. I never heard a word!" Olsen was a good man, and Carl wouldn't want to see him get his ass in a sling because of Sorden. And he was grateful to Olsen for giving him something to laugh and smile about.

The feelings didn't last for long. Back in the hootch his earlier emotions of anger and hollow depression swept through him again. He stripped off his Nomex and tossed them in a heap on the floor, flakes of dried reddish-brown blood crumbling off. Too early to start drinking, even though a dozen 3.2 beers would have gone down fine.

He stood there for a few minutes, feeling warm and sticky, even though he was wearing only the OD boxer shorts. No breeze came through the barricaded walls. Nothing to disturb the musty odor of unwashed clothes, rotting wood, and sandbags. Maybe a shower would help. He took a towel and walked across to the shower stalls, kicking up little puffs of dust with every step. He hadn't bothered with the shower sandals, but he had long ago gotten used to the slippery scum on the wooden shower floors, and all he wanted now was the cool water pouring over him. Outwardly it felt good. He just stood there under the fall of the liquid, ignoring the initial gurgling of rusty water, and relaxed as it flowed over him, washing away the grit and grime. It felt good on the skin, but the waters of all the oceans in the world couldn't erase the sights that were burned into his mind.

Trying to sleep while his body was still cool from the shower, he was plagued by nightmarish visions of fiery explosions and screaming children, faceless ones reaching out scarred arms to embrace him. Several times he jerked awake, the screams still echoing through his mind, sweat pouring off his body to soak into his cot. He finally gave up on sleep and just lay there, staring at nothing, trying to feel nothing.

XV.

Approaching his eighth month in-country, Carl was still bothered by the memory of the dying girl, but like all the other deaths he had witnessed, he accepted it and lived with it. Some of them would fade in time; others like the girl, he knew, would be a part of his life forever. But still it was a part of the Game, and he was going to see a lot more of it before he was benched. He was already to put in for his extension as soon as he became eligible. He still wanted to stay on the playing field. It was where the excitement was, not watching the Game from that stateside bench across the ocean.

The continuing combat assault missions and hot log flights kept the pace going fast after that one short lull when he hadn't been able to get in the air very often.

"Not again!" Carl grumbled at Wells when the lanky platoon sergeant had smilingly told him who his pilots were for the day. "I can't stand that . . ." He caught Wells's warning look. Still had to observe some of the formalities from time to time. At least he had a good pilot again, teamed with Olsen once more. One of these days, Carl thought, that idiot, Sorden, is going to be an AC. He knew that when that happened, the lieutenant would be watching for any little screwup.

"Guess I can't get out of it, huh?" Carl asked without much hope. When Wells smiled again, Carl asked if he could at least get his pick of gunners, to which Wells did agree.

Olsen filled them in with more detail as they approached their destination. "They've got a reinforced rifle platoon down there that's been chasing a small force of NVA, also estimated to be platoon size, but they haven't been able to pin them down. Support elements working with them are two ships from the 1st of the 9th, a hunter-killer team. As a matter of fact, there they are now." He pointed forward through the Plexiglas.

Carl stepped out onto the skids for a better look. Sure enough. Cobra up at altitude, cruising high over the jungle with its deadly arsenal, a dark snake ready to drip its deadly venom onto anything that the hunter might find. Harder to spot was the hunter half of the team, the fragile-looking recon chopper that was circling over the lush greenery of the jungle. Those were the ones that Jolley had said were the real crazies. Carl had heard a lot about them during his time in-country and was considering extending for a transfer to 1st of the 9th scouts. It seemed like there were write-ups in the division rag about the exploits of the 1st of the 9th all the time, and he wanted to get together with some of the people from one of the troops and find out some more about them.

He continued to glance back at the *loach*, the local term for the OH-6A scout helicopter, and wondered if they might shut down at the fire base while Carl's ship was there.

For several hours, 312 made the trips in and out, back and forth from fire base to moving platoon locations, keeping up a steady supply of ammunition and water to the men on the ground.

"Mayday! Mayday! Taking fire! Going down!" The suddenness of the radio blaring in his ears made Carl jump. They had just dropped off a load of supplies to another platoon and were en route back to the fire base when the message broke. Another message followed almost immediately, a different voice, different ship.

"Mayday! Mayday! Low bird down at Whiskey Tango 365461. Repeat. Aircraft down at Whiskey Tango 365461." The voice came rapidly, urgently, but with steadied calmness.

Olsen knew the general area—they had been working that vicinity part of the day—and he quickly banked the ship hard over to the left and responded to the distress call on the Guard channel.

"This is Papa One Eight. En route your location. Be there in zero-five mikes. Over."

Carl was already staring out into the distance, trying to spot where the Cobra was. It had to be the Cobra that was still in the air. Charlie must have taken the bait and brought the smaller ship down somewhere out there. He saw the smoke a couple of miles out at the same time Olsen spotted it. The Cobra was there, diving toward the ground, one man firing while the other pilot gave Olsen their radio frequency and a situation report.

"Papa One Eight, this is Red Two Four. My low bird's down and burning. Hostile fire in the area. Low bird made it to a clearing before going down. Enemy muzzle flashes approximately three hundred meters to the sierra of crash site. Over."

"Roger, Red. I have you and smoke visual. Keep us covered and we'll go in," Olsen fired back. Then he hit the intercom. "Eyes open, gentlemen. We'll be going in low and fast from the north, but there still may be someone who wants to shoot at us. We'll be there in less than two minutes. Go ahead and get the first-aid kits off the walls now."

Neither of the men in the gun compartments bothered to respond. Carl and Kurtz both reached the kits on their respective sides about the same time and were back in their positions within seconds.

Carl had wanted to meet up with some of the scouts, but not under these circumstances. Burning ship didn't sound good. At least they had powered into a clearing. That meant someone could still be alive and waiting for a rescue ship to pull them out.

That hope faded moments later as they swept into the clearing, guided by a diminishing smoke cloud. There wasn't much left of the small ship. A pile of gray ash, the remains of the aluminum-magnesium alloy that made up the bulk of the ship's hull, provided the focal point for their attention. In the midst of the smoldering ash was the lone pillar of the power train while around the fringes of the fine powder were the tips of the main rotors, part of the tail boom, and what at first appeared to be a pair of burned logs, conspicuous by their presence in the open.

"Damn," Carl breathed softly to himself as the realization hit home. The charred, stubby logs were part of the crew of the ship. He glanced around away from the ship, searching, probing the clearing and the treeline. Only two bodies visible. He knew that the 1st of the 9th scouts carried a three-man crew, pilot and observer up front, a gunner in the rear. Nothing moving on his side. He looked back at the two blackened bodies just as Olsen brought the ship down. Probably the two front seat men. The missing soldier was likely to be the gunner, who would have had a better chance to get clear of the ship if he hadn't been picked off on the way down.

Carl gave one quick yell for Kurtz to move when Olsen gave him the go motion, and both men dashed into the swirling ash as the Huey's rotors stirred up the air.

Carl, closer on the jump-off, reached the bodies first and dropped sharply to his knees, trying to ignore the biting smell of the roasted flesh. Kurtz arrived gasping, more from the sight than from any physical exertion.

"Check the other one," Carl ordered harshly, channeling some of the sensory impact of the scene into his voice. He touched the blackened corpse gingerly, flaking off pieces of charred clothing, the remnants of the flame-retardant Nomex that had been fused to the flesh. He placed one hand over the openings that had been the man's mouth and nose, carefully trying to avoid touching the scorched face. He had seen and handled a lot of dead and dying men and children, but these burned-out shells of humanity were the worst things he had seen. The face below him with its charred crust and burned-away eyes represented his own private terror. It was no way for a man to die. Not in agony, feeling the flesh sizzle, boil up, and burst. He prayed that the soldier was dead and was grateful when he detected no trace of air from the mouth or nose. Maybe the guy had taken a hit and been killed before he burned. He hoped so.

"Oh, God! Weird! This one's still alive!" Kurtz's scream was almost pure panic.

Carl scrambled across to the other crewman, feeling a rush of dizziness flood through his brain. He flopped down next to the body and shook his head to clear away the fogginess. No time to get sick or freak out. Inwardly, he was a little surprised at himself for his reactions. Weird Willy's got to be tougher than that. Can't let a couple of crispy critters shake a man up.

Again he checked to see if the soft breath of life was in evidence. Just as the gunner said. A faint breath of air was passing between the tightly pulled-back blackened lips. First-aid measures for burns had already swept through his head and he knew that there wasn't a hell of a lot that he could do except get him back to the rear as fast as possible and hope for the best. He motioned Kurtz to take the man's legs, and they carefully lifted him up and carried him back to the ship. For the second time in recent weeks a casualty of the war was laid out on Carl's seat, the regular troop seats having been left behind. The ironic difference in the cases was not lost on Carl. One, a girl, a Vietnamese, he had hoped would live. This one, a fellow countryman, he hoped would die, quickly if he was going to. He knew that the survival instinct was a strong one, but he also thought that if he were inside that burned husk he would rather be dead.

He peeled off his chicken plate and slid it under the

soldier's feet in what he recognized was probably a futile attempt to ward off shock. The trooper was probably already in that stage and past the point of feeling pain.

"Go get the other one on board!" He turned away from Kurtz and plugged in his mike. "Any ideas about the third man, sir?"

Olsen shrugged. "Check around that area of the treeline, but don't take too long. NVA's probably on the way here right now!"

Carl gave him the two clicks with his button and hastily whipped his AK-47 out of its bag. Slapping a magazine in it as he ran, he dashed across the open area, watching for any sign of the third crew member. Judging from the way the wreckage of the ship sat, it had come in along the line that he was following. If the missing man had dropped off along the way . . .

Pushing into higher grass near the jungle fringe, he almost stepped on the soldier's leg before he saw him. Some crushed-down grass with smeared blood darkly staining it marked where the man must have fallen, then rolled or crawled to where he was now, a small sanctuary of brush at the edge of the jungle.

Carl swept aside some of the tangle with the barrel of his AK and dropped down on one knee, carefully rolling the crewman over onto his back. The broken arm was obvious, twisted unnaturally, but not serious. Some bad burns along the left side, but again, not as bad as the other two men. This man was still alive and Carl thought he might stand an even chance of surviving, making it back to the World still resembling a human being. Dark hair showed under the flight helmet, making the soldier's face a tricolor with pale skin serving as a backdrop for a finger-painting swirl of dark blood from a long rip in the right cheek, a rip opened wide enough for pink gums and dull white teeth to show through.

He sprang back out of the brush and waved for Olsen, who, anticipating the signal, was up and sliding over the ground instantly. Carl shielded the downed man's body from the flying dust and debris as best he could until Olsen dropped the chopper thirty feet from Carl's position and Kurtz jumped out to help him. Carl laid the broken arm across the man's chest and they hustled him into the ship while Olsen nervously scanned the jungle's menacing border.

At the edge of the ship, Carl paused to change his grip and glanced up at the pilots. For an instant he froze in disbelief, staring into the lens of Sorden's 35mm camera, watching as the lieutenant's finger pushed the button. Sudden rage boiled up, a fiery heat burned at his brain watching the fat butterbar grinning behind the camera. He jumped up into the ship, pulled the scout in after him, and, crouching, whirled back to Sorden.

"Put that damned camera down!"

Sorden's eyes flinched, but only for a second. Then, with an arrogant sneer, he aimed the camera again, this time at one of the charred corpses.

Rank meant nothing. Fuck the regulations. "You son of a bitch!" Carl screamed at him, a savage joy registering in his heart at the look of shocked surprise on Sorden's face. A look that changed for a split second to fear as Carl swung his left hand around hard, smashing the camera from Sorden's grasp and sending it to the floor. Carl snatched up the camera and thrust it toward Olsen, his hands shaking furiously. "Did you see what that—"

"Get to your gun, soldier!" Olsen's sharp voice cut off Carl's angry outburst and snapped him back to his job. "Get to your position! Now!" Olsen repeated angrily. "We'll take care of this when we get back to base." He stared both men down and stiffly ordered Kurtz to look after the third man while Carl slipped back into his place with the still living burn victim. Carl was still burning inside, not only with anger at Sorden, but now angry with himself as well. They were still on a mission, on the ground with enemy troops nearby, badly wounded men on the ship, and he was wasting precious drops of time fighting with that asshole.

Now he had done it. He continued to seethe over Sorden's callous behavior while he did what he could to keep the charred soldier from shifting and rolling with the motion of the ship. Taking pictures of dead and messed-up GIs for his lousy scrapbook and having the balls to smile at him while he did it. Carl had just barely restrained the impulse to smash the camera back into Sorden's face. Should have gone ahead and done it, he thought. Sorden would probably have him up on charges anyway for insubordination or some shit. He looked down at the human misery on his seat and checked to see that the man was still breathing. In the whirling air around the ship it was almost impossible to tell, but he thought the soldier was still alive.

Olsen was still on the controls and had the ship zipping along at red line speed for Tay Ninh, passing on information to the gunship that had been requested.

Carl had heard the Cobra pilot's strained voice over the static hiss of the radio asking for identification of the casualties by rank. Still working procedure, no names over the air. Carl began a careful scrutiny of the burned man's neck and collar area for any of the black rank insignia or dog tags. A metal chain around the neck showed where the dog tags probably were, buried under a layer of crust that was what remained of the Nomex shirt. The chain itself was embedded in the charred skin and Carl left it alone. He slid out of his hole to check the other corpse, but Kurtz motioned him back, shaking his head.

"Nothing recognizable on the one with me," Carl informed the pilot, "and Kurtz says there ain't nothing on the dead man, either."

"This guy's got enough to see," Kurtz took up. "Spec 5, name tag says Anderson, sir."

Olsen rogered and passed on the sketchy information, using the soldier's initial, and then broke contact with the Cobra.

Dropping down once again onto the dust-off pad, the ship was swarmed by the medics and orderlies, the new caretakers of the grisly cargo. Expressionless for the most part, only a couple of them showed any emotion, and that merely surprise that the one badly burned man was still alive. The tired, lined faces had seen too much of the human wreckage of war pass through their station, day after day, to be shocked by anything. Carl was glad that he only had to deal with the passing on of these men and not the job of trying to put them back together.

A lull in the activity finally gave them a chance to shut down at the earth-walled base for chow. Both pilots stayed in the saddle until the blades came to a stop. Olsen was out first, and as soon as Kurtz had the blade tied down, the pilot ordered him into the base to get some food.

"And don't be in a hurry to get back," Olsen called after him. Kurtz signaled that he understood and disappeared into the clutter of the camp.

Oh, shit. Here it comes now, Carl thought. The steady hours of work had calmed him down and given him too much time to think. It wasn't the fear of anything that the green machine might do to him that bothered him. Mentally, he was already challenging any charges. *What the fuck you gonna do to me? Draft my ass and send me to Vietnam?* He really hadn't done anything except yell at Sorden and knock the camera out of his hands. Article 15 stuff at worst if Sorden pushed it, and Carl didn't think that he would, not if Carl pushed back a little. Carl remembered somewhere an item forbidding photographing dead or wounded, trivial but usable, maybe. Hell, everyone did it with the enemy, but shooting shots of GIs, under the circumstances, might be embarrassing for the lieutenant. Carl had been thinking hard on the situation and remembered the nervous look on Olsen's face while they had been sitting there on the ground. Olsen watching one side for Charlie and good ol' Sorden sitting there clicking his shutter.

It wasn't any punishment that worried him. He didn't think it would go that far. But he knew Olsen. The man was cool, but he was an officer and had his duties. Carl could recognize that. He was in for an ass chewing and then, the part that already grated on his nerves, he was probably going to have to apologize to the son of a bitch!

"Front and center, Specialist," Olsen ordered sharply. The order also carried a note of disgust, the implication that the AC had better things to do with his time than screw around with a pair of jerks. "Explain your actions, Willstrom." The midnight eyes were not friendly.

"Kurtz and me are busting our asses trying to get those dudes on the ship, and this . . ."—he caught himself—"this lieutenant's sitting there taking pictures like he's on some kind of vacation. And there's some kind of regulation, I think, about taking pictures of friendly casualties. Regulations aside, sir, I think it sucks."

Sorden started to say something, all puffed up, face flushed, but Olsen cut him off. "You'll get your turn, Lieutenant," he snapped, even sharper than he had at Carl. The "lieutenant" came out with stress, reminding Sorden that Olsen was the aircraft commander even if the overweight lieutenant outranked him officially. Olsen turned back to Carl. "Your points may be valid, but your actions are out of line and dangerously close to insubordination."

"Close!?" Sorden's yell was indignant. "It *was* insubordination and I'm going to nail his ass!"

"Back off, Lieutenant," Olsen growled warningly. "This incident isn't going any further than this spot right here. It's going to end now! Understand? That applies to both of you."

Carl nodded quickly, wanting to smile, but kept a tight rein on his expression. Sorden was clearly pissed off, but after a moment under the no-nonsense glare from Olsen, he, too, nodded his acceptance.

"I don't need any more of this shit, Willstrom. I want the rest of the day to be smooth, no friction. I'm not going to order any of that handshake-and-apology routine, either. Just do your job. Now get on into the base, get some chow, find Kurtz, and get back out here to watch the ship while we eat."

Carl nodded, avoided looking at Sorden, and left. Just before entering the base, he paused and looked back toward the ship. Sorden and Olsen were already going at it. Carl smiled, and whistling up a little tune, kicked up a puff of the fine red dust and strolled on in for lunch.

* * *

Walking back to the ship with Kurtz, Carl saw another man approaching their ship. The man's black Stetson riding proudly on his head identified him as a member of the 1st of the 9th Cav, probably one of the gunship pilots or someone from the crew of a new scout ship that had been sent in.

Carl and the gunner arrived at the same time as the stranger, who introduced himself as Captain Jacobs. Olsen and Sorden both saluted and then shook hands with the tall, darkly tanned officer.

"I'm the scout platoon leader, Apache Troop. I just wanted to thank you gentlemen for pulling my men out of there today."

Olsen held up his hands, warding off the thanks, but the captain continued in a drawling voice, reminding Carl of an old John Wayne cavalry picture. "Gunner's going to be okay, thanks to you." He paused for a moment, tilted the wide-brimmed hat back on his head, and let out a deep breath, looking suddenly tired. "The other one, the pilot, didn't make it. Just got word that he died on the medevac en route to Bien Hoa." He stared up at the sky, beautifully blue and clear.

"Sorry to hear that, sir," Olsen finally said. "There wasn't much we could do for him on our ship."

The captain nodded slowly. "Thanks for the effort, though." Extending his hand again, they shook, saluted, and the cowboy departed.

Carl had been watching Sorden during the conversation, and the lieutenant had seemed very uncomfortable while the captain was thanking them. He wondered what the cowboy would have done if he had told him that butterbar had been taking pictures of his comrades in their misery. But he had promised Olsen that the matter was finished.

"Crazy bunch of people, those scouts," Olsen remarked as they watched the Stetson go. "That man should be used to losing people. Fish bait is what they are. Charlie's the fish, scouts are the worm, Cobra's the fisherman. Sometimes the fish gets caught, sometimes they lose the worm. Hell of a way to make a living!"

Carl thought so, too, but what a living! He had his mind made up for sure now, burned crewmen notwithstanding, he was going to get one of those hats. He was going to extend for the 1st of the 9th scouts.

XVI.

March swept in and passed on with hardly a flicker. Day in and day out the olive-drab Hueys rose up into the skies, disappearing into the distance like alien insects in search of new plunder. Again Carl went through days of dull, slow business, missions dragging on endlessly. Another slow cycle of action had found them, and the only thing that Carl looked forward to was his thirty-day special leave for extending and the extension itself. Three weeks had gone by since he put in for the extension. He hadn't heard anything yet, but that didn't bother him. If there were no snags in the paperwork, it would only take the army forever to get it done; if there were problems, it would only take twice that long. He knew that the extension would be approved. Doorgunners were always in demand, and he had heard that the scout crews had a high turnover rate, not from short-timers DEROSing, either.

During this slow cycle, life at Tay Ninh for Carl had lost one of its more pleasant diversions. Kim had failed to show up one day, and when Carl questioned a couple of the mamasans, all he could find out was that she had moved on. Where? They didn't know. Why? Same blank look and answer. They didn't know. People moved without records, without traces, all over Vietnam, swarms of refugees always hoping that the next stop would be their last and final home. He couldn't figure out why she would have skipped out of Tay Ninh, though. She had a good job, and he gave her a little extra, not like paying for a whore, but like a kid spending money on a girlfriend. As days went by, though, he realized that she was gone for good, and had to turn to the five-dollar quickies again, in the small, dank back rooms off the main streets of the city. Clap city if there ever was one.

He didn't see much of Sorden, either, but when their paths chanced to cross, he always rendered the salute and proper greeting, still transmitting the message of contempt, and Sorden only smiled each time, as if to say, "I'm gonna get you, fucker."

Fast and sudden action suddenly boiled up in the opening days of April. Fire bases were constantly under attack, and Tay Ninh began to live up to its old nickname from hotter times. "Rocket Alley" had incoming mortar and rocket fire on a regular basis. For six days straight, Carl could have set his watch by the morning barrage and the six o'clock evening toss-ins from enemy gunners.

Combat assaults were the order of the day, and Carl was burning through several thousand rounds a day on some of the hotter missions. Company choppers were taking more and more hits as the NVA units seemed more inclined to stand and fight against the GIs instead of fading back into the jungles and lighting out for the sanctuary of Cambodia. Even the fast movers, the jets flying air strikes, were being fired at more frequently by increasing numbers of the .51-caliber or 12.7mm heavy machine guns.

Carl looked over the ghastly scene as the ships swept into the landing area just outside of Fire Base Green. The entire platoon had been sent out to support the infantry there after a savage night battle involving at least three NVA battalions. The Americans had repulsed the attack and were going to use the choppers for fast assaults to try to cut off the NVA force before they could pull back into Cambodia.

A light, early morning mist was just rising off the field in the pale light of dawn, creating a surreal vision. Dead, twisted figures everywhere. The concertina and wire aprons were literally stuffed with corpses. Here and there were trails of bodies marking places where the enemy had breached the wire or been channeled into narrow corridors, right up to the foot of the berm, that dark wall of earth that marked the final line of defense. There were a few of the small brown bodies sprawled across the top of the berm, marking the deepest penetration of the attackers.

"Must have been one hell of a fight," Chrissen, the AC, remarked, echoing Carl's thoughts.

Nobody said anything, but Carl noticed that it hadn't been a one-sided affair. Inside the base he had seen a long line of spread-out ponchos, boots sticking out from under the ends like dirty headstones.

The ships didn't have long to wait before grunts began to pour out of the base, some eager to continue the killing, most just tired, glassy-eyed, performing their functions on auto pilot. They pushed through the blasted corpses. Without glancing down Carl figured there must be well over a hundred.

Chrissen, still one of the youngest pilots, almost twenty, was listening to final instructions that were being passed down to the flight leader from the C and C bird, command and control, that had stayed in the air. Carl grinned, thinking about Jolley stuck up there away from the action and with Sorden as the copilot to boot. Flying the brigade commander around to direct operations was going to make for a dull day, and Carl was glad he hadn't drawn the assignment.

The grimy foot sloggers loaded up with no talking, the ones on Carl's ship all seemingly grateful for a few minutes to relax and close their eyes on the ship. Kids mostly, kids with faces of old men. The kinds of faces that Carl had seen on the evening news back home when he was still in high school. And they were still here.

Somewhere in the jungle were other Americans, a company-size force following the blood trails of the retreating Charlies, trying to maintain contact, but moving slowly to avoid ambushes and traps.

From what Carl had picked up on the radio, it sounded

like the helicopter-borne force was going to act as the anvil for the enemy units to be smashed against.

Beating steadily through the sky, the ships made a wide loop out away from the base area, and after a roundabout flight, they soared back into an LZ far in advance, they hoped, of where the NVA main force was projected to be. No fire from the gunners unless fired upon. Even the guardian gunships remained quiet as the landing was made. The grunts poured out of the ships, small green insects swarming out away from their mothers to become one with the lush, high grass.

The glass-eyed mother ships swarmed back into the sky, returning in the same roundabout fashion to pick up the second and final sortie for this portion of the operation. The second phase went just as quietly as the first, and the guns remained cold and unfired. Nothing to do then but sit back and wait for contact.

The sun was well up into the sky and the heat was already pounding down on the work crews at the base who were clearing away the bodies. Carl thought about trying to have some fun with Rossi, his gunner, who had only been around for a few weeks, but decided that a few minutes of shut-eye would be better. After a quick check of the ship with the pilots, Carl climbed up on top of the helicopter, stripped his shirt off, and rolled it up for a cushion. Stretching out on the top deck, he relaxed, faceup, hat over his eyes, and let the warmth of the burning solar orb soak into his body.

Chrissen's yelling brought him back to the real world, and the pilot's blue eyes almost sparkled in the sunlight as he looked up at Carl. Carl still thought of the boyish-faced pilot as a kid, but the kid knew how to handle himself now, a far cry from the Chrissen Carl remembered from almost five months ago.

"Wake up, Sleeping Beauty!" He was already strapping on his chest protector. "We're moving out!"

A few minutes later, engines cranked, everyone in place, Chrissen passed on the newest information. "We're going to Fire Base Grayson for a combined CA with some first platoon ships. The head honcho wants to try to catch another bunch of dinks that intelligence just got wind of."

Carl couldn't help comparing Grayson with the devastated base they had just left. Grayson was one of the few fire bases in the sector that hadn't been hit that night, and life was pretty relaxed. The grunts were moving easily around inside and outside the perimeter. Troops with sweat glistening on their backs were engaged in the never-ending task of strengthening and improving the defenses, stringing more of the flesh-stripping concertina wire, packing sandbags, and checking claymores and trip flares in the wire. Even though the work was serious, it was being done in an easygoing manner, deliberately and carefully, without haste or sloppiness. Living on the fringe of death, in the midst of Charlie's realm, the soldiers never knew when that extra ounce of careful preparation might mean the difference between a happy homecoming and DEROSing in a body bag.

"We've got a few minutes before the troops are ready to load, so if you want to grab some fast eats, do it now. Could be a long mission," Chrissen told them.

Carl scrounged through his box of goodies and came up with a can of peaches. The C-ration cans of fruit were about the only things he ever carried on the ship, those and the cans with the crackers and army-style candy bars. The rest of the meals in the boxes he traded or gave away if they had no value on the C-ration exchange market. Some of the food nobody ever seemed to want. Even some of the ragged-looking Vietnamese kids would throw back some of the stuff, proving that they weren't really as hungry as they pretended to be.

As he hastily slurped the peaches and juice down, he eyed the can that was fastened on the side of his machine gun. Good old army spaghetti and beef chunks. That can's main function in life was to keep the ammo belt feeding into the gun smoothly, but it could be eaten if he needed more solid food. For a few months he had kept an old can of ham and lima beans on the gun until the hungries started twisting his guts one day. They hadn't been too bad, despite the fact that the date on the can indicated that they were two years older than he was. The new can was almost cherry, less than ten years old. For a moment a ridiculous vision was captured in his mind, gentlemen in fashionable attire seated around a huge polished oak table, sifting and savoring vintage C rations, commenting on the color, the sparkle, or bouquet. He raised his olive-drab can to the imaginary scene. Cheers, and he gulped down the last of the oversweet juice.

The ship with the brigade commander and Carl's best friend and enemy, Jolley and Sorden, slid into the landing area and hovered down toward the lead ship. While Carl watched, a short man in what looked like starched jungle fatigues and highly shined combat boots jumped from the C and C ship and darted to the mission leader's bird with a map for a quick conference.

A minute later the man raced back to the control ship and it promptly lifted into the air. A message buzzed down the row of waiting ships, and a moment later they lifted off, each ship now brimming with troops who had boarded during the brief conference. Looking around at the human cargo, the range of expressions on the young faces, Carl felt a sudden chill roll through him. Not fear, not that easy to define. Something else, a hint of foreboding, a feeling of something intangible, not quite right. He shuddered involuntarily, shaking off the effect, looking back into the light of day and the string of ships.

On the radio the flight leader was handing out final instructions, once again changing the formation. Carl's platoon went into a staggered trail, ready for descent, while the second "V" stayed in orbit. This time the gunners were to have free fire going into the LZ, and Carl could already see the grayish smoke rising from the artillery prep that had just started smashing into the LZ. He knew the NVA were down there somewhere. If they were close to the LZ, the barrage would alert them to where the lift was coming in at, giving the enemy the option of moving away from there or engaging the Americans. A third choice was available, and Carl had seen it used several times. Charlie might leave a covering force around the most prominent LZs along his route of retreat to slow down any pursuing force. But one way or the other, they were down there. He knew it.

The flash-boom from the impacting artillery suddenly ceased, and the first group of ships started in, saddled by the gunship escort. A thousand meters out, the Cobras began their runs, lacing the LZ with rockets and miniguns. A few seconds later the order for the doorgunners to open up came over the radio. Flashes of flame licked out from both sides of the ships as gunners and the infantry on board added their portions to the battle din. Carl fired into the grass, the trees, anywhere at all. With no one firing back yet, one place was as good as another.

They were almost to the ground, the grunts poised at the edges, ready to spring off, when weapons in well-concealed positions suddenly blazed fire at the hovering choppers. Grunts pitched out of the ship, crawling or rolling away a few yards, while Carl fired back at a muzzle flash, trying to cover his ass and the grunts as well until they could bring their guns to bear.

Radios were screeching in his ears, ships taking hits, warnings of gun positions, the roar of the turbines, weapons blasting all around, and through it all, he had the feeling that the unseen face behind the muzzle flashes directed at his ship was zeroing in on his head. Troops out, flight clear up, the ship lifting, burning lead still seeking out targets from both sides.

Carl's head suddenly snapped back, slapping with force against the transmission wall, his brain ringing and blinking black. A second pressure pushed in on his chest accompanied by a sharp metallic popping sound and a splattering of something warm and moist on his face. He reeled forward, pulling himself back into firing position, trying to focus his eyes. Through the dark visor everything was blurred and it took him a moment to realize that there was a reddish smear across the visor.

Damn. Hit. Fucked up, just can't feel it yet. He had seen a lot of soldiers with horrible wounds who hadn't known that they were dying or even been hit. He tried to move his arm up to raise the visor and was surprised to find that it responded normally, no numbness or awkwardness. With his vision unobstructed by the besmattered face shield, he glanced down, afraid of what he might see. Jesus Christ! His entire chest protector was covered with a sickening film of red-smeared goo as if his flesh had been converted by some mangling force into a pulp of ground meat.

Can't be hit that bad. Still don't feel anything. A twinge of pain shot through his head. Well, almost nothing. The throbbing in his skull told him that despite the messy exterior, he was still capable of feeling pain. He wasn't dead yet. It clicked. The damned stuff splattered all over him *was* ground meat. He wiped some of the goo off his visor and licked it, savoring the taste of the tomato paste from the exploded spaghetti can. Laughter broke out, relieved, for a moment uncontrollable. The short seconds that had elapsed since he felt the first hammering impact against his head had carried the ship clear of the ground fire from the contested LZ, and Carl was thankful for small favors. Where the C-ration can had been snapped onto the side of his gun, there was now only a blurb of its contents. Sauce and noodles streaked the dark steel of the weapon, and the feed tray mechanism looked to be jammed with heat-baked noodles and beef. He snapped up the cover.

The tray and chamber were clogged with blackened food that had been pulled into the weapon while he was firing in that split second before the impact ripped his fingers away from the triggers. He peeled off one glove and jerked the closed bolt back, pulling some of the mess out with it. He half turned in his seat to reach for a small screwdriver that he kept in one of the seat pole brackets next to his operating rod persuasion device. At that moment, Jurgens, the freckle-faced rookie copilot, chose to glance back in his direction.

"Jesus Christ!" The sudden yelp caught everyone's

attention. "The crew chief's been hit," he almost shouted, jerking his head back in Carl's direction.

Chrissen didn't bother to look back, but quickly commanded the gunner to get to Carl's side.

Carl, recovered from Jurgens's yell, resisted the magnificent opportunity to have some fun with the others. Not a nice joke to play, at all. Besides, he reasoned, they would probably throw him out of the chopper once they found out that he was really okay. Instead, he keyed the mike before Rossi could get in motion.

"Negative on that hit, sir." He gave the open-mouthed copilot a big grin. "I'm covered with spaghetti." He wiped a streak of it off his chicken plate and sampled it to show the rookie that he hadn't been turned inside out. "Lousy bastard down there blew the shit out of my ammo feeder can."

Chrissen half turned in his seat, straining to get a glimpse of his crew chief. When he saw the chicken plate buffet, he broke out laughing. "Damn it to hell, Weird Willy, if you don't look like a dust-off case. No wonder my poor old rookie here thought you were hit. You sure you're really not hit somewhere under all that mess?"

"Don't think so, sir," Carl replied cheerfully. "Something smacked into my helmet and rang my bell for a few seconds, but I think I'm all right."

Chrissen nodded and turned back to the task of keeping the ship from midair mergers with the rest of the flight. The remaining minutes of the flight were spent by Carl in trying to clean up the gun, getting it back into working order for the next lift. After a difficult moment or two, a few choice words, and a scraped knuckle, he jacked the bolt back and forth a couple of times, chambering and ejecting rounds. Satisfied that it would work reasonably well until he had a chance to clean it out properly, he began cleaning up his own appearance, wiping off some of the paste, mostly just smearing it around. He finally gave up the effort in disgust just as the flight came down to pick up the second lift. The grunts didn't even seem to notice. Maybe they thought it was normal to wear their food for insect repellent or for camouflage.

They didn't look too concerned about their trip out into the jungle, and Carl figured they must have already gotten the same word that he had picked up on the radio. The first lift, after the initial flare of resistance, had swept the area clean, sending the NVA packing or neutralizing them.

Neutralize. Carl liked that one. It sounded so impersonal, but indicated a high degree of technical proficiency. A task to be done, an objective accomplished. He thought for a moment of all the meanings the word implied and smiled sardonically, considering the language differences of the soldiers and the big brass. The politicos and the top brass could soften or impersonalize the ugliness of the war with terms like neutralize, eliminate, terminate, and all the other big words. But it should be personal, hard, and "waste 'em" was as good a phrase as any. It all meant the same in the end, and the Game didn't care what dictionary was used.

A sudden image of a drill sergeant flashed through his head, bringing another smile. An image of the DI yelling at his assembled recruits, "What is the spirit of the bayonet?" and the obedient maggots yelling back hoarsely, "To neutralize!" Just didn't have the right ring to it. The bloodlust response that Carl and a million others had savagely screamed back, "To *kill*!" was what it was all about. A personal matter to him, this killing of men. Each time, a small personal triumph, their guns against his, and for the moment he was still alive, not defeating the Game, merely existing, surviving within its fluid boundaries.

"Now, that's a helmet to be worn when telling war stories," Chrissen said, blue eyes twinkling in the bright sunlight. He tapped Carl on the top of the helmet. "You're damn lucky it didn't take your head off."

Carl pulled off the fiberglass helmet, inspecting the damage for the first time. He let out a low whistle, tracing the entry gouge and the furrow that started near the top center of the helmet and followed the curvature over and down, coming out of the back of the headpiece. He had heard of such strange hits before, even knew a gunner in the third platoon who had taken a hit like this in the helmet. He examined the point of entry more closely. No biggie. Even if it had hit him, it probably wouldn't have been much more than a scalp crease. But it damned sure looked impressive! "Hell, sir, I lead a charmed life. Too handsome to die," he laughed.

The rhythmical *whop-whop-whop* of a single approaching ship drew their attention. Carl recognized 372, Jolley's ship, from the off-color battery nose cover.

"Probably bringing in the brigade commander to check out the prisoner, see what kind of news they can get out of him in a hurry," Chrissen remarked, waving a greeting to Lieutenant Richter, 372's pilot.

The ship set down a short distance from the rest of the flight, and while Jolley and Kurtz moved up to open the pilots' doors, the brigade commander remained in the ship, headset on, waving one arm and evidently engaging in a highly animated discussion with someone. A moment later, he jumped out of the ship and stomped toward the fire base. Even from where he stood, Carl could tell that the full bird was pissed off about something.

After the big honcho was clear of the area, Carl grabbed his helmet and headed for Jolley's ship, eager to show off this latest close call. Approaching the ship with an air of nonchalance, he carelessly tossed the helmet back and forth, one hand to the other, and whistled a little tune until the sound of angry voices reached him.

Jolley and Kurtz spotted him at the same moment. Jolley, with a big grin on his face, motioned him not to come any closer, slapped Kurtz on the shoulder with a "follow me" gesture, and started out to meet Carl. Behind them, on the other side of the ship, Carl could see Richter angrily talking to Sorden. He couldn't make out the words, but it sounded like Sorden was getting raked over the coals. Carl looked back at Jolley, who was still smiling and rubbing his hands gleefully. Sorden must have really screwed up good this time.

Less than ten yards separated the crew chiefs when Carl heard it. That high-pitched whine that heralded the onslaught of a mortar barrage, fired from hidden tubes somewhere in the surrounding jungle.

Jolley had heard it, too, and in that split second between the hearing and the impact of the shells, both men dove to the ground.

"Incoming!"

The trailing part of the warning was drowned out by the explosions of the first mortars, which also covered the whistling scream of the next salvo coming to earth. His ears ringing from the first nearby blast, Carl raised his head just enough to jerk his helmet over his ears for better protection against shrapnel. The ground under his body seemed to be shaking, but he couldn't tell if it was from the explosions or his body trembling. No way of fighting back against this. Just stay put and ride it out. He forced himself to stay calm and resist the urge to jump up and try to run for shelter. Through the ringing in his ears and the now somewhat muffling effect of the helmet, he could hear people yelling somewhere.

A nearby blast that definitely shook the earth under him made him press closer to the ground, wishing at that instant that mother earth could absorb him. Dirt and rocky chunks rained down over him, and for a moment he couldn't hear anything. Then the screaming broke through the blocking deafness.

The screaming turned into a hoarse, tortured cry, and Carl twisted his head toward where Jolley and Kurtz had gone to ground.

Rasping animal noises were escaping from Kurtz's mouth as he thrashed crazily on the ground, writhing in agony, his right arm ending at the elbow in a stub of red and slick white bone.

For a second Carl stared uncomprehendingly at the scene, wondering why Jolley didn't move to help his gunner.

"Jolley!" The scream ripped out of his throat as he scrambled across the twenty-five feet that separated them. "Jolley!" He reached the old-timer's side, dropping to his knees, ignoring the fall of the mortar fire.

Jolley was lying spread-eagle on his back just a few feet

away from Kurtz, who was only moaning, babbling, now. The ground was already soaking up the crew chief's blood, a large pool spreading around the head and upper shoulders, enriching the earth as it stained it.

Carl's numbing mind could only manage one low curse. Jolley's head was almost completely severed from his neck. Only a ragged strand of skin and flesh still connected the head to the body. For a moment Carl felt the blood rushing, pounding with a fiery heat into his own head, and he wavered, fighting to maintain self-control. A groan from Kurtz cut through the fog and brought him back to the task of saving the still living. He forced his eyes from the grotesquely twisted head of his old comrade. He moved quickly to the gunner's side, drilling his concentration on the soldier's arm, taking action to keep his brain in motion.

Somewhere in his skull, he became aware that the shelling had stopped and more voices were cutting into him, men yelling, running, the confusion and chaotic action slowing back down to what passed for normal. The crackling of flames nearby also registered.

"Must've hit one of the choppers," he muttered, surprising himself with the tightly controlled sound of his own voice. Unnaturally calm. Good old adrenaline.

He forced Kurtz to stay on his back and cut away a piece from the gunner's other sleeve with his survival knife. Kurtz stared up at him, no sign of recognition in the dark eyes. He was still babbling, nothing intelligible, just a drooling noise. Carl wrapped the length of sleeve around the arm just above the elbow and knotted it, using the knife handle for leverage to shut off the blood flow. Footsteps running toward him made him look up.

Lieutenants Richter and Sorden were almost there. Richter slowed up, took a quick glance at Jolley, and then bent to help Carl lift Kurtz. Once they had gotten the gunner to his feet, Richter lifted him on his own and started for the chopper with him.

Sorden was just standing there staring stupidly at Jolley when Carl picked up Kurtz's forearm a few feet away and held it out by the wrist to Sorden. The beefy officer looked at Carl questioningly without making any move to take the wretched piece of flesh.

Carl impatiently flipped it to him, almost smiling at the panicky look that flared into the lieutenant's eyes as he caught the arm on instinct. Sorden took a stumbling step backward, turning unsteadily to leave, and almost stepped on Jolley's corpse. Catching himself, he cautiously side-stepped around it as if somehow afraid of the death it portrayed.

Sorden's eyes caught Carl's for a brief second, and Carl saw the fear in them. "Where's your fuckin' camera now, you son of a bitch?" Carl put the question to him threateningly, grimly pressing out each word for emphasis. "Go on, get the damned thing and come on back and take a picture . . . and I'll kill you."

Just the two of them. No one else to hear or see. And Sorden saw hate in those eyes. Hate and the reality of the threat. He backed away, spun awkwardly, and struggled back to his ship after the pilot.

Turning his back on the retreating officer, Carl knelt down next to Jolley's lifeless body. He wanted to cry, to let the anger, the sorrow, go from his mind, but the tears wouldn't come.

"Dammit, Jolley," he said softly, staring at the ruined head. The old crew chief's dashing handlebar mustache was matted with his drying blood. The mirror-lensed glasses lay close by, one of the silver teardrops shattered, reflecting fragmented images. He slid one arm under Jolley's legs and carefully worked the other arm under the armpit, twisting to cradle the dangling head in one hand. He carefully rose, gripping the chief's sandy hair, and carried his friend back to 372, where Richter and Sorden were making preparations to lift off.

Richter was in the cargo bay trying to get Kurtz comfortable. Sorden was in the pilot's seat. Richter took Jolley's legs and gently lowered him onto the silver-gray floor panels. Richter's eyes met Carl's.

"Sorry, Weird." There wasn't much else to say. Jolley

had been around in the unit for a long time. He had been friend to many, officer and enlisted alike, people who had shared the edge of life and death with him.

Carl nodded and stepped back wordlessly as the engine began to hum and the rotors started their buildup. Out of the corner of his eye he saw Sorden staring at him. No longer the arrogant sneer. There was still a shot of fear in those eyes, and Carl wondered if he was the sole cause of it. Something wasn't right. Richter had been hollering at the butterbar just before the attack came. He shrugged his shoulders, suddenly feeling drained, empty. The reaction was setting in, and he walked back to his own ship on rubbery legs, trying to think about what was going on with the rest of the flight, channeling his energies and thoughts away from Jolley.

One ship had taken a direct hit farther down the line where the first platoon had landed their ships. Nothing left of it now, except for a pile of ash and a section of the tail boom. Looked like they had enough people around there to handle things. Someone had hooked a lump of charred meat and was pulling it out of the fringe of the ashes. Carl wondered what had happened to the rest of the crew. He hoped they were some of the men standing around stomping out the burning grass near the wreckage.

At his own ship nobody said anything. They had seen what happened after the shelling stopped and knew there was nothing that really could be said. They all went quietly about their work, checking out the ship for any damage from the attack. Carl studied the ship carefully until the wave crashed into him. The legs suddenly would not support him anymore, the lungs closed up, refusing to let the air work its way through the body, while his throat tightened painfully, wrenching one long gasping sob from him. He sat down quickly, before he lost control of his legs, and let the flood pour out.

A cold rage burned through Carl's veins as he turned over the rumor he had just heard, piecing it together with what he had seen.

Word was going around that the unusual midday mortar attack might have been drawn out by a certain second lieutenant who, in a flagrant breach of radio security, had announced that they were bringing in the brigade commander, identifying him by name and rank instead of using the colonel's call sign. Those tubes could have been there for some time, just waiting for the right moment, and had seized upon that target of opportunity.

It all fit together. The colonel had acted pissed off about something. Richter had been jumping in Sorden's shit for some reason, and Jolley had thought something was pretty funny. And Sorden's reaction, the wide-eyed fear, for good reason.

In his mind, Carl had already fixed the guilt, but some part of his brain told him to verify the rumor. How? He couldn't very well walk right up to Sorden and put the question to him and expect a truthful answer. Neither would Richter be likely to tell him. Jolley was dead and Kurtz was probably halfway back to the World by now. Somebody at the fire base operations center would know, though. He wanted the next log mission going out to Grayson. If the rumor was true, then Sorden was quite likely responsible for the deaths of three men and the wounding of several more, including Kurtz, maimed for life. And if it was true, Carl grimly resolved that there would be a fourth death. Sorden would die in Vietnam, a victim of enemy fire, one way or another. He looked down at the spare barrel bag under the edge of his cot, thinking about the AK-47 resting in it. And there would be plenty of time. The rage wasn't a burning flash, short-lived and then extinguished. It was an icy fire that would last for a lifetime.

XVII.

Sixty-five days before his first year ended. He wondered what the World would be like. Probably hadn't changed much. They didn't hear a lot about what was going on stateside. The Pacific edition of the *Stars and Stripes* wasn't designed to cover all the news in the world, and the letters from home didn't tell much about what was happening outside of the home. That leave was still two months away and a lot could happen in that time. Jolley had been down to less than sixty days when he bought it.

Since that day, the Game had become a more personal duel, with Carl's life in the balance. Before Jolley's death, Carl had always assumed, except for frozen moments in time, that he would always survive whatever was thrown at him. Now he wasn't so sure, and he still had a mission to accomplish.

He had gotten back out to the fire base and had located the soldier who had been on the radios that day. The young private had been more than happy to relate what had happened and confirmed the rumor. Evidently, though, no official action was going to be taken. Poor judgment, radio security breach, coincidental attack, nothing further. Carl could wait a little longer.

Enemy activity continued at a near-feverish pitch through most of April, more assaults on fire bases, more ships getting hit.

Lieutenant Rawls was speaking to the remnants of his flight platoon, now short four men because of the month's shooting-gallery activities.

"Gentlemen, I'll make it short and simple," he began,

his bushy, red walrus mustache hiding the movement of his upper lip. "We've got a big mission tomorrow, not just the platoon, but the whole company and then some." He waited for a moment while the buzz rippled through the men. "Wake up at 0400, lift at 0500. Ten cans of ammunition for each gunner and crew chief in addition to full minigun cans. Sergeant Wells has already given your crew assignments." He paused and looked to the tall staff sergeant, who nodded affirmatively. "Each man will draw a C-ration meal from the mess hall at breakfast. It's going to be a long day, so get some rest tonight. Pilots will give you the rest of the details tomorrow, after they get them. That's all."

It was still dark, but warm, when Wells came through the hootch to roust everyone out. Carl snapped awake instantly and dressed quickly, joining the heavy traffic to the latrines and washbasins. A quick shave, minor nicks, and he was on his way to the mess hall. Breakfast at this hour was even more tasteless than usual, but it satisfied the needs and he picked his favorite Cs for the day.

His gunner for the mission was one of the platoon's newer replacements. Pfc Ryan looked like he should still be in high school back in Iowa or wherever the short, red-haired kid hailed from. Not a particularly impressive-looking specimen, but he would have to do. Carl had worked with a lot of rookies since becoming crew chief and never put too much trust in any of them until he had flown with them at least five or six times. Ryan seemed likable enough, but the weak chin and short stature made Carl hope that the kid was tougher than he looked. He wasn't real pleased with another part of his team, either.

Sorden was already at the ship with Olsen, the black pilot's face almost invisible in the early morning darkness. This was the first time since Jolley's death that Sorden had been on his ship, and the thought sprang to mind easily. Big mission, probably real hot, lots of ships, people shooting everywhere. Problem . . . how to do it without endangering the others? Patience. Wait and see.

He smiled unpleasantly at Sorden in the flashing bursts of

the running lights. He hoped the lieutenant felt uncomfortable and tried to think of some mind-fuck games to play with the man.

All up and down the lines of revetments, the company's ships were starting to crank, and there was a flurry of activity across the runway where one of their neighboring helicopter companies was located. It looked like every flyable chopper in Tay Ninh was getting ready to move out. As a dull glow began to spread across the eastern sky, he could see more ships moving into a line behind his company and could hear their sister company's call signs on the air. Had to be Cambodia.

As if reading his mind, Olsen came across on the intercom. "Cambodia, troops. The man in the White House says we can hit 'em. Practically every ship in the division is going in. Can you imagine what the NVA are gonna think when they look up and see a couple of hundred choppers coming down on them?"

Yeah, Carl could imagine it. They'd probably go apeshit. This was one that nearly all the GIs in the border provinces had long awaited, whether they were grunts, armor, or fliers. The chance to storm in on Charlie's sanctuary and really kick ass had only been a dream until now. Maybe after this the NVA wouldn't feel quite so smug when they tried to pull back across a border to escape pursuit.

"How long is this play going for, sir?"

"According to our final briefing, fearless leader in the big house over the ocean has given the green light on a two-month operation. Got to be out by the end of June, but what the hell. It ought to shake them up pretty good. The ARVN are already inside, but I don't know what they're doing."

A cackle from the radios signaled that the lift-off hour had come, and in steady sequence the ships came up, by platoons, companies, a huge mass of flying machines migrating west. Carl had never seen so many ships in the air at one time, and a warming thrill ran through him. This was history. He was helping to make it. Maybe not the

D-Day invasion or the Marines at Iwo Jima, but this was about as close as he would ever get.

Once in the air, things began to move quickly. The ships split into several groups, each heading to designated fire bases to pick up the infantry for the assault. Choppers were fun, but to take ground the infantry had to be there.

They swarmed aboard, faces lit up with eagerness, a hint of nervousness, fear here and there. Understandable. This could be a real field day for the Americans, or it could turn into a turkey shoot for the NVA. It was an enormous operation and the little brown men had a damn good intelligence network. If they knew what was coming, it could be a real trial. He looked over the helmets and faces of the soldiers to where Sorden was. Maybe, just maybe, his old reputation for losing copilots would reassert itself today. No guilt. If an enemy bullet were to put Sorden out of everyone's misery, fine. If not, he intended to do it himself. Murder, murder without remorse. He was only slightly surprised at how easy it was to contemplate. Would it be that easy when the time came? Patience.

A veteran buck sergeant wearing an NVA canvas ammo pouch grinned at him. ''Numbah one hunting today!'' he shouted above the roar of the engines.

Carl smiled back and patted his machine gun, an old and comfortable friend. ''Right on! Gonna kick ass and take names!''

Last time, it had been a small recon mission with secrecy as a prime consideration. This time they were going right into the heart of the enemy's strongholds. Lots of little brown dudes down there with lots of big guns. On the command channel he could hear the lead ship advising about the arty prep that was going into their target LZ. He leaned out into the tugging air, squinting against the rushing force. Smoke pluming up in the distance marked the spot. Hope they're blowing the hell out of them. Of course, the artillery would alert the NVA that something unusual was happening, but the confusion and the short reaction time should play well for the assault.

''They've been doing that for quite a while now,''

Olsen remarked. "The prep started out early with B-52 strikes and then this." He paused for a mock dramatic flair. "And finally, we sweep down upon them, the heavy hand of retribution!"

Well, let's get to retributin', Carl thought. He could hear the C and C bird directing the flight, breaking it up into sections, ordering the descent. His ship was in the first section, and as they started down, the Cobras materialized, a group of six, three on each side of the flight. Get some, Carl sent a mental wish.

The artillery fire stopped and the lift ships streaked down, leveling out a scant fifty feet over the treetops, racing for the LZ as the first pair of gunships whipped past them higher up, loosing their fury of fire.

"Gunners, engage any targets, fire at will!"

Almost simultaneously with the firing order, Carl saw things that he had never seen in the jungles before. Surprised but acting, he swung his barrel down and opened up on the olive-green military-looking truck that he had spotted.

"Trucks right under us!" he rapped out excitedly, squeezing off a fast burst into the vehicle. "There's some kind of road down there," he added, continuing to fire into the jungle highway that was only partially concealed by the upper canopy of the jungle.

As the truck flashed out of sight, away from his visible field of fire, he heard the reports coming in over the radio from the ships ahead of him. They were starting to receive sporadic ground fire. His ship crossed the edge of the treeline into the vast clearing and he saw for himself the lack of resistance to their initial thrust. Only a few isolated muzzle flashes and they were being smothered by the gunships.

Leaning out over the edge, Carl checked out the landing area by sight and by ripping up the surrounding turf with his gun. No traps were visible and the probing bullets failed to detonate anything. The NVA had missed a good bet when they didn't put up any defense at this point. Very anticlimactic.

The grunts lunged off the ships into the high grass, and

the ships flocked back into the sky without incident. Not anything to get the old adrenaline flowing, disappointing in a way when a big fight was anticipated. For Carl at least. Some, he knew, were breathing great gulping sighs of relief right now. But the danger, the fighting, was what it was all about. When the shooting was in full swing, both directions, there was a feeling in Carl of such intense emotional inflow and outflow, a swirling current of life force, that it was unequaled by any other experience he had ever encountered. That essence, the awareness of life while death stood by, was like a natural high, and coming down was the reaction to what the body had felt. He knew how easy it was to lose yourself in those moments, seeing nothing but your target, and wondered if that sensation was kin to the berserker's rage of the Vikings, those fierce warriors who had terrorized the coasts of Europe a thousand years earlier. He liked the comparison, but today there would be no rage, no violent flood of bloodletting.

More lifts, and more lifts. The thrill of the big invasion wore off quickly as the mission became routine insertions. During one break the news came around that the infantry sweeps were meeting very little resistance, but were already reporting huge finds of weapons, munitions, medical supplies, and rice. Word also had it that some of the cache sites showed evidence that someone knew the Americans were coming and had taken out the larger guns. No wonder they weren't hitting much resistance. Charlie had been tipped and pulled back his biggest equipment and most of the troops, leaving only a few security units to slow down the GIs.

Only once during the day did Carl get a decent opportunity to engage some of the left-behinds, and even while he was blasting away at the hidden machine-gun position, a Cobra rolled in on it with a brace of rockets and obliterated the offending Charlies.

"Glad someone's having a good time," he muttered, disgustedly firing off a stream into the jungle at nothing in particular.

* * *

Day followed routine day. Most of the assaults were over, and the Hueys were being restricted to mostly logistical missions. Take some C rations here, a mailbag there, this platoon needs more frags. And take away Charlie's toys! Every day they loaded up the ships with piles, small mountains of captured stocks. Carl checked it all out, looking for some more goodies. Most of the equipment was brand-new, grease-covered with precise little Chinese markings. A few older, worn-looking weapons were loaded up from time to time, mostly Russian-made AKs, but the majority of the RPDs, mortar tubes, and assault rifles were Chicoms.

The constant strain of long hours of flight became a gnawing, eroding drain on man and machine. Carl knew that there was some regulation about how many hours pilots were supposed to fly in a given period of time, but nobody had ever paid any attention to it. They still didn't. The total concentration of effort needed to keep the ships flying was being sorely tested. Day's-end landings became clumsy affairs, maintenance crews worked themselves ragged into the small hours of the night, chiefs and gunners were slower on their responses. But somehow they survived. Ships took hard landings, bullet holes, blade strikes, engine failures, and men walked away. Nobody in the company died and the only injury came during a night mortar attack on Tay Ninh. Still a few Charlies lurking around the door while most of the action was in the neighbor's yard. Cilino, one of Carl's contemporaries and down to his last three weeks, took a foot-long piece of shell-shattered board right in the ass. The wound was painful in the extreme, and Cilino had thought he was dying just as he was getting short. The platoon's hilarity at his discomfort only pissed him off.

New guys continued to form a steady stream into the unit, leaving a large number of combat-untested crewmen to replace the old-timers. Kids who had only been in the unit for a couple of months but who had gone through the cycle of action just prior to the invasion were almost considered old veterans. And the stories that the new kids were bringing in! Carl had heard brief mention in the *Stars and Stripes* of some of the things, and knew that a lot of people were against the war, but some of the tales were almost incredible.

"Can you believe that shit, Weird?" Riglos asked, raking oily fingers through the gritty, sand-colored hair. "Bunch of NGs running around shooting college kids. Guess this tourist trip of ours into Cambodia really stirred up some people."

Carl nodded his head slowly. The talk had been circulating for several days about some Kent State place where National Guardsmen had opened fire on student protesters. Reaction in the platoon had been mixed.

"Shoot all them fuckin' protesters!"

"I'd be protesting this damn war right now if I hadn't been drafted."

Carl wasn't sure where he stood on the matter. The only thing that he understood was that the people protesting the invasion of the "neutral" country didn't understand what it was like along the border. They didn't seem to know or care that Americans were dying in attacks launched from that same neutral nation. He wasn't real sure that he wanted to bother with his thirty-day extension leave. Not if people were going to be spitting and screaming at him.

Carl marked through day eleven on his short-timer's calendar. The wild-eyed figure, almost completely covered now with colorful patches, had an oversize helmet covering most of his head and a set of combat boots that reached clear up to his neck. In a way, the calendar was a lie, but Carl kept it blocked in for tradition's sake. Hell, he was coming back for six more months. Got to get short all over again. But with a little more rank now.

The army, in its infinite wisdom, had decided that he ought to be a Spec 5 if he was going to stay on in the tropical paradise, and the platoon leader had given him his stripes the night before in a brief ceremony. No wild party or foolishness. Too tired for that. Here you are, congratulations, thank you very much, lift-off at 0500.

The promotion board had been very informal the month before and the chances of not getting a promotion had been slim indeed. More money. A whole five hundred bucks a month, counting the overseas pay, combat pay, and flight pay. At least there were no taxes to worry about. He thought they might be earning their combat pay again. In the last week things had started to heat up. NVA units were pressing the line troops and their bases. The entire world knew that Nixon had promised that the invasion would be a limited one and that all Americans would be out of Cambodia by the end of June. That date was fast approaching and the operators in Hanoi knew that if the GI pullback could be delayed by even one day, they would have a tremendous propaganda victory. Carl could just see Uncle Ho denouncing the imperialist dogs who wouldn't even abide by their own declarations.

These political considerations had a tangible effect on Carl. Such effect being that with four days left to get all GIs out, Carl had to work with an extraction of an infantry company back to its Cambodian fire base and from there back into the Republic. Down to eleven days and the dinks wanted to play games.

Carl wouldn't have minded so much, but the company he had to keep grated on his nerves. Still, that, too, might work out for the best.

"Some really bad stuff out there, sir?" Carl asked Jurgens.

The stocky pilot nodded, smiling. "Man as short as you shouldn't be out on this kind of trip, Weird." Then the smile faded and reality voiced. "One, maybe two battalions of NVA have got these guys pretty well pinned down and are staying right on top of the grunts. Making it tough for air support, even for the gunships."

They had been in tight situations before, pulling troops out of the boonies just ahead of the enemy. "No sweat, sir. Our ship won't have any trouble. I'm too short for this unit to get shot up."

"You ain't short until you're out of here," Sorden snorted.

Carl grinned unpleasantly at the fat officer, thinking exactly the same thing about Sorden. He interpreted Sorden's remark as "Hope you die, fucker," but he didn't care. "I know I'll make it," he said carelessly. "Will you?"

The gunner popped in with the ammunition, and Carl helped the Sad Sack load up the heavy weight. Pfc Slaker hadn't changed much in the months he had been there. His uniforms were still baggy enough to hold three men his size, and even the smallest flight helmets available wobbled loosely on his head. Not very creative, probably wouldn't last long on his own if they ever got shot down and separated, but he made a good follower. Did what was asked, hard or dirty, always with that goofy-looking smile.

Carl slapped him on the back as they loaded up the last of the ammo cans and motioned for him to climb aboard. Time to go.

In the air the flight was joined by the slim-bodied protectors, two sections of gunships. Their shark mouths smiled hungrily as they cruised through the higher currents of the invisible ocean.

Below the humming ships were a seemingly infinite number of bomb craters, dotting the landscape like a thousand carefully constructed circular swimming pools, with azure-blue water catching the sunlight and mirroring it back to the heavens. Newer craters stood out distinctively with their light-colored halos of earth surrounding them, sometimes overlapping into the older craters and the green carpet ringing them. Mother nature was working constantly to try to heal the scars of the war, and Carl knew that if the bombing ever quit, it would only be a matter of ten years or so before the giant craters became just shallow depressions and then the jungle would reclaim them completely. If the bombing ever quit. It was already the longest conflict in the history of the United States. Carl remembered a science fiction book by Edgar Rice Burroughs about a faraway planet where two nations had fought each other for centuries, the only legacy from one generation to the next being the continuous destruction of improving technology. Would that be Vietnam's fate, war unending?

The flight leader's instructions for the staggered trail approach broke into his musings, and he watched as the other ships slid into their slots. Good clear field of fire this way, but spread out. Listening to the radio traffic made Carl's blood start to speed up as he got the picture more clearly. The flight was going to come in directly over the enemy-held section of the LZ, fast and hard, with as much suppressive fire as the gunners could put out. Down quickly into the far end of the clearing where the grunts were, and some of the NVA as well, load 'em on and get the hell out, straightaway from the ground fire. That meant that Carl's ship, flying as tail-end Charlie, would be closest to the heaviest concentrations of NVA and their weapons. Maybe the Cobras would make them keep their heads down. While the Hueys hit from one direction, the gunships would be coming in from the opposite direction, giving the whole thing the look of some kind of military flying drill. He had never seen an operation worked out quite like this one was supposed to go. Sounded good the way Jurgens passed it on. But then, recruiters sounded good, too.

Carl took a deep breath, letting it out slowly, thumped his chicken plate to make sure that it hadn't gone anywhere, and steadied himself. The lead ships hit the clearing, and even before the chopper guns went hot, Carl heard the chatter of the Chicoms opening up on them. He half crouched over his gun in his compressed kingdom and angled his barrel down, trying to pick up on the sharp, crackling reports of AKs being fired straight up at the ships. Then his ship broke over the clearing and the flashes from dozens of guns in the treeline revealed the enemy's determination to make this operation a real bitch. No difficulty in finding a target, just point and spray.

A hundred typewriters rattling, each tapping out the same message of finality. His entire world narrowed down to the flashing muzzle fires and flitting shadows in the jungle that could only be the NVA moving forward. He kept the triggers back, no need for the prescribed short bursts, and poured an unbreaking stream of fire at the shadowy figures and the pulsing lights.

"Coming down. Keep firing but watch for friendlies your side, Sad Sack. They should be breaking out any second now!" Jurgens's voice was broken, excited.

Sad Sack cleared the right, Carl cleared the left and kept on firing, shifting his aim further to the rear as the ship settled down and was stormed by the grunts, sprinting from cover despite their heavy loads. Carl heard the snapping fire of their M-16s as they joined the gunners in trying to keep the enemy down. Another section of Cobras made their pass, unloading a salvo of rockets into a section of the jungle's edge where Carl was concentrating his own fire as the ship hovered up and forward. The rockets blasted just inside the fringe, blowing out a tattering rain of dirt and vegetation along with one black-clad form, tumbling and rolling to a stop. Carl laced the still figure, jerking the body with his hits, just for good measure, and then shifted back into the trees.

The flight worked past the danger point and broke hard to the left, giving Carl a chance to relax some and check around. His passengers certainly seemed a happy bunch. Out of the fire. He listened in as the flight leader checked out his gaggle for damage. Pretty damn lucky. No major damage on any ships, and by some miracle, despite the heavy volume of enemy fire, there had been no casualties except for a couple of the grunts with minor wounds from the short dash to the ships. Incredible. But as he continued to listen, other news, not so good, came over the air.

The ground commander was relaying a constant stream of rapidly changing status reports. With his force cut in half now, the NVA pressure was becoming heavier.

Jurgens was also following the reports carefully. "We picked up a few holes, Weird, but nothing to worry about. Let's try to keep it that way. Things are heating up on the ground, so cover us tight. Quick turn around here, so don't relax too much."

Carl grinned and clicked his mike button twice. He was looking over the grunts at Sorden. The copilot looked absolutely scared from this angle, his face slightly turned toward the instrument panel. Sorden had raised his visor now that they were away from the LZ and was wiping sweat from his puffed-out face.

The flight dropped down to the relative security of the fire base, where waiting Chinooks would take the troops the last leg of their journey back to Vietnam. The grunts tumbled out, laughing and smiling. One of them reached past Carl's gun and took his hand, shaking it enthusiastically, yelling a word of thanks. Great to be appreciated. He watched the man's retreating form as the ships began to move out and wondered how many of the men they had just pulled out had been saved just to die in some other meaningless place of jungle and craters.

He considered his own mortality as the ships winged back to the disputed LZ. He had often thought that he would have some premonition of death's coming, some Seeger-like vision of his own rendezvous with the Master of the Game. The image of a dying, crazed Wiley could easily be his personal harbinger of the dark shadow, but that nightmarish visitor hadn't intruded upon him in quite some time. He wondered briefly if it would be better to know when your time was up or to be happily unaware of the final moment. Then the approach to the LZ for the final extraction commanded all of his attention.

The Cobras were still working out, had been, in fact, for the entire time, trying to retard Charlie's advance and suppress his fire. The ten lift ships hit the clearing, adding the fire of twenty guns to the effort, crinkling Carl's nose with the acrid air. The air was heavy with the biting smell of burned powder and Carl loved it.

More muzzle flashes than before, closer to the landing area, lashed out their hungry tongues of flame, searching, reaching for life to feed upon. Carl responded in kind, trying to brush back the probes from the gauntlet of fire. Above the sounds of the engines and his own gun he could hear the crackling fire of the enemy and the slapping sounds of rounds punching through the fragile skin of his ship.

"Coming down!" Jurgens spoke loudly, a tremor in the voice, showing the strain of his efforts.

Down? Here? Too fuckin' close! "Clear down left! Charlie's right on our ass!" He kept the triggers back, aware that his gunner was still alive from the sound of his gun going nonstop. The blood was starting to pound now, images flooding in like slide projections. The ship rocking as soldiers desperately scrambled on, hitting the skids before the ship touched the ground.

At the same moment, Sad Sack's voice screamed through the ship's intercom, almost incoherently. "Gooks coming! Gooks! Get us outa here!"

The gunner's fire sputtered, and Carl could hear hoarse shouting, M-16 fire from inside the ship, and the sharp crack of AKs firing from close range. Then Sad Sack's gun opened up again, rattled off a sporadic series of bursts, and stopped.

"I'm hit! Help me, Weird! Goddamn! Help me!"

Carl screamed at one of the grunts as Jurgens started to lift the ship. "Get my gunner! He's hit!"

The sweat-soaked soldier nodded and turned toward Sack's position. Carl heard someone scream above the gunfire in the confined hell of the helicopter.

"Get him!"

"Jesus . . ."

The screams were cut short by a deafening explosion that jerked the ship like a model on a string being yanked violently. The ship was shoved sideways and half rolled up on its left skid, bodies sliding and tumbling out of the cargo bay, chased by an intense light flash and a second explosion.

A giant hand threw Carl out of his cubbyhole, ripping his hand away from the machine-gun triggers. One hand grabbed at the AK that he had placed next to him, and it accompanied him on his chaotic, tumbling flight to the ground. Somewhere a gear in time slipped, and everything went into slow, painfully slow, motion. Even in the act of tumbling through the brief airspace, photographic images registered in his brain. Click. The rotor blade biting down into the dirt, gouging a hole before the fragile honeycombed blade snapped. Click. Frightened faces, cartwheeling torsos, arms and legs flailing in the air as the helicopter disgorged its contents.

The impact of the ground almost knocked the wind out of him, but he tried to control his roll and almost came up on his feet, only to be crushed to the ground by the weight of one of the grunts slamming into him. The screaming all around, the roar of the guns, sent a swelling tide of fear through him, almost a tangible object trying to grip him, and for a moment he forced himself to lie flat, regain control. The grunt who had crashed into him rolled away.

Somebody grabbed his shoulder, shaking him and yelling above the din of the surrounding battle. Carl shook off the hand, indicating to the person that he was able to move.

"Get to another chopper!" the soldier shouted, on his knees, firing over Carl's head at a target somewhere in the trees.

Carl twisted suddenly, trying to locate his ship. It was still there, having settled back on the skids after recovering from the half roll. The entire right half of the ship seemed to be in flames, but there was still movement inside from the pilot's seat, and Carl launched himself forward. He clawed at the door, threw it open, and helped the struggling Jurgens get out of the jammed harness. The flames were lapping at the back of the pilot's head, searing away the hair not covered by the helmet, and the pilot threw himself out of the ship as the safety harness separated, crashing into Carl and sending him sprawling to the hard ground again. Jurgens regained his feet first, pulled Carl to his feet, and yelled at him to move out. Carl glanced at the burning inferno that had been his ship, but Jurgens yanked on his arm.

"They're gone! Let's get the hell out of here!"

Carl's glance had told him as much. Most of the ship was a roaring blaze, and through the heat distortion and shooting flames he could see the outline of Sorden's form, still strapped in his seat, head slumped forward. Where the Sack should have been there was nothing but white heat. He joined the pilot and the surviving grunts in a rush for the nearest ships.

Two of the infantrymen were skip-running as fast as the burden of a wounded comrade would allow, while a fourth soldier held back, giving covering fire to his buddies. Jurgens stooped and grabbed up a fifth man, obviously dead, and Carl fell in with the cover man, adding his AK fire to the grunt's as they retreated.

This is fuckin' crazy, a voice inside him was yelling. Turn around and run, you stupid shit! This ain't some John Wayne movie. He kept on firing, short bursts, calmly aware that he had only the one magazine in the rifle, but also aware of the beautiful gunships that were rolling in, trying to take the heat off the retreating men. Even in that moment of fear, he thought he had never seen such a gorgeous sight as those slender-bodied merchants of death.

All too soon, the bolt on the Chinese-made weapon locked back and then Carl gave in to that screaming voice in his head. With a warning shout to the grunt, he turned and raced for the safety of the ships.

The grunt waved him off, emptied the contents of his magazine toward the jungle, and joined in the headlong flight.

Carl couldn't feel any sensation in his legs in that final burst of speed, but the rest of his body was making up for it. His lungs seemed to have carried the fire from the ship with them, and the pounding in his head threatened to explode through his temples.

Don't let 'em shoot me in the back. Don't let 'em shoot me in the back. The ship was almost in reach. Suddenly hands were grabbing at him, pulling, grasping at him urgently as the chopper's skids lifted off the ground. The grunt, a step behind Carl, jumped for the skids, arms outstretched, slipped a foot off the runners, and grabbed Carl's legs, slamming his rifle into Carl's knee. Carl gritted his teeth and hung on to the arms that were hanging on to him.

As the ship cleared the battle zone more hands reached out, and with considerable effort he was hauled into the ship along with the soldier. He flopped back against the transmission wall, next to the crew chief, a dude from the third platoon that he knew slightly. He grinned weakly, trying to pull his reserves together before he got the shakes. His legs were already beginning to quiver with that sickening rubbery feeling. It occurred to him that he might be hurt, but a quick scan didn't reveal any damage other than a skinned knee and a few rips in his uniform. The knee stung a little now, but the feeling passed with a weak wave of dizziness that rolled through him.

He looked around the ship, spotted the grunt who had been running behind him, and yelled at him. "Did you see what happened back there in the chopper? What hit us?"

The soldier, a young black, tired and grimy-looking, nodded. He shifted over a little closer to Carl. "Fuckin' dinks charged outa the bush, Jack. One of 'em nailed your gunner before we snuffed him. This other bastard jumps out of the trees with an RPG and pops us before we can get him, too. Shit, man, I thought we were all fuckin' dead," he said, shaking his head as if he couldn't believe that most of them had made it out.

Carl nodded his agreement with the unspoken thought and fell into silence, thinking about what they had left behind. The grunts were out, not all alive, but at least they were out. Back in the LZ were the remains of Sorden and Sad Sack, their ashes mixing with those of his dead ship. No more baggy-looking Sad Sack shuffling around the hootch. No more Sorden, either. He couldn't feel any loss from Sorden's death. Charlie had just saved him the trouble, but even though he had intended to kill the fat lieutenant, he hoped the man had bought it quick and clean, not by the burning.

He leaned back against the padded wall again and closed his eyes, floating with the ship, feeling the reassuring pulse of the blades. Damn.

SCOUTS

XVIII.

God, this felt better. Back again. Nam. Home. The World had been a terrific place to be for the first few days. Being back in his own house, seeing his parents, had been great at first, but then the conversation bogged down. What was there to say? "Gee, Mom, ten days ago one of my friends was burned to a cinder and they almost got me, too." No way. Mom didn't need to hear that kind of stuff. His father would have understood. He had been down that road before, but it still didn't make talking any easier.

That first night around the dinner table had been bad. His mother had hopefully asked if he was going to be stationed close to home. He had dreaded that kind of question. He hadn't written home about the extension, and now, face to face across the table, he had to tell them that he was going back for another six months. His mother started to cry, his father had just leaned back, arms folded across his chest, and looked at him. In the blue eyes was a mingling of pride and sadness.

Wandering around town looking up his old high school friends hadn't been any better. He ran into one of his former running mates who wanted to know where he had been keeping himself. When Carl told good old buddy Bill that he was just back from Nam, buddy Bill made some comment about how rough it must be over there, and then began telling him how tough it was in college.

After his fourth day back in the World his interest in it and the people dropped to about a half point above zero. He had taken to staying in the house most of the day, watching TV and drinking beer. The nights were more of the drinking in small bars, rediscovering round-eyed women, neither of which satisfied him. Too much missing. He could see it in the news at night.

Vietnam in live action, straight from the battlefields. More action from around the nation. Protesters, shouting, waving banners, filled the screens. He quit watching the TV. It all had seemed so trivial, so unimportant, compared with the reality of being there. He wanted to get back, and at night, in his fitful sleeps, he could feel the Nam calling to him in his dreams. They slipped into his unguarded mind at night and the recall was there every morning. The muzzle flashes were as bright as ever, the Cobras still diving in over the dark jungle. They were strangely undisturbing. More like messages than nightmares, from the unseen corners of his mind, giving him the missing ingredient of life.

The departure had been a tearful one for his parents. He had assured them that he would be okay, even made up a little lie for his mother's benefit about the kind of job that he was going back to. Just before turning to walk the final distance to the plane, his father had clasped his hand firmly. Carl could still remember the look in those eyes and the final words.

"We haven't talked much, son, but I think I know you pretty well. I just want you to know that I'm proud of what you're doing, and maybe even more important, I'm proud of what you haven't done."

XIX.

The hot sun of Vietnam soaked into him, warming him like the embrace of an old friend. He stood there quietly, taking in the brilliant blue sky, the familiar sights and sounds of the air traffic. The other rookies were already swearing at the heat as they struggled across the PSP strips with their duffel bags to the assembly area where they would be assigned to temporary barracks. After that they had the usual rookie work details to look forward to until they were sorted out and given their unit assignments.

He laughed at one new guy who tripped and fell, using his hands to break his fall, then bellowing at the touch of the hot metal. He recognized the kid as the same one who had sat next to him on the flight over. What an asshole. The kid had been full of questions. Wanted to know if Carl had "killed lots of gooks," and when Carl shrugged off the question, the kid kept on talking.

"Man, I'm going to kill a bunch of them little bastards. I hate those slanty-eyed fuckers, hate all of 'em," he had stated emphatically.

Carl had looked at the youngster quizzically, half amused. "You ain't even been there yet, slick. How come you already hate them?"

"Well, my brother was in Nam and he hated those gooks, so I hate them, too."

Whatever the kid had expected Carl to say to that, he didn't know. But the rookie did look a little shocked when Carl told him that his family heritage and intelligence level left a lot to be desired. Just the kind of liberators they needed in Nam. He hoped the kid would draw an assignment in some place where he wouldn't do much damage. There was already enough hate on both sides, some blind, some deserved, without adding more like this kid.

He cleared through the reception station and wandered around Bien Hoa's Castle Pad until he found a chopper that was going back to Tay Ninh.

It really was like coming home again. Being back in a chopper, even as a passenger, felt good. He loved the rush of the air against his face as the reliable old workhorse thumped its way across the sky, passing majestic Nui Ba Den. That towering mountain, jutting up from the earth like some ancient dragon's tooth, told him that home was near.

XX.

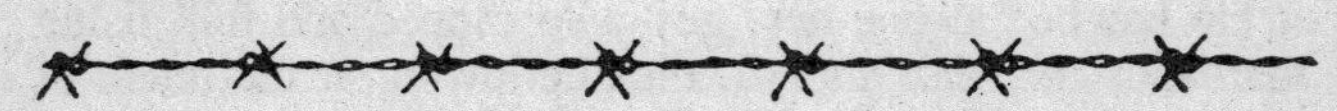

It was easy to identify the section of the base that belonged to the air cavalry troop, "A" Troop, 1st of the 9th Cav. The bright yellow crossed sabers with the squadron and regiment numbers were painted almost everywhere. The black Stetsons worn by most of the officers and quite a few of the enlisted men also served as a clue.

Carl found the orderly room, handed the clerk his orders, and was instructed to wait for the first sergeant. A wooden bench seemed to be the only seating facilities, so he sat back and relaxed, studying the walls of the orderly room. Along one red and white wall there were news articles and captured war materials, both proudly proclaiming the prowess and accomplishments of Apache Troop. Looked impressive. Just where he wanted to be.

A door marked "First Sergeant Grimes" creaked open, swirling a small puff of dust, and his new topkick stepped out into the room. He glanced quickly at Carl, took his folder from the clerk, and motioned to him.

"The captain's in right now, Specialist Willstrom, so you might as well see us both in one shot." He knocked on the CO's door, paused for a second, then opened the door and stepped in, Carl following. "New trooper here, sir. A Spec 5 Willstrom. Extension for the scout platoon from the 229th." He handed the commander the file and stepped to one side.

Carl stepped forward to the captain's desk, snapped to attention, saluted, and made his report.

"At ease, Willstrom. Have a seat, First Sergeant," he said, motioning toward the only extra chair in the room.

He looked Carl over for a moment, then opened up the file, scanning through the pages of army mumbo jumbo.

Carl took the opportunity, in turn, to study his new bosses. First Sergeant Grimes didn't exactly fit with his image of the typical army first sergeant. He appeared to be in his late thirties, light brown hair, and light blue eyes that just looked too damned cheerful for a topkick. He didn't have the traditional white sidewalls and looked to be a couple of inches shorter than Carl. The man was friendly-looking, not a common trait for first sergeants. But he was a soldier. Carl noted the CIB and the airborne wings above the pocket, and on the right shoulder he sported the winged-sword patch of the 173rd Airborne Brigade.

Captain McKenny looked more like he should be the sergeant. A craggy-faced individual, his closely cropped black hair made the hawk nose seem more prominent than a nose should be. Like the first sergeant, he was at least a second-tour man, wearing what was commonly called a "Cav sandwich," a 1st Cavalry Division patch on both shoulders. Looking at that reminded Carl that he, too, was now the filling for such a sandwich.

Captain McKenny looked up at Carl and settled back comfortably in his chair. "Looks good, Willstrom. We can always use men with solid experience. I see your extension request and approval is specifically for the scout section."

"Yes, sir!"

McKenny leaned forward, drumming his fingers on the worn desktop. "Any way we can convince you to change your mind?" Seeing the questioning look in Carl's eyes, he continued. "Here's our position, Willstrom. For a rare moment we've got a full-strength scout platoon, and our lift section, the Hueys, happen to be in need of a good crew chief. You've been a crew chief on those ships and we could use that experience." His eyes, a dark match with his hair, drilled into Carl. "On extension cases we always honor the man's request and I'm not going to order you into the lift platoon, but I do need to explain this. If you stick with scouts, you'll have to rotate with the other observers, not much flight time, maybe two, three times a week. On the other hand, if you go to the Blues, you'll have your own ship and all the flight time you want." McKenny leaned back, waiting.

Inwardly Carl was squirming. This was damned uncomfortable. He didn't want to get on the CO's bad side by demanding the scout platoon, especially if there was a legitimate need for him elsewhere, but he had been looking forward to this for five months.

"Sir, with all respect to your considerations, I extended for scouts and that's what I really want. As you said, sir, I've already spent one year with slicks, and I'm looking for something new. I've heard a lot about Apache troop scouts and that's why I'm here." He paused for a moment, letting out a slow, controlled breath, trying to hide his nervousness. "I want to fly scouts, even if it is on a part-time basis." He watched McKenny's face carefully. That was about as polite and tactful as he could be.

McKenny leaned back onto the desk again and turned to Grimes, a smile spreading across his rough features. "Man really wants to be a scout. Top, send a runner over for Sergeant Hearndon."

Grimes nodded, got up, and stepped out of the office while McKenny rose and reached out a dark brown hand. "Welcome aboard, Willstrom. I didn't mention it, but it's a fact of life around the scout platoon. You probably won't have to be on rotational duty for long. There is a rapid turnover rate." He sat back down, not needing to explain the nature of the turnovers. "Now, before your new platoon sergeant gets here, are there any questions that I can answer?"

Carl felt a lot more relaxed now. He was in. He eyed the black Stetson hanging from a wall peg. "Yes, sir. I do have a couple of questions. I'd like to get myself one of those hats."

McKenny laughed easily, glancing at the colorful mark of the air cavalry squadrons. "No problem. Just give your hat size to the clerk. Of course, you realize that the hat is not a standard issue item. Comes with a twenty-dollar tag, but well worth it for the man who wants one. Another question?''

"Yes, sir." Now to find out what kind of crap was happening. "A friend of mine at my old unit said some pretty strange stuff about fire restrictions and changes in engagement rules." He stopped, noting the ripple of annoyance that flickered across McKenny's face.

"There have been some changes, but generally speaking, they do not affect the scout and weapons platoons. Most of the areas that you will be operating in will already be cleared for free fire. There are exceptions, but I'll leave that to Sergeant Hearndon, who is out there now evidently."

Carl took that as his dismissal, came to attention, saluted, and exited the office. In the orderly room Grimes introduced him to a short, stocky staff sergeant. The compactly built NCO extended his hand and flashed Carl a quick smile.

"Welcome to the best. We've got a full platoon right now, but we'll find room for you somewhere." Southern accent.

"He's all yours, Joe," Grimes told him. "Better get him geared up before everybody splits for chow." He turned back to Carl and added his welcome-to-the-club comment.

On the way to the supply hootch, they went through the usual questions, checking each other out. Hearndon wore his Stetson with the brim turned down, shading his face from the broiling sun. He appeared to be in his late twenties, no right sleeve combat patch, but Carl figured him for a career soldier anyway. From their conversation he learned that his guess was correct. Nine years in the army, first tour in Nam, and happily counting down his last sixty days that separated him from a wife and two children back in Georgia.

After they picked up the last of his gear, an M-16 and a well-worn .45, they turned toward Carl's new home. "You keep your pistol with you all the time. The rifle can stay in the scout hootch when you're not using it. Our own little arms room."

"Question, Sarge." Carl was still toting around his bag with the AK in it. "How's unit policy on using captured weapons?"

Hearndon pulled up next to a little collection of ragged sandbags that had been stripped away from a large hootch. "Officially, of course, army regs say no use of enemy war materials. I'm sure you know that. But half the people in this outfit use toys other than what Uncle Sam issues. Lot of my people prefer the AK-47 for the oscars since they're shorter than 16s and easier to move around in the front seat."

"Hold up a bit, Sarge. I don't know your local lingo. What's an oscar?"

Hearndon decided the same thing and gave him a quick air cav vocabulary lesson. Carl learned that besides the pilot, the scout ships in this unit carried an oscar, or observer, and a torque, the back seat doorgunner. The three flight platoons also had special designators. The scouts were the white platoon; the weapons platoon, the Cobras, were the reds; and the lift platoon, which was made up of Hueys and an infantry platoon, went by the name blues.

"Your job for the first month or two, depending on Charlie, of course"—he paused and smiled—"will be working as an oscar, flying front seat with the pilot. That means looking after the radios, making some of the calls, watching the maps, and keeping your eyes out on the left side of the ship. You ever get any flight time, actual flying on the Hueys?" Carl nodded and Hearndon went on. "Part of your job will be learning how to fly the ship in case the pilot gets hit. If you can make one of those clumsy slicks move, you won't have any trouble catching on to the loach. She's fast and responsive and a hell of a lot more fun." He stopped again to see if Carl was getting all the information.

"I'm still with you, Sarge. I read about some of this stuff in the division magazine."

Hearndon nodded. "Most of the time all you have to do is sit there with your rifle in your lap and a red smoke grenade in your left hand. If you get in over your head, you drop the smoke for the Cobras. You'll have plenty of time to pick up on our operations, just pay attention to what the others tell you. Meanwhile," he said, smiling, "this is your new home." He patted the side of the hootch. "Come on in and get settled."

Hearing that bit of information, Carl backed up a step and surveyed his new dwelling. Not much different from his previous home. Must have been the same architect. The only distinguishing feature was the narrow rotor blade from an OH-6A, a loach. It was mounted just above the hootch entrance and at one time had been painted bright red. The sun and rain had conspired to wear away the paint, but the white lettering still stood out: "SCOUTS DON'T GIVE A DAMN." An impressive statement. It spoke of boldness, reckless daring, pride to the point of arrogance. From what he had heard, they lived up to that image, and that was part of the reason he was here.

The interior of the hootch had also been done by the same designer. Same old corrugated metal roofing, creaking wooden floors, ammunition crate decor, and the faint odor of decaying wood. The hot air would have been stifling except for the presence of a small plastic PX fan that kept the warm air circulating. At the far end of the hootch two sweating soldiers were swatting at flies while trying to work through a game of checkers. Both seemed to appreciate Hearndon's interruption and rose to greet the new arrival.

The platoon sergeant made quick introductions and then left Carl in the care of his new family. Sergeant Slute motioned him to sit down on a grenade case. He was a sharp-looking black, and his bearing gave the impression of a professional. He, too, wore the Cav sandwich, a subdued cloth CIB marking him as a former grunt, and his flight wings. Just above the left side Cav patch, Carl noticed that he wore a little scroll tab proclaiming the wearer to be a member of Apache troop scouts with the unit numbers. Another one of those little unofficial additions to the uniform.

"Welcome to where it's at, m'man," Slute said in a deep, firm voice. "We got a nice little family here. Extension?"

Carl nodded. "Yep. Used to be across the active, down at the far end. 'A' Company, 229th. Did a year with them, and thought I'd try something different."

Slute flashed an understanding smile. "It's a whole different ride here, man. Most of the scouts are either on extensions or transfers from line units. We got a little saying around here that says it all. 'Slicks are for kids, guns are fun, but scouts is where it's at.' It can get pretty fuckin' hairy out there, but it's being alive, man, and if you can dig that, then you're in the right place."

Carl looked at Slute for a few seconds, remembering some of the times that he had already been through, and considered telling the man a little of his background. No need for it. He knew he had played for high stakes already. Carl simply smiled a humorless grin. "You can see where I am."

"All fuckin' right!" The other man slapped Slute on the arm. "Another worm for the hook!" he exclaimed, grinning like a man who had been out in the sun too long.

The man's name tag read Marvin, but Hearndon had introduced him as Psycho, and Carl could see where the name might have come from. Overly large and slightly bulging eyes set off by a tangle of wild red hair and a gap-toothed smile made him look slightly demented.

Psycho turned his grin on Carl. "Don't let old Slute mess with your head. Just 'cause he's in line for Hearndon's position don't mean he can't talk no shit. Things been dull as hell around here for the last three weeks. We've only had one ship take any fire, and that was probably from some old dink farmer dipping into too much rice wine." He rolled his eyes around crazily and then laughed as if reading Carl's thoughts. "And me, I'm only half as crazy as I look!"

Slute laughed. "Psycho's always talking shit, but there is some truth in what he says. Things have been a shade slow around here since the Cambodian pullout. That's why we still have all six of our ships operational and a full platoon.'' He looked around the hootch slowly. ''But we may be saying good-bye to all this peace and quiet and a definite good-bye to this place. We're moving out to Song Be in two weeks.''

Song Be. Nice place if you liked living, breathing, and looking like red dirt. Carl had been there a few times. It was a cross between a fire base and a base camp, a reddish-brown blob on the face of the earth where the hootches were only glorified aboveground bunkers.

''You be gettin' here just in time for the move. Gonna be a real pain in the ass,'' Psycho grumbled, then glanced at his watch. ''Speaking of moving, let's hit the roach room before they serve up all the water buffalo.''

Just like back home with the 229th. The food never changes.

XXI.

The next two weeks were fast and hard. His flying was only on a spotty basis, and he spent most of his time getting the unit packed up for the move. And when he wasn't flying or working details, he was with any of the other scouts on the ground, learning the workings of the OH-6. In the evenings when his exhausted body was no longer needed for work details, he got to know the other men in his family on a close, personal basis.

He quickly learned that platoon pride and unity was a large part of the air cavalry unit. In his previous flight company all of the platoons had the same type of job, but in the air cavalry troops each flight platoon had a different yet intertwined mission. This interaction and dependence made the men in the troop tight. Other chopper units worked for the division, carrying cargo, hauling troops from all over the division, getting support from other units, people they couldn't see. In the 1st of the 9th the only troops that rode in the Hueys were the troops' own infantry platoon, part of the family, and when they needed support, it came from the weapons platoon. When the downed ships needed cover, the Reds came in to cover while the Blues landed and provided security and recovery on the ground. It was, effectively, a self-supporting unit, and there existed a close bond between the men within it.

Carl liked the feeling and was accepted as almost an equal among the others, needing only to get into the action with them to complete the weld. They had to be sure of him, these men in their small machines, dangling over the heads of hungry shapes in the jungle. No room for doubt or lack of trust in the scouts.

On the few flights that he made before the move, he learned the routine of the scout missions and got a chance to take the controls long enough to wish that he had gone to flight school. This was the only way to fly. Low level, the jungle rushing up and past under the lower Plexiglas bubble, a blur at high speed, a panoramic jungle stroll at search speed. It gave him the feeling of a predator, gliding through the currents of the invisible ocean above the dark, shadowy jungle floor, waiting for his prey to dart from cover. But the little brown men never came out while he was up, and the only thing he saw was the everyday sight of farmers struggling through the paddies with their buffalo and the seemingly peaceful jungle.

The big move came and it was the pain in the ass that everyone knew it would be. The advance parties had already staked things out, and as the troops arrived in Song Be, by truck and by chopper, they were directed into their new Nam Hiltons.

"Just like a bunch of fuckin' bums," Lighter told him as they pulled their gear out of the chopper's back seat. "Someone leaves and we gotta jump in and try to take over before the damn rats do."

Carl looked at the skinny blond torque who was trying

to wipe some of the grime off his black-framed army glasses. He didn't mind moving into someone else's left-overs. Sure as hell beat building your own quarters. Not that that was a problem anymore. Since Nixon had started the slow withdrawal of troops from Nam, there were more than enough places to move into.

The slightly rectangular building was nothing more than an aboveground bunker with two large openings, one at each end, shielded by a sandbag barricade. Inside the barricade the place resembled a dilapidated dungeon. The entryways formed the open ends of a six-foot-wide corridor and served as the main source of light during the daytime. A single weak bulb suspended from the center of the corridor lit up the middle section. In the dull glare, Carl could see four cell-like holes on each side of the hallway, each about four feet wide, six feet deep, and less than head high. He looked around with some distaste at his surroundings.

"Man, this is a claustrophobic's nightmare!"

Lighter gave up with his glasses. "No shit. At least you're a short fucker." Lighter was a good six foot four, and there wasn't enough headroom in the main corridor to allow him to stand up straight.

Swanson, the short red-haired surfer from California, stuck his head out of the cell at the far end. "Ain't this some classy hole? Whole place looks like it's just waiting for all of us to squeeze in before it collapses."

Carl had to agree with that opinion. "Guess we don't need reservations to move in here. I suppose we'll get used to it. Matter of fact, in a couple of days we'll probably love it."

"Yeah, well, anybody who extends for this shit deserves whatever they get," Swanson remarked. "You guys just been in this country too long. Sun's done got to your brains. Half the fuckin' rats in Nam probably live in this hole. Gonna have to get a shotgun just to scare 'em off at night!"

"Shotgun won't do more 'n piss 'em off, Swan," Lighter informed him. "I'm gonna use frags on the little bastards and hope they don't throw 'em back at me!"

"Hey, you bunch of lazy bastards!" Hearndon's gentle call reminded them that there was still a lot of work to be done, and they threw their gear into whichever cell was nearest and trudged back out into the glare of the sun.

Carl's body felt like it could use a thirty-day leave on his cot. They must have unloaded several tons of munitions and filled up the ammo bunkers. And the gritty dirt was going to have to stay for a while. Someone had forgotten to fill up the showers and everyone was bitching about it.

When he hit the bunker, he found some of the scouts seated around some piled-up crates playing cards under the glow of their one light. Slute looked up at him, grinning hugely.

"Yo, Weird Willy, my man!" They had adopted his name as easily as they had taken him in. "Hearndon says that since you and Lighter worked so hard putting all that ammo up, you dudes deserve first shot at using it up. You got first light with Animal at 0500!"

Lighter just groaned and flung an imaginary grenade at Slute.

"Oh, but that's only part of it," Slute continued happily. "The man says to pack along beaucoup frags and ammo, heavy on Willie Petes and incendiaries. Didn't say what kind of numbah, but sounds like it might be exciting."

The rumors that had been circulating popped into Carl's mind. For the last week, the talk going around said that they were going back into Cambodia soon. Not the whole army, not even the division. Just a few helicopter units, supporting the ARVN who hadn't been included in the pullout order from Nixon. The ARVN had stayed on in Cambodia, and that presence was now being countered by a fresh rush of NVA. His thoughts drifted back to his last time in that country. It hadn't been so bad, now that it was behind him, but he was glad that his ship had been destroyed. He had felt a little shaky after that, and some of the feeling had carried over into his leave. Now here they were. Poised on the edge again, maybe getting ready to cross the red line. Well, if it were true, it would definitely do away with the monotony that all the scouts had been complaining about.

On a suggestion from Slute that they all turn in and get some sleep, he peeled off the sweat-stiffened shirt, halfheartedly rubbed some of the dirt off with the filthy garment, and collapsed onto his cot, falling immediately into a deep sleep that ended too soon.

The cogwheels of his brain were slogging through a muck of glue and quicksand. The runner's hand shook him awake, but he had trouble clearing the cobwebs out of his head and almost slammed his skull into the low ceiling of his cell. A stumbling near collision in the corridor with Lighter told him that it was going to be a great day. Still no water and he didn't feel like a dry shave, so he trudged to the mess tent for a tasteless breakfast, only the coffee serving to make him feel a little less zombielike.

Lighter downed the last of his coffee and signaled that it was time to go. The sun would be breaking its first light soon and they had to be in the air by then.

Animal, a gigantic hulk of a first lieutenant, was already at the ship, preflighting under the beam of his flashlight. Carl hadn't flown with him yet, but everything he had heard told him that Animal was even crazier than the average scout pilot. In a ten-month time span, the bearish pilot had reportedly accounted for a couple of hundred enemy KIAs, even shooting at some of them with his pistol while using one hand to control the ship. It hadn't been all give and no take, though. In that same period Animal had been shot down three times and lost an oscar and two torques.

Carl couldn't help but think that Animal was an unlikely pilot for the lightweight scout ships. At six foot three, tipping an easy 240 pounds, the aircraft had to be overweighted on his side.

Animal grinned at him, a strange mask in the low light of the flashlight. "Don't worry. We'll make it off the ground,'' he said, laughing, ''but it wouldn't hurt if you had some more weight on your bones. Maybe we'll just sling a bag of grenades on your side to help out.'' He paused and glanced at Lighter. ''You got all the goodies ready?''

Lighter nodded and pointed to the grenade case in the back seat. ''Just what you wanted. Expecting to find something interesting out there?''

Animal's grin widened, but he didn't say anything.

Animal broke the ship to the left once they had passed over the perimeter and began their early morning check of the area around the base. A new area, but no different from Tay Ninh except in size. Enough light now to see the same ramshackle huts, the early morning traffic through the garbage-littered streets of Song Be itself. As their circle widened out, they crossed over the rice paddies where the farmers were already struggling through the muck with their obstinate beasts. Most of the people paid no attention to the spying insect, but here and there a few of the dark-skinned children in their tatters and rags would turn their faces skyward, waving at the ship.

''That's right, you little junior league VC. Wave and smile and maybe you'll live another day,'' Lighter mumbled into the mike.

''Be nice, GI,'' Animal cautioned him. ''You know my rules.''

''You know something, Animal? One of these days some of those innocent little fuckers are gonna blow your shit out of the sky, and I hope to hell I'm somewhere else!''

More stuff Carl had heard. Animal was real particular about the kinds of targets that he let his gunners fire up, and Lighter was on the other end of the street. Carl had already heard about some of Lighter's exploits where the KIAs hadn't all been VC or NVA.

Lighter's train of thought about how to handle the war ran closer to Sorden's way of thinking, but at least the torque had some guts, even if Carl didn't like some of the things he had heard. And it wasn't just Lighter. His attitude seemed more the rule than the exception, and people with Carl's still-simplistic view of things were a definite minority.

The red dawn broke over the landscape, flooding the country with warming light. More and more traffic was appearing on the roads and trails, but nothing that was worth a second look.

"All right, troops, let's go have some fun," Animal finally said, breaking off the first light patrol. "We've got a search area, possible infiltration route, right on the border northwest of here."

Carl had the feeling that they might "accidentally" end up on the wrong side of the border if Animal could find anything worth going after. Navigational errors happened all the time with units working in close proximity to the red line.

Animal announced that they were at their destination, but the solid line on the map failed to appear on the ground below them, and as far as Carl was concerned, they could be deep inside Cambodia. None of this area was familiar to any of them, but the Cav gunship had guided them here, and here was where they would begin their work.

Animal dropped the ship down on the deck and began a leisurely roll across the jungle, he and the torque covering the entire right side, front to rear, while Carl tried to find anything off to his side and forward. The jungle below them was not as thick as some places Carl had seen, but it was dense enough so that the best chance for spotting a target was when they were almost even with it and it was slightly off to the side.

"Trail at three o'clock," Lighter announced.

"Got it." Animal swung the ship into a tight circle to the right, giving himself and Lighter a better view of the trail.

Carl had flown scouts just long enough to know that he hated this part of the mission. It was great that they had something besides trees to look at, but when the pilots put the ships into those right-hand orbits, it left him with either a crazily tilted view of the jungle through the front or a clear picture of the sky over Vietnam. Of course, he could always try to see past the pilots, but they invariably bobbed and rocked into his field of vision, and with a pilot like Animal there was no chance at all.

"Hard-packed, running echo-whiskey," Animal called up to the gunship. "We're gonna take a little trip, follow it to the whiskey."

West. Nothing but Cambodia in that direction and everyone in both ships knew it. Several minutes passed as they scouted down the trail, losing sight of it from time to time, but always picking it up again. From his position Carl couldn't see the trail and nothing unusual was visible on his side. He could hear the reports relayed up to the cover ship, changes in direction, evidence of recent traffic, and other things that the scouts were supposed to pick out.

Carl started to press his mike button, but the other two were already seeing what had suddenly appeared below and all around them.

Well-camouflaged hootches were barely visible through the tops of the trees, but they were there, with little trails connecting groups of them together.

"We have large number hootches, mostly ten-by-tens, no visible personnel," Animal advised the gunship. "We'll do a recon by fire and see who we can pull out of the woodwork."

Animal sent the ship into a hard right turn and pointed out a hootch for Lighter. The sudden rapid explosions of the machine gun seemed a hell of a lot louder than the gunfire in the Hueys, but it was a welcome sound to Carl. Even if he couldn't see what Lighter was cranking up on, the steady clatter had the sound of an old friend.

Animal broke away from the first target after getting no response and locked the ship onto another set of hootches. Lighter's gun opened up again, sending its lethal probes into the yielding thatch roofs of the hootches. Carl heard that old familiar sharp crack at the same moment that Animal started yelling.

"Get him! Get him!"

The ship jerked hard around, pulling at Carl's stomach

with a nauseating wrench, but for a flash of a second he glimpsed a dark-clad moving figure on one of the trails below. Then Animal's bulk blocked his vision and only his ears could follow the unfolding minidrama on the jungle floor.

Lighter's gun was firing continuously, and in his mind Carl could see the bullets pursuing, catching, and spinning the running figure. He wondered what had made the man break from cover, exposing himself to the certain fire from the chopper.

"Good shot," Animal said, more calmly now, just after Lighter's gun became silent, indicating the end of the one-sided duel. "Now let's check out that hootch and see why he was in such a hurry to get away from there. Go ahead and fire it up!"

Lighter opened up on the hootch while Animal called in one enemy KIA to the gunship. Both actions were rudely interrupted by a deafening explosion, sending shock waves rushing through the air to buffet the small craft.

"Son of a bitch! Pay dirt!" Now Animal was back to his excited stage. Huge billows of flame and smoke were cascading up from the former location of the hootch, searing the trees, crackling the thinned-out underbrush into balls of fire.

"Hey there, gunner. I do believe that you just created a fuel shortage for the local NVA. Look at that shit spreading down there!" Animal leaned back against his seat so that even Carl could see the results of their hunting.

There were several fiery streams flowing away from the area of the hootch, some kind of flammable liquid that for reasons unknown hadn't exploded in that first searing fireball. No wonder that dude had risked the machine-gun fire!

Animal put in an update to the Cobra while he kept the ship circling around other hootches, letting Lighter alternate between his M-60 and the incendiary grenades that he had loaded up. No big bangs, but their search pattern was marked by flaming or smoking hootches. Carl could see that some of the structures had been recently done over with fresh green thatching while others were turning yellow-brown, discolored by age and heat. Must have caught Charlie in the middle of his spring camouflaging.

Animal was still wired from the fuel find, Lighter was happily blowing away every hootch they came across, and only Carl and the Cobra seemed to be left out of the fun. He knew that he was going to have to get on the stick, find some action, get to be the gunner, anything but this observer business. His first contact mission in the scouts and all he was doing was watching the sky.

"Hey, oscar, keep your eyes open! Where there's fuel, there must be something that uses it, and I don't think Charlie would have barrels of the stuff sitting out in a hootch unless he was getting ready to put it to an immediate use."

Made sense to Carl. He knew about the hidden highways in the jungle. Charlie had been damned clever about cutting roads through the seemingly impassable jungle, leaving enough of the upper canopy to conceal the bamboo interstate from the eyes of anything except the low-flying scouts. He had seen a few trucks, supplied by the Soviets or the Chinese, during the big Cambodian invasion, but none before or since then.

He loosened his harness some and twisted his body, leaning out as far as he could to get a better view. He caught sight of another hootch, must have found at least a dozen by now, and Animal pulled the ship around to let the gunner tear up the flimsy structure. Still no signs of anything resembling a roadway big enough for any kind of vehicle.

Animal was seeing the same thing. "Well, troops, if it was a fuel point, they probably carried it out by foot or bicycle to some other place for the actual refueling. Oscar, go ahead and drop a smoke on my order and we'll let the gunship use up some of his fireworks." He wheeled the ship toward the heaviest concentration of hootches and gave Carl the nod.

Carl was glad to get rid of the red smoke grenade. Didn't have to screw around with putting the pin back in.

He let it roll out of his hand, didn't hear the tiny pop of the fuse, but saw the spurt of smoke from the canister before it went through the trees.

Animal flipped the agile craft away from the direction that the Cobra would be coming in from and went into a steep climb, hitting the gunship's former orbital altitude just in time to level off and see the Cobra pulling out of its first pass, a faint plume of mingling red smoke and whitish gray from the ship's rockets. No tracers followed the ship back up. They knew that there were more people down there, but without infantry to dig them out, there wasn't much that could be done. The Cobra made a few more passes and then Animal took the ship down for a final check.

It was easier to spot the hootches or what remained of them now. The gunship had used his "nails," the small steel dartlike objects released by the hundreds from the heads of the rockets as they raced toward their targets. The tiny darts, capable of nailing rifle stocks to the bodies of their owners, had stripped away the leafy covering in a couple of places, and the high explosive rockets had ripped away many of the branches and even downed a few of the smaller trees.

What the Cobra hadn't hit, Carl's ship finished off, using Lighter's assortment of grenades. Animal kept the ship at a slow walk around the area, and despite the lack of any serious resistance, Carl was beginning to get edgy. He knew that the standard method for finding the enemy was to make yourself a good enough target, but this was fuckin' ridiculous. He glanced over at Animal, who had the ship almost at a dead hover now. No doubt about it. The stories he had heard about this crazy bastard must all be true.

The hulk in the pilot's seat really seemed to be enjoying himself, tempting the Charlies, daring someone to try to blow him away. Carl liked the element of danger. That was what had brought him back to Nam, to the scouts, but he also wanted to survive to be able to tell his children and grandchildren what the war had been like. But he couldn't let Animal know that this sitting-duck routine bothered him. Got to play it like it was an everyday game. When with the crazies, act like a crazy, be a part of the madness or at least pretend to be.

Finally, even Animal had to realize that the fish weren't going to try to snatch the worm today, and after making sure that all the hootches were well on their way to being ash piles, he lifted the ship back into the friendly skies and turned east.

The platoon stayed overstrength and the flying stayed sporadic as the days crept by. Ground time was a real bitch because of the work details. It seemed that their new home had been on the condemned properties list. Almost every other day, one structure or another in the camp area would collapse or require some kind of major reconditioning effort. Carl wound up scavenging some discarded lumber and propping it up in his cell to prevent the thing from caving in on him. The thought of sleeping outside was put into practice by only one of the scouts, Psycho, who had boldly announced his intentions to the others in the cell block.

"Ain't no fuckin' way I'm gonna spend another night in this shithole! Sand came pouring through a damn crack last night. Woke up and thought I was in fuckin' Miami Beach, it was so sandy. And the rats! Bastards ate the front half of my boot last night! Not one more fuckin' night! I don't care if Charlie shits shells on us all night long!" He struggled out of the bunker with his possessions, almost tearing his cot apart going past the outer barricades.

As if on directions from the man upstairs, the camp had

its heaviest mortar attack in six months that night. Carl woke with a start, not-so-dull thuds hammering into the ground nearby, shaking the already tortured cell block. He rolled out of the cot, fumbling in the dark for his pants, found them, and slid them on. Under the cot his fingers grasped the edge of his steel pot and he capped it on just for good measure.

A deafening thunder exploded just outside the bunker sending a fine shower of sand raining down on Carl's naked back from some crack in the ceiling. At the same time there was a crashing and thudding sound of a human body slamming into the outside bunker wall that sent Carl groping for his AK. Not a ground attack yet. Too much stuff still coming down.

Psycho's yelling relaxed his heart and lungs, as the outdoorsman stumbled into the bunker that he had vowed never again to sleep in. "Dammit, dammit, dammit! Don't nobody say nothing!" There was a moment of silence between shell impacts, and somewhere in the bunker someone tried to suppress a laugh.

The attempt failed, and in a moment the entire bunker was filled with demented laughter, punctuated by the falling mortar rounds that were still impacting in close proximity.

Be a part of the madness. Carl tried to fight back the tears from the almost hysterical laughter, but it only made his stomach knot up painfully, so he gave in, letting the laughter run its course.

The following morning things didn't seem quite as funny. Carl straggled out with the others to do some early morning sight-seeing and find out what damage had been done.

He could hear Skull grumbling just ahead of him, the gunner's rumbling joined by the voices of the others as they walked out into the light of the early morning.

"Would you look at this mess!" Skull, one of the veteran torques, had planted himself just outside the barricade, his stocky form looking very much like an angry bull standing his ground just before charging. "Here we spend a couple of weeks trying to fix this place up and what happens? Does Charlie blow away the old messed-up places? Fuck, no! Assholes hit the bunkers that we just finished rebuilding!'' His already swarthy complexion was turning a little darker and Carl could understand the feeling.

The troop area had taken quite a few hits, and most of the damage had been done to the structures that they had put in so much backbreaking labor on. More detail work, and to foul up things even more, they found that one of the scout ships had taken some shrapnel from a near hit and was going to be down for at least two days. That meant more men for the work details and less chance of flying.

Their own creaking rat trap had some repair work due where the shell that had chased Psycho back in had blasted a section of the sandbags into shreds, leaving a small sand dune at the base of one side of the bunker.

Slute had gone back into the bunker and reemerged with an armful of the OD sandbags, throwing them down next to the damaged wall. ''Let's go get some chow. This is gonna be a fucked-up day,'' he said disgustedly. He was doubly pissed. He had been scheduled for a trip into the same general area where Carl had been with Animal, and had been looking forward to it. Naturally, it was his ship that had gotten messed up during the mortar barrage.

After breakfast, one group of scouts headed for their ships, shit-eating grins on their faces as they sauntered by Carl and a few of the others from his bunker who were already sweating generously from their labors.

Dutch, the tall, sturdy Italian from New York, smiled at Carl as he passed. ''While you're fixing things up, how about adding an extra layer or two around my crib, Weird?'' He had to duck and run to dodge the shovel of sand that Carl flung at him.

Carl wanted to make some remark, telling him that he hoped they got shot down and that Charlie would make them build bunkers all over Southeast Asia. But men didn't say stuff like that to each other when they were getting ready to fly. Around the mess tables, over the cards, it was fine for joking, but not just before the mission.

* * *

For three days he did nothing but sandbag details, and in his restless sleep at night he soared low level over endless mounds of sand and their OD baggies. Mornings came painfully with tight, cramped fingers and hands that were curled, as if gripping an invisible shovel. Cold water from the showers loosened them up slowly, and by the time he got to the mess tent, the fingers were able to respond to the brain's commands. At least he was able to grasp his fork and shovel the food into his mouth.

Watson, one of the oscars who shared the same bunker, and many of the same work details, had joined him at the table. The serious-faced young man attacked his bacon and eggs as if they were an enemy force to be disposed of ruthlessly. Maybe they were. There were enough food stories in the army, but Carl had never heard of the food actually biting back. Fighting back, yes. In the forms that kept the supply rooms out of toilet paper, food poisoning, and the like, things that made life just a little more degenerate.

"Sandbags again, Weird?" Watson asked as he crushed food chunks in his jaws, discoloring the long scar that ran across his chin.

"Hell, no! Sarge said I could slide on that today and give Skull a hand on his ship's maintenance. I've filled so many sandbags since we've been here that I think my brain has turned into one."

Watson laughed knowingly. He had been a grunt for five months before accepting one of those offers put out by the various chopper units when gunners got scarce. He had seen his share of bag-filling details and was used to the work.

"Just thought I'd check. Me and Andrews and a couple of guys from the other bunker are goin' down to the ammo point to break down some of the cases, and I thought you might want a change."

Carl shook his head. He knew that the guys working the ammo wouldn't be pushing too hard, but he'd rather work on the ships. The sarge might let him up on a mission a little sooner that way.

After the morning meal, he and Skull headed down to the ship and managed to keep themselves busy or at least apparently busy for the better part of the morning. The easy pace gave them a chance to talk about what they thought was going down. Skull's real name was Skaul, but long ago the other scouts had tagged him with his alias, and he liked the sound of it. He had even gotten his hands on the skull of some dead NVA, painting his name and a set of crossed sabers on it. Back in Tay Ninh he had kept it on display on an ammo box next to his cot, just like the fancy nameplates the big brass used on their desks. He had a dozen stories about how he had gotten the skull, but Slute had told Carl that the grisly relic had been the object of a trade for some of the white powder that was so plentiful in Nam.

"Just before we moved out here, I boxed that fucker up and sent it home to my old lady! Wish I could be there to see her face when she opens that thing up!" Like the platoon sergeant, Skull was married and his wife was waiting for him in Georgia.

"Just better hope those jokers at customs don't check the box," Carl told him. "I know there's something in the regs about stuff like that."

"What the hell they gonna do? Draft my ass? Besides, it ain't like I was trying to smuggle back guns or smack. It's just a lousy skull that would be out in the jungle rotting somewhere if I didn't have it."

Carl shrugged it off and checked his watch. Too early for lunch and the ship was finished, ready to go immediately if needed. He looked over toward the ammo bunker. Nobody in sight. They were probably finished with their work and just laying low until chow time. Skull nudged him, nodding his head toward the bunker.

"They're probably sacked out in there. What say we sneak over there and shake 'em up a little?" he asked with a sly smile.

Carl gave him a thumbs-up and off they went, circling

to the side in case someone popped out of the bunker. They had closed to within fifty yards of the squat, sandbagged structure when Carl suddenly heard muffled shouting, a hysterical scream as a man shot out of the entrance and tried to dive over the entry barricade.

A deafening blast erupted from the small opening, shock waves picking the man up away from the barricade and slamming him to the ground five yards away, his clothing blazing from the enveloping tongue of flame that had ripped out of the bunker. Carl saw it all as he instinctively dove for the ground, eating the dry red dust.

The bunker was being destroyed from the inside by continuing explosions, but Carl couldn't see that. He was keeping his head down until he heard Skull screaming frantically at him.

There was more screaming, and he twisted his head toward Skull, who was pointing at the source of the second noise.

The one man who had made it out was still alive and roasting in his own uniform, evidently unable to move or do anything except let out gut-twisting screams of hellfire agony.

Even though it was undoubtedly the fastest low crawl he had ever done, it felt as though he were trying to flail his way through a quicksand bog. Nothing would move fast enough, and the only thing that really registered in his mind was the red, blistered face of the man ahead of him. He couldn't even tell who it was. The eyes were seared and the hair had sizzled away. The jaws worked with each fresh scream, chin digging into the red dust, but the rest of the body lay there, a nerveless flesh heap.

Skull reached the man first, smothered the trooper with his own body, not daring to kneel in the face of the still-exploding munitions in the bunker. Most of the grenades had already gone off in the first few violent seconds, but there were still isolated larger boomings mixed with exploding small-arms ammunition.

Carl arrived a split second later, kicked his legs around,

spinning on his belly in the hot dirt, and slapped Skull to let him know that he was there.

Skull rolled off the burned, mindlessly screaming form, and grabbed him under one shoulder. Carl did likewise, and on Skull's dry-throated yell, they both sprinted up, toes and knees digging in, and dragged the soldier away from the bunker, staying as low as they could. Carl stumbled, tripped, and brought the three of them down after less than ten yards, but they struggled up again, chests heaving, nostrils clinching from the stench of the burned flesh that they carried.

They stumbled down again, stayed this time, far enough away from the collapsed bunker. Skull, swearing miserably, rolled the man over onto his back. The screaming had stopped after the first fall, and for a second Carl was afraid that they might have killed him in their haste to get away. A drooling, gurgly sound from the raw lips told him that the man was still hanging in there. He thought, from the general build, that it might be Watson, the one who had asked if he wanted to work on the ammo detail earlier.

A hand clamped down on Carl's shoulder. One of the medics knelt down in the dirt with him, motioning Carl and Skull to back off, giving him room to work. Carl didn't even bother to get to his feet, just back-shuffled on his knees, stirring up small puffs of dust. A little more dirt in the air wouldn't hurt. Where Watson had been lying on his face, the sand had embedded itself into the boiled-up skin.

Carl rocked back onto his heels and slapped down into a sitting position, blowing out a deep breath of air while the medic worked. He glanced over at the smoldering remains of the bunker, where only isolated pops were now sounding. Wouldn't be anything left of the men who were in there.

Other troops had come running almost immediately after the blast, and now some of them, a few officers and sergeants, were cautiously approaching the bunker shell, ready to eat dirt if anything big went off. Carl wondered why they were even bothering until things were completely safe. They had to know what he knew. His eyes caught the motion of the medic slamming down his aid bag, turning his head away from the burned soldier, looking skyward, jaw quivering.

Carl knew what he was looking for. Why? Why couldn't he save him, why do young guys get fucked up like that, why? But the medic knew, and Carl knew, that the sky wasn't going to give up any answers. It was the question that would haunt some men for the rest of their lives. Others would try to forget the question, but Carl didn't think that he was going to be one of those who tried to forget. He had come to experience, and experience suppressed is no experience at all. He stared at Watson's lifeless body. The experience of death, of course, is only for the living. This is weird, he told himself. Man's lying here dead, and you're sitting here in the fuckin' dirt trying to be a philosopher. First man he had seen die since that last big operation in Cambodia when his ship was blown up. He wondered if this calmness was part of a new acceptance of death. Had he seen enough of it now? He shook his head, slapped away some of the dust on his fatigues, and pulled Skull up with him. He patted the medic, mumbling some meaningless phrase, and headed to join the others at the bunker.

The cause of the explosion at the ammo bunker was never determined, but everyone figured that a faulty grenade must have been the prime factor. The cause didn't matter anyway. The results were all that counted. Four men dead. The three who had been in the bunker were unidentifiable, and there wasn't enough left of all of them to do more than fill a sandbag. More closed coffins. Carl had gotten to know all of them, but not as well as some of the other men had. It stayed real quiet around the two scout bunkers for the next few days. They were used to losing men, but not to losing four at a time because of some fucked-up accident.

Hearndon had told him when he first arrived in the scout platoon that they had never stayed full strength for long and that Carl probably wouldn't be on a rotating flight schedule for long. Now they went from the luxury of overstrength to the standard of understrength. Lots of flight time for everyone, and three days after the ammo bunker disaster the pace was picked up as they were assigned to work for an ARVN infantry division in Cambodia, scouting ahead and locating the enemy for the South Vietnamese.

There was a lot of grumbling from the men when the news was announced, not because of the duty, but because of the conditions attached. The entire unit was to be under the control of the ARVN division commander, and in case any ships were shot down, the security and rescue teams were to be South Vietnamese reaction units who would come in on the lift ships. The infantry platoon wouldn't be able to do anything because of Nixon's orders that there were to be no ground combat troops in Cambodia. The Blues were disgusted at being replaced, and some of them offered to try to disguise themselves as ARVN so they could help support their fellow troop platoons. The scouts were upset because they were the ones who usually got shot down, and many of them didn't have that much faith in their allies when it came to hot life-and-death situations.

"But that's the way it's going down, gentlemen, and there's not a thing that we can do about it," Lieutenant Reiner told the assembled scout platoon, pilots, and enlisted. "We'll just have to be extra careful out there and hope the Cobras can keep Charlie off if you go down. Bravo troop commenced operations southwest of Snoul"—he indicated a small dot on his map—"and the reports that we've heard indicate that NVA regiments are back all along this area"—a sweeping gesture across the border areas—"and they've got a lot of fifty-ones with them."

The olive-skinned lieutenant smoothed down his mustache and looked over his disgruntled bunch. "Cheer up, troops. At least, you're going to get all the action you want, maybe more than you want." He straightened up, dismissed his officers, and turned the rest of the briefing over to Hearndon.

Carl found himself teamed up with Skull and WO1 Reeves, a sour-faced individual who wasn't known around the platoon as being a big talker. Reeves was kind of an exception to the usually hard-partying scout pilots. He was a loner, didn't say more than two words to Carl or Skull at the ship the next morning.

Carl didn't care about that as long as the man knew his stuff. Evidently Reeves did. He had survived over nine months in scouts, going on the down side of being a two-digit midget.

Silently they hummed through the air, crossing the border, officially this time, not just screwing around. Carl mentally tracked the time and checked the map. They were going a lot deeper into bad-guy country this time. Lotta Indians out there, boss. The reaction teams had to stay back on the Vietnamese side of the border. Somebody didn't even want the American choppers to touch ground in Cambodia, and that told Carl that if they had the misfortune to go down, it would take entirely too long for the rescue teams to get there.

They hit their search grid, and with only a few words passing between Reeves and the gunship they dropped down onto the deck to begin their runs. From an even higher altitude than the Cobra, Reeves was directed into specific areas by the C and C ship with an ARVN colonel on board. No telling what this dude wanted them to do, Carl thought, as he scanned the jungle below. Probably just the routine stuff, find NVA regiments, get shot up a little bit, let the Cobra blast away for a while. Maybe then the ARVN would come in later and check out the area.

The area below them was not as dense as most of the Vietnamese jungle areas. Scattered clumps of trees made islands in fields of head-high waving grass, which were, in turn, islands themselves in the middle of a scraggly, half-dead jungle maze. Lifeless trunks and limbs contrasted sharply with the green of the surviving trees, a graveyard of stark skeletons among the living. Whatever had caused it, Carl was thankful for it. It made it a hell of a lot easier to see what was going on down there. So far, no trails, no hootches, no signs of anything out of the ordinary.

"Ain't nothing down here, sir," Skull finally said after a half hour of trolling without a nibble. "Did they think there was something in particular in this area?"

"They didn't tell me." Short and to the point. Reeves kept his eyes focused on the ground 45 degrees out to his front.

The terrain didn't change and the ARVN colonel kept them flying their pattern. Carl recognized the danger that was already beginning to set in, that slackening in looking for details, the urge to look around to other places out of his search zone, and pulled himself back onto target. It took an effort to maintain full alertness when there was nothing happening, but he knew that the effort was worth it. Lot of kids didn't make it back because they let their guard down during those frequent moments of false security when the war seemed a thousand miles away.

The radio suddenly blared in his ears, startling him, even as Skull's M-60 opened up on something Carl couldn't see or hear.

"Taking fire! Taking fire! Small arms, only one!" Reeves fired the information up to the cover ship and banked the loach around to the right in a long loop.

Carl couldn't hear anything besides Skull's gun, never heard the other gun at all, and was a little surprised by Reeves's order for him to open fire, but he complied and rapped out a couple of short bursts with his M-16.

"What the hell are you doing?" Reeves yelled at him. "You trying to help Charlie kill us? Keep shooting!"

The warrant's face shield wasn't dark enough to hide his expression completely, and Carl could see in a quick glance the anger in the twisted lip, heard the trembling note of fear in the strained voice. The man was afraid.

After nine months of this kind of work, the strain had gotten to him, Carl thought. Maybe that's what happens when you start getting short and you know you're going home. You think too much about the dying and forget to concentrate on the living. But he knew better than to argue. Obediently, he emptied the remainder of the magazine into the jungle and popped in another, spraying the contents of that one into the greenery as well.

Skull's gun suddenly came to a stop. Carl still couldn't hear anyone shooting at them, not that he doubted that someone had. Skull must have heard the shooter because he had opened up even as Reeves was just starting the "taking fire" message.

"Did you get him?" Reeves asked sharply, still an edge to his voice.

"Never even saw where he was," Skull replied. "Just heard the shots, sir. Sounded like an AK."

Reeves turned back toward Carl, and Carl supposed that he was being glared at angrily. "All right, oscar, drop the smoke," he said quietly, and contacted the Cobra, informing the cover ship that they were putting out a smoke in the general target area.

Carl relaxed his hand and let the smoke roll out, watching the firing lever spin off. "Smoke out."

Reeves took the ship up to altitude and then divided his attention between the Cobra and Carl. "I suppose you never heard that it was part of your job to shoot back when someone's shooting at us. What the hell do you think we have you riding there for?"

Carl knew that Reeves wasn't expecting any answer, but he took the moment of pause to provide one. This pilot was pissing him off. "I never heard the shots, sir. There wasn't anything happening on my side and I—"

Reeves cut him off, almost yelling. "I don't give a damn. When you hear me yelling that we're taking fire, you better open up. There could be Charlies everywhere down there."

Carl felt his face reddening. Yeah, right, there could be dinks swarming around down there, and it'd be a shame to blindly waste a clip and maybe get caught by their fire in the couple of seconds it took to change magazines. As for trying to draw Charlie's fire, they had already done that and Skull was doing a good job on his gun. But he voiced none of those thoughts to Reeves. Swallowing his anger, he nodded his head. "Yes, sir." He stared out the open door, avoiding the pilot's glance. Maybe the "yes, sir" hadn't come out quite right.

They stayed up for several minutes longer while the gunship played games, blowing up trees and grass, and then the two ships again traded places.

Skimming over the trees just a little faster than before, Carl couldn't see that anything had changed. A few shredded trees, some swirling puffs of grayish smoke where rockets had started fires on some of the dead trees, but that was it. No bodies, no signs of anyone, although that didn't mean anything. The little brown men had been playing this game for many years against many contenders. Frankly, he was surprised that they had been shot at by a single gun. Either an excited rookie down there or someone who just couldn't resist the slow-moving target, and must have thought that they were in a fairly safe position to fire from. Could be an entire bunker complex down under all that brush, with the entry trails several klicks away.

Finally, even the ARVN colonel got tired of flying a nonproductive area and shifted the operation farther west a few klicks, near a more civilized area.

Reeves was talking to someone, himself, Carl, Skull, maybe the wind. "Great, just fucking great. That lousy gook up there must know I'm getting short and wants to see if he can get my ass blown to hell out here. Look at that shit."

The ARVN colonel wanted them to scout around a large village that marked the intersection of two hard-packed dirt roads, highways in Cambodia. Carl still thought Reeves was losing his nerve, but he had to agree that it looked like an excellent place to get blown away in. Smatterings of jungle broke into the rice paddies around the village, some of the fringes within three hundred yards of the remains of the abandoned place. Easy machine-gun range. Great field of fire for anybody on the ground who wanted to shoot at curious helicopters that were checking out the village itself.

Reeves was still talking to himself, but not on the intercom anymore as he brought the ship and began checking out the devastated village and the road intersection.

Carl felt naked and exposed, flying low and slow over the burned-out hootches and crumbled walls. He kept his eyes scanning back and forth from the rubble close in to the treelines farther out. A lot of places to hide, but he also reasoned that if there was anyone concealed in the ruins, they probably wouldn't want to reveal themselves to the Cobra's firepower. Ruins and rubble might be great for ground fighting, but in such a small area as this village, it wouldn't do to take the risk of an air strike just to shoot at a loach.

The road intersection made a natural partition, quartering the village and surrounding paddies, and they worked the search along those lines, starting from the intersection and working out.

"Charlie must have really liked this place," Skull remarked as they passed over another old machine-gun pit. They had already seen several of the "doughnut" positions, a favorite pit style for NVA .51s employed against aircraft. Circular in shape, the gun pits had an island in the center, a mound of dirt on which the machine gun was placed, giving the gun crew an unobstructed 360-degree arc of fire. Ordinarily well camouflaged, these lay open and exposed to their scrutiny, leftovers from the first Cambodian invasion, no doubt. They found some in the village itself, more along the treelines. Could have been a real hot spot for choppers, Carl thought. Get sucked in by the ones in the village and then catch it from the trees.

After a long fruitless search, the ARVN ordered them to do a route recon along the road heading south, and when he was satisfied that there was nothing of concern in that direction, he turned the ships loose for refueling.

* * *

"Aw, don't sweat it, man. Reeves is always like that," Skull told him that evening. "Most of the other pilots'll tell you oscars to hold back on your fire unless they give you the word or unless you've got a target." He paused, grinned at Carl, and punched him none too lightly in the shoulder. "Or unless there's a whole bunch of people shooting at us!"

"You never saw the dudes, right?"

"That's a Roger. Sounded like just one gun, but it didn't have the same kind of sound that you usually hear when they're shooting directly at you, unless they were shooting from quite a distance. As skimpy as that stuff was out there, I suppose it could've been a dink several hundred yards away who got a clear shot at us for a second."

Carl nodded, still pissed at Reeves, but glad to hear that Skull didn't think he'd screwed up. It made sleep come easier.

XXIV.

Carl shifted lazily in the sun, watching the ARVN play with the instamatic camera. He didn't know what they expected to get out of it, but they sure seemed to be having a good time, hamming and snapping shots of each other. He didn't mind that it was his film they were shooting up. Some interesting pictures might come out of it. Just like a bunch of kids with a new toy. He couldn't help smiling at the ARVN lieutenant, a buck-toothed man with the standard tight-fitting tiger-striped fatigues that the ARVN loved. The guy was trying to come on like John Wayne, posing for shots, brandishing his pistol, pretending to fire a machine gun with one hand while making a radio call. His men were enjoying the show and laughing it up, some of them getting into the pictures, striking up fighting stances next to the lieutenant. As long as they didn't try to steal his camera he didn't care what they shot. They were just trying to break up the boredom that everyone was feeling except the crews in the air.

Every day for the last week, they had been flying all the involved ships out to this strip near An Loc, using it as their staging area for the trips into Cambodia. Generally, they ran two scout missions at a time, leaving the rest of the ships at An Loc until it was time to rotate duty. The time in between missions dragged along. No place to go, and not a hell of a lot to do. Pulling maintenance on the ships and cleaning the guns didn't take that much time.

The sound of approaching footsteps made him prop his hat back to face the glaring sun. Just old Marvin the ARVN bringing his camera back. Probably no pictures left in it. He smiled at the lieutenant and accepted the camera, glancing at the back plate. Sure enough, shot the entire roll.

The lieutenant squatted down next to him, sun rays sparkling off the gold and enamel smile. Carl couldn't tell what the eyes had in them. Like many of the ARVN officers, this one sported the mirror-lensed sunglasses, just like the ones Jolley had worn. Even without the shades, he probably couldn't tell anything about the man's thoughts, inscrutable Orientals and all that crap.

"What's happening, *dai uy*?" Carl asked, using the word for captain, stretching the ARVN's smile.

The lieutenant pointed to the camera. "GI numbah one. You souvenir me pitcha?" He made a shutter-snapping motion with one hand.

Might not ever see you again, Jack. "Sure. Maybe five, ten days," Carl told him. What the hell. Give the guy something to show his grandkids, if he lived that long.

The officer laughed, a high shrill note, and nodded his head happily. "You numbah one GI. Numbah one!" He patted Carl softly on the leg and then rose, turning and trotting back to his troops, chattering up a storm.

"Yeah, we all numbah ones, ain't we, Weird?" Slute

was resting in the back seat of the ship. They were a team today with WO2 Langer, a second-tour pilot who was just as crazy as Animal.

"Right," Carl agreed, "but I wish they weren't such a touchy bunch of people." He hadn't gotten used to the way the Vietnamese men treated each other. They could always be seen, arms linked, almost hugging each other, or walking hand in hand.

"Don't sweat it, man. It don't mean nuthin' over here, it's just the way they are. Personally, I don't care if they're glued to each other as long as they fight when the time comes."

"I hear you. They sure look like they could be some mean-ass fighters if they wanted to. For sure, their cousins with Uncle Ho are a tough bunch." Carl looked back at the ARVN. Sharp uniforms don't always mean sharp fighters.

Shouting from the temporary operations tent drew their attention. Langer came bounding out of the flaps, long legs eating up the ground, whirling one hand over his head.

"Scramble! Scramble! One Seven's down!"

The quiet strip suddenly burst into a flurry of activity as men scrambled for their ships, throwing on shirts and helmets. Carl got the blade untied just as the red-faced pilot reached the ship and threw himself into the seat, yelling for clearance. Carl gave him a thumbs-up and sprinted around the front to take his place next to the pilot. In a matter of seconds they were ready to lift off, the engine almost up to operational RPMs. Langer was still breathing hard, but normal color was returning to his face, allowing the flaming red handlebar mustache once again to dominate his features.

They had to wait a few more seconds for the Cobras to get cranked, then like a gaggle of geese late for a flight south, all the ships lifted and headed for the border. Langer filled them in on the situation, stopping every now and then to hear the latest status reports from the control ship.

"They were checking out some hootches near the edge of a plantation area, doing a recon by fire when they started taking fire from small arms. Ship lost power and started down and then the cover ship saw the ass end explode. Ship was maybe fifteen feet from the ground and hit hard." He stopped and they all listened in.

Two Three, the cover ship, had just spotted at least one survivor near the wreckage and wanted to know how long the reinforcements would take to get there. More traffic rattled back and forth, leading gunship giving an ETA, lift section leader getting a picture of the landing conditions, everybody interested in the enemy situation.

Enemy situation was definitely hot. The gunship was taking fire while trying to cover the downed ship, so evidently whatever force was there wasn't inclined to move out.

Carl checked his gun, made sure the bolt was all the way forward, magazine tapped in place. One Seven was a warrant named Reiner. Short, dark-haired dude. Easygoing, but a real teller of war stories. Carl had flown with him a couple of times and been favorably impressed with his flying skills. Lighter and Swanson were flying with Reiner, and he wondered who it was that the Cobra had seen. Too early to start worrying about who was alive and who wasn't. If one of them had made it out, there was a good chance that all of them were alive.

Now Carl started to feel the excitement, the danger, the rush, and he willed his responses to match his thoughts. Stay cool. He went over the procedures for any eventuality. Just like baseball, he thought. Got to know what to do with the ball no matter how it comes.

The building charge of adrenaline suddenly evaporated. He heard the call from Animal's ship as the pilots organized the cover and rescue operation with the control ship. Animal's loach and the lift section were going down to the crash site while the Cobras covered and the other scout ships stayed on top, out of the way until or if they were needed.

Langer grumbled, frustrated, but took the ship up above the circling gunships and fell into orbit with the other two scouts.

The lift ships went in with no ground fire, surprising every man in the operation. Maybe the threat of so many Cobras, five of them, had made the NVA hold off on trying to hit the downed ship, or maybe they already had. News was painfully slow getting out, and Carl was feeling the itch of not knowing.

Animal's voice broke the air reporting no sign of enemy activity in the area of the crash. Charlie must have gone to ground.

"We've got survivors," the pilot from one of the lift ships suddenly announced, and Carl could almost feel the mental cheer that everyone gave. "One Seven's on board and his oscar is okay," the voice continued, and Carl felt the cheer hush. "Golf element didn't make it."

Carl's throat tightened up, a knot forming in it.

"Shit!" Slute said it all. Anger, pain, loss. He and Lighter had been scout gunners together for a long time, as a scout's life was reckoned. The tall, lanky gunner had been getting short on his extension, down to less than sixty days, but hell, that was a lifetime in the scout business.

Carl listened in on the subdued radio traffic that continued. Lighter's body was brought out, and what was left of the downed ship was blown in place to keep Charlie from using anything on her. The lift ships lifted back out, and as soon as they were clear, all of the gunships started rolling in on the area, one after another, devastating the surface of the earth in that one small corner. Animal's ship was staying on station to continue the mission with two cover ships while the rest of them began a silent flight back to An Loc.

Carl stared out across the jungle below. Two ways of looking at it, he decided. Take the positive point. Two of them are still alive and that was a hell of a lot better than it could have been. He found out later just how lucky those two had been.

"Man, one minute we flying around, firing up a couple of bunkers, and then these dudes with AKs start firing at us," Swanson told the scouts who had crowded around to listen. His voice was stretching higher than normal and it was obvious to all that he was controlling it with effort.

"Reeves pulled the ship about to let Lighter hit on those dudes and the next thing I knew, something slammed into us and exploded. Damn, I thought we were all dead. I heard someone yelling, must have been Lighter, and then we smashed into the ground and whatever was left of the ship broke up. Reeves told me on the way back that he thought we must have taken an RPG in the ass." His voice trembled a little as he relived the action in his mind. Slute handed him another beer, and he went on, needing to talk about it. "Reeves and me crawled away into the brush." He looked down at his beer and then back up into the faces of his family, a look of helpless frustration. "He was dead, man. Wasn't nothing we could do for Lighter." He lapsed into silence, staring moodily at his beer again.

Carl and most of the others said a few things, clichés on surviving, still being alive, to comfort him, and drifted away, while a couple of his closest friends stayed on for support.

The bold scout motto, "Scouts don't give a damn," was only partially true. About most things they didn't give a damn, but when it came to life and death in their own close-knit family, they were like everyone else.

XXV.

"Scramble! One Five's down!"

Carl leaped out of the front seat where he had been reading an old paperback and dashed back to get the blade tie-down. He was back inside the ship, jerking the helmet roughly over his head, before Harrier got to the chopper.

Harrier, a plain-faced experienced pilot of eleven months,

arrived at the loach just the way Langer had only three days before when Reeves had gone down. The wind sprint from the operations tent left him huffing and puffing, and he didn't start with the details until they were already in the air.

"He's down just about a half klick from where Reeves crashed," Harrier finally said. "Fucking dinks must have something in there that they want to keep. Damn ARVN haven't done anything about it!"

ARVN reaction to what was being found had already become a major sore point with the scout platoon. They had the understanding that the scouts' job was to find evidence of the enemy and then the ARVN mechanized infantry battalions were supposed to go in and follow up. It wasn't working out that way. Since Reeves had gone down, the scouts had been concentrating on the area, found all kinds of signs of large unit activity, but the ARVN commander just kept sending them back into the same area over and over again without committing his fighting forces.

As the ship approached the area, the radio messages from the cover bird suddenly became urgent. He was reporting increased ground fire, taking hits, and over the hissing static everyone heard the background noise. Someone was swearing and moaning into an open mike and there was a heavy rushing sound of air.

"Two Six has been hit. I can't tell how bad, but someone better get here in a hurry. I've got to get out of here," the Cobra's pilot informed the listening audience.

One of the gunships that was with Carl's loach called in, telling the stricken Cobra that the cavalry was almost there. "Give us sixty more seconds, then break station. What's the ground picture?"

"One Five went down on the edge of the river, no explosions, no signs of survivors, either, but they may be under cover. Many small arms and at least two fifty-ones within two hundred meters of the ship, so keep the cover tight," the control ship told the rescue force. He went on to organize the effort and Carl tightened up on his rifle when Harrier got the word to take their loach down and try to find survivors.

"All right, troops, keep your eyes open. This is gonna be a hard ride. Skull, you see anything, you just make sure it's not one of ours before you open up!" Harrier sounded calm enough and it made Carl loosen up a bit.

No reason to be flying slow over this area. They already knew that the place was crawling with NVA, and if there was anyone still alive from the ship, they wouldn't be trying to hide from the choppers.

Harrier dropped the ship sickeningly, plunging toward the leafy jungle deck well before they got to the crash site. From the treetops he took up a fast zigzagging course, guided by the control ship while three cover birds patrolled the sky, responding to ground fire from the long-reaching .51s.

Carl tried to keep all of his concentration on the ground, but the faces of the three men who had gone down kept popping up. He and Langer had just been out here days earlier responding to a downed ship and now Langer was down, and with him were Slute and Psycho. They were all experienced men, but experience didn't mean shit if they had gone down in the middle of a regimental base camp. He couldn't imagine it being anything less than that. The NVA usually wouldn't mess with three Cobras, so it had to be something big, and, he figured, it must be well concealed underground, a regular city, maybe.

"You'll be right on top of it in ten seconds," the control ship warned, and Harrier jerked the fragile ship up and then back down again, having spotted the area.

"Hang on," he said quickly, matching the movement to his voice. The ship bent around hard right as they skirted a tiny grassy spot near the river's edge, and then whirled back sharply to the left.

Carl was having trouble trying to get his eyes to stay focused on the blurring ground and felt a rising heat sensation in his throat. The ship was ploughing up and down, pitching, twisting, trying to avoid getting nailed by the AK fire that Carl suddenly heard. He couldn't get a line on anything from the left seat position, but the hammering explosions of Skull's machine gun told him that someone had a target, even if only for a second.

Harrier continued to make the ship dance to an impossible beat, slowed for a moment, fluttering by the downed loach, then sent the ship back into its wild gyrations.

"Ship's down, front end in the water, partially submerged. Oscar's still in the ship, strapped in. I think he's dead. No sign of the rest of the crew," Harrier reported to the control ship. "Hang on, Weird, and see what you can spot. I'm bringing her around. Skull, be ready on that gun again."

Carl found himself staring at the wrecked chopper, saw the dark form slumped forward in the observer's seat, moving gently with the flow of the muddy green water through the ship's cockpit. Some of the water slowly swirling in the loach's interior had a darker shade to it, a dirty brown turning darker near its source, Psycho's body. Little details stuck in Carl's mind, crystalline images, a leaf passing through the open portals of the scout ship, ripples from their own rotor wash sweeping across the water, an arm floating lazily, bobbing up and down in the current swells next to the ship.

Nothing else was visible from his position, and the strangeness of the moment passed, the war on again, the Game master shifting the scenes.

"Sir, over there, four o'clock, on the ground!"

Harrier whipped the small craft back in a sharp, rising turn, then flattened out, tempting the fire of enemy gunners who had become silent again. A quick spin around something that Carl couldn't see and Harrier was back on the radio.

"Get that security team done here quick!" His voice carried an excitement that the sight of the broken ship and dead oscar had failed to evoke. "We've got a flight helmet on the ground fifty meters south of the crash site. Ground around has been kicked up, like there might have been a fight." He bent the ship off in a new direction and slowed down again. "Keep your eyes open. One of them might have gotten captured. Might leave a trail for us to follow."

Carl leaned out a little farther, angling his rifle down. He could hear the control ship talking to the lift section with the ARVN security forces. Sounded as if they would be hitting the area in just a minute, and the thought crossed his mind. Charlie knew that a reaction team would be coming in. Maybe they were holding off their fire on the puny scout ship, waiting for the bigger targets to swarm to the bait. The thought made him feel a little more comfortable for his own safety, but it was short-lived.

A staccato burst of fire from their front, almost directly in their line of travel, dispelled the trap idea. The fire, the sound of Plexiglas shattering, the sudden jerk of the ship, pulled his attention toward the front glass bubble. A slow-motion wave of inward rushing, glittering, twisting fragments broke across his legs and he jerked his head back, instinctively throwing up one hand to guard his face. Stinging lances drove into his legs below the knee, but somehow he knew that they were only shards of the brittle plastic, and while they were immediately painful, he blessed the pain. He had always thought that if he could feel the pain instantly, then it couldn't be that bad a wound.

The ship lurched again, but from Harrier's controls, not from the ground fire. "Smoke out!"

Carl released the red smoke and joined Skull's fire into the jungle below. Whoever the helmet had belonged to would have to take his chances if he were still alive. Too many little brown men down there, all over the place. Besides, the lift ships were on their way in and the gunships needed to try to clear the area for them.

"All right, gentlemen, let's get the hell out of here for a while." Harrier took the ship straight out to the south at high speed for about a klick before climbing into the sky, passing the flight of five Hueys with their ARVN passengers on the way in.

Carl wished them a silent good luck and good hunting, hoping that some good news might come out of the mess. So far, the situation looked pretty damn poor for the downed ship and crew, and their own chopper had some problems. The giant ventilation hole that had replaced the lower Plexiglas bubble allowed a steady rush of air that felt good on Carl's legs, soothing the stinging sensation. Now, away from the danger zone, he took the opportunity to examine the damage.

"Well, Weird, what's the verdict? You gonna live or die?" Harrier asked.

"Guess I'll make it," Carl replied with a wince as he tried to pull a trouser leg away from the flesh. "My leg feels like a pincushion, though. Just the right one, got all kinds of crap stuck in it." He tried to pull out one of the larger pieces, an exposed two-inch-long icicle, but decided the pain wasn't worth it for now.

"Any other damage that anyone can see?"

Skull checked out the back of the ship while Carl looked over the instrument panel and radios. Harrier wiggled the ship around and eventually came to the conclusion that aside from the windshield they were in good shape. No red lights, no vibrations, blades were still going around, keeping them in the air and traveling where the pilot wanted to go.

Within the circle of ships orbiting above that contested piece of jungle, they listened to reports from the control ship. The ARVN officer in charge of the force on the ground had to relay directly to the control ship for anything that he needed. His English wasn't good enough to speak straight to the supporting gunships or the lift ships that were once again in the air.

According to the information that was coming out from the C and C pilot, the ARVN were in contact with an enemy force of unknown size, and Carl had the feeling that most of the messages coming from the ground were urgent requests for extraction. The ARVN had gotten Psycho's body out of the ship, confirmed dead, bullet through the head, and one squad had recovered the helmet along with an M-60 in the brush near it.

"The bastards must have gotten Slute," Skull growled,

and Carl heard a thud from the back of the craft as the gunner punched at the ship's wall.

Carl didn't know whether to hope that Slute was alive and captured or dead. He had thought about that subject quite a bit in the last couple of weeks, since they had begun this Cambodian junket without the benefit of American ground support. He had long ago gotten over the idea that the Americans were the guys in the white hats and could do no wrong. As a kid growing up he had believed that, but Nam had shattered the idealism. Both sides in this fucked-up little war did the same thing to each other that opposing forces had been doing to each other for six thousand years, only now there were rules that said some of those traditional favorites were frowned upon.

He had heard enough about how the VC and the NVA treated some of their prisoners to come to the decision that if he were ever down and it looked like capture or death, he would take death. He could understand small enemy squads not taking prisoners. They couldn't afford to—too much trouble to feed, to guard, and POWs could jeopardize a mission. That part of the game was just one of the facts. But he didn't want to end up staked out in the brush with his balls cut off and his eyes burned out before they killed him. He hadn't seen anything like that, but he had enough sense to know that all the stories couldn't be made up. And, of course, he had studied many of the wars waged by the Orientals and knew that quality care of prisoners had never been a high priority.

Slute was only a sergeant, so that right there was bad news if the NVA did, in fact, have him. He wished they had the backing of the entire division. A handful of ARVN wasn't going to do much, and when he saw the lift ships start down, he knew that they had given up.

"Reaction force is being extracted. No signs of the pilot or the gunner, but an ARVN infantry battalion has been alerted at Snoul and should be here in three, maybe four hours. The C and C's going to stay here for a few minutes and organize a continuing search by air with one of the other pink teams," Harrier informed them. "They want us to link up with Two Three, Langer's cover ship. They had to set the ship down at Snoul 'cause of a warning light. They took an engine hit when the pilot got hit, but they just radioed in, said they think they can make it back okay. We're just gonna keep them company." He pointed down at the shattered bubble. "Besides, we've got our own problems to work out back at base. Sending all of us cripples back together."

Carl looked back at the river, the small dark spot at its edge. Three men gone. Men he knew and liked, especially Slute. Part of the family, and there wasn't shit they could do about it. All in the hands of the ARVN. Well, at least there was an ARVN unit in force moving into action now. That was something that they had been pressing for ever since this area was discovered. He thought back about the number of guns that had been reported down there. One battalion of ARVN wasn't going to be enough. Whatever force was down there had already shown that they weren't afraid to take on anybody who wanted to try them. Some hard-core dudes.

The flight to the ARVN fire base at Snoul, about thirty klicks from the crash site, was made in silence. Nothing to say that needed any words. The only break in the quiet came when Harrier called into the base to make contact with the Cobra. He couldn't make a connection with base control. Maybe none of the ARVN were monitoring the radios or maybe they didn't have anyone handy who spoke English. He switched back to the unit frequency and raised Two Three.

"Nice to hear someone talking," the Cobra copilot replied. "Nobody here seems to want to talk to us, but at least I got a medic to look at Two Three's arm. Not bad, just right for a purple heart. Engine's probably gonna be okay, but I want to take it easy going back."

"Roger that," Harrier answered. "We've got a small problem, too, so we don't need to be going high speed, either. Ready when you are."

Carl heard the Cobra make their call on the fire base frequency. Since nobody had answered any of their previous calls, the gunship pilot didn't bother to request clearance for departure. He simply gave notice that he was departing their control area and indicated his direction.

Straight ahead of them they could see the Cobra rising up, slowly moving forward, the broad blades beating at the air for support. Carl's ears were suddenly assailed by a shrill chattering from the fire base frequency which was drowned out by two tremendous explosions, one following the other so closely that their roars blended into each other. The struggling Cobra disintegrated in a blinding flash less than five hundred meters in front of them, vanishing in midair like some stage magician's disappearing act.

XXVI.

"I'm gonna kill some fucking ARVN! That's all there is to it, Weird. I'm gonna blow those little bastards away!" Skull was saying what all of them felt at this stage of the game.

It was bad enough that they had lost two scout ships to enemy ground fire in only three days before the ARVN had decided to take action on the ground. Now they could scratch one gunship as well, blown out of the sky by an ARVN 105mm howitzer. A search team had found only a few teeth, tiny bone fragments, and loose bits of flesh scattered over a hundred-meter area next to the fire base. Not much to show for two human beings.

Carl was still unnerved from the experience. Too much stuff going down too fast. He had watched a proud ship vaporize only fifteen minutes after seeing one of his friends dead inside a downed ship, another comrade missing from that same crash, one dead three days earlier, and four from the bunker accident obliterated. The platoon had been overstrength at thirteen when he arrived. Now, looking around at the small group that remained, he wondered how long this kind of action could keep up without wiping all of them out.

They all knew the hazards of scout life, but none of the surviving older scouts could remember when they had lost so many men in such a short period of time. And this was the first time in over a year that one of the gunships had been lost.

"Damn ARVN!" Skull was still carrying on about what he was going to do next time he got close to the ARVN base.

He was the only one who was doing any talking. The remaining five men were subdued.

Hearndon, down to his last few days with the platoon, came into the hootch, now the single home for what was left of the enlisted scouts. Usually he would have had Slute with him, a wide smile of ivory across the jet-black face, but not anymore. Nobody had even thought about who was going to have to take over in Hearndon's place now that Slute was gone.

Skull stopped his one-man tirade and turned to face the platoon sergeant. They were expecting news. The ARVN infantry battalion had hit the general area of the crash a couple of hours earlier, and while none of them really expected to hear anything good about their missing men, they at least wanted to know that the South Vietnamese were exacting repayment from the NVA.

"ARVN pulled back out just before dark," Hearndon began. "They were getting their butts kicked. Wandered right into a regiment-size force, the same thing that we've been trying to tell for the last two days. From what we could hear it sounds like they lost almost a full company. Naturally they didn't find any traces of our people. I don't even think they made it as far as the crash site." He looked around at the mumbling from the men, let it subside, and continued. "And that's just the beginning of the bad news. VNAF planes are running air strikes on the place, going all night long, and we're going back out there in the morning to assess the situation."

"Meaning they want us to go out there and get our butts assessed," growled Skull.

"Meaning they expect us to do our job," Hearndon replied sharply. "And I expect you to do your job, no matter how fucked up the ARVN end of this operation is. Shit, soldier, you think you're the only one who lost friends here. Most of these guys have been in this platoon with me for a long time. I've lost a lot of scouts, but you men here were around so long that you really have become my family, and now, in my last few weeks, I'm watching that family die. Sure, it's fucked up, but you gotta live and do what has to be done."

Behind the reddening face Carl could tell that the man was almost in tears. This was hard, losing so many so fast, and he could tell that the platoon sergeant was being twisted by his happiness at going home to his real family and a sense of desertion of his adopted family at a critical time. He was glad he didn't have any of those responsibilities to deal with right now.

"Enough of that. You men are still in a war. There's no one available outside the platoon right now to take my place, so I've got a choice of two E-5s here."

Carl looked up, startled. He was one of the E-5s, but he sure as hell didn't want the job. Hearndon met his stare and smiled grimly.

"Relax, Willstrom." He turned to Dutch, who looked just as uneasy as Carl. "Dutch, you've been here longer than Weird Willy, so I'm making you the acting platoon sergeant. It'll only be temporary. Top has already requested a replacement, but it may be a week or so before we get one, and I'm gone in two days."

Dutch opened his mouth to say something, but Hearndon cut him off. "No use bitching about it, Dutch. Someone's got to do it and you're the man. In addition, I'm making a few new assignments to cover our losses until more replacements get here. Dutch, you and Swanson are now torques, so make sure you check the arms room out, tell the man that you need two more sixties, tonight, 'cause there ain't gonna be time to mess with that in the morning." He drew himself up and folded his arms across his chest, taking a deep breath. "This next bit isn't very well timed, but it needs to be said. We've got two men missing and presumed captured out there. I'm gonna tell you in all seriousness, no John Wayne bullshit, if you go down out there and you think you're going to get captured, you'd better keep one bullet for yourself. Bravo troop's scout platoon leader got shot down this afternoon about fifty klicks southwest of our area. His oscar and torque must have been killed when the ship went down. They were found near the ship, like they'd been dragged away from it and then chopped up pretty bad. The platoon leader must've been taken alive. He was found, stripped, nailed to the ground with bamboo stakes."

Hearndon's voice started to quiver and he bit his lip, stopping again. The words came out slowly, with effort, anger, and desperation crawling out with them, as if he were feeling the pilot's dying agonies. "The bastards stuck an incendiary in his crotch and smashed another one into his mouth and pulled the pins. When the reaction force found him, there wasn't much left of his face or midsection. Gentlemen, I hope to God that our men didn't go through that, but I'd keep that in mind. It's not a bullshit story. Came straight from the CO. He just wants you to know the score out there." He dropped his arms, looking suddenly old and tired. "Morning comes early. Let's get some sleep."

Carl wasn't sure that he was going to get any sleep after that. Just thinking about what Hearndon had described made his balls tighten up. The incendiary grenades that they carried on the ships burned at over 2,000 degrees centigrade and could melt gun tubes. He had a sickening vision of a helpless man having his teeth broken and shattered by the cylindrical body of the grenade as it was brutally thrust into his mouth. He wondered how long, how many seconds of that fiery heat it would take to kill a man. He shuddered involuntarily, more resolved than before that he would kill himself before he would let the NVA take him.

He was thinking what some of the others were saying. Be bad news for any Charlies that they might find for the next few weeks. Blood was boiling, heated by fear, revenge, frustration. Carl was against the idea of torture, but killing NVA had always been a part of the Game. He had viewed them as people just doing their job, same as he was doing his, killing without hate, but that view was changing. It was hard not to feel hate for men who did those things that represented the dark horror of the Game. And that hate would manifest itself when there were targets on the other end of the gun. Some of the little brown men might die hard deaths if they got caught in the open. In his mind, in troubled dreams, Carl saw Slute, the handsome black face no longer flashing a brilliant smile, but contorted in silent screams as unseen devils worked over him. Scenes chased by, him lying on the ground, trying to move, but unable to escape from whatever was coming after him.

The three scout ships and their companions, five gunships, flew into their jumping-off point, dropping off two of the scouts and three Cobras. Carl's ship, with Skull as gunner and Reeves doing the control work, had the first mission, and Carl was glad to see that the gunship escorts were being doubled. Might make all the difference in the world if the shit hit the fan.

Reeves, tense and jittery-looking, had warned him right at the start about firing. Carl had the feeling that the combination of getting short and having been shot down just days earlier was making Reeves a flying risk, but he didn't want to agitate the warrant any further, so he kept his mouth shut and nodded.

Carl glanced back at Skull. Hell, they were all on edge. Part of their mission today was back in the same area where they had already lost two ships, and they were supposed to keep an eye out for their missing men, just in case they had somehow eluded the NVA. Carl figured the chances of that were about nil from the evidence that had been reported about Slute's helmet and machine gun.

Their early passes swept out near a couple of small villages, still occupied by peasants who were either too stupid to leave or more afraid of becoming refugees than they were of the NVA or Americans. The peasants in Cambodia looked just like the farmers in Vietnam to Carl. Wiry-framed, brown leathery skins, same ragtag clothing, working the paddies with the ever-present water buffalo. Same problems as in Vietnam, too. Trying to stay alive in a cross-fire area where each side always assumed that you were helping, or at least cooperating with, the other side.

He was glad when the ship swung away from the villages and began searching the jungle edges a couple of klicks away. As much as he wanted to find some NVA to blow away, he didn't want to be working out around the villages. Skull was in a foul enough mood and Reeves was freaked out enough that it wouldn't take much of an excuse to make them waste an entire village. And angry, scared, frustrated as he was, he didn't want to have to make those kinds of choices. There was still that lingering notion that war was for soldiers, consenting partners in his game.

Reeves bounced the ship, tossing it through the air, using more evasive maneuvers than scout pilots usually used. Usual method of drawing out the enemy was to be low and slow enough to tempt them, but everybody knew where they were at now.

Carl kept his eyes scanning, stopping every now and then to focus on a suspicious-looking dark spot or shadow that seemed to have moved. Most of the area that he could see was rice paddy mixed with isolated tree stands, and an occasional finger of jungle extending from the side where Reeves and Skull were watching. Looking farther out, he suddenly noticed a lone military vehicle, a jeep, lying upside down in rice paddy ooze next to a small dirt road. He started to press the mike button, but Reeves beat him to the punch.

"This is where the ARVN who came in yesterday got

hit. A few of them made it into the green, maybe a company or so, before the NVA decided to spring the trap. Most of the ones who made it into the green didn't make it back out, so we may see a lot of stuff and bodies around." Reeves glanced across Carl's front, nodding to show that he had seen the jeep.

For several minutes, Reeves worked the ship back and forth near the point where the narrow road vanished into the jungle, and then he began to push the loach deeper into the canopy area, crisscrossing the road from time to time.

"Got something, right below us," Skull warned. "Think it might be some dead ARVN."

Reeves brought the ship around quickly, banking at such an angle that even Carl was able to see the still forms sprawled on the ground. Maybe a dozen or so, all of them ARVN probably. Most of them had been stripped of weapons and uniforms, and even though Carl couldn't see the black swarms, he knew that the bodies would be covered with gorging, egg-laying flies by now.

"Hey, sir. Some of those might be NVA playing dead, just waiting to ambush our friends, the ARVN, the next time they try to bust in here. How 'bout if I shoot 'em up just to make sure?"

Carl could tell from the way the question was asked that Skull just wanted to fuck up some ARVN, dead ones or live ones, made no difference to him. Carl thought about saying something, decided it wasn't worth the effort, and let it slide. The NVA wouldn't have left anyone alive down there and the vengeful bullets wouldn't hurt the dead men. The ARVN commander in the control ship wouldn't have to know what they were shooting at, just another recon by fire.

Skull kept the trigger pressed for a good fifty rounds, extracting a partial revenge on the dead for the destruction of the gunship by the ARVN artillery at Snoul.

"Enough, Skull. Don't waste all your shots on them. We might find something better," Reeves said, sounding less jittery now that the opening rounds of the day had been fired.

All along the route that wound through the jungle they spotted more dead ARVN and a pair of burned-out APCs. No sign of the NVA. In their own yard Charlie could dispose of his own dead with ease, adding to the frustration of the searchers. Plenty of time to carry the bodies away, wipe out the blood trails, re-cover anything that needed camouflage work. None of that surprised any of them, but even Reeves was curious as to why nobody had shot at them yet.

"They haven't been bashful about it in this area lately, and I'll bet those ARVN didn't put any scare in them. Those little bastards know they can bring us down anytime they want. That's what it is. They're just trying to mindfuck me," he said, swinging the ship violently around.

Carl looked closely at the warrant. Those last words had come from a voice that was almost cracking. Reeves was going up and down, cresting with a false bravado, then bottoming out into fear, open and dangerous. He could sympathize with the pilot's feelings, having felt that same way after his Huey had been destroyed in Cambodia, but he hadn't had to fly anymore. He had gone back to the World on his extension leave and recovered. This man hadn't gotten himself back together, and Carl was more afraid of this man in the pilot's seat than he was of the men on the ground.

Reeves worked the ship back down the general area of the jungle road and broke north, scouring the treeline and giving Carl the rice paddies to look at. The paddies and the jungle, side by side, hardly seemed to belong to the same world. Dead men and burned-out vehicles in one world, lazily soaring birds and docile water buffalo wallowing peacefully in the other.

Carl watched a herd of twenty or more out to their left front. Some of the ungainly beasts were rolling in the ooze of the paddies while others stood, flipping their tails endlessly, brushing away the eternal flies. Around their feet small birds fluttered, hopping, enjoying the feast of water bugs. Carl noticed that some of the small dark birds unconcernedly had stationed themselves atop the broad, gray backs of the horned beasts, looking for whatever creeped or crawled across the tough, leathery hide. What a life, fun in the sun. Watching the animals relaxed him, eased out some of the tensions that were building to pull at his nerves.

Reeves's voice crackling through the system caused him to look at the officer who had spotted the buffalo. "Hey, Skull, check this out!" He slid the ship toward the quiet gathering, a smile playing around his lips.

The small ship humming through the air caused stirrings in the ranks of the large creatures, some of which began to rise to their feet, warily eyeing the approaching ship, and Carl could sense their uncertainty, even as he could feel the chill of what he knew was coming next.

"Look at those stupid bastards," Reeves hissed. "Fuckin' NVA probably been using them for pack animals and fresh meat." He brought the ship down, hovering so low that Carl could see the heads, the wickedly curving horns, almost across from the pilot.

"Hey, sir." Carl's mind was now racing desperately, seeking some kind of excuse or reason to stop what was in the wind. Reeves glanced at him, a cruel light flickering in his eyes, and Carl knew that compassion wouldn't count for much. But he had to try. "The buffs ain't doing nothing, sir. There's people in those villages who are depending on those animals for a living. If you kill the buffs the NVA's just gonna have an easy supply of meat and they won't even have to piss off the villagers to get it." He knew even as he said it that it was a feeble attempt. "Besides, we make a damn easy target sitting here like this!" At least that got his attention.

Reeves glanced back at the jungle, suddenly aware of how exposed they were, but then the smile returned. "Best hurry up, then. Skull, short bursts, head shots!"

Skull didn't respond by voice, but let his machine gun roar its approval, firing the short bursts into the now panicking cluster of wild-eyed beasts. The sound of the animals, the gun, the engines, and the screaming in his own brain was too much for Carl. He desperately wanted to do something, but the only possible means of stopping this small carnage might well cost him his life. Threatening to kill, or even killing, the pilot was the only way, and then they might all die. With a frustrated sob, cursing himself for a coward, Carl wrenched his head around and savagely jerked the trigger on his own rifle, spraying the entire contents of the magazine out into open space, leaving the empty clip in the weapon, a futile gesture of protest.

Reeves heard the chatter of the M-16, and, unable to see Carl's face, misinterpreted the firing. "All right, now you got it, oscar. Load up again and I'll bring the ship about. Let you get in on the fun!" The action matched the words.

Carl found himself staring down at the slaughtered animals, most of the herd sprawled in the mud, a few with legs jerking in their dying spasms. The muddy water was turning a darker, murkier color as the flowing blood from the wretched animals merged with it. Maybe half a dozen animals had bolted away, stupidly staying in a cluster, slowing now that Skull had stopped firing.

Reeves slid the ship along sideways, giving Carl an excellent shot at the broad backs and thick skulls as they half trotted toward the treeline a hundred yards away. Carl fumbled with a new clip, stalling for time until he sensed that Reeves was reaching the end of his patience. Angling the gun downward at the buffalo directly underneath, he fired a short burst into the mud next to the animal, hoping to stall a little longer and speed up the animals' flight for cover. For a moment the tactic worked, and most of the animals picked up steam, lumbering through the muck, still together except for the one that Carl had fired next to. That one bolted off at an angle away and to the rear of the ship, out of everyone's sight except Carl's.

Another short burst held Reeves off for a second longer, then Skull's voice shot through the earphones. "He's not getting any of them!" Skull had been poised with his machine gun to finish off any of the buffalo that the M-16 only wounded, but there weren't any wounded to finish.

With a sharp curse Reeves swung the ship around giving

Skull the time to finish the butchery before the beasts could make it to the cover of the trees. Carl tried to block out the slamming sound of the machine gun, a noise that he had once found so sweet to his ears. Now it was the peal of chaotic madness, death without purpose, and Carl wished the madness would take him and free him to do the thing that no sane man would do. Too much the thinker, too much the coward, all the same. He couldn't shoot his own pilot or fill his own ship with holes to force the situation.

Through red brimming eyes one small spark shone through as he saw a motion at the treeline and recognized the bulky shape of a sole survivor, the one who had bolted off at an angle away from the ship. The creature had reached the edge, and he held his breath, mentally willing the buffalo to move on into the cover before anyone else saw it. It moved slowly, almost as if it had no cares in the world, forgotten now the slaughter of the others of its kind. Finally, after forever stretched moments, the animal vanished into the protective blanket of the jungle.

Reeves swung the ship back across the paddies, admiring the gunner's handiwork. At least Skull had made a quick job of it. No animals were struggling or thrashing in the mud. "Good work, Skull. NVA won't be using that bunch for anything." A dry cackling sound, a chuckle, punctuated his remark. "This early in the day, meat'll start to spoil before Charlie can slip out and butcher them. *Sin loi*, Charlie, no steak tonight." He turned to stare at Carl, shaking his head. "Don't know what to think about you, oscar. You don't seem to have your shit together."

Carl continued to stare out at the jungle, unwilling to meet the pilot's eyes or to even make any answer. His mind was in a frenzied turmoil and he didn't know what was happening to him. His war was a storybook war, still the Game, but getting uglier all the time. He was now a part of the wanton destruction, the madness, the exercise of power wielded by those who had the means. And this fucked-up pilot, running hot and cold, acting like a man on the edge of a breakdown, and then admonishing Carl over his performance without malice or anger this time.

"How you fixed for ammo, Skull?" Reeves turned back to a more responsive person.

"No sweat on that, sir. Still plenty. All I need is some more targets," Skull replied.

"Gonna fix you right up, then. The man upstairs wants us to head back down the road and then work our way north to the crash site. Bound to be something there."

Through the confusion of thoughts stumbling through his mind, Carl heard the warrant's remarks and couldn't believe that it was the same man at the controls who had been there earlier. Firm, solid-sounding. The only explanation had to be the killing. And despite that same reason, Carl knew that he had to pull himself together to get through the rest of this mission. After this mission, well, anything was possible.

A few klicks down the road revealed nothing new. The ARVN force from the day before hadn't made it that far, so there were no bodies or vehicles to be seen, and on instructions from the control ship they turned away from the road area. The man in the control ship evidently thought they might find out if the NVA were still in the area where the other ships had gone down.

Why not, Carl thought, send in one more and see if it gets blown to hell? No sweat off his balls. But he kept his eyes open. Still angry over the buffalo incident, he forced his attention, knowing that the luxury of self-pity and preoccupation with the event could get them all killed when the war once again became man to man.

Reeves ran a back-and-forth drawn-out "S" as the ship worked its way to the site, carefully skirting the edges of the numerous clearings, large and small. Ahead of them Carl could see a series of fairly large clearings spreading out, ideal places for enemy gunners to set up antichopper positions. Hitting the edge of the first open area, Reeves cut short his curve and made a straight line along the side of the football-field-size space.

Carl saw the first gun pit, a too dark tangle of vegetation, just before the heavy .51 opened up. His M-16 and the enemy machine gun spat fire at each other almost simultaneously, but those two guns alone couldn't account for the thousand typewriters that Carl suddenly heard, coming from all around them.

The licking flames from the concealed guns at a dozen different positions slowly reached out for him, spreading their fiery arms, seeking to merge with his body, and in that moment he knew that they were all dead. He emptied the first magazine, felt the ship lurch under the small metal fists that were slamming into it, heard the screams from Skull's side. There was a roaring in his ears, not the blasting of the guns, but something that sent waves of heat rolling into the front of the ship. Without looking around, he knew that the back end of the ship was in flames, knew that there was a case of grenades sitting right behind him, knew that it didn't make any difference.

Another magazine in the gun, spraying at the flashes. Out of the corner of his eye he saw the looming trees, a thin line of them separating this clearing from an adjoining one. Hope swelled up. Maybe, just maybe. He just didn't want them to go down in this clearing. No chance if they couldn't make it over the trees.

The bolt locked back, another empty clip, and as he pressed the magazine release button he looked down through the lower bubble just in time to see three men step out of the trees under him. The clip slid out, falling between his legs, his hand dipping into his bag for another. The three men raised their assault rifles, flashes, white lightning leaping from the muzzles.

Too slow, the bubble burst, the plastic of the console splintering, a hundred pieces of control panel flying through the air, and then the ship was over them, past the trees and almost as suddenly into the next clearing.

Carl couldn't believe that they were still alive after the gauntlet of fire, but he knew they weren't out of the woods yet. He knew that they were getting ready to hit, wanted them to get to the ground quickly now. Nobody was shooting at them in this spot, not yet, at least, but the ship wouldn't last much longer. He was now aware of the burning sensation biting at the back of his neck, and the specter of burning alive exploded back into his senses. Skull was standing out on the skids next to Reeves, batting at his burning clothes futilely with one arm, holding on to the ship desperately with the other as the speed of the aircraft fanned the flames.

"Hang on! We're going in," Reeves gasped, fighting the controls of the stricken ship.

Too scared to acknowledge, all thoughts of the water buffalo gone, Carl reached over, deliberately concentrating on the task, and locked down the pilot's seat belt harness and then his own.

The ground rose up to meet them and even though it was a partially controlled landing, the ship hit with enough force to snap off the skids, rolling the loach into the ground.

Momentarily dazed by the impact, Carl struggled up in his seat, saw that Reeves was trying to get out of his harness, but didn't realize that Carl had locked it in place.

He reached across and quickly released the lock on both of the belts and then threw himself sideways out of the door onto the hard ground. The blades were still going round, tilting drunkenly, dangerously low, flames from the burning aft section rising up into the wobbling arc. He expected the ship to blow any second, but reached back into the seat, feeling for a magazine.

His hand locked onto the rectangular shape. Too light. Another one, again too light, empty. Where the fuck was his ammo bag? He looked around quickly, trying to take in everything. No use. The pilot was already moving away from the ship, running hard for the treeline farthest away from the enemy. Skull was close behind, uniform no longer on fire, but half melted to his body on the right side. A new threat, an explosion twenty meters behind the ruined loach, made up his mind completely.

Scrambling, half crawling away from the still-moving blades, he came to his feet in a rush, sprinting across the open after the others. Gaining rapidly on the slower-moving gunner, Carl couldn't feel his legs pounding the earth. In his mind he could see some NVA sighting in on his back from the other end of the clearing and spun sharply on one foot, starting a zigzagging course. The foot failed him, slipped, and down he went, rolling to the side, flattening out face-first on the ground.

Despite his wounds, Skull had glanced back to see if Carl was still with them. Seeing the oscar sprawled out, he stopped and started back.

"Go on! I'm okay!" Carl shouted, waving Skull back. He could see that Skull was bleeding from the right arm, where, even at this distance, he could see a chunk missing out of the upper arm.

Skull motioned for him to get the lead out, and took up his original direction following Reeves, who was just hitting the edge of the trees. Carl glanced back at the ship, some thirty yards behind him. Two more explosions erupted near the ship sending up plumes of smoke and dirt, then a third explosion went off directly inside the ship. It was like a photograph in his mind, someone shooting rapid film sequences. The slow-moving blades sped up their motion, no longer attached to the central hub, but free-flying with other twisting segments of shredded metal, showering the ground around the ship.

Again the explosions galvanized him into action, and he finished the dash to the spot where the others had vanished into the trees. Without slowing he launched himself into the hole that presented itself, joining Reeves and Skull, who were looking around nervously from their own shallow shelters.

For several seconds they all crouched there, trying to listen for outside sounds over the pounding of their own hearts and heaving lungs. In the distance the sounds of the Cobras rolling in on the other clearing was a comforting noise.

"Hope someone saw us get away. Someone of ours, I mean," Carl whispered. He was sure that there must already be scores of NVA swarming through the woods toward their location. Images of the Bravo troop scout platoon leader hovered up uncalled. He swore nervously, looking around at what they had with them, and caught Reeves doing the same thing.

Reeves grinned at him, scared, but still a show of teeth that made Carl feel better, even if it totally convinced him of the pilot's mental state.

"Got any rounds for that?" Reeves asked, pointing a stabbing finger at Carl's M-16.

Carl suddenly felt very stupid, hoped that he would live through this to be able to joke about it. "No, sir. I was trying to find a fresh clip when things started getting too hot. My ammo bag must have gotten knocked loose when we hit." He didn't know why he had hung on to the empty weapon. Without bullets it was simply a large, awkward club.

Reeves nodded, looking around. "Well, maybe you can scare somebody with it. How about your forty-five extra clips?"

"One in, two in my pocket," Carl answered, then added, "and a knife." Carl saw Reeves's mirthless smile and knew what the warrant was thinking. If those little brown men got close enough to use a knife on, they could all hang it up. Time to use that last bullet. If Charlie got in that close, it meant that the NVA would be trying to take them alive. He looked down at his .45 Colt. He had only fired the thing a few times for practice. Three of them with three pistols, and one of them wounded, against too damn many Charlies with AKs, RPGs, machine guns, grenades, and probably mortars. Not enough against too much. He looked over at Skull, who was holding his pistol in his left hand, the right arm hanging uselessly at his side.

Reeves glanced around furtively, then carefully slid over to Skull's private foxhole. "Let's see what we can do for you, firebug." He pulled out his survival knife and cut off a piece of his sleeve. "Not the most sterile thing in the world, my man, but it'll have to do."

Carl wanted to watch the work, but someone had to watch for moving shadows in the jungle. Eyes trained intently, he knew that the NVA could move to within ten yards of them without being seen, if the NVA knew where to look. Reeves was staying quiet, and only once did Carl hear a stifled growl of pain from Skull. Carl figured the gunner was still under the adrenaline effects of the shoot-down and feeling little or no pain most of the time. But that wouldn't last for long. He shot a quick look at his watch. Still early in the day. It seemed like half of his life had passed this morning, maybe most of it, if someone couldn't get down to them. He knew that the reaction teams would already be in the air, but they were at least fifteen minutes away, maybe more, and fifteen minutes down in the jungle could be a lifetime.

At least they had these holes to hide in. Without closely studying his cover, he decided that the holes must be old defensive positions left unfilled by ARVN or American forces during the big spring push into Cambodia months earlier.

"Well, torque, I don't pretend to be a doctor, but it doesn't look like you're going to die on us, and *when* we get out of here, I'm pretty sure you'll find that this is going to be your ticket home."

Carl wished he felt as optimistic as Reeves sounded. He was scared shitless, but in control of himself. In control enough to realize that every minute they stayed on the ground made their chances of rescue or escape a little less likely. He was already trying to think of what they could do if the rescue ships didn't make it in soon. He figured that the same wheels must be turning in the pilot's brain, too, because the warrant was looking back at their former ship and then up at the sky. If they stayed here too long, the dinks would be all over them despite the cover of the gunships.

A new sound filled the air, turning all their heads in the direction of the source. "Hey! It's the control bird!" shouted Reeves, suddenly mindless of the possible presence of the NVA. He sprang out of the foxhole, grabbing Skull by his good arm. "Let's move! They're coming in for us, and I don't want to keep them waiting." Half pulling Skull up, he ran to the edge of the treeline, made a quick scan of the area, and motioned for Skull to take off.

Carl covered the rear, not out of any sense of bravery, but only because he was a little slower getting out of his protective home. Nothing visible closing in, so he, too, bolted for the ship that for reasons he couldn't imagine had landed near the center of the field, just a couple of blade lengths away from the ash pile that had been their ship.

Fifty yards and closing fast. His only fear now was that, so close to rescue, some Charlie might shoot him as he ran. No time for zigzagging this time, though. The Huey sitting there in the open was a far more tempting target than the men running toward it. Thirty yards. Besides, if they shot up the ship, they would still have the men on the ground to shoot at, maybe even a few more. Ten yards. He caught up with Reeves, who had slowed to help Skull, and both of them pulled the gunner a little faster. From six feet out they all dove for the ship's floor and felt the floor panels rise to meet them as the Huey pilot pulled the ship into the air.

Above the thundering of the blood pounding through his temples, Carl heard the first enemy fire as NVA gunners on the ground tried to target the rising ship. He wasn't the only one who heard the stammer of the guns. On both sides of him, the steady, familiar sound of the doorgunners' weapons answered the call from below.

After a few seconds of hugging the floor, Carl swung up to a sitting position. Across from him was the man who had been sending them into these places, day after day. The ARVN colonel smiled at him. What the hell did that mean? They all smiled at Americans. Reeves had already inserted himself between the pilots, talking rapidly, excitedly to them. Even Skull was looking pretty good. Looking any way but dead seemed pretty good to Carl.

He leaned back against the back of the pilot's seat, stretching his legs out over the floor. He didn't trust them enough to prop them up. He was beginning to get the shakes after the adrenaline rush, and he didn't want it to be any more noticeable to the others. Replay of the crash and burn began to filter through his mind as he tried to keep his thoughts occupied. He could almost feel the heat, hear again the screaming from the burning gunner. Shit. Those images would be with him for the rest of his life. He had thought they were all dead a half-dozen times in the ten minutes that it had taken for the entire drama to unfold. Ten minutes. It had seemed like a lifetime. Maybe it had been.

XXVII.

Nights came hard, restless, dreams driven by torrents of blind, howling things, undefined shapes that became wild-eyed beasts, collapsing, falling into bottomless bogs, changing even as they fell into burning helicopters with small, flailing torches hanging on them.

His eyes were taking on that dark, haunted look from the troubled sleep, and only the shut-eye in the forward areas gave him the undisturbed, if short, sleep that his body needed to keep on functioning.

Hearndon had packed his bags and left for the World without ceremony or party. Just too much action going down, too many men worn thin from the constant strain and the attrition. No replacements had made it in yet, and the manpower situation was getting critical. Skull had been evacuated back to the World by way of the burn unit in Japan, and only five remained of the once overstrength platoon. Dutch had worked out a deal with the Blues so that the scouts could still field three loaches, using alternating oscars from the infantry platoon, an arrangement that the Blues enjoyed. They were tired of doing nothing while the chopper platoons were getting into all the action. Dutch also shifted Carl up to the gunner's position and gave him a ship of his own, 016, which Carl promptly painted up with his *nom de guerre*, Weird Willy, in bright yellow paint to match the crossed sabers on the front.

The assignment and the identity with the ship restored his spirits, but the war had changed. The crash and burn had been scary as hell, but it was the memory of the slaughtered animals, his own weakness in the situation, that haunted him. He rationalized and pulled mental strings trying to convince himself that there wasn't anything he could have done, and a crazy idea kept popping back into his mind about the entire sequence of events. He didn't know if there was a God or not, but he knew something of other religions, and in the land that they were in people might have regarded their being shot down as instant Karma. The ship that did it had gone down, the man who did the actual shooting had suffered the agony of fire. Rational or not, the idea made him feel better and made it easier for him to concentrate on his job of finding the enemy.

The first day back up in the air after the crash and burn stretched his nerves, each clearing promising to suck him back down to the ground again in a burning coffin, but nothing had happened. For that he was grateful, but he recognized the validity of the old saying about climbing right back into the saddle again after being thrown. He had the feeling that if he stayed on the ground for a few days, he might lose his nerve and become a liability in the air.

Finally, as if grudgingly, one replacement filtered in, a blond-haired, thin-faced kid from Oregon who had been trained as a slick doorgunner. Blackthorn barely had time to draw his flight gear before he was up in the air, flying as oscar with Carl and Animal. Carl had given him a crash course on the duties of the observer the night before, about two hours after the new guy had signed into the unit, and the kid was clearly nervous. He knew why he had been rushed up to the unit.

"Shit, slick, you'll be a hero before you know it," Carl told him as they zipped away from their forward staging area. "This is definitely the place to be if you want all them Air Medals, DFCs, and, of course, that hard-to-get Purple Heart.''

Animal laughed at that, but Blackthorn didn't see the humor in it and didn't even pretend to put up a brave front.

''Medals are for assholes and idiots. And dead men,'' he replied. ''I may just be a rookie, but I'm not stupid. I don't want to be a hero. Mama didn't raise no fool.''

Carl liked him already. Not bad for a rookie. Not scared silly or full of hot air like some newbies he had seen. Just honest fear.

With the two high shadows following their movements and a trailing form, the control ship, directing them, the small loach ran a pattern across several winding roads, through patches of jungle, and skirted around several occupied villages.

Carl's muscles tightened every time they veered off toward the collections of huts and the inevitable fields with their wallowing water buffalo. He already knew what his actions would be if the same situation ever arose again. He was the man on the gun now, the power was more in his hands, the power of life and death over all that they came across. Today, with Animal as the pilot, he knew that there wouldn't be any problems. They were both of the same mind in many respects, and that would make the work easier.

''Coming around,'' Animal warned, shifting the angle of the ship, banking on Carl's side, and taking up a course that paralleled a narrow road that connected two of the villages they had worked around. ''The man upstairs wants us to check out this dude on the bike up ahead.''

Carl leaned a little farther out of the ship, keeping both feet planted firmly on the skids, and glanced ahead. Five hundred yards away and closing fast was a small brown figure putting down the road on a moped, raising a floating trail of the powdery road dust. Nothing particularly unusual about the scene. War or no war, people still traveled the roadways, on foot, bicycle, ox cart, anything that was available.

Animal pulled the ship even with the man and matched speeds with the puny motorbike. They were close enough for Carl to see the man's eyes and he saw fear in them. With good reason. Carl knew what the Cambodian was seeing. Grim-faced men, eyes hidden by sinister dark face visors, machine gun carelessly angled in the direction of the traveler. That was enough to scare anyone caught on a road, whether they were NVA or civilian.

The dark brown skin crinkled up and the man nodded his head meekly, teeth flashing in a nervous smile, as the ship stayed right with him, barely twenty yards away. He took one small hand off the handlebars to try to wave, but had to clamp it back down to steady the smoking machine in the ship's rotor wash.

"Fucker probably thinks I'm gettin' ready to blow his ass away," Carl told Animal.

"He might not be far off. The man upstairs wants us to check him out." Animal had been in contact with the control ship, but Carl hadn't followed the exchange. He had decided a few days earlier that if he didn't need to monitor any extra channels, then he wasn't going to.

Carl looked over the object of their scrutiny. Shorts, sandals, peasant shirt. No bags, bundles, or packs visible, nothing to indicate that he was a soldier, but in this kind of war that didn't mean anything. For all Carl knew, the dude could have been Ho Chi Minh's secretary of defense.

"All right. I checked him out. Big deal, now what do they want us to do?"

"Nothing suspicious, right?" Animal asked, just to make sure that both of them were in agreement.

"Hell, sir, the road looks suspicious, the trees look same-same. Everything in this fucking country looks suspicious to me now, and this guy just fits in with the rest of the place."

"Roger. Understand nothing more unusual than ordinary," Animal replied, then broke to the control ship to pass along their report. Seconds passed and the ship stayed parallel to the moped and its worried rider. "Marvin the ARVN up there says we should stop him and destroy the machine. Some shit about not letting the enemy have access to motor vehicles.''

''Ten thousand damn mopeds in this place and that asshole thinks we should waste this one. I don't like it, Animal.'' The muscles were starting to tense up in his shoulders. He didn't like the direction that events were taking.

Animal was listening to the control ship again, shaking his head. ''You gonna like this one even less. The man has decided now that this dude is NVA, or at least, very likely NVA. He wants us to waste man and machine.'' Animal sounded more amused than angry. ''I got control of the ship, but you've got the big gun, Weird.'' He left the unspoken question hanging in the static waves.

''I'm not going to shoot him,'' Carl said flatly. ''I might shoot up the bike if I can separate the two, but I ain't going to shoot the dude.'' With one hand he swung the machine gun to bear on the already frightened man and thrust out his other hand in a gesture he hoped the man could read as a signal to stop.

The man's eyes widened watching the barrel of the weapon, but he didn't slow down. Carl couldn't tell if he was too scared to stop or if he didn't understand the sign. He pulled his arm back and repeated the motion twice, but the windblown figure only bowed his head, an idiotic grin frozen on the brown features.

''This ain't getting us nowhere,'' Carl muttered disgustedly, and got a firm grip on his weapon. Shifting the barrel slightly forward, he squeezed the trigger, held it back for a half second, letting several rounds zip into the road just in front of the moped, slapping up puffs of dirt as they hit.

The man on the bike almost lost control of the thing, veering wildly off to the side of the road. Carl was amazed when he saw the man regain control and continue down the road with the ship still shadowing him. ''This fucker must be nuts!'' When he was sure that he had the man's attention once more, he tried again to signal him to stop, with the same results as before. In his mind he could picture what must be going through the rider's thoughts in this strange chase. The dink probably thought that he was going to die, and was too scared to do anything but keep on moving, just waiting for the helicopter to finish its catlike playing with its victim.

"Come on, asshole, just stop the fucking bike." Another burst, longer this time, closer, sprayed dirt around the front wheel of the moped, but the driver, looking more terrified than ever, only ducked his head nervously and raised one arm in a gesture that reminded Carl of someone trying to pray. That was enough for him.

"To hell with it. Animal, let's get out of here. No more of this shit."

"Roger. The game's getting boring. I'm sure Marvin's got something more useful that we can be doing besides making work for the Cambodian road repair department." Animal sounded glad for the episode to come to an end. Probably two divisions of hard-core NVA in Cambodia and they were hassling one man on a moped.

Carl watched the diminishing figure as the loach sped away from the road. A different gunner, a different pilot, and that lone figure would have died there on the road. There always was the chance that the man was an enemy soldier, but Carl couldn't bring himself to cut down an unarmed man. Too much idealism left, even after the fifteen months of Vietnam. Individual responsibility hadn't completely vanished.

The control ship sent them into the rubber plantation area for their second sortie of the day, and Carl felt more comfortable with that. The rubber plantations were notorious for hiding NVA bunker complexes even though they lacked the heavy canopy cover of the untamed jungles. Their primary advantage was based on economic considerations that were a sore point for the scout and gunship troopers. The rubber plantations, a remaining vestige of the French colonial days, were still owned and operated by big-business groups who insisted on compensation for any of their trees that were destroyed by the Americans' bombs or artillery. Uncle Sam was only too happy to comply with these desires, but didn't want to have to spread out the big dollars, and the end result for the troops was that heavy support for operations in the plantation areas was extremely limited. No massive air strikes or huge artillery barrages could be used to make life uncomfortable for the NVA units who knew when they had a good thing going.

"Check it out! We got bunkers," Animal reported happily, sending a message up to the cover ships. "Weird, see if you can make anyone come out and play!"

Carl answered with a long burst, firing almost straight down at one of the entrances of the large bunkers. Beneath the green cover of the trees they had found at least a dozen of the underground shelters, probably all interconnecting and multilevel. Hard-packed trails all around them told of recent and heavy traffic in the area, but Carl really didn't expect anyone to come up and bite at the almost hovering bait. He rested the M-60 in his lap and reached back for a pair of grenades, holding one out where Animal could see it. The pilot nodded his huge head and Carl pulled the pins, holding the levers down until Animal had the ship right over one of the square entrance points. Using just a bit of wrist flip to get them to the ground faster, Carl sent them out.

"Frags out!"

Animal gave the ship a little power, pushing it away from the overhead area, but keeping it close enough so that Carl could see the effect of his grenades.

"Bingo!" That from Animal as one of the frags went off inside an entry area. The other had bounced away from the opening and exploded in the open. Animal laughed. "Oh, well, maybe you got some communist bugs with that one."

That's about the best I could hope for, Carl thought. If the NVA made their bunkers properly, a grenade sump would probably limit the effectiveness of the other one. Those little guys down there weren't dummies and everybody knew it. Carl knew that most GIs hated the gooks, but they also had a healthy respect for their fighting abilities and attention to detail.

They continued to prowl around the bunker area, firing, dropping grenades, staying low, but it evidently wasn't enough to tempt any of the dwellers in darkness. Animal reported in sizes, number of bunkers, trail directions, and left in the hands of the control ship.

"If that colonel wants to dig these Charlies out, he's going to have to bring in some of his valiant ground forces again," Animal remarked. "Air power is great, but even I must admit that there are times when the infantry is the only one that can do the job properly."

"Yeah, especially when the game card says you can't bomb the little bastards back to the Stone Age." Even Blackthorn had been here long enough to learn the score. "Too bad we gotta be so careful with our dollars when we're trying to crush out the evils of communism."

"Well, maybe we can get them nasty commies somewhere else. Our fearless leader upstairs wants us to check out a building next." Animal didn't sound very respectful of the man in the control ship, but then, none of them felt much respect for the ARVN commander.

"You mean a hut, or a shack, don't you, sir?" Carl asked. Hell, there weren't any such things as buildings in Cambodia—at least, none that he had seen.

"Man says it's a building, right out here in the middle of all this. Can't imagine that any self-respecting NVA would be foolish enough to stay in something that obvious, but we're going to check it out." His tone suddenly lost its flippancy. "While they might not be stupid enough to stay in an open building, you can bet that they might be smart enough to have some guns in the area to make it hot for anyone who noses around, so keep your eyes open!"

Nothing like a building to draw attention away from the commonness of the rubber trees. Perfect place to set up a trap for bothersome little flying bugs. Carl hoped Blackthorn wouldn't miss anything. He knew that his own eyes would be on the structure, looking for whatever might be there.

Following a vector from the control ship, Animal took the loach right into a small open area, a scout ship's nightmare, and circled the house from a distance. It was indeed a house, the first such that Carl had seen in Cambodia. Must have been built by the French, he figured. It had seen better days, but was still livable and was presently occupied, although he didn't think it was by the NVA.

Inside a small fenced area was a stretched-out line with peasant-type clothing drying in the hot air, and there were two bicycles leaning up against one side of the house. A couple of scrawny chickens with dirty white feathers pecked mindlessly in the dirt by one wall. No sign of any people, but that didn't surprise Carl at all. Anyone with any sense would hide when they heard ships coming over, or if there were really civilians who felt like taking chances, they might stay out in plain sight, smile and wave, and hope for the best.

Carl and Animal both checked out the trees surrounding the house, but found nothing unusual. No gun pits hiding in the shadows, so they moved in to circle the house. The laundry on the line flapped a little more in their wash, the chickens continued to ignore them, and the house remained silent. Carl scanned it carefully as they came around it once more, still moving slowly, invitingly.

No sandbags or signs of being fortified. Cracked dull red tiles covered the roof and some broken ones lay in pieces on the hard-packed dirt around the base of the house. The aging whitewash showed long weblike cracks in the walls and the empty window frames showed only darkness within.

"Man would have to be a real fool to use an easy target like that for a hiding place," Animal remarked, "but the colonel wants us to fire the place up anyway."

Carl had figured that there would be some such order or instructions coming down, but he didn't mind winging a few rounds across the area. He shifted his machine gun, aiming at the laundry, and fired off a short burst as the ship circled around to the front of the structure. He pulled the barrel back slightly, swinging into line with the pair of bicycles, and started to pull the trigger. A faint outline lying inside the shadows of the door stopped his finger.

"Let's get out of here, Animal. I'm not going to do any shooting around here."

Animal had noticed it, too, and sidled the ship in closer for a better look. Just inside the doorway area was a ragged-looking doll, a large one, about the size of a baby, and for a moment Carl had felt the tightness clap in his throat until he realized that it was only a doll. Old and battered, but still the plaything of children. Rapid-fire thoughts had fled through his mind, ideas of how an enemy might leave something like a doll visible on purpose, hoping for exactly the kind of reaction that Carl gave. With a mental "fuck it" he relaxed his grip on the machine gun. If there was any chance that there were kids, civilians, in the house, then he wasn't going to shoot it up. Too many head games to have to play with later.

Animal reported something to the control ship and veered away, back out over the jungle and the rubber plantation.

XXVIII.

"Fuck that son of a bitch!" Dutch threw his flight helmet at the closest tree, shattering the extended visor in a shower of dark crystals.

Carl watched him carefully, but didn't get up from his spot under another tree. Dutch wasn't the sort who usually showed so much emotion about anything, but now the hollows under his eyes were red and his cheeks were flushed with rage. The black eyes glittered hate and a desperate frustration as he stood there, chest heaving, staring at his helmet in the dirt.

Dutch's oscar, Blackthorn, had silently moved in behind him, looking more sick than angry. Nobody had been shot down, no scrambles, and Carl hadn't heard any unusual traffic from the radios at the operations tent.

"Hey, Blackthorn, what the hell's going down?" Carl asked the oscar because Dutch didn't look to be in any frame of mind to answer questions rationally.

Blackthorn turned his head slowly, as if not sure who was talking to him. Carl sat up and motioned the drained-looking kid over. "Hey, what happened out there, man?" Carl repeated.

Blackthorn looked at him, a dazed look in his eyes. "He killed 'em, Weird. He just rolled in and blew them away. Wouldn't stop, even when our pilot was screaming at him over the radio. He just came back in again." The trembling voice broke, the last few words coming out in a gasping sob. Blackthorn stared at Carl, as if expecting him to do something to erase whatever had happened.

"That bastard Slater's the one who did it," Dutch growled savagely behind him. Carl turned to watch the grim-faced gunner, waiting for an elaboration. "We were cruisin' near this ville, popped over it for a quick check, usual bag of kids, mama-sans, and old gooks. We just cleared the hootches when we hear this pop, maybe a gun, and Harrier calls in taking fire. But we stayed on station, Weird. The oscar didn't even pop smoke! Harrier figures we can check one round and handle the situation." He looked up at the sky for a moment as a ship passed overhead. "Never even heard the guy say he was rolling hot, just heard the fuckin' explosions of his rockets hitting the ville. Christ, Weird, we were still down there checking things out, and he comes rolling in with miniguns and rockets. Harrier was on the horn hollering at him to break off, telling him there was no threat, but that son of a bitch circled high and came back in again!" He swept his arms helplessly across the front of his body, drawing Carl's attention to the dried blood smears that he hadn't noticed earlier. "The kid died in my arms. I couldn't do anything to help him!" He plopped heavily to the ground.

Blackthorn's strained voice took up again. "Harrier set the ship down in the middle of the village figuring the guns wouldn't make another run with us there, and me and Dutch tried to help some of the villagers. There was bits and pieces everywhere, kids and women screaming and hollering. Dutch picked up a baby that was screaming. Kid didn't have any legs left, Weird, just bled to death right there while Dutch held him. Too many of 'em to deal with. I didn't know what to do for them anyway, and Harrier started yelling for us to get back on the ship. On the way back he told us that the control ship wanted us out of there." He looked helplessly at Carl. "What the hell for? He must have killed twenty or thirty of them at least, and more's gonna die 'cause there's nobody gonna help them. Why? Why'd he do that?"

Carl stared him straight in the face. No answers to that one, unless something had snapped in the gunship pilot's head, or unless he was operating under someone's orders. His mind went back to earlier times, jumping from dying animals to a small girl who had died in his own arms despite his efforts to save her. Those had been bad enough, but this new slaughter was bringing the blood heat up.

A shadow fell over the three as Harrier appeared, looking nervous, angry, confused. He eyed Carl carefully, then addressed the other two. "What happened out there never happened. Dutch, Blackthorn, you got that? Nothing went down out there. No arguments, no shit about it." He turned to Carl again. "Weird, if you heard anything, just forget it." He could tell from Carl's eyes that the story was already out, and he glanced down into the dirt. "Routine mission, nothing unusual. Just do your time and get the fuck out of here." He turned and strode quickly away toward the operations tent.

"Cover-up starting already," Carl told the others. He started to tell them that he was going to do something about it, but decided against it for the moment. Pressure from highers and peers could do some strange stuff in the green machine. He'd chickened out during the buffalo slaughter, but he wasn't going to let this get by.

* * *

The chaplain listened intently, earnestly, as Carl poured out what he had heard of the story, even to the point of naming the names and the location of the village, which he had gotten from Dutch after half a case of beer. Carl hadn't been able to think of anyone else within easy range other than the chaplain. He could always write a letter to the IG, but that would take too long. He had never been to see a chaplain about anything before and felt a little uneasy at first, but in the warming, fatherly smile of the chaplain, he loosened up and emptied the tale.

"All right, Specialist Willstrom, I'll check into this and see what I can find out. This is serious business, and I think you did the right thing in coming to see me." He showed Carl to the door of his little office, and Carl went out into the heat of the sun.

Carl stepped into the coolness of the colonel's air-conditioned office, and his stomach tightened. Behind a long table were seated three men. The chaplain, still with his fatherly smile, the squadron commander, a lieutenant colonel who bore a more menacing smile, and the last of the three, Captain Slater, the Cobra pilot responsible for the havoc in the village.

Carl cursed himself silently for being an idiot. He could already see how this game was going to be played out. The chaplain had bucked straight to the colonel.

Carl reported to the colonel, saluting and remaining at attention.

"It seems that your story wasn't quite accurate," the chaplain began. "The colonel assures me that our ships were not involved in the tragedy at the village. It was a horrible error made by a South Vietnamese artillery unit and every effort is being made by us to help those unfortunate people." He continued to smile at Carl.

The colonel, a squat, double-chinned man, took over from there. "Now, Willstrom, I hope we've cleared up that matter for you. I was just looking through your records. Very impressive. You seem to be an excellent soldier and getting down to that last couple of months."

He smiled almost painfully at Carl. "Want you to be careful out there. I wouldn't want anything to happen to a good soldier." The meaning was unmistakable, both in words and the glint in the eyes. "Especially since you're getting so short after all this time over here." He stared very deliberately at Carl for a moment, then dismissed him with a curt nod.

Carl saluted, turned, and left the room, feeling the three sets of eyes drilling into his back. Inside he was fuming, but he was also worried. They'd be watching his mail now. Anything to the IG would never make it, and even homebound letters might not get there. The bastards had him by the balls and they knew it. He hadn't been an eyewitness to the massacre, and it was a safe bet that Dutch and Blackthorn would get fresh messages, advice, to keep their mouths shut. The colonel had only hinted, but he might as well have told him straight to his face that if he tried to make waves he wouldn't leave Nam alive. That gunship pilot hadn't looked at all worried. He had all the big guns on his side and Carl had nothing.

Even while he wrestled with the situation he knew there was only one choice. He had fought, bravely, been shot at, shot down, and shot up by the enemy and was beginning to think about making it home. To hell with that next extension. He wanted out of Nam now. Too much shit and he didn't want to come this far and get killed by some "accident." There were a thousand different things that could happen to a man over here even when everything was going right. A village had died and he wanted to live. And that knowledge of his own weakness only made the coals fan hotter.

XXIX.

Carl was still raging inside. He had known after those first few flights around Song Be months earlier that this unit's missions were going to be carried out differently from what he had experienced in the slicks. He had heard of these things happening, knew they happened, even been a part of them on a lesser scale, but the cold-bloodedness of the attack and the sense of betrayal afterward turned his blood to a boiling, almost consuming, fire in his veins.

The night before, he had written off a letter to home, and for the first time had given his parents some indication of what was happening. After finishing the letter he had held it tightly, almost crushing it up, then stuffed it angrily into a grimy envelope and threw it in the troop mailbag, and tried to sleep.

In the morning coolness he was still hot. He jerked his machine gun off the cot and paced the distance out to his ship. He quickly checked the grenades, positioned everything where he wanted it, and started on the preflight before the pilot arrived. At least today on this mission there wouldn't be a repeat of the senseless slaughter. His pilot, Animal, despite the name, was similar to Carl in nature and actions. He couldn't help wishing that it had been his ship with Animal at the village. Wishes were futile, though, and he got his mind back on task. He knew that having this in his mind could cost him his life. When a man was on a scout ship, all of his senses had to be alert to the dangers and signs of danger in the jungle. A moment's distraction could kill, especially in the areas that they had been operating in.

Blackthorn and Animal wandered out to the ship, still

with their coffee cups in hand. Together the three of them finished up the checks with only small talk passing between them. Carl hadn't told any of the others about what had happened between the chaplain and him, but everyone in the platoon knew Carl's feelings about the event.

"Hey, Weird, lighten up some," Animal finally said, tired of the tenseness and noncommunication. "Things are going to happen that you've got no control over. All you can do is ride it out and make the best of a bad situation."

Carl stared at the hulking officer, then shrugged resignedly. "Do what you can when you can, huh, sir?" Animal nodded. "Well, just try to keep us away from villages, sir. Let's fight soldiers."

"Ought to be easy to do today. We're going back into the rubber. ARVN commander wants us to check out a grid before he moves his troops through there. There's supposed to be an NVA regiment in there somewhere. Make sure we've got plenty of everything. It's probably going to be a long hot day and we took first mission." He pointed over to two Cobras that were warming up. "There's our baby-sitters for the day."

"Hope two's gonna be enough," Blackthorn said quietly. He hadn't been around the unit very long, but he knew from a short, violent experience that even three cover ships wouldn't always guarantee the survival of the loach and its crew. In South Vietnam, yes, but in this section of Cambodia there were no guarantees.

Animal lifted off quickly and climbed rapidly up into the skies with his escort ships rising slightly above him. Carl had taken a quick look at the map before takeoff and knew that they were heading in a straight line shot toward a rubber plantation just slightly west of Mimot, almost straight north of Tay Ninh. By the time they got on station and started their pattern, the other pink teams would be coming down at Tan Linh, the jumping-off point for missions around the Mimot area. It made Carl feel more secure, knowing that there would be other ships within a hard fifteen-minute flight of the recon area. The heavy action and losses of the last month almost demanded that the forward area be as close as possible to where the diminishing numbers of scout ships were operating.

If the pace kept up, the last forty-two days were going to be tough ones unless the platoon got some more men and a couple of new ships. While Animal guided the small helicopter toward Cambodia, Carl mentally checked off what was left of the scout platoon. Not much to work with. Only three flyable ships and they were wearing thin from overuse. The manpower situation wasn't much better. There were only six enlisted men left in the platoon, only two of whom had been there when Carl arrived in the troop. Faces of the others, those first friends in the scouts, flashed through his mind. Most of them had made it back to the World, but only one of them had gone by way of regular DEROS. His mind wandered back to the political cartoon that he had seen in the paper before the village. A general had been pointing up at a sky over Cambodian jungles, a sky filled with jets, bombers, and helicopters, some flaming toward the ground as crews bailed out. "Oh, those aren't combat troops. They're just fliers," the general had been telling a suited figure representing the American public.

We who fly also die. Carl liked the way that sounded and wished that he could tattoo it in blood on the butts of some of the assholes who were sitting on their duffs in Washington.

He shifted slightly on the floor, edging forward more and sliding his ammo box and grenade crate closer to him. He figured they must be crossing the border about now, once again into the enemy's sanctuary, with nothing but the ARVN for ground support. He glanced up to see the comforting sight of one of the snakes, lean and menacing in profile, the painted shark's mouth along the front adding to the illusion of flying death.

"There's the plantation," Blackthorn announced, drawing everyone's attention to the even rows of rubber trees in the distance.

Carl leaned out even farther, enjoying the tug of the wind, and looked through wind-blurred eyes at their target area. Just like any of the other plantations that they had worked over, nice neat rows, relatively undamaged by the passage of war around them. "I'd like to burn every one of those damn things down. Think maybe we can blow just one of those trees away?"

"We'll see when we get down there, Weird. If the place is wall-to-wall bunkers like I heard, then I imagine that we can do some bang-bang shoot-'em-up without costing Uncle Sam more than a few hundred thousand dollars."

Carl, like most of the scouts, didn't give a damn about the economics of the situation. Damn government wanted to save money, he figured they could blow away all the fucking rubber trees and the NVA hiding in them and save a lot of GI insurance money on the men who were getting killed in there.

"That's a big chunk of rubber," Animal commented as the ship drew ever closer. "Must cover a hundred square klicks, easy." He glanced down at his map and then turned his eyes back toward the plantation. "We're going to start on the northeast corner and work a quarter section at a time. Enemy contact extremely likely, free fire all areas. Remember, communicate and shoot." He turned slightly toward Blackthorn. "Keep that smoke ready, but don't release it until I give you the word. We'll see what kind of trouble we can stir up before we let the guns work out. No reason why they should get to have all the fun."

Blackthorn gave him two clicks and readjusted his M-16 in his lap. When Animal began the drop down toward the search area, the observer pulled one of the red smoke grenades off the wire, held it outside the aircraft, and pulled the pin, which he left hanging on his finger.

At the same time, Carl edged out a little more, most of his weight resting on his feet on the skids. He shifted the machine gun into firing position, barrel angled slightly forward, and made sure that the belt wasn't tangled. Satisfied that all was in order, he craned his neck upward, spotting the pair of Cobras taking up their protective orbits out of range of small-arms fire.

The tops of the rubber trees loomed up closely below

the ship before Animal pulled out of the rapid dive and settled in just a scant few meters above the green caps of the ocean jungle. Without any waste of time he started the first run along the inside edge of the plantation's northern border.

The steady thirty-knot speed and the relatively unobstructed view of the ground would make it easy for the enemy or his bunkers to be spotted. Carl also knew that the reverse side of the coin was true. Those same factors made it a lot easier for the NVA to spot the ship and bring their guns to bear on it. His blood began to race and his finger tightened on the trigger. That part, the anticipation, never changed. Gone were the thoughts of the village now. The great dollar war, the fellow fliers who had died, all that had vanished from his mind. Only the awareness of the ship, the radios, the ground below, and the heavy steel in his hands remained. The bulk of concentration in that tiny universe was centered on the ground, looking for shapes, figures, movement.

The ground below the rubber trees was even, dark brown, possessing the texture of coarsely ground, rich coffee. On many of the trees, Carl could see the grayish white of oozing rubber drippings from cuts in the trees. He felt a brief wave of bitterness toward whoever owned this plantation. They expected payment for damages, yet they allowed the NVA to hide in there. Fuck 'em. While he kept his eyes focusing slightly forward and out, he also scanned down the rows for obvious positions as they passed, but nothing turned up on the first lap. He braced himself as Animal banked into a sharp turn just before hitting the east end of the section. The pilot didn't want to get the ship out past the treeline where any Charlie could get a clear shot at him. Animal had already picked out his search markers and was beginning the cruise down the eastern boundary. Carl agreed with the pattern, decreasing concentric boxes, one section at a time. That way, both the pilot and the gunner kept facing the inside of the giant fishpond.

"Bunker, four o'clock!" Carl said quickly, and immediately opened fire, sending a flurry of bullets toward the oblong hump of earth with a small square opening at one end.

"Got it!" Animal banked the ship hard right, giving Carl the dizzying view almost straight down to his target and leaving the oscar with only the Cambodian sky to look at. "Looks like someone forgot to cover up. Maybe we disturbed them. See if you can put a few rounds right into the entrance."

"No problem." With the bunker entrance right below him, a distance of less than a hundred feet, Carl knew he could have rung their doorbell with his M-60 if they had one. He squeezed on the trigger and held it down for a two-second count, kicking up dust around the entryway with the first few rounds, the rest disappearing into the darkness of the shelter. He let off the triggers and took a quick look around to see what else might be nearby. That was one thing that he had finally learned to do, thanks to the scouts. The old target fixation that used to hit him during the shooting games had finally passed.

"More bunkers, Weird. One o'clock, fifty meters!" Animal exclaimed. "Targets!"

Carl had spotted them just as Animal voiced his warning and started to bring his gun to bear while the pilot shifted the chopper's course.

This time they were expected. From two of the dark holes leading into the bunkers muzzle flashes lashed out, short tongues of flame licking hungrily toward the ship.

Carl heard the thwack of something hitting the ship close to him and knew that the NVA weren't shooting blind. Walk the rounds in and concentrate. Little puffs of dust, dancing dirt and leaves marked where his shots hit, and he closed in on the nearest opening, making the unseen soldier draw back into the cover of his shelter. For a brief segment of the ship's tight orbit the other shooter couldn't draw a line on them, and it must have been a brave or foolish man who thrust his head and shouders up through the bunker entrance to keep the ship under fire. Carl saw the upper portion of the body as the brown-skinned soldier exposed himself, AK grasped tightly in one hand, the other hand pulling him up to a firing position. Carl squeezed the trigger. Right on the mark. The first burst took the man square in the back, between the shoulder blades, slamming his face into the ground. The second burst kissed the ground next to his head, and Carl let the ship's motion carry the slugs into the jerking head, ruining the closely cut black hair. The body quit twitching and slid slowly back into the dark opening, dragging the tightly gripped AK with it until the assault rifle wedged across the opening and the hand broke free.

"Good shooting, gunner. Stay alert, though. Look at all those damn bunkers!" Animal jerked his head and Carl followed the motion with his eyes. The dark mounds of earth were everywhere, some with unconcealed openings and signs of very recent outside activity. Animal widened the orbit but stayed slow to give Carl plenty of time to use the gun. No one was visible, nobody else fired at them, so Carl took his time, firing into the open entrances until he spotted some equipment at the base of one of the trees.

"Five o'clock, sir," he reported, and used his barrel to indicate his sighting. Animal veered the ship toward Carl's line of fire and started another series of tight circles.

"Looks like we caught someone in a real hurry. Must have been laundry day and they decided to go on a picnic," Animal said, laughing. "Go on, help 'em with their wash!"

Down below them were a couple of sets of the standard black pajama-style uniforms, a cooking pot, and a reinforced frame bicycle, the kind commonly used by the NVA and VC to carry supplies on. The last of the abandoned garments lay at the edge of one of the dark mounds, and Carl cut loose on it first to make sure it wasn't covering the entry hole and hiding someone with a gun. Seemingly solid earth under the riddled shirt, so he moved to the other items, and in quick order added one dead rice pot, a dead bicycle, and several black shirts to his list of victories in the war. Despite the dangerous proximity of unknown numbers of NVA, he couldn't help but smile as a mental image whisked through his mind of a general presenting him with a medal in front of stiff-backed soldiers and wind-whipped flags, ". . . for heroism above and beyond the call of duty in fighting against the aggression of communist rice pots."

The whimsical vision faded fast with the sharp reports of automatic fire that weren't coming from his gun or the oscar's.

"Taking fire, straight ahead!" Animal yelled, taking evasive action to get them out of the line of fire while giving Carl a shot at them.

"Shit! Fifty-ones! I'm on 'em!" Carl shouted, taking the concealed gun pit under fire. The huge white flash from the heavy machine gun seemed to be right in his face for a split second before the pilot pulled the ship out while the gunner dropped his red smoke grenade on Animal's order.

Carl knew that he hadn't hit the other gun during the short exchange, but he didn't mind not having more of an opportunity. He had dueled at close range with the powerful Chicom .51s before and knew that in areas like this, where there was one of them, there were probably going to be several more with interlocking fire zones.

Animal had been calling in his spot reports to the gunships and they were ready at a second's notice to roll in on any large targets that the scout ship couldn't handle. When they heard the pilot call in "taking fire," the lead Cobra started to roll in from three thousand feet.

Animal knew the first Cobra was coming in, ready to break off if the scout helicopter was out of danger or ready to continue if he gave the word. He got the ship clear, making his call at the same time. "Papa Two Seven, roll in! Targets, fifty-one and many bunkers. Red smoke out." The Cobra with Carl's old savior, Lieutenant Sanders, at the helm came streaking earthward as the small scout ship soared up and away from the plantation.

"Now, gentlemen, we'll just float around here for a while and watch the fireworks. No lights on, but I know that we took a couple of hits. Anybody see anything real obvious?"

The pilot's question was followed by a short silence

while they turned and twisted their heads looking for those unauthorized ventilation ports. Carl knew that there must be one near him, but he couldn't see it and didn't really care. As long as no warning lights came on and the ship continued to function smoothly, there couldn't be much in the way of serious damage.

"Can't find shit back here, sir," Carl finally replied.

"Nothing on this side, either," Blackthorn said. "But, then, they'd have to have been in their own damn chopper to have hit this side. I spend so much time looking at the sky that I'm beginning to feel like a fuckin' astronomer," he added seriously.

Carl laughed. "See there, I knew the army was training you for a good civilian job, and all you want to do is complain. You'd probably even bitch and moan if Charlie shot off one of your balls!"

Animal interrupted their joking by banking the ship around to the left, finally giving the oscar a good view of the action. Carl slid back completely on the floor and leaned against the wall to watch the Cobras making their attacks in comfort. At this altitude he didn't have to worry about anyone trying to blow them out of the air, especially since the NVA were probably well occupied by the diving gunships. They made a magnificent sight, slender, lethal shadows, turning sharply in the sky, swooping down spitting fire, and then pulling out, rolling away and back up to repeat the savage game.

"That gook's got some balls," Blackthorn decided. "I don't think I'd be sitting there trying to take on a Cobra all by myself."

They were watching the tracers racing up from the rubber trees. The NVA gunners were hanging in there, trading shot for shot with the oncoming snakes, and even Carl was impressed for a moment. So far, only one .51 had been firing. Maybe his earlier feeling had been wrong. This might just be some crazy motherfucker who didn't care if he got his shit blown away.

One of the Cobras—he couldn't tell which one—reached the bottom of his gun run at less than a thousand feet and let loose with a final burst of 40mm grenade fire. Suddenly, there was shouting on the radios and Carl realized that there were at least four different lines of tracers criss-crossing the airspace around the Cobra.

"A trap! A fuckin' trap!" Animal yelled, and almost threw Carl out of the ship with a violent jerk, bringing the loach back to a clockwise orbit.

"We're hit! Two Seven's been hit! I don't think I can pull out!"

Sanders had been hit, that red-haired, freckle-faced son of a bitch is hit. Carl could see it in his mind as the Cobra plunged closer to the ground. He must have fallen forward on the controls and the copilot couldn't get him off or get control of the ship. "C'mon, c'mon, pull up, get her up, dammit!" The tracers were still reaching up, converging on the gunship as it raced closer and closer to the ground. Two Seven's copilot was still broadcasting but coming in brokenly.

"I'm hit. Can't . . . out. Don't let . . . me . . ."

"Two Three, we're going in to try to cover him," Animal advised the other Cobra. "Get ready, Weird. We're going in fast. This is gonna be hairy." He switched back to the other ship. "Two Three, we're going to stay tight on Two Seven. Blast those motherfuckers all around us!"

"Roger, stay alive. I've scrambled the reaction forces. They'll be here with the rest of the guns in one-five mikes or less."

So much for the good news. Carl braced himself tight and pulled his ammo belt into his lap. No one was going to make it out of that Cobra alive unless the copilot did something quick.

"He's flaring!" Blackthorn's voice almost cracked, near the breaking point in the tension.

For a short second in his field of vision, Carl saw that the Cobra was indeed flaring out, maybe two hundred feet above the treetops, but steady streams of tracers were still eating into the ship. Somehow, the man had managed to slow the ship's dive and pull back. He was still going to hit the trees, though, and Animal's descent, a fast spiraling drop from the sky, wouldn't get them there before the snake hit.

Animal's voice, suddenly calm and measured, outlined his plan. "When we hit those treetops, Weird, I'm going to make a fast spin right around the ship to check for survivors and to let you blow back anyone who is trying to get to the ship. It's going to be a yo-yo ride, up and down, sideways, uneven as hell, and hope we don't get our ass shot off. Oscar, I want you hanging over that side as far as you can stretch. Don't worry about the smokes, just unload your rifle on anything that moves." He paused for a second, then amended the instructions. "Check that last. For God's sake don't shoot up our own people if anyone makes it out."

"Roger," Blackthorn replied, sounding more confident now that he had a solid task to perform. "I got over twenty magazines in my pouch."

Might need every fucking one of them, Carl thought. When he had first started as an oscar, he kept a whole claymore bag stuffed full of magazines. He reached back and slid the grenade case in a little closer. His throat was dry and it took an effort to swallow. This is some scary shit. Dinks all over the place down there, just waiting for us to come in. The pace of his heart was picking up, almost strong enough to move the chicken plate, he thought. Won't make any difference anyway if I get clobbered by a .51. Cut through this like it was wet paper.

"Shit!" He watched as the Cobra struck the treetops tail-first and plowed over, rotor blades shearing off in a spray of leaves and small branches as they ate through those and made contact with the heavier limbs of the rubber trees. It disappeared. A ragged hole in the treetops swallowed the ship while Carl was still over five hundred feet above.

"No explosion! Hang on!" Animal spun the frail loach straight for the gaping maw in the green cover. "Stand by," he commanded needlessly.

Carl was keyed to the point of that battle phenomenon that he had experienced so many times before. Three hundred feet off the deck and flaring hard, turning, still dropping, slowly, unreal, everything blending, but still each motion precise and detailed.

Over the ragged branches, his eyes covered the ground and the remains of the gunship. Leaves were still drifting down slowly, spinning, falling on the dark earth or coming to rest on the broken body of the Cobra.

It was on its side, no fires, no smoke. No movement, either. Through the shattered canopy he could see the still forms of both the pilots. Movement, yelling.

Blackthorn was emptying a magazine as fast as he could. "Gooks! All over the fucking place!" A pause and then the firing started up again with a fresh magazine.

Small brown forms rushed from the surrounding trees, racing for the downed ship, and firing up at the scouts at the same time.

Animal lurched the ship, spun it crazily, trying to keep the NVA from getting an easy shot. Carl sprayed steadily, trying to keep on target with the bucking ship. Too many guns down there. He could hear bullets hitting the ship, could feel them hitting. Two men stopped in their charge to the gunship and stood their ground to get a better shot. Across the back again, Carl laced them both, spinning and dropping them to the ground. Move on, next target, engage. Several reached the edge of the ship and began firing into the canopy until Carl raked them down, pressing his fire into them until they were almost unrecognizable tatters of flesh.

"Die, you bastards, die!" A red blur was forming around the focus point of his vision, and bodies began to merge together under the sweep of his gun. Something slammed into him, pushed him back for a second, then his hail pulped the head behind an assault rifle, and he shifted to another target.

The ship lurched, screams from the front, Plexiglas flew back into Carl's area. He heard Blackthorn yelling something, not using the intercom, just yelling. The oscar's gun wasn't firing, but the man was still screaming as the ship turned nosedown. "Animal's hit! He's hit!"

Carl swung up, forgetting the gun, disregarding the scores of NVA just meters below, and reached through into the front compartment to grab the pilot. Animal's weight was all forward, blood rolling down his neck from under his helmet. Straining, grasping, Carl pulled the heavy man back, only to lose his grip as the ship crashed into the trees nose-first. More Plexiglas caved into the ship's interior, blades snapped. Carl flung himself back neatly into a ball, heard a harsh rupturing sound as the tail boom broke away, letting the oval frame of the ship fall free for the last yards to the ground.

Noise. Men yelling, not close to the ship. Gunfire still. He lay there in the crumpled egglike body. No pain, no fear. Senses still at work. A warm, flushed feeling spread through him, content, no hurry, no cares. Nothing wanted to move. He could hear the explosions and the buzz-saw sound of the Cobra still working out, but it didn't matter anymore.

Footsteps, running quickly, stopping at the edge of the ship. A brown face looked over into where he lay. Small little people. The footsteps faded back with the face, only to become louder as the man came around to Carl's side and stared down at him. Never can tell what they're thinking.

The slender brown hands lowered the AK-47 slowly, one hand releasing its grip. The other, fingers wrapped around the pistol grip and trigger, brought the warm tip of the barrel to rest against Carl's forehead. No expression, still unreadable.

The scattered rays of warm sunlight felt good. Warm and caressing. Across an infinite void of time and space, a thousand light-years away, he saw the delicate, small brown finger tighten on the dark steel of the trigger.